I0824516

One's soul leads the way to wholeness

SATCH

WHY IS LIFE SO HARD?

NOT FOR CHILDREN...
BUT ADULTS WHO WISH THEY WERE AGAIN
AS A CHILD...LOVED AND FREE

J U L I A N F A G A N

SATCH

Published by
Illumify Media Global
www.IllumifyMedia.com
"*Let's bring your book to life!*"

Library of Congress Control Number: 2025902801

Paperback ISBN: 978-1-964251-42-4

Cover design by Debbie Lewis

Printed in the United States of America

This story is dedicated to my siblings, children, and friends who have shared my journey, and Brad, the demanding stickler that it be told.

May you smile, laugh, and cry. Most of all I hope you feel and understand.

Contents

Foundation Statements...vi

Chapter 1 The Challenge of Growing.............................1
Chapter 2 Glimpses from Childhood.............................18
Chapter 3 Senior Year and Grit.....................................32
Chapter 4 One Lonely Drive 43
Chapter 5 Sulk and Sour or Step Forward.....................55
Chapter 6 So You Had a Bad Day.................................67
Chapter 7 The Smiths...75
Chapter 8 Family and Church 86
Chapter 9 Hell and a Horse Ride 108
Chapter 10 The Sinkhole..120
Chapter 11 Grumpy..139
Chapter 12 Tunk..153
Chapter 13 Rooms 172
Chapter 14 The Girls, Sherbet, and a Spittoon.............187
Chapter 15 Seduction 200
Chapter 16 The Revenant..218
Chapter 17 Crows and Eagles..239
Chapter 18 Stay Stuck or Fly...256
Chapter 19 Backward Good 270

Chapter 20 The Boys 283
Chapter 21 Not a Kitten 307
Chapter 22 The Burn Pile..332
Chapter 23 Wholeness 344
Chapter 24 The Return 359
Chapter 25 Then..369

Foundation Statements

"Why should they among the peoples say, 'Where is their God?' "
Joel 2:17 (NASB95)

"For ever since the world was created, people have seen the earth and sky. Through everything God made, they can clearly see his invisible qualities—his eternal power and divine nature. So they have no excuse for not knowing God."
Romans 1:20 (NLT)

"So where does this leave the philosophers, the scholars, and the world's brilliant debaters? God has made the wisdom of this world look foolish."
1 Corinthians 1:20 (NLT)

God—Father, Son, and Holy Spirit—originated the cosmos and put a ripening earth at the center. The sun, moon, and other bodies are circling under the cupola of the heavens. This tiny planet is seemingly surrounded by multiple other developing universes, each being granted the distinctive spirit capacity to progress of its own natural powers. All are made partners, free in design—with mankind as the center of Their focus and purpose—to reveal genuine life and meaning.

"What are people, that you should make so much of us, that you should think of us so often?"
Job 7:17 (NLT)

" 'For I know the plans I have for you,' says the LORD. 'They are plans for good and not for disaster, to give you a future and a hope.' "
Jeremiah 29:11 (NLT)

"Go out and stand before me on the mountain," the LORD told him. And as Elijah stood there, the LORD passed by, and a mighty windstorm hit the mountain. It was such a terrible blast that the rocks were torn loose, but the LORD was not in the wind. After the wind there was an earthquake, but the LORD was not in the earthquake. And after the earthquake there was a fire, but the LORD was not in the fire. And after the fire there was the sound of a gentle whisper.
1 Kings 19:11-12 (NLT)

"That is what the Scriptures mean when they say, 'No eye has seen, no ear has heard, and no mind has imagined what God has prepared for those who love him.' "
1 Corinthians 2:9-10 (NLT)

"And if our hope in Christ is only for this life, we are more to be pitied than anyone in the world. . . . What I am saying, dear brothers and sisters, is that our physical bodies cannot inherit the Kingdom of God. These dying bodies cannot inherit what will last forever."

1 Corinthians 15:19, 50 (NLT)

Chapter 1

The Challenge of Growing

Hi, my name is Satch. This tale is of my life story. The subtitle points to how hard life can be and asks why it is so. Let's be honest with each other. Not everything in life is hard. There is always somewhere, at some time, a gentle kindness that comes. There is an occasional, perhaps brief, cheerfulness, joy, even an unexpected exhilaration. Randomly, there appears a season of happiness. Beauty interjects herself in unexpected ways. Intermittent music invades the soul. Think about that time when a young child looked at you with that smile of hers. She opened her arms and reached for you and touched your face with her hands. Then she hugged your neck, pulling you to herself. You melted. An unspeakableness filled your soul. What just happened? You cannot explain it, but you experienced it. That is in no way a hard thing.

Even the most difficult life has its good parts. Simultaneously, we are surrounded daily with examples and experiences of seemingly unending suffering and hardship. Perhaps the toughest in life is the unalterable fact that all that seems precious to us will, in some way, sooner or later be taken away. Our kids grow up and leave, friends move away, others disappoint us and damage us, loved ones die, our health declines, hope vanishes, or we are taken out by some catastrophe and we die. Even our faith and values suffer—things change, our notions, beliefs, emotions, our plans alter. Foundations that once anchored shift. Doubt slinks in, the bottom collapses. We are left wondering what is solid enough to believe in. There is no anchor. What, who truly can be trusted? Where is safe?

What results when these damaging things happen to a young child, when pain and suffering are thrust upon him? He is defenseless. His life becomes swamped in uncertainty, a heavy negativity regarding the meaning and purpose of life. What is the sense and value of life when such evil surrounds you? In this life how do you discover value and worth that will last and carry you with some hope? You must work for it.

When older you can examine your life as you look back over your shoulder. You can, with some experience, seek its meaning and purpose. One longs to find the truth of one's destiny. Perhaps the best way to reveal truth is through a story. We all have a story. Mine begins with my first memory. From that day forward I was uncertain about my mother and did not feel safe with her. Nor could I trust women after what another woman did to me that day in front of my mother, who though watching did nothing to stop it. At the same time, I developed a paradox within me, an unknown desire and a simultaneous aversion for some women that I could not understand or describe. How can you at age two and a half?

It wasn't long until I felt this great tension, an enigma between disdain and love for my father. This led to my not knowing what was coming next from him. I never knew what to expect. I was born the eldest of four children. As the younger ones came along, our parents presented us to the church folk and community as the model children our parents were rearing—the perfect family unit. We were dressed up and shown off to the public who always commented: "What a wonderfully behaved and ideal family you have! You are the consummate Christian family. Your children are exemplary."

We were like show ponies, groomed by the owners to be admired. But in the trailers they hauled us around in to take us places and in the stables it was another story. In time my life experienced grandparents, static religion, affairs, abuses, betrayals, and rejections that were accompanied by unexplainable contradictions without affection shown or affirmation being given. So a core question arose in me: Why is life so painful and uncertain? Children who grow up abused suffer for years while seeking answers. They simply want to feel safe and to be able to trust. To find that path takes movement away from what and whom they have known to a secure place. But how does a child do that? Where and who is safe? It is like life is a puzzle, with scattered and missing pieces, yet with an abiding sense of eternity in it.

This incident still haunts me. I cannot forget it.

It was summertime in the humid, semitropical South. Southern summers can be close to unbearable. At times you can drown in sweat from the mugginess. It feels like you cannot get your breath. On the cooler days your skin just seeps, but you still need a towel. It was hot as blazes. My mother took my little brother, Fletch, and me to the public swimming pool. She wanted to meet some of her girlfriends, along with their children, for a break from the heat and a playtime for the kids. I did not know who we were meeting. I carried Fletch's and my swimming suits, towels, and sunscreen. My mother carried my little brother and her personal bag and purse with all her lady's stuff.

The swimming pool was an oval structure with the dressing rooms downstairs. As we approached, I smelled the warm-wet mixture of chlorine and mildew combined with the smell of sopping bathing suits. Kids, dripping wet, were standing in line to buy snacks at the concession stand. The men's dressing room was to the right, the women's to the left. The pools were upstairs.

We were headed to the big pool for a fun time. We loved the big concrete pool and the smaller pool too. It usually meant friends, Fudgsicles, and candy bars, as well as wrinkled fingers and toes.

I was walking just behind my mother until we reached the concession stand. After she paid, she turned toward the women's dressing room. I didn't want to go in. I had been through the men's dressing room before, never the women's. Even at age two and a half, I knew I should not go into the ladies' dressing room. I told my mother I didn't want to. I had this terrible, uneasy sense within me. She stopped, turned around and snapped at me and said, "Come on!" I resisted, and then begrudgingly followed her with this troubling feeling inside.

I walked warily into the dressing room. There was a center aisle with green wooden benches on each side with lockers in front and behind every bench. I noticed everything. I was feeling everything around me. I stopped again. My mother turned, pointed at me, and said, "You come here, NOW!" I walked through the puddles of water. Everything was damp—the floor, benches, lockers, and walls. The sound of women giggling overshadowed everything.

Fletch was about a year younger. I guessed she was carrying him because of the heat and distance we had to walk from the car. Otherwise, Fletch would have been walking We were healthy, stout, big boys. I didn't know why I balked at entering the women's dressing room.

Inside the dressing room was a group of young mothers, some with children. These women, some of whom must have been acquaintances of my mother, were in the process of getting themselves and their children ready to swim. I had never met or seen any of them. The women just stared at me and giggled and said things like "He is too young to know." Well, I didn't, but it began that day. If I had been a little older, I may have lost my mind inside the women's dressing room. I almost did—dismay and shock came.

My mother sat down and was trying to help Fletch get on his swimsuit. She looked at me and firmly instructed me to change clothes. My mother was exceedingly reserved and modest. She wouldn't dare change into her suit until I went upstairs. I looked around. It seemed like all the women were staring at me. So, I just stood there, frozen. I couldn't do it. The women were undressing and putting on their swimsuits in front of me. My mother, still sitting on the painted wooden bench, had her back to the lockers and all the women behind her.

I was on the other side of the bench, looking down the hallway to the stairs ascending to the pools and facing the disrobing women, listening to their laughter. I couldn't move. I was petrified. They kept peering and smiling at my timidity and snickering between glances. It was intriguing, disgusting, and humiliating all at the same time. They all were in various stages of dress and undress. It didn't seem to faze them that I was standing there watching. I was stunned. I had never seen anything like it before. I do not know how to describe it.

Their faces seemed to say they enjoyed disrobing in front of me. Little brother got on and off the bench. He was a handful, so my mother didn't notice what was going on behind her. She scolded me for not putting on my suit. To do that, I had to take off my clothes. I couldn't believe my ears and couldn't close my eyes. I was seeing things, shapes, forms that looked very different unveiled—things I didn't even know existed. I was so uncomfortable, and yet, I was drawn to it.

Then I noticed one woman. She had positioned herself in the very next locker across the aisle and behind my mother. None of the others could see her. She kept looking and smiling at me the whole time, slowly undressing until she was completely nude—all the while staring and smiling at me. As she hung her clothes in her locker, she would turn around and look back at me over her shoulder. She was a pretty brunette with a beautiful smile, big brown eyes, and multiple other attributes about which I had yet to form a considered opinion. But I was developing one in a hurry and was feeling funny. I remember her breasts, the stretch marks on her stomach, and a bruise on her left thigh. What I remember most were those brown eyes and that smile—that look in her eyes—that grin on her face.

My mother yelled, "Put your suit on NOW!" She was angry. I turned away. As I tried to change with my backside to her, this woman walked buck naked straight to me and stood next to me holding her bathing suit, totally comfortable and unfazed that my eyes were stuck to her like glue. She smiled and just stared at me. She stood right there in front of me, chatting with my mother, with her blue one-piece bathing suit flipped over her left shoulder. They were having a conversation.

When I looked down the aisle, some of the others were still looking at me, and some were on their way up the stairs. The pretty one just kept on looking at me and grinning. She watched me while talking to my mother. She said to my mom, "What a handsome and well-developed little boy. That's the finest looking boy I have ever seen." She did not take her eyes off me but looked me up one side and down the other while standing there naked. When she did leave, she turned and smiled over her shoulder as she swayed back to her locker. Then, she turned to face me and slinked into her suit, grinning at me the whole time. I jumped into my suit and ran out of the women's dressing room, past the concession stand, through the men's dressing room, and upstairs as fast as I could. From that day forward I refused to go into the women's dressing room.

No one ever knew about this, but I could not forget it—and never have! I didn't know what a voyeur or seductress was then, but it had just happened to me. Fifty years later, a psychologist diagnosed it as trauma. I wondered why my mother didn't protect me. That hurt. I don't think all the other ladies realized what was happening, but some did. The brown-eyed one liked what she was doing. It seemed intentional.

Going after children, the little ones, is evil. Such is the nature of evil, a shadow growing in the dark. It chafes, smears, and expands like poison in the blood. And there was more—time and again after that. I don't want to talk about those other instances. Why were these things allowed to happen to me? God, who are you?

Satch and Fletch

A child does not have the answers, but he does have questions. The biggest question of all is, Is there a God? In the spirit of truth, the answer is not in man's intellect or in the honest efforts of science, mathematics, or physics alone. All of these worthy pursuits are valuable, begin with theories and questions, and lead to more questions unanswered. Some of the most fascinating discoveries even come by accident.

There are no provable facts regarding God's existence. But the godness and goodness of God and his fatherliness have been received and exampled to us in our very flesh. We are made in the image of God, and we are made like Him. Belief in God rises beneath and beyond controlled methods of proof. When one does believe, then the questions become: Who is this God? What is this God's true character?—and Who am I? Broken people are torn apart longing to know.

In my seventh decade I was still trying to understand why life is so hard. How did I deal with it? Poorly. I was angry at not having answers to the quandaries of my life. I was like any trained self-reasoner who had been taught and had firmly carved out a box for God within the safety of a logical or systematized formula. It is hard to learn and grow when you start out being told you have been given all the right answers. Growing up I was told, "Here's the way it is. Just do what you are told; do the right thing. Work hard!" *Perhaps the most important light in the entire world is the light you cannot see.*

After a lengthy process of discovery, I received, in increments, insights that contradicted and exposed what I had been taught my entire life—things that had never before entered my mind or heart. I discerned things that required me to make deep adjustments to my core convictions. God began to show me some of the things He has prepared for those who love him. Many others helped me grow in my understanding. A wise, compassionate, and experienced person can be of great value in interpreting and understanding one's life. We all need help and a community that supports us. I certainly do.

I spent most of my life feeling broken. This story is about that and my path of restoration. I am going to share many other incidents and people that affected me deeply. But hold on a bit. Let's talk briefly about the way we see things, things essential to understand, like our belief systems, perceptions, protocols, and acquisitions. The way we ourselves attend the world and the attention we pay to it with our subjective tendencies results in what we interpret and conclude in the natural and deem unnatural or miraculous. It also determines what surprises us.

Many unprovable and deniable experiences in unseen worlds have happened over thousands of years to people of all cultures. These experiences have been both transmitted orally and recorded. Such encounters seldom would be entered voluntarily. You certainly have heard about encounters with Satan, ghosts, demons, angels, and deceased family members. You know stories of visits to hell, Gehenna, the underworld, Sheol, and Tartarus, and near-death experiences. Books and movies abound with these themes. Wanna go there?

J. R. R. Tolkien takes you to Middle Earth's Mount Doom and the fire of Mordor, Sauron, and Balrog's fire spirits. You may want the power of the secret flame of Anor and the precious. Those must be destroyed to have genuine life. C. S. Lewis takes you to the grayness of hell with available weekly bus trips to heaven. Through these fantastic tales, we can see the pain and cost of defeating evil in ourselves and see the real and true life. Desire for genuine life and courage are required to discover and hold a life-giving identity, an authentic wholeness.

Many people look at fantasy as unnatural, paranormal, out of this world! They see it as only entertainment. Yet every person has beliefs centered in what he or she cannot scientifically or intellectually prove. You hold onto hopes and have fears, especially those of heaven and maybe hell—perhaps annihilation's nonexistence. You have hopes for which you long but think you will never deserve. Where in you does that come from? At a minimum, you wonder if it could really happen. Why? Because of an inmost sense of knowing that it could. Just take the library of the Bible for one. The Bible is the portable written treasure trove of an ongoing conversation about and with the living God. These extraordinary encounters are not uncommon but a part of every culture's history.

There is a distinction between real and true. Reality or what we call real has a substance and existence in the world around us in spite of feelings, experiences, or encounters. Reality or what's "real" rests in our eyes as what exists. What seems to be so real is often explained or challenged by a seeming contradiction called truth—a dimension or explanation of spirit which points toward a depth, width, and height beyond what appears to be real. Empirical data is gathered from living in what we call normal reality—yet experiences, encounters, observations, and incidents can reveal more than what one sees as real.

We receive these insights from the senses. We also observe with our senses and our spirits. Our senses are connected not only to the physical body but to the spirit in us. We sense spiritual connections. The imagination is a vehicle for gaining understanding, insight, and wisdom. To see, hear, and even glimpse what nature and God are communicating to us, our minds must move beyond the familiar and natural, what we call real. The real as we think of it cannot see beyond the material. The extrication of the mind's bondage must take it beyond the ordinary and physical. Our minds grow numb, and our attention must be awakened to discover genuine truth. What you touch is real. What about what touches you?

You may be asking, "Why is he going into this real-truth distinction?" That story I just told was real. Yes, it was. *It still is*! But what is the truth in it, behind it? Is there any? What was going on with my mother, that woman, those women, God…me? What were they thinking and doing? Why? I was two years old! It's simple. Real is what happened; the truth of it is vital. For anyone to understand the extreme difficulty of choosing to pursue the journey described in this story, you must understand that life is tough but can resolve into a peaceful wholeness. Likewise, the journey from abuse and rejection to the discovery of meaning is hard. It brings stress. It does not at all mean you should avoid it, but be aware that change will cost you, because it feels threatening. So, heed, take good counsel on the front end.

Most lives are beset by troubles. If your life has been or is easy, this book may not be for you—not yet. *Whether it is that you feel successful, landed here on a pile of riches—or you have the ambition or temptation of the need to have and grasp for fame, knowledge, money, pleasure, possessions, power, or especially a religious superiority—the longing to be a higher somebody—don't.* Those who do are not happy. They pretend. A deep sickness lies within all such perceived prideful treasures, like a nakedness to be revealed on stage. I have been there, done that. If the certain confidence or desire you hold is prestige or esteem, it is a dreary shadow, absent assurance. It is a trap, which leads to soul death. Is such a fading treasure worth your integrity? *The needs to have do not meet the need to be, which gives meaning and purpose and leads to peace and wholeness.* Pursue the need to be. Should you choose to stay with me, there is a reason. I cannot know your motivation. Lost, hurting, searching, wandering, or just being curious are places I have sojourned. *Aspiration is the way, not ambition.* I invite you to stick with me.

When we lose the will to choose goodness, we lose our true being, our connection to trust, and any felt pillar of safety we may have had—especially with God. Your heart is yours to give to whom or what you will. Just decide what you will do with the time given to you.

I want to introduce you now to one person who has provided tremendous help for me. He knows the journey through brokenness. His name is Yeesa. No reason for you to know him—not yet, unless you have read one of his books. He died almost a century ago. Yeesa is a Native American Sioux Indian who became a medical doctor and government representative to his own people. He is very open about his faith and his struggles. He chose not to blame the gospel for those who misrepresented and misused it. He dealt with presidents, senators, and politicians. He writes about how the public constantly gave these officials applause, praise, and money. But neither they nor their bureaucrats ever understood or helped his Native American people. Some said they were public servants and cared for them, but their actions never proved it. People tend to follow power, not truth. These ambitious and conning people knew the contest well and could not help themselves. They were takers. He told me how each man will protect his own honor. A man without honor is a man without sorrow, and a man without sorrow is a man without love.

For now, just receive Yeesa as the spirit of an Indian who had died. I realize this is different. We think of the dead as gone. They are not. He is not. I encountered him face-to-face in a different way. He told me that he had observed me for my entire life as a member of what Scripture describes as the great cloud of witnesses. Members of the cloud of witnesses are not sitting in armchair swivel recliner rockers floating on heaven's cloud observing earth's goings-on below. Some are active participants in lives as Jesus asks them as messengers to help God's children.

Yeesa was asked to observe my life and not to interfere until the time was right. It took a long time for that moment to arrive. Though this is my story, I need his help in telling it. When I met him, he knew me better than I did myself and says some things better than I am able. Yeesa is my friend and a spiritual guide. **Yeesa and I both share with you as narrators, voices or speakers in telling segments of the story. We indicate that at each transition. As you read or listen, we ask that you do so thoughtfully and picture Yeesa and Satch as being together inside the story. When I am not the one speaking to you, Yeesa is. He knows me well.** I have asked Yeesa at this point to help by sharing some of his observations.

Hi, my name is Yeesa. I am speaking to you now, and I want you to know this tale chronicles only glimpses of Satch's life. But just to read or hear it can bring a heaviness. To engage such a path is arduous. A lot of people just want all the gritty, grimy details like the specifics of abuse, failures, divorce, and other broken relationships. Satch was very clear to me that some things should never be told. They are not necessary. They are only harmful.

Shallow and nosey "inquiring minds" want to know and gossip the stark secrets of another's life. At the same time there is a hushed, instinctive awareness within them that their own world does not approach the big picture of life—the kingdom of God, the network of creation and the universes—the connectedness of all people and things. We do not want to face something that mysterious and huge, that far on the edge, that costly. Yet it is always near you and in you. Therein lies hope. If you can acknowledge the felt discomfort of life or just the anguish of enduring, your inner being may enhance your boldness to move you beyond your tiny, incomplete world. To do so takes courage.

Bravery and courage are not the same thing. Bravery is being adrenaline filled and can be reckless. Bravery is dauntless with no fear of an enemy. Courage is being afraid and confronting an enemy in spite of your fears. Brokenness is an enemy. To face our brokenness requires an effort that may kill what you feel is your life, but it won't. Someone, something bigger than you matters more than your fear. Be not afraid and nameless. Have courage. You are not alone.

An ordinary man does not listen to the voice of the imperishable flame in him, the light that dispels the darkness.

The seemingly small things keep evil at bay. It is the sound, a song far off from deep inside that compels; but you do not have to answer. Yet it sings. This internal flare leads you forward against external and internal enemies, which smother and drain your authentic life. Hold not ill will in yourself. Fight the shadows. Reclaim yourself. You want more, but you cannot do it alone. Only the inner light can give you strength and courage to confront your pain. *At times, all things seem right on the surface, while deep down inside, nothing is right at all.*

We cannot play the victim and continue to excuse accountability for our own lives. No conclusion or position is greater than God's approval. God wants us to live from a center of love and absolute assurance, a place of wholeness rather than from a place of lack, a place that strives to aspire. Satch was determined to find that certain surety. You make choices and fight your way frontward from love's assurance, while confronting and adjusting. If you choose the status quo and want to stay dissatisfied with your life, just sit there and shrink away. Satch refused to do that.

You should know on the front end that Satch tried to build his own little kingdom but felt he was an unworthy failure. Something foundational was missing. Now, why would Satch, who was a successful student, athlete, lawyer, politician, preacher, and administrator with a good family feel like a failure amidst all that success? Why did he not feel good about himself? Satch once asked, "How much of my life has been just for me and spent using my understanding and interpretation of the gospel as a way to advance myself?" Why did he feel he should always ride in the back of the team's second bus? Yet, he refused to throw in the towel. Satch and I hope this partial walk-through of his life will reveal something that matters to you. Stay awhile. You'll find out.

Yeesa, OhiYeesa (Oh-Hi-Yee-Sa) (Dr. Charles Alexander Eastman) Sioux Indian 1858-1939.

Photos from Google Images. A partial list of books authored by OhiYeesa – Yeesa,

Dr. Charles Alexander Eastman: Indian Child Life, Wigwam Evenings Sioux Folk Tales Retold, Indian Heroes and Great Chieftains, Indian Boyhood, The Soul of the Indian, Indian Scout Talks a Guide for Boy Scouts and Camp Fire Girls Fully Illustrated, The Indian Today, The Indian Today the Past and Future of the First American, Red Hunters and The Animal People, From the Deep Woods to Civilization, Old Indian Days, Indian Boyhood, The Raccoon and the Bee Tree.

CHAPTER 2

Glimpses from Childhood

There is a core issue all of us need to understand. For a child to know well-being, his connection with a primary authority figure also must feel safe. Satch's did not. What does a child do when he cannot trust anyone and finds no one safe? Safe is not just a place, it is a secure reliance. A distrust has to be uncoiled and removed to go forward in life. He did not know what to expect from his father. It took a long time to understand his mother and the other authorities in his life. His mother even changed her middle name and celebrated a different day as her birthday from that on her birth certificate. What was going on inside her? He grew up feeling very insecure.

Our ideas about God are most often influenced by our parents, especially our fathers. Therefore, children see God as they see their earthly father. Their earthly father is the authority mirror, the model of their heavenly Father. When an earthly father is fractured, he cracks the mirror of God's character, and the picture of our heavenly Father does not come through clearly. For Satch, God was not safe nor trustworthy.

Satch did not know how to make good choices. Who could he rely on for a safeguard? He did not have an encourager or protector. His father and God were inscrutable riddles. Emotional safety was unknown. Only by being compliant, performing and striving to please could he find any scant approval or acknowledgement. These efforts as a mechanism for acceptance do not work.

In order to have a fullness of life, it is essential to know what one cannot do. He eventually learned the only choice for him was to avoid staying in relationships that made him feel something was deeply wrong with him. He had to find a way to distance himself from the authority figures and groups that made him feel unsafe or were abusive and untrustworthy. The true God helped by dropping him down a sinkhole.

The greatest influences and forces come from within, but like the wind, they are incomprehensible. Satch was dazed, bewildered. He needed and wanted to wake up what was in him, to revive his better self, not just with external, second- or third-hand propositions directing him. He wanted to work out his own life, his own salvation. Psychology calls it individuation. Jesus says it starts with being born from above.

Satch told me about the suffering life had inflicted on him—as well as his reactions. I have no question about his integrity. My observations are included, but this is his story. He has spent his life asking questions, reading, listening, paying attention, and noting his best recollections of significant events. His exhaustive search covered over half a century, and his recollections, while knotty and disjointed doesn't mean they are untrue. Should you find meaning in his life story, it should not be mine or his, but yours. Revealing intimate things in honesty and being vulnerable is unusual and exceptional.

It is no picnic either. Do not harshly appraise him too quickly. He used to be somebody whom others labeled as smart, self-righteous, intense, hubristic. We all have been something else. That is what he "was." People want to define us by our past. The "I am now" is what matters.

Satch is of a different kind. Has been since a child. We are all truly unique, but Satch is a minority in his makeup and emotional complexity, which all likely developed in his struggle for emotional survival. Some might describe him as messed up, all twisted and broken inside. He is not exceptional, genius, or moronic—just apart; not a normie. According to personality profiles, between one and two percent of the human population have his personality niche, and it's not a comfortable one. His personality is multifaceted. Like all of us, he too has sub-personalities. We each have all dimensions within us and could benefit by understanding, valuing, and utilizing each aspect. Satch wears a lot of different hats. His personality is complex. At times it is torturous, but he also has dimensions of a real faith and demonstratable fortitude.

Satch is a paradox. He has been described by his counselors and others as intense and quiet. He is both bold and timid, strong and weak, hard and soft. He can be rude and sensitive, ascensive and humble. He is equally obsessive and practical, structured and impulsive. He is smart and foolish. He is mutually inscrutable and vulnerable, confident and unsure. In a way, he seems split. He partly wants to stay but is strong enough to walk away. He demands yet has compassion. He rattles people's cages. He changes things and at the same time tries to help re-establish them correctly.

Satch carries multiple thoughts in his mind, wants everything but knows it is not possible. Then he tries to do it anyway. In some ways he is spectacularly dysfunctional. He is no hero but often is viewed as a villain, especially by the religious. All the while, he feels abused, unaccepted, and unloved. He is not neurotic but is often socially awkward. His difficult manner of living engenders fatigue and resentfulness—and often pushes others away. At times, he wishes his life could be free from the pale of his name.

In a single moment, a life can be changed. With multiple negative occurrences, the damage can be devastating. Shun and kick a dog enough times, even he will think he is nothing, of no value—and that it is his fault. When that tilt happens, an indwelling, lingering melancholy often results. Satch's predicament reached a heavy hopelessness, a lifetime of low-grade unworthiness. He lived in the poverty of shame—a sorrow so deep it never faded from his memory. These wounds included the sexual and spiritual abuses Satch experienced at such a young age and later his own failures and affairs. Together they grew into a mountain of traumas that tore apart the depths of his being. His was a bleak world. It caused a breach in his soul, sabotaging inward parts. His deep wounds maimed him, resulting in a spirit of desolation.

Satch would not equate them with PTSD, but were some variant thereof. If they did not completely alter him physiologically and psychologically, they sure affected his neuro and immune systems and his relationships with others and within himself. The traumatic events that have happened to Satch and his negative reactions borne out of his pain are many.

His church elder father was a rule-enforcing merchant with a leather belt, a Sunday school teacher, and chairman of all the church committees. He was president of the local school board and of the board of trustees of a religious college. He was a thirty-third degree Mason, head honcho in the state. Fletcher and Satch found their dad's hidden key in a refrigerator in a storage room at the house. Fletch took it and inspected the rented locker where their dad kept his liquor and pills. He also secretly maintained a regimen of available women—including other men's willing wives.

Fletch followed a different path than Satch. Fletch did not like school, and he was the most gifted athlete in the entire family. He was drafted and sent to Vietnam. He served as a sniper, once staying in the top of a tree for two days, surrounded by the enemy. When he escaped, he finally made it to the convoy which on exit was blown up. Fletch was the only survivor. Multiple times he wrote letters to their dad, asking if he was okay and would he accept him. Their dad never wrote him back. Their sisters were younger. They would have to tell their own experiences.

Their dad held memberships in three different country clubs and various men's clubs in different towns. As a Christian he was rigidly legalistic, and as a worldly man, he was as sensual as a decadent Roman Gentile. His dad was an imperfect father. Both Satch and Fletch became imperfect sons. The ones sinned against likely follow suit, becoming infected, take in the sin and inflict on others that to which they were subjected. It is passed down and learned. Satch and Fletch came to grieve not being the fathers they wanted to be to their own children.

Satch's mother knew about her husband's dalliances but never mentioned them. Resigned to the fact, she became introverted and remote, stoically intent only on duty, unable to show affection to Satch and his siblings. Four or five days each week, his parents took him to some church function as obligatory service. Satch bought into religion, sorta. He resisted the forced religious duty, and, in time, Satch concluded that institutional religion was crippling rather than freeing. Any corporation, institution, or government as an entity is not a person. It has no heart, no feelings.

Stach's paternal line included six male preachers. He became the seventh, and later two female cousins became ministers, one of whom has now been in four marriages. Despite the male preachers, it was his paternal grandmother who wielded the religious power in his family. When Satch was three days old, in front of the entirety of both sides of the family, she pronounced, "This one is my preacher grandson." The family and community adopted this prophecy. As he grew older, Grandma pushed him into the ministry, as though it were necessary to continue the strict tradition of priesthood as a mandatory role handed down to a priest's sons generation after generation. His mom's mother, Nanna, gave him a Bible for high school graduation. He asked her why. Her response was, "I wanted you to have something you could use." Satch already had three translations beside his bed.

Satch's paternal grandmother, Grandma, was not without a heart, but she was driven by rules and law and had a radical penchant to manipulate. She held to the extreme legalistic, brutally rigid fundamentalist right side as opposed to the radically promiscuous and scientific left side of the Enlightenment, which is expounded today in the cagy and deceptive virus of woke postmodernism. Both sides seek to humiliate and indoctrinate rather than inform and educate. Their extremist views are saturating the internet and social media, utilizing smart devices as their carriers. Developers and manufacturers of these devices are largely proponents of these views, rebelling against culture's foundational values. Providing a young child with such a smart device or smart phone is like allowing a strange man into your house who takes your young daughter (or a strange woman your young son) into a bedroom and closes the door, while you leave them there and go shopping. These devices can be treacherous in immature, unwise hands.

Neither excessive right nor left extreme views lead to wholeness. Religion, philosophical and social theories, and politicians cannot and will not save you. You want someone else to come and fix it. They won't. Stop being silent if you want to live in a meaningful world with any degree of integrity. Courage—declare, live what you believe. Do not be afraid to be seen.

Satch's Grandma shamed a state senator's wife for wearing a pantsuit to her Sunday school class. She told her not to return until she was "properly dressed for church." The respected lady returned in a proper dress. Grandma, like a gargoyle with a mix of identities mounted outside the building as a warning, entered through the church door in her very personhood, unleashing a dark force lying within. She, the family, and the entire community treated Satch as being the one who was responsible for doing right. He understood nothing about it until his late forties, when his aunt, who had witnessed the "prophecy," told him about it. She was astonished he did not know, saying, "I cannot believe you have not been told about that!"

You need to hear the following experiences from Satch himself.

I, Satch, think it may help you to understand that my mother sent me to school at age five. I felt that I was always the youngest child in my class. I was immature, emotionally unprepared. I would beg my daddy to let me go to Wednesday night prayer meetings before I was age ten. That was the only time I could spend with my dad. On the few occasions I was allowed to go, I was the only child in the chapel. I both honored and resented my dad, creating a confusing and incoherent mistrust. I viewed God as I did my father, with apprehension and anxiety. I would ask questions of the preacher and other adults, looking for answers—ultimately to determine whom I could trust and with whom I could feel safe.

In November of my tenth year, I killed my first quail. My dad had never shown me how to use that .410 single shot shotgun or any gun. He handed it to me with a shell and told me how to load it. We arrived at the site and met his hunting partner. Shortly thereafter, the dogs slowed and pointed, revealing they had located a covey of quail. At the covey rise, my dad and his hunting partner shot several times, emitting a thunderous sound I had never heard before. Birds fell. My dad collected the birds and walked off, chatting with his partner. They proceeded down the hill and out of sight. A few minutes later, they commenced the shooting of singles disbursed from the covey rise. Then it happened.

I was just standing still in my tracks. Stunned, I did not move. What I call a sleeper was hidden in the grass. The quail did not leave with the covey but secreted itself a long time. When the bird suddenly burst forth, almost from under my feet, I took a long aim and pulled the trigger. Shockingly, the bird fell. It was flopping and still trying to run away. Back then I did know how to wring its neck. I thought, *There are only tiny pellets in this little shell. If I hold the bird at the end of the barrel and pull the trigger, it would only put small holes in the bird and then it would not suffer anymore.* So I held the bird by its head at the end of the barrel and pulled the trigger.

Following the explosion nothing was left of the bird. There was only a voluminous floating cloud of feathers, many of which settled on my head and shoulders. There was no more bird. I was left holding the bird's head between my thumb and forefinger. I had almost shot off my left hand. The injured flesh stung badly and bled. I cleaned and wrapped my hand as best I could. My dad never asked what happened, and I never told him. It would have done no good. I still do not know why my dad took me on that hunt, but the event evolved into a frightening, unforgettable experience.

My youngest sister was born on the same morning as the infamous hunt. On the way to the hunt, we had visited my mom and little sis, Ellie, in the hospital. She was my parents' fourth child, born at 4:00 a.m. Neither of my parents had chosen a name for my little sister. No name, no blessing. I could not believe it, so I named her that morning. I saw she was distinct.

The next month on Christmas Day, the seventeen grandchildren on my mother's side got in trouble for egging the roof of a grouch lady's house next door. The lady had called the police again—for the third year in a row. "They are playing outside and making too much noise," the police reported her as saying. We grandchildren responded with mischief and egged her roof. My mother blamed me. Not a word was said to the other sixteen grandchildren by any of the parents. I was "the one" who was never to do such things. My mother made me, the scapegoat, earn the money to clean the lady's roof. I had no idea what that could cost. She never told me.

With an allowance of twenty-five cents a week plus what I could otherwise scrape up, I could only accumulate $7.50 over many weeks. I kept the change in a paper bag. Then, over a two-week period, my mother drove me three different times to the lady's house to apologize and pay. We parked on the street, and I walked up to the front door. I knocked and waited every time. Each trip as I stood at her front door knocking and ringing the bell, I heard the lady stirring around inside the house, but she would not answer. Finally, after continually pleading the obvious, my mother allowed me to leave the money with a note in the lady's mailbox. But only after my mother approved the language in the note. I was humiliated, but at least it was over. She spoke not another word to me on the drive home.

As an eleven-year-old seventh grader, I started on the sports teams and made straight *A's* on my first report card.

That evening after practice, it was dark. I rushed home on my bicycle to show the only person who mattered, my daddy. I caught him headed to his bedroom. I called to him. He would not answer. I had to knock on the door to get him to come. I showed him my report card. My dad looked at the card and shoved it back in my face. I said, "Dad, I made straight *A's*." He retorted, "That's what you're supposed to make!" Then he slammed the door in my face.

My little brother, Fletch, and I traveled by train the next summer to a boy's camp in the Blue Ridge Mountains. Every Friday night, the camp staged a Native American Indian celebration higher up the mountain with authentic native costumes, campfires, tents, and rugs—including a ceremonial tent. Every boy wore a headband indicating his rank. The fourth week's session found the Big Chief standing proud in his moccasins, split fringed leather pants, beaded shirt, knife in belt, and eagle-feathered knee length headdress. I received a promotion each of the previous weeks, but no first-year camper could be awarded the rank of Little Chief. He announced the recipients of the highest award for first-year boys. Even though I had succeeded every week in all tasks, my name was not called. I hung my head. I could not envision how I had failed or disqualified myself. I was filled with an overwhelming sense of unworthiness. I tried to hide my tears, but they dripped from my cheeks. I had failed again.

After all awards had been given, the Big Chief, who owned and ran the camp, stood silent. He struggled to find the right words. The drums stopped their reverberations, no sounds came from the gathered. Nature grew hushed all around. A stillness filled the mountain. The Chief finally broke the silence. "We have had something happen this year with which we have no previous experience. We decided to create an honor level above our previous highest level that can be achieved by a deserving boy in his first summer with us. The new title for that is Pathfinder. Two first year campers deserve this tribute—the only two in the long history of this camp." At that point, one other boy and I were called forward. I had no idea of the honor's significance or the path I would eventually discover.

I was humbled but did not know how to hold the affirmation. The feeling came quickly like a flash from a camera. It burned into me then faded as a glowing light from a bulb that is turned off. Any sense of unworthiness clasped me like Velcro. I did not know how to interpret or receive praise. The next summer, I returned to the camp. After meeting all the required goals, I was nominated for and confirmed as Little Chief. Camp officials encouraged me to select my own Indian name. I felt I was not good enough to wear the name of an honored, powerful, and strong leader among the Native Americans or that of a revered animal or bird. I chose Little Chief Hustling Spider. I did not then realize this was to be like a coming-of-age ritual, my bar mitzvah, my transition to manhood. I had no idea of my true identity, except that I tried. So I had no clue of the pathway I was to be given. My soul eventually found me on the path I was walking. You cannot rush the tide. It just happens. Then you know.

One summer night of my fourteenth year, Fletch and I slipped quietly out of the house to ride bicycles and meet a couple of buddies. I was gone less than an hour. I slipped quietly back into the unlit house—still sweaty from August's heat. It was before midnight. I listened to the barely audible sound of footsteps easing down the fifteen stairs to our bedroom. My mother, now beside my bed, said, "Do you think you can get away with anything in this town without us finding out about it? We have already had several calls about your being out. Where is your little brother?"

When we had arrived at the first stop sign, Fletch turned his bike in a different direction. I did not know that Fletch was going to do that or where he went. I called for Fletch but received no response. He just took off down an opposite hill. After I told my mom what Fletch had done, she snapped, "Get in the car!" She drove me around for over half an hour demanding I tell where Fletch had gone. I had no idea. Then, she pulled to the side of a street and stopped. She cut off the engine and stared at me. Pointing her finger, she declared, "You need to know that twenty minutes of pleasure is not worth it." I almost laughed aloud but held it and turned my head. I could not help smiling. I was ignorant but not dumb. I knew she was talking about sex. When she said it, I thought, "How do you make it last twenty minutes?" From that time on, my parents would not allow me to spend a night away from home.

On Halloween night of my sophomore year in high school, I attended a party at a friend's house. The fifteen kids there wanted to go into the locked and gated town cemetery across the street. All fifteen went. I walked with them but refused to go in because I considered such an act disrespectful. Despite my feelings, the others climbed the gate while I sat outside leaning against one of the bricked columns. When they returned, the partiers laughed at me and called me names. Pay attention to this: I believed my parents. In my mind, they were right about everything. Even as a fourteen-year-old, I still believed in Santa Claus—at least until I found new bicycles in the car trunk on Christmas Eve. They had misled me! I felt ashamed and foolish.

The next year, my parents let me attend a school dance as long as I arrived back home by 10:30 p.m. Remember when those numeric flip clocks came out? My dad had one. After my night at the dance, I came home and ran feverishly up those same fifteen stairs to check in. I always had to check in. I stood beside my dad's bed. His clock read 10:31. "Dad, I want you to know I am okay, home and safe," I said. As I spoke those words, the clock flipped over to 10:32. My dad did not even turn over to look at me, but in an irritated grump retorted, "You are late. You are grounded. Do not plan anything for the next two weeks!" I later discovered that as a teenager my dad came home after curfew one night. His mother locked him out of the house, forcing him to spend that night in their yard.

CHAPTER 3

Senior Year and Grit

In my senior year, sports analysts and fans projected our football team would be the best in four years, when the team finished undefeated and ranked number one in the country. A week before the first game, some of the thirty-six seniors on our team called a senior meeting. All came. They proposed a strict abstinence—no drinking, smoking, or girls—as evidence of total dedication to the team's success.

Although I was only sixteen years old, I knew my teammates. I knew they could not keep such a commitment. It ran contrary to who they were. I knew it was a huge mistake. "Please don't do this," I pled. "What are you going to do when a teammate violates one of these proposals? This will cause division." They responded, "Tell the coaches." They all belittled me for opposing the proposal. When the votes were cast and the decision made, I knew immediately that disaster awaited. It came quickly. Some of them at that very meeting when they voted already had dates and beer iced down in their cars outside.

Less than three weeks later, some teammates made a spectacle at a school-sponsored senior dance monitored by teachers, sponsors, and coaches.

One of my friends, who was a starter, entered the venue accompanied by other teammates. My friend and his date and two other friends were clearly drunk and pranced around like fanned-out peacocks. The young drunkards strutted up to me in the middle of the dance floor. They were so loud the music stopped playing. With students, teachers, and coaches watching, my friend simultaneously taunted and challenged me: "What are you going to do now, big boy?" It was so public everybody knew about it.

The next week, as the seniors had insisted, two of my close friends and teammates came and said I had to be the one to report it to the coaches. I asked, "*Why me?*" The two were certain and firm that it was my responsibility. Together we begrudgingly reported the incident to the coaches, knowing they already knew. I had given my word, and as much as I hated doing it, I intended to stand by it. *Doing what you believe is right does not always make you feel good. Suffering can come from doing right as well as wrong.* At that point neither I, nor my two teammates with me, understood the hypocrisy of Southern culture or how to deal with it. I knew all my coaches regularly partook of alcohol. I pled with the coaches not to punish them, because it would destroy the team. My two teammates supported my request to the coaches, but the coaches did not listen. The punishment brought wave upon wave of destruction. In the aftermath, I was denounced and ostracized for acting according to the agreement made between our coaches and teammates. No one else was blamed.

The coaches kicked my friend off the team. It was a disaster for the team, the season, and the school. We lost several games because of discord. The team, the school, and the community blamed me. Schoolmates sneered and walked away calling me names. No adult in the school or community would talk with me about the matter. Rather, they greeted me with surliness and stares. Football is a god in the South. And mobs and crowds don't have a mind, only a dangerous mimetic momentum, which I learned quickly. I was rejected. I was labeled *persona non grata*, ostracized like a skimmington.

They wrote derogatory names for me on the stadium walls.

Vandals destroyed our family property. They cut the tires on our car, rolled our yard with toilet paper, and trashed our outdoor furniture multiple times. Different hostile groups at various places confronted me. They threatened and pressured me to meet them at late hours in dark locales, but none of the bullies would go to the gym and put on boxing gloves to settle the issue. An anonymous person retained three out-of-towners to knife me at the senior prom. God must have intervened, and the police caught them. Neither of my parents would listen or talk to me about all that happened or the potential assault. I had embarrassed the family. They did not know how to be the good stewards of my life as God intended.

Some so-called friends did not have time for me anymore. Girlfriends turned out to be deceivers. Coaches said one thing while doing another. Hostile schoolmates, betrayals, and rejections—it all took a toll on me. Sure, I injured others and made my own mistakes and failings. *Hurt people hurt people.* The sum total of these moments multiplied and continually cloned themselves in various persons and circumstances.

They fostered an inner wretchedness and a beleaguered soul within me. I felt no comfort or strength.

On the day of high school graduation, as I approached the entrance to the auditorium with my cap and gown in hand, a classmate came up to me and said, "Well, you did it again!! They just kicked another classmate out of the graduation line for being drunk. You told on him too, didn't you?"

I had no idea what he was talking about, but I had had enough. I was pissed. I went in the school looking for a person in authority. The school counselor was walking down the hall. I asked if we could talk. She agreed and we went into her office. "Please tell me why not one teacher, not one coach, not one administrator, not one person in authority—not even you—for over the last nine plus months, would stand up and deal with this situation. You have allowed it all to be placed on the shoulder of one sixteen-year-old boy! WHY?" I asked. She dropped her head and would not look me in the eyes. Her only response was, "I do not know." I felt like life had treated me like a baby does a diaper.

Now let me, Yeesa, tell you what happened to Satch thirty years later. Satch met again with his counselor friend, for three all-day sessions. Brad was leading a conference in another state. Satch told more of his upbringing—stories of the tension from the contorted tenets and codes. Much of Satch's sharing centered on his family, church, and college days, but he also told of that day he chose his Little Chief name. His friend asked, "Well, did your parents give you anything good?" All he could say was, "Yes, material provision and grit!

Stubborn grit." The real gifts of determination and courage have benefited him all his life, even though many years passed before he could appreciate them.

Satch recognized these traits within himself during his first professional football preseason. As a college senior, Satch suffered a second knee injury, which caused his draft status to drop from an early rounder to the very last round—then the seventeenth at #430. Essentially, he was a walk-on! Minimum salary.

NFL teams work by capitalizing and depreciating players. They use most draft picks and free agents as guinea pigs for training camp's endurance process to test the players they hope to keep. Players are like equipment, replaceable objects. They stuck Satch at wide receiver. He had not played that position in three years! Further, they placed him in the fourth slot on the depth chart. Back then, most teams only used two wide receiver slots—one outside on either side of the formation. The team would keep only three. This team already had their experienced receivers in camp. He was a wideout on one side of the formation, splitting plays with an All-Pro receiver. Satch became a fill-in for as long as he could last.

The July heat in West Texas provided the perfect crucible for weeding out the pretenders. Only the players with the greatest resolve could bear up under the grueling, daily practice routine. Satch was running twenty to forty yards per play, sprinting on passing routes, cutting, jumping, catching passes, and jogging back to the huddle to do it over again and again—all in a 104-degree pressure cooker for over two hours, twice a day.

One day midway through camp, Satch lost fourteen pounds from morning weigh-out to evening weigh-in.

The team practiced the kicking game for which he was drafted at the end of the afternoon practice. By that time, Satch was exhausted. They had drafted another player in an early round for the same specialty punter position as Satch's. He stood or sat every practice on the sidelines flipping a ball. Satch knew what was going on. The team's medical doctor checked the records daily and came to Satch. "You cannot do this. You cannot lose this kind of weight!" Satch responded, "Well, you tell me what I can do about it. I know what they are doing, but I am telling you right now, they are not going to win this! You just watch."

At the end of the pre-season, the head coach called Satch in and told him they would keep only one punter. Satch was traded. These teams have a hard time admitting they make mistakes, some of which are obvious. Satch outperformed that other kicker the years he was in the league. Grit helped him face the tough stuff, but Satch still did not know the true source of his determination. While the world focuses on money and notoriety, Satch directed his focus elsewhere.

He never earned much money playing football, but he saved as much as he could. In those days, Satch knew he was searching for something but did not know what for or why. Regardless, he felt compelled to keep searching.

One thing that hurt Satch immeasurably was his parents' refusal to discuss the suffering and vilification he endured in high school. That and his dad's and mom's inability or unwillingness to look him in the eye and say, "I love you, Son." Such aloofness plagued men of that generation—especially a World War II fighter pilot shot down twice in the Pacific. Displays of emotion were not manly.

His mom became detached and withdrew into her shell, not unlike an ascetic, due to the pain of her husband's behavior which she knew about—producing her own traumas. Neither parent could affirm him. Their own damage would not allow it. Satch had much experience with pain, grief, and loss. They can trounce you.

The state of Texas may or may not have had more churches than the county where Satch was raised in the deep South, but Texas also wasn't simultaneously the world headquarters for the Ku Klux Klan! When you have God turned backward, it causes multitudes of suffering. Spiritual abuse, perversion, and non-affirmation transferred to children as being culturally acceptable causes calamity physiologically and psychologically. Genes even modify. The effects of such sin, which is missing the mark of one's and another's true identity, is passed down this way. It is not just a problem, it brings death. Incredulous? I watched it all happen! Denying the goodness of Good, the truth of Truth, rejecting and refusing to acknowledge the very Spirit of God is often called the unpardonable sin. *Someone must break the cycle and repair the tear in the garment handed down before an authentic life can begin.*

One can avoid dark places out of fear or be light to them. Tough, challenging news can make one spiritually deaf to the truth. A piece of wood will yield to the carver's hand. A human heart—that's a different story. Satch in time learned forgiveness was a way to honor his parents. When that happened, the weightiness of the fog eventually lifted as he remembered the good his parents did for him. Since then, he has forgiven and blessed them. Satch now realizes his dad, mom, and family were like tutors—God's potter hands molding the stiff, hardheaded piece of clay into a small vessel that would become a man who one day might hold a tiny glimpse of the goodness and love God wanted to place in his soul.

Satch chose to meet again with his confidant—this time at Nashville's Vanderbilt University where his friend served on the faculty. He also coached leadership teams who constantly clamored for his guidance. He had been reared in Mexico as the child of a missionary couple. He enrolled in seminary but became bored with the doctoral program and transferred to Vanderbilt for his doctoral degree. He told Satch, "You are the classic example of what a religious culture can do to a child. You have to tell this story."

Long before the day his counselor friend urged Satch to tell his story, the seed had already been planted in him that what had happened to him needed to be told to help others. Satch had seen similar pain in so many other people. Satch and I have known each other now for several years since the night he fell into the mound. Satch was born in the rural, conservative Deep South but has traveled all over North America. He has lived in Houston, Fort Worth, New Orleans, and New York—plus multiple small towns in the South. But the struggles to overcome the issues addressed herein are not limited to the southern USA. Watch the Netflix documentary on Satch's fellow football player Aaron Rodgers. He grew up in California.

Satch has followed a nomadic spirit, relocating about thirty times as he continued searching, testing his soul. Those who go their own way without a star get lost in an unfathomable darkness. In about half of the stops along his journey playing professional football and practicing law—both before and after pastorates—Satch took his family. Although Satch remained married for four decades, he ended up divorced. He now administers a business for his family.

This may seem strange, but what folks might say and do is not always their root reality. With much introspection one can move from saying and doing to being. Satch learned to be grateful for all that had happened, whether done to him via the weeds tied to the roots of his life—culture, traditions, and his family's behaviors—or when done by him to others. He now understands and accepts that *an indefinable corporate network of sin unbiddenly assaults everyone*. He has faced, named, and slayed many of his dragons, along with making amends as best he knew how. He is no longer a moral gardener pulling the tares from the wheat, the evil from the good. His suffering and failures have been and will be his teachers. Religion, family, and other influences were not simply mistakes. They formed a learning ground, the process of matriculation in faith. He began to see that resentment, murmuring, blaming, and a complaining spirit further disintegrated his own personhood.

Any proud, rule-based, climbing-back-to-God religion tries, at least in part, to teach the importance of identifying and participating in what is right and good—to be the very best and noble person one could be. It taught Satch the necessity of the fear of God. That will set some boundaries. He now sees the dangers of blindly repeating mistakes. He now appreciates the failures, sins (whatever you want to call them) and their pain. Through them, he has come to better understand that God is not as He is taught in most religious systems, which is an ambiguous and arbitrary ruler to be feared. A renewed mind results from a lifelong process of learning, unlearning, and relearning. It is essential if one expects to find peace.

Satch's advanced years and diminished physical health have limited his activities. Despite these limitations—and in part because of them—he has identified and continues to face his subconscious shadow and has become healthier in mind, emotions, and spirit. He experiences peace, at least most of the time.

Satch judges less, since his own self-righteousness and unworthiness have been exposed. He has learned to trust again after being betrayed. Measuring comes back on you. Deluded minds and divided hearts require hard lessons and a lot of suffering. Broken and moaning hearts need a lot of healing. Most times, both suffering and love are required. Satch is learning to contemplate, celebrate life, and pursue meaning.

He has a cordial relationship with his former wife and his children. He remembers and prays for them but has learned to let them be whom they choose. Now, he lives away and alone with minimal social contact, but he is not lonely. He is comfortable with himself. He loves his little farm. Some evenings, he still sits beside the cedar tree, which now tilts toward the former sinkhole shaft into which he fell. He misses his bird dogs and horses but enjoys his barn cats. He says they are fascinating to watch. He's right!

Satch was taught and thought many things about God and himself, but most of those have been turned upside-down. God is not up there somewhere totally outside oneself and separate but inside, both immanent and transcendent. God's grace and mercy comes it seems out of nowhere, flowing, seeping down like water through every narrow crack and crevice to the dimmest, deepest, darkest places in the underground dungeons of our beings that we didn't know existed. Together, they pool up there, enlightening and soothing our griefs and heart's darkness, quenching the barren dryness of our souls. Satch has been and continues to go through this ringer of life but has become more sensible and joyful in truth. God is always good, and loving, even of ol' broken Satch.

Everyone can encounter and come to know this authenticity, but it does not come from a kingdom of this world. There is no such thing as luck or chance. It is indeed a mysterious wisdom, a hidden secret, a paradox which intellect and logic cannot conceive. It is energy of the sacred. Yet it is revealed to those who would again become a child in heart and spirit, willing to see and act toward the good and become original. Imagination helps one to begin. *Get used to the different.* Be patient with Satch and yourself.

CHAPTER 4

ONE LONELY DRIVE

I, Satch, want to tell you about my old farm where I was going to live now. It is located six or so hours away from my last house, which my wife received in the divorce settlement. The farmhouse was at the peak of the hill. The land sloped west down to the boundary creek and was flat the next three miles to the river. The property angled down to the road in front of the house. Houses dotted the landscape to the state highway a mile away to the west. The bottomlands, where no one lived because of the river's flooding, lay beyond the highway. The river, which occasionally rose, entered and swelled the creek on the west side of the property. Across the river bottom land ran a gravel road from the highway, down across the railroad tracks and to the river and the remains of an old bridge. Although no longer in use, parts of the old bridge remained and served as a hangout and fishing hole.

This trip to the farm took place months after the divorce was final and everything was settled. During this lonely and long drive, I looked down at my gas gauge and noticed my tank was close to empty. I needed a fill up. I knew a store at the next intersection and decided to take a break, fill up, and get a bite to eat. I pulled over, filled my tank, and went inside. I was standing in line paying for my drink and snack when I started thinking about how all this started when I was two years old. When I got back on the road, my mind started recalling all of these incidents, jumping back and forth, all over the place.

That episode at the swimming pool along with subsequent experiences of sexual and religious abuse, betrayal, rejection, and my confusion about and fear of God seem to be my deepest issues. There were two girls in particular, one in high school and one in college, who played with, used, and deceived me. Later in my forties and fifties, I was enticed and betrayed by two other women when I was serving as a pastor. Those relationships cratered my life. For a while I could not get away from them. Thankfully, I was finally able to do so.

My counselor told me that events in our childhood can impact us for the rest of our lives until you face them and get to the truth at the bottom of them. Too often family, religion, and rejection—especially betrayal—confuse and compound issues for a sensitive child who feels neglected and forced to comply with traditions. Those issues vibrated within me, but there was more, the contradictions lived out by my daddy and my mother's withdrawal into herself. As a result, both parents were unable to show love to us children. This affected all four of us in different ways. In my sixties after my divorce, I called a family meeting where I confronted my father about what had been done to my mother. All three of my siblings were there. It happened like this:

I asked my father and siblings to meet with me at the farm because I had questions only they could help me answer.

I was surprised *they all came.* I laid the groundwork by telling them what I knew to be true about my mother. I related to them my experience growing up with my mother and asked them to share theirs. Each of them told the same story. Then I said to Dad, *"When Momma dies and nobody cries, something is wrong. You have never shed a tear over her. Neither have we. What happened to our mother?"*

My dad dropped his head and looked at the floor. His only response was, "You are taking me places I have never been." He remained silent. He would not say another word.

I loved both my parents. All four of us children were grateful for our father's material provision, but I had little respect for him. I had more respect for my mother, because I knew how she had suffered. I never understood how my father could demand we live one way while he lived in stark contradicting contrast. Well, eventually I did. I had walked a related path and have to face the consequences.

All four of us knew our mom loved our dad. Divorce in those days was completely forbidden. She knew about his liaisons but did not address them. Instead, she became dispirited and withdrawn. She isolated herself, eventually staying home all the time. She had no outside relationships, and only left the house for the beauty parlor once a week. That was probably for dress up Sundays. Eventually, she told all of us children not to come visit for Christmas. Both of our parents provided well for us materially, but they were not able to show us love.

Our mom became cold and aloof. None of the four of us remembered her rocking, holding, feeding, kissing, or telling us she loved us. Our dad was home only at night and hardly spoke to us, but he disciplined us ruthlessly. We were not allowed to embarrass the family. My father was simultaneously an important religious and community leader but a total negative incongruity in his alternative, secret life.

We children found it strange that he would show up at our practices and watch for a few minutes, then leave. Could it have been because he was president of the school board or was it the only way he could demonstrate his connection with us? He did not speak about it. We never knew why. Both our parents attended all our games and performances, even my college and professional football games, but they never complimented me. My mother kept extensive statistics on our games and recognitions, but we did not find out about that until after she died. She wrote down and kept everything, but she never said a word.

My mom's folks had some money, but you wouldn't have known it. I did not until I handled my grandfather's estate when he died. They were unpretentious and lived simple lives. The assets in my family came from them. My mother had more income than my dad. My maternal grandfather completed only the sixth grade, but he was a whiz who had businesses in several states.

All the men in my dad's family were preachers. My dad's mother was the force. Her four daughters married preachers. That tradition continued all the way through each of her children's family lines, including mine. All of it was a conundrum for me.

I became a performer as a child, seeking approval from academics, athletics, and church. That was expected of me and all I knew. Unfortunately, the affirmations never came. Rather, I received deflating feedback from my parents, such as, "That's what you're supposed to do" and "You can do anything you want, just excel at it; be at the top of your class." They even gave me a board game titled: "Top of the Class."

Then I thought about my divorce. In short, my marriage went to hell. And no wonder. So, there was the sexual abuse, spiritual abuse, and psychological abuse in my childhood, and I had no idea how to deal with it. Then there were my affairs. They were my fault, as was the divorce. I was disobedient to God. I can't think any more about that now. My heart aches at the thought of it.

Then there are the words of my counselor when I was going over all of this with him. I couldn't believe my ears when he said, "But you have been so successful!"

"And just what does that mean?" I chirped. "When I received as a rookie that NFL Oscar in Chicago on national television, I said to myself, *Is this all there is at the top?* The questions I received from the media and attendees were "How does it make you feel? Do you think you can improve and do even better next year?"

I asked my counselor if he knew the children's story *Hope for the Flowers*? It's the story of a caterpillar crawling on top of other caterpillars to get to the top of a pillar. Once there, he thinks there must be more. He looks up and sees a single caterpillar crawling out on a tree limb making a cocoon. That sole caterpillar constructs a cocoon and becomes who he truly is. He had it in him all the time—but didn't know it. He turns into a butterfly. One caterpillar/butterfly was never compelled by the competition for the top of the pile. Well, I don't know how to do that. I'm in my seventh decade. Answer me this, When you get to the top, how do you get back down? Well, the others knock your ass off! That's what happened to me!

How do I become a butterfly now? I am stuck, drowning, while corroding inside. Whatever joy and happiness are, I have yet to meet them.

I thought back about all the places I had been and the things I had done. During and after playing ball, I practiced law for a decade before entering the ministry. I earned two theology degrees and pastored churches for twelve years. I had an affair, got kicked out of the church, and went back to practicing law for over a decade. Then a friend called me every day for eighteen days in a row to come help him lead a very large congregation. We moved again. After several years there, I got emotionally involved with another woman.

Then Maggie jumped back into my mind. I pondered on how and when my marriage to Maggie began to disintegrate. That was the slam dunk that ended my former life. What caused this? Maggie and her family were clear and outspoken about their feelings regarding my becoming a preacher instead of a lawyer. Her mother said to me, "We don't need any more preachers. We need Christian lawyers." My own father told me, "You are too damned old now to make a mistake."

My wife loved living close to her mother and the life she enjoyed as an attorney's wife. We had just moved into our new house and were expecting our third child. She was happy, as were our children. We had good friends and exceptional pediatricians. I knew she did not want me to go into institutional religious ministry.

She followed me anyway and gave birth to our third child while I attended seminary. My first full-time pastorate was in the same state we had left and wasn't terribly far from her mother. But the next stop was a large church in another state. Each of my children had to adjust to different public and private schools with each move. It was a constant variation in life for them and the family. Our two oldest girls had a very difficult time. After the first year, the older one started college and within a year wanted to get married. Our second child struggled with not being as accepted at a new school as she had been in the former town, so we transferred her to a private school where she excelled. In her new school, she received recognition socially, in academics and sports. After high school, she attended college in that same state and did very well. Both our girls and son are now exceptional and capable people.

At the last senior pastorate, we lived in a rented house for four years, being unable to find anything we wanted to buy. We were not comfortable with our life in that situation. The church was large and demanding—big staff serving three thousand members. They expected the pastor to minister to each one and be available as a speaker at every club event in town. One of the leaders said my twelve-year-old truck was not suitable for their pastor and told me I needed to buy a new one.

I seldom spent time at home. On one Wednesday evening, I hurried home after the service to pick up a file I needed for another meeting. I carried the burden of the church people in my heart, but these constant administrative duties and meetings sapped me. After retrieving the file, I rushed to the door to return to the church when my young son appeared in front of me. He said, "Daddy, what are you doing home?" His question stopped me in my tracks. I worked seventy to eighty hours a week; my family had become a small sidebar. The situation was bad, and I knew it. I was failing as a husband and father.

At the same time, I had begun to transition from my limited grasp of theology to an understanding of the connectedness of all things in union with God. I tried repeatedly to share it with our six seminary-trained staff. They rolled their eyes but admitted having no idea what I was talking about. I felt alone in a foreign land. My wife and children were not happy. Neither was I.

One night when I finally got to bed, I wanted to talk to my wife, the only person I had left with whom I thought I could share trust. She was lying in bed with her back to me. My reading light was on. I kept talking about the struggles we were facing, hoping she was hearing me. Then, she rolled over on her right elbow, looked me in the eyes, and said, "Satch, I've made up my mind. I'm going to stay with you and raise my children. I don't know what you are going to do. Good night." She rolled back over and went to sleep. I knew then I was all alone.

After that, other incidents occurred. The marital relationship moved into dire straits. That's when the first of the aggressive "other women" appeared, and I could not resist. Four years before I had sent the same woman away after one counseling session. This time I couldn't. Feeling lonely, I rationalized that I needed someone to listen and care for me. When the affair became known, I resigned. The woman and her husband betrayed me, Maggie, and themselves by confessing it all during a church service. The gossip spread like the government's COVID. It went everywhere.

Suddenly I remembered what one of the few friends I had in that town told me the afternoon after I resigned. I was sitting beside the rental house located on a corner lot. I was watching the parade of church members' cars pass by as the inquisitive occupants glared at their discredited pastor's house. They wanted to see or learn more. As I watched, my friend drove up and parked at the bottom of the hill. He knew where I would be. We had sat there many times and conversed. As he lumbered up the hill, I rose and met him halfway. He hugged me and then looked me in the eyes and said, "Man, I am so sorry, but now you are one of us." I jumped back at him saying, "What are you talking about? We have hunted quail, traveled together, shot crows and feral cats, turtles, ridden four-wheelers, sat by the fire at your farm, shared meals in each other's homes. We have always been with each other and with some other guys."

"Yeah," he said, "you were with us, but you never were one of us—but you are now, aren't you!"

And it hit me, the realization, the exposure was not just my secret becoming public, I saw myself to the core for the first time, as I really was, a rebellious sinner. I was exposed to myself in my own eyes. I was just exactly like my friend and all other people. I was undone. I will be forever grateful to him for his love, courage, and honesty.

But we moved in shame. Maggie and I spent eighteen months in counseling, driving week after week to Nashville for all-day sessions. I thought the issues had been resolved, but they had not fully. During this time, which included a nine-month interlude living in another town, unemployed with dwindling financial resources, we moved back to the town where I had practiced law before. I spent seven years longing and trying to be accepted for another pastorate. Nothing but rejection due to my affair. After more than a decade of law practice there, we moved to another city so I could help guide an even larger church as the Executive Pastor. I refused to preach there. We were there a number of years, but our marriage continued burdened.

That's when the second woman appeared. I wasn't looking for a relationship, but after several years I became emotionally involved. I bit the sour bullet again. As I thought about these things, I came to realize that I initiated the marital issues by choosing to go into what I understood was "the ministry." Well, I blew it twice, and I knew it. My wife and I went to four different counselors together—all of whom she chose. At her urging, I agreed to go separately to a fifth—a religious counselor—who she had already seen. I complied with her wishes, but it was obvious I did not need to stay long.

I told the counselor what I knew my wife had told him, and that he was number five to be consulted. Then I left. The counseling saga had gone on for more than a year. Then my wife received counseling from a sixth—a family member of hers. He must have told her what she wanted to hear.

We agreed to a separation. After about six or seven months on a Friday afternoon, Maggie called and asked me to come look at the computer in the home office. She said there were issues with it. I knew she didn't use the computer. I sensed something suspicious, but I went to help. When I arrived my two daughters and my granddaughters were already there. I knew something was awry. I greeted them and then went to look at the computer. She stopped me. I sat on the couch. She would not sit down. Instead, she unloaded on me in front of the children and grandchildren whom she had invited to witness her announcement. She detailed my faults and advised me that she had filed for divorce. I tried to talk her out of it. I told her that I didn't want a divorce, but at that point knew I had to find an attorney in a hurry. I felt that she did not want the divorce either, which was not clearly revealed until after our final mediations and the final decree was already sealed and entered.

I got up and went to look at the computer. There was nothing wrong with it. Soon both my daughters came in and said we had to work this out. I told them I had tried and would continue. They asked me what the other issues were. I was not going to talk about it. There are always two sides to an issue. Whatever she told them was up to her, but I was not going put her down or say bad things to them about her. Her pain drove her actions in planning what she did. I confessed to them I had been wrong and apologized to them for my failures, as I had done with their mom. I could do nothing more.

I was then about an hour away from the old, four-room farmhouse, which gave me some time to consider the way the church responded to my inappropriate actions and the resulting rejection. These unpleasant thoughts caused me to pull to the side of the road and sit for a while. I thought, *All I know to do is ask God for help.* I pled with God to realign me. For that, I knew I needed a lot of help. I could not fix myself or anyone else. After that honest prayer, the only thing to do was wait to see what God might do. But how was I going to respond?

I just had to keep going. The prospects in front of me would not be fun. The condition I was in was deeper than sad. It hurt like I had been cut wide open with a circular saw and left exposed, bleeding and unattended. I was laid bare. I felt so alone. I began to realize I had to find a new way, a new life. Despite the grief I felt over this biggest regret and failure, I knew I must start over. My mindset, my environment, and my tendencies had to change. I couldn't fight back. I had to press forward.

CHAPTER 5

Sulk and Sour or Step Forward

Some wounds time alone cannot heal. They go too deep. I have learned you cannot go back. You can only stay stuck or move forward. *Hurts only increase the sadness and bitterness until each wound is acknowledged, faced, named, and addressed.* I knew that moving does not always change things. Perhaps it can lead to discovery but often becomes only a geographical exchange. After months of separation, then a year's worth of negotiations, the divorce was final. If my wife had not filed, I would not have. She was taken care of financially and had a lot of support. Now I had to move on.

I had friends close to the old farmhouse. I decided to move there, seeking the encouragement I needed to press forward. I had spoken with them, and we looked forward to seeing each other. *I hoped to find one friend who would be a true brother, upon whose shoulder I could lay my head and cry. I needed a soul friend.* In that kind of acceptance, you are understood and loved as you are, with no charade or pretense. I sought those who would care for me that way. I longed for the serenity and fellowship of a healing presence.

I gathered my belongings and headed for the place that held special memories—my dogs, horses, barn, and the little farmhouse. As I pulled up to the farm, I stopped my truck in front of the property. I looked at the horses in the pasture and the little white farmhouse at the top of the hill. I remembered the first time I saw it. It looked like an Indian Mound. I drove up the gravel driveway and parked between the cedar trees and the house.

I unloaded the truck and began to make the small house ready to be a permanent home—an activity that kept me busy for several weeks, until the eagerness faded. The emotional burdens again began to reach for me when I went to bed and when I woke. These voices and thoughts came to me unbidden, bombarded me, haunted me. They pronounced I was not good enough. They uttered and gazed at me in the mirror when I brushed my teeth and combed my hair. These weights of abuse and rejection sat on the table with me as I ate breakfast and were co-pilots when I drove my truck. There came no glow of the sun at dawn or in its setting at dusk. A gloomy haze filled the days' skies. Even the daylight felt dark. They all came back uninvited and squeezed the life out of my soul all over again.

My phone's hot spot then satellite Wi-Fi enabled me to continue to manage the family business remotely. This responsibility offered little satisfaction—except maybe because it was the one thing I was doing right. After several weeks of melancholy, somehow my preacher cousin popped into my mind. I had not thought about him in years. He too had left the church, his wife, and children, but to be with the woman he loved.

Hutt agreed to meet with me. Hutt was the name by which we all knew him. Everybody called him that, except his mother and father, who was also a preacher. He was smart and a gifted communicator. As I drove to Kentucky, I thought about how Hutt had divorced and then married a lady who had been in his congregation at a church where he formerly pastored. He was very capable as a preacher. He had left the original church for a large church on the East Coast that paid him well and provided him a beach home in the summer and extended vacation time. I wanted to know how he was able to walk away from everything, deal with the emotional and psychological fallout, and manage whatever guilt he felt.

I arrived at their apartment, and we greeted each other. I spoke to his wife, who received me warmly. We went outside to talk. The outdoor fountain spewed water over the fountain urn's edge. It created something of a mist hovering over the splashes in the pool. Sometimes the water bounced off the surface of the pool onto the fountain's brick base. It was hot, so the occasional spray felt good.

We sat there talking, looking at the fountain, the setting sun, and each other. He was several years older than me. I had always looked up to him. We were extended family and knew all our relatives, half being preachers. During our younger years, at the family gatherings, we always played ball together, but we were not close. All the boys in the family played sports, so every chance we had we were throwing, shooting, hitting, or kicking a ball.

On this day, both of us had moved well past that desire. There was a much deeper issue I wanted to discuss. I needed his help.

As we sat by the fountain, I explained to him my reason for coming. He had never discussed or talked about what he had done and been through with anyone in our family. I had come to try to understand. Maybe that would help me. He told me his story. He asked no questions about mine.

One Sunday morning, Hutt got up early, packed his bags, put them in his car, and headed to the church. The monthly deacons' meeting was scheduled for 8:00 a.m. He waited in his office with the door closed. When he knew all the men were seated in the meeting room, he walked in and closed the door behind him. He was not one to waste words. He told them he was resigning, effective immediately. He turned and walked out. He got in his car and drove to his house. He went into his bedroom and found his wife in her slip. She was standing in front of the mirror and getting ready for church. He told her he was leaving her and their three children, returning to their former town and going to marry Andrea. He told her that she and the children could have everything he owned. He would give her three-fourths of everything he earned for the next ten years. Then he walked out, got in his car and drove away with only his packed belongings.

That day, he drove across several states to the woman he had loved for years. While we were sitting by the fountain, Andrea was in the kitchen cooking supper. She was gorgeous, kind, a very good cook, and sharp as a razor. She was also ten years his senior. She always supported Hutt and encouraged him. That was why I was there, to understand their mutually rewarding relationship and his walking away from the church and his family.

I knew about affairs from my own experience. It was tough—marriage and ministry—but that wasn't unusual in my family of three plus generations of preachers. A lot of pretending went on. My issue: I simply did not understand. I needed Hutt to explain to me not only how he had done it, but why and how he was able to deal with it. Nobody in our family had a clue, and he had not spoken to anyone about it.

He spoke straightforwardly: "My wife turned out to be just like my mother. She was all about what she wanted. She had her own life that had little to do with me. She did her own thing as she wanted, went where she fancied. She supported me only by her presence during the services she chose to attend. She never complimented me nor went with me to engagements. She didn't ask about my day or how I was doing.

"The church became a droning experience, same thing over and over. I beat my brains out to be creative and helpful—to give them something. The leadership was always comparing how we were doing in regard to certain other churches in terms of attendance, buildings, budgets, and baptisms. I received no personal support or encouragement at home or at work, or from parents. The church paid me well but demanded more; there was always something to prove. I just had enough, so I walked away. It was time to live my life for me. I had no guilt.

"My parents don't question me anymore. I rarely talk to them. You need to hear this: *The best day of my life will be the day my mother dies. The second-best day of my life will be the day my father dies. Maybe then all this will be over*. Now, let's go eat."

I just looked at him. I did not understand—not yet. Although I did not fully grasp his loaded words, I did feel his frustration and his hurt. More than that, I knew what he meant. We grew up in the same system of beliefs and culture.

He said no more. We stood up and walked toward the drifting aroma of a well-prepared meal. We have not spoken of it since.

That night, I slept at Hutt's home. As I thought about the conversation, I recalled my sessions with the three psychologists I saw in the months before I moved to the farmhouse. They were not helpful. A good one is hard to find. I knew I had to face my pain. I needed to meet with Brad again. That night I called my long-time friend and counselor who was in North Carolina leading a conference. The next morning after breakfast, I said my goodbyes and drove to the conference site. I spent three days there talking. It was there I discovered a core issue in my life. It happened like this:

At one point my father came up in the discussion. Brad observed, "Satch, you are just like a little boy in his baseball cap looking up at your daddy asking, 'Am I okay yet?' He cannot and will not ever tell you. You were born with honor. It cannot be granted or taken away. It can only be forsaken, shamed, or given away. You must stand up to him and find that out for yourself."

Then he pulled the old chair trick. He placed an empty chair in front of me and moved his own chair and sat behind me. "Now," he said, "Your daddy is sitting in that chair. Tell him how you feel."

I stared at the chair for two to three minutes. Many thoughts raced through my mind like a tape on rewind. As I remembered all the incidents from my life, my eyes filled with tears, and my throat squeezed shut. I could not speak. I finally turned to my friend and whispered, "I don't think I can do this."

"Then get up out of the chair, go out the door, and get in your truck and go home. If you're not going to face the issues, I can't help you," he said.

I had always thought he was such a nice guy, but I recognized I had come to a significant issue that I did not know how to address. I realized I had to face this. It was a huge, harmful heartache for me. So I began as best I could. After a time, my buddy did it again.

"Now you've told him what he did and didn't do. Tell him how you feel."

As I thought about how my father's actions made me feel, the emotions crushed me. I cried as hard and as long as I had ever cried. I heaved and sobbed until my friend stood up behind me, wrapped his arms around me from my back. He squeezed so hard it hurt. I began to gather myself. My handkerchief became so soaked that I had to use my sleeves as a towel. My friend just sat quietly behind me. He finally broke the silence.

He asked, "Do you know how lucky you are?"

"Yeah, I'm really a piece of work, aren't I?" I quipped.

"I'm serious! Most people would have gotten up and walked out that door. Now that you are aware of this issue in your life, it's time to face it.

"Satch, you received all these academic and athletic honors in high school, played college football, graduated with an overall A average. You had enough course hours in three subjects to have three majors. You were a runner-up Rhodes Scholar. You made All Southeastern Conference, Academic All-American, and All-American in football—at least second team or honorable mention on writers' lists. You were on the law journal in law school, made All-NFC team in the NFL. You were three times elected to political office. You earned a doctorate and pastored and co-pastored big-time churches. Do you not yet see ambition is a dungeon that imprisons your heart? You feel on the inside like a little boy who still needs affirmation from his father.

"Listen to me. Your father is never going to affirm you. He cannot do it. He will not do it. So, face it and go see him. Get up right now and go to that house you grew up in and face him."

I jumped out of my chair and exclaimed, "That will not do one bit of good!"

"You are exactly right," noted my friend. "Now go see it for yourself. The honor of your personhood cannot be taken; it has to be given away. Do not give it away to him. So go! And when you get back to the farm, start writing your story again. Just look at your cousin Hutt. YOU have to tell your story!"

I got in my truck determined to face my father. I knew it was too long a drive to make it that day. I spent the night on the road. I slept off and on through the night and woke up early for the remaining drive to my hometown.

On the way, I detailed my strategy. My sister Rachel lived in the same town. I hoped she would be at home, because I needed to tell her about my discovery. She accepted me warmly, and we sat in the den from late afternoon to evening—just talking. I told her about the nuggets I had gleaned from the three days of counseling with my friend. As I revealed the details, tears began to run down her cheeks.

"Got to you too, didn't it?" I asked.

"Yes," Rachel conceded. "But I never knew it hurt you like this. What are you going to do?" I told her my plan. Rachel said, "He will be mad. He won't like it." She looked uneasy.

"I know," I said. "That is why I am going to do it that way."

Strangely, on that day, none of her children or anyone else stopped by her house. Her husband came in for a minute to fix a sandwich and left again saying it would be late when he got back. She helped him with the sandwich and made a couple more for us.

When we finished eating, I looked at her and said, "Dad's the reason you left home and got married, isn't he? We all know the pain you are in with issues and losses in your family, and I know you won't talk about it. You are reserved like Mother. Guess I'm more bull-headed like Daddy.

"I just want you to know I'm here for you. I sent you the paper I put together on the waves of grief. Find someone you trust to talk to about your grief. I want you to know I am for you and will be there if you want me. Thanks for listening to me. I needed to talk to someone about all this. You have helped me just by listening."

She remained silent for a long time. Finally, she said, "I'm going to be okay. I don't know anyone I can talk to. I've made up my mind to deal with my loss and grief on my own and in my own way without bothering anyone else." She spoke no more about it. I knew to leave it alone.

The sun had long set by this time, and Rachel was getting nervous. She was afraid of what our father might do. It was getting late. She urged me to call him. I said, "Look, I have thought this through. He goes to bed every night at 10 o'clock. I will call him at about 9:45. He will be sitting in his chair watching television. Mother will have already gone to bed. He will answer the phone and say, 'What are you doing? Where are you?' I'll tell him I'm at your house but am coming to see him and want to spend the night there. He will get testy and tell me I had better hurry up because he is about to go to bed. Then I will respond."

"Satch, I'm concerned," she replied. "This will not go well."

"Sister, it is okay," I reassured her. "We had a good visit today. We understand a lot more about each other and our family. This is something I have to do for myself. I hope you will also be able to do it in your own way."

"What are you going to say?" she inquired.

"It will not take much, and it will be fine," I explained. "You will not be affected. I will call him at 9:45."

And I did. My dad responded just like I had told my sister, virtually word for word. On the phone I told my dad I would be there before 10:00 p.m., so he could go to bed. I left in time to arrive at my family home before 10:00. I unlocked the garage door, walked up those same fifteen steps, and marched into the family room. My dad sat there in his pajamas, pretending to relax in his favorite chair. He was flipping channels with the TV remote control in his right hand. He was clearly mad as a hornet. I said, "Dad, I have been visiting with Rachel at her house but wanted to stop by and see you and spend the night. Tell me how you are doing."

Without even looking at me, he said, "I am just fine. If you had been five more minutes, I would have been in bed!"

I looked at him without a flinch and said, "Well, get up and go to bed because I do not care!"

My dad jerked as if having a seizure. He fumbled with the remote and almost dropped it. He stood up and stared at me. Without another word, he stormed out of the room and around the corner. I heard the bedroom door slam. I turned, walked back down the fifteen steps to the bedroom in the basement where Fletch and I had spent most of our growing up years. I brushed my teeth and went to sleep. Next morning, I got up early, made the bed, and said nothing to either of my parents. I walked out the door, got in my truck, and headed for the farm. I already felt better about myself.

Neither my dad nor mom ever mentioned it, but that day, things began to change for me. I began to feel like a different person as I drove back to the farmhouse. It was a beginning, but only one step. My counselor friend had told me to finish telling my story and think about all of the people who have been damaged in the same type of family culture. Driving home, I kept thinking about all the people who have been negatively impacted by family beliefs and traditions—especially non-affirming, religious ones.

Later on, I discovered what had happened throughout their lives to both my parents. That began to change my understanding of the frailty and damage that comes to all people. I remembered one man who once told me how much my dad helped people and concluded, "Your dad is the best man I have ever known, including preachers!" I began to learn that blaming others can be self-destructive, but the heaviness in my heart took a long time to dissipate. Honoring your mother and father is not higher than honoring God. To love parents more than Jesus does not honor Him. Jesus came to bring a sword of division in households and more. Knowing Jesus accepts you with your shortcomings can cause hatred and rejection by other people, even those closest to you.

As I pulled the sheets back on the farmhouse bed, I kept thinking about how my family had raised and treated my siblings and me, and how it had affected each one of us—especially our image of God. But their rearing had also negatively affected them. I resolved to write my story as best I could.

CHAPTER 6

So You Had a Bad Day

Several months passed since I had confronted my dad. I had come to enjoy quail hunting, but this year's season was almost over. My long-time friend Scott and I loved to go hunting together, but we hadn't been able to go much. In addition, the quail population had been decreasing rapidly for several years, leaving fewer places to hunt.

Maybe I could have a good end of season hunt—followed by a meal of fried quail, biscuits, and TJ Blackburn syrup. Plus, I still could not get the haunting questions about God's character and my life out of my mind. I called Scott and told him I was leaving the farm and would be ready at his house before 1:00 p.m. Somehow, I talked him into going. Scott was ten years older than me and had made many more hunting rounds. He was not super excited.

The town where Scott lived was situated in a river bottom and was flat as a flitter. The town had been given the nickname Stabhurt for a number of reasons. A sign outside another small town about five hours away read "Home to 300 Good Folks and a Few Old Soreheads." Stabhurt had more than their share of hardnosed religious soreheads in every class level. They held their prejudices and would unhesitatingly give their crusty corrections and admonitions to anyone crossing their traditions. They held incontrovertible positions and opinions. They did not hesitate to share them forcibly and measure you on the spot. So the nickname was applicable. Every town across the US has some real soreheads. After I arrived at Scott's house, we loaded our dogs and shotguns in Scott's truck. With a peanut butter and banana sandwich, chips, and Coke in my hands, we headed up the road. I was excited.

The highway through the town to the east rose out of the river bottom and crossed hills all the way to the hunting site.

It was a good road, but its yellow lines warned drivers against passing for long stretches as it wound over hills and around curves. We drove for several miles with me munching my lunch. Scott kept looking in the rearview mirror and then the side mirror. We chatted, but Scott kept looking behind us. About eight miles out, we were about to reach the highest point in the county, but Scott's focus on the rearview mirror disturbed me.

"What is going on?" I asked.

"He's been on my bumper since we left town," Scott rejoined. "He keeps trying to pass me."

I looked behind us. Scott was right. This car was right on our bumper—way too close. The road was one hilltop and curve after another. Scott would not drive over the speed limit. He was an aerial applicator and would not take a chance on any violation that could affect his pilot's license and his living. I understood. He was aggravated. He recognized the car and driver.

As we approached the high point where another highway to the south intersected, I saw a maroon midsize Chrysler top the hill coming our way. At the same time Scott said, "He's going to pass us."

Just as the Chrysler passed us in the oncoming lane, there was what sounded and felt like an explosion, like a bomb went off at the rear of Scott's four-wheel drive pickup. The entire truck shook side to side. What was left of my sandwich and chips flew out of my hands. I exclaimed, "What was that!?"

"He tried to pass me and hit that car head on," Scott said.

A 1973 yellow four-door Ford LTD sedan (the same size as a big Lincoln) and a small Chrysler crashed head on. Smoke billowed from each vehicle. The Ford smashed into the Chrysler, knocking it straight backward five or six feet in the same lane. The cars sat there facing each other with both front ends crushed.

I said, "Stop, I'm getting out. Go call for help."

Scott pulled over at the intersection. I jumped out. Scott said there was only the driver in the Ford. Neither of us knew how many occupants were in the Chrysler. As Scott pulled away to find a phone at a nearby house, I ran to the driver's side of the Chrysler. I saw a small woman totally squashed against the steering wheel. The windows were up. I tapped on the window and spoke to her. No answer. I could not tell if she was breathing. I could not get the driver's door to open. I ran to the front door on the passenger's side. After pulling and pushing, I finally pried the door open.

I crawled into the front bench seat and spoke to her. No response. I placed my hand on her shoulder. No movement. She was not breathing. I searched her neck and wrists for a pulse—again, nothing. As I crawled back out of the car, I looked in the back seat—nothing there. Before I closed the car doors, I looked on the front floorboard and under the front seats—nothing. I opened the back door again but didn't see anyone or anything on the seat or on the floor.

As I closed the back door, I looked toward the yellow Ford with its engine smoking. I could not see any occupants but walked over and looked in the driver's window—no one. Then, I noticed a yellow cup sitting upright on the floorboard on the passenger's side. I walked around the car. The window was down. As I stuck my head in the window, I smelled something. A yellow plastic Solo cup was sitting upright on the passenger's floorboard. I walked around the car and reached through the window and carefully picked up the cup. There was an inch of amber liquid still in the cup. I raised it to my nose. It was whiskey. I gently returned it to its original position on the floorboard.

I was fuming mad. I walked in front of the Ford and heard a moaning sound. I bent down and looked under the Ford and saw nothing. *Where was he?* On my knees I looked under the engine of the Chrysler—there was a man lying on his back, his feet toward the rear of the Chrysler. *How did he get there!*

The man struggled to say something.

I told him, "Be very still and don't try to move. Help is on the way."

Through all the smoke from the vehicles and the aroma of oil and burned metal, I could still smell alcohol emanating from him. The injured driver mumbled something. The man slobbered, "I shore hope ain't nobody hurt."

"Don't move one muscle and do not say another word!" I screamed.

As I stood up, a woman came running to me from across the highway and exclaimed, "I know her. Is she all right?"

"No, I believe she is dead," I replied.

"What about her child?" the woman inquired.

Taken aback, I exclaimed, "What!?"

"She has a baby boy," the woman explained. "He has to be with her."

"There is no one else in the car," I declared. "I have checked!"

"He has to be with her," the woman insisted. "She would not leave her child at home. Please look again. Is there not a child's seat in the back?"

I had already looked but went again to the Chrysler. I opened the back passenger side door again. The ceiling, seats, and floorboards were all black. The sun was glaring down, so it was hard to see. As I reached under the driver's seat, the partial form of the bottom of a black child restraint seat came into focus. It was stuck under the driver's seat. I felt underneath the child seat. Something was there—a child! As carefully as I could, I held the back of the car seat with one hand while holding the child against the seat with the other. I gently slid the seat and the child from under the front seat.

I stood up and held the car seat with the baby in it. He was the most beautiful blond-haired baby I had ever seen. He was still breathing but had bad contusions. His eyes were bruised seeping blood, his entire forehead was a deep purple, and blood was running from his nose and mouth. His car seat was not buckled in, nor was he strapped into his car seat. He was precious. I loved him. I wanted him to live. My heart broke. I was enraged.

As I held the baby boy, I turned to the lady who was acquainted with the mother. Immediately another woman ran across the highway and stood beside her. She said, "I am a nurse. Let me take him. He just now turned a year old."

I asked, "Do you know this family?"

"Yes, where is her other baby?" asked the nurse.

Shocked, I exclaimed, "Another baby!!!"

"She had a baby eight days ago—another little boy," said the nurse. "He has to be in the car with her."

"He can't be!" I replied. "I have looked in the front and back and under the seats and around the car. There is no one else in that car."

"He has to be in that car," the nurse insisted. "Please check again."

I looked again in the back seat, under both seats, under the mother's seat, and under the front passenger seat. I could not find anything but a purse rammed under the driver's brake pedal. I backed out of the car again and saw Scott standing with the women.

"Were you able to call and get help on the way?" I queried.

"Got an ambulance and the sheriff's department coming," Scott replied.

I looked at the nurse. She said, "Please look again, he has to be in that car."

I climbed in the car again and repeated my steps. I looked again under the seats and on the front and back floorboards. I lay on my stomach again and looked up and behind the glove box but could not see anything. I reached up behind the glove box and felt my way to the front firewall. I felt something. It was soft. I felt gently from one side to another. Could it be the little boy?

How does a baby get thrown up under the dashboard, and concealed behind the glove compartment between and next to the firewall? I do not know how I got him out. He was completely hidden and stuck up in that dark, narrow space. As gently as I could, I brought out this precious eight-day old little boy. He was still alive but bruised from head to foot, and his head was swelling. The newborn whimpered. I walked toward the front of the car holding that little boy. Both the ladies were overcome, tears coursing down their faces. I was sad, angry, and numb.

With sirens screaming, the paramedics arrived at the same time as the sheriff's deputies. I handed the baby to the paramedics and told them the mother was dead, but they should check and make sure. I told the deputy all I had observed, and that the other driver was lying under the engine of the Chrysler and did not appear to be seriously injured. I looked at Scott and then at the officers. I told them I had to leave.

We got in Scott's truck and headed farther east toward the hunting spot without saying a word. We turned off the highway down a gravel road to a spot where previously we had found a covey of birds. Scott parked the truck. We grabbed our stack-barrel Browning shotguns and reached for our hunting vests lying in the bed of the truck. As we did, we looked at each other across the truck bed and dropped the vests. Without saying a word, we put the guns back in the window rack, closed the doors, and headed home. When we passed the scene of the wreck, I asked, "Do you know who that son of a bitch is?"

"Yes, he drives that car every day around town while drinking," Scott said. "Occasionally, they lock him up 'til he gets sober and then let him go. He has had several DUIs."

Both of us were so hurt and so mad, we could not talk. Sheriff's deputies took the man to the emergency room before arresting him. I drove to the hospital that evening to check on the children and their dad. Their father had already left. Those two little boys died that night at the hospital. The drunk driver made bail and was released. A year later he pled to a felony with time to be served in the county jail. Before completing his first year in jail, he was appointed cook. Within a year, he was making beer in the kitchen of the county jail. That's Stabhurt for you. This man had killed the mother and her two infants.

I was a livid melancholy. I will never forget them or the babbling drunk lying under the car. I wanted to care for him, but I could not. Where is the good mixed with this evil, this kind of hell? God, why did you allow this to happen? I could not figure it out. Between the accident and the struggles within my own soul, hell had burst forth again.

CHAPTER 7

The Smiths

"Yeesa, will you tell them about what happened with Ron and the Smiths?"

"Sure, Satch, happy to," agreed Yeesa.

The next day for Satch was a swirl of heartaches. Satch's heart was torn, and his mind could not yet fully face the sadness of that mother and two little boys dying because a frustrated drunk wanted to pass on a hill. Then he remembered he needed to take care of the horses. After finishing his chores at the barn, he took a walk through the national forest. Then he crossed his neighbor's land until he reached his friend Ron's property. As he got close to the paved road, he turned around to head back.

He looked up and observed an astounding sight—the largest red oak tree he had ever seen. He stopped and stared. He had been on this property before but had never seen anything like it. He called Ron and a game warden friend, who brought Ron and his son-in-law with him. They touched hands in a circle, and the four could not reach around the oak. The warden measured it and contacted the wildlife department biologist who determined it was the second largest red oak tree found in the state.

Later that night Ron came over to Satch's barn to ask about the wreck. The sky that night shone like blued steel shot full of stars. There was a cold wind howling out of the north. Thirty miles away city lights gave a warm vanilla crème flavor to the northwestern sky. They were sitting in the porch swing at the barn enjoying the warm glow from the gas heater Satch had bought years ago to watch his son's baseball games. It was the only light, but it was not as bright as the sky. He was trying to stay warm and moved to stand next to the heater. Ron was wrapped in a saddle blanket with his grandpappy Amos's hat over his ears down almost to his shoulders. He looked like a gorilla wrapped in a chimpanzee's shawl.

Satch's legs were starting to warm up when Ron looked at him and asked, "How old were those little boys?" Satch told him the whole story of what had happened. Then he did not want to talk about it anymore, so he asked Ron, "Were you not aware of how big that red oak is? It is on your property."

"Well, actually, it is not mine," Ron explained. "It belongs to my wife and her mother."

"Come on, man, I know you have seen it a hundred times," remarked Satch.

"Yeah, but never paid no mind to it," Ron admitted. "It's just a big oak."

"The second biggest one in the whole state," Satch asserted. "That is something. It's a beautiful, amazing tree. Today was the first time I noticed it. That is why I called you and the game warden."

Ron interrupted, "Why do you spend time with us?"

Caught off guard, Satch replied, "What? What are you talking about?"

"Seriously, you being a lawyer and a preacher with all that education, why do you spend time with folks like us?" Ron asked. "You know, just plain, uneducated country folk? I want to know. It's not normal."

"Ron, I've been around a lot of wannabes and upper crusts, and I've seen lots of charading and posing," Satch explained. "You are genuine, honest. I respect you. I like you. Where is that coming from?'

"You are just a better man than I am," Ron declared, and he said it twice.

"How do you figure that?" Satch wondered.

"You just are," Ron said.

"Were you taught there are people above you and below you, like a class system?" Satch asked. "How did you decide I was better than you? What led you to that conclusion?"

"You're a lawyer," Ron noted. "You got education and have made money. You're just better than me. I tell people I can't figure out why you spend time with us. You are at least two levels of people above us, and you hang around with us. I can't figure it out."

From that point on, the questioning proceeded in rapid-fire succession:

"So, who was better than you growing up?" Satch asked.

"Everybody—especially the ones who lived in the big white houses," Ron replied.

"Where'd you live?"

"In the shanties."

"How come they were better? What made them different? Did you not spend time with any of their children?"

"Nope, weren't allowed to."

"Ever talk to any of them?"

"No, never saw any of them. We just didn't associate with 'em."

"Never?"

"Uh-uh."

"What about school?"

"Didn't finish but the eighth grade," Ron answered. "Sometimes I never got a report card, because it was time to move back across the river to harvest other crops. Only one of us ten children ever finished high school. Nobody was lower than us."

"You sure?"

"Yep. We were the lowest of the low. You couldn't get any further down the line," Ron said with a laugh. Ron had a great sense of humor and could laugh at himself.

"Do you mean to tell me your mom and dad and grandparents, none of your family, ever told you not to associate with some people?" Satch asked.

"Well, no. There were some of them that were just sorry."

"What do you mean?"

"They worked in the same fields, but they weren't like us."

"What do you mean? Give me an example."

"Well," Ron said, "there was this family. One winter it was snowing, and their baby was crawling on the front porch in diapers. That baby fell off the porch. The parents were gone. Nobody watched any of the children. The baby just lay there. Left the children there by themselves all the time. Never bathed. Just sorry. We couldn't have anything to do with them."

"So, you were taught certain values like money, power, education, work ethic, and cleanliness made people better."

Ron looked at Satch with a quiet, blank stare. Satch hoped Ron would never get mad at him. Ron resembled Paul Bunyan—six foot four, two hundred seventy-five pounds, country strong, like an ox, yet with the gentlest spirit. Ron looked confused, not knowing what to say. Satch was not making himself very clear. It was hard to convey feelings about values and family systems and how one gets absorbed into and infused by them. Satch continued, "Well, what was the most important thing to you growing up?"

"Survival," Ron said. "We just tried to make it. It took all of us to just make it. We all worked in the fields. At age ten, I was paid full labor for hauling water to the hands. That was my job."

"Tell me a story about something you learned growing up and how it affected you."

"My job was to haul the water," Ron said. "There was one bucket. I went to the well, hauled the water to the field hands—men and women—and they drank it all. It was hot, man. I would go straight back to the well. It was that way all day long.

"One day ol' Bobby caught me on the way back to the well. He handed me a package of cigarette papers his daddy had told him to take care of. His dad must have had them in his pocket. They were soaked with sweat. Bobby was supposed to spread them out and dry them. We tried to separate them, but they began to tear. Bobby said, 'You do it while I run to the house.'

"I worked at it for a while but couldn't do any good with it. Every piece would tear. Bobby didn't come back. I had to take the next bucket of water. I didn't know what to do, so I just buried them right there in the cotton rows. I figured it would all be on Bobby. He was always getting into trouble. Nobody knew I had anything to do with it. So, I ran back to get the next bucket of water.

"It was a long way in the field to where they were picking cotton. On the way I got to thinking that Bobby was going to tell on me. I was going to get into trouble. I'll bet it cost Mr. Simms a whole day's pay just to buy that pack of papers. I had watched him many times. He would take a break and try to get in some shade. He would take out his pack of papers and slide one off the top. Then he would get his pouch of tobacco and drop a pinch into the paper and start to roll it up. Then he would lick it and find a match that wasn't wet and light that cigarette. He would do that on breaks. It bothered me. I couldn't face Mr. Simms. I had lost his papers and cost him money none of us had to lose. I grabbed the bucket and ran all the way back to the well and then back to the field with the bucket sloshing.

"All the way I was thinking, I have to find those papers. I couldn't find where I buried them among so many long rows of cotton. I couldn't remember where I put 'em. I scratched around but couldn't find the place. I got back to the well and sat down behind the tree. Wasn't long 'til Daddy showed up. I was crying. I told him the whole story. 'I can't face Mr. Simms,' I told him. I begged Daddy to talk to Mr. Simms for me. He told me to go home. It never bothered Bobby."

Ron looked over at Satch. Changing the subject he said, "I would like for you to talk to Momma some time. She is ninety-four. And you need to meet my brother Larry. Maybe you can help him, but I doubt it."

Satch grinned and said, "I would love to."

They talked long into the night, until they both were shaking with cold. Nature forced them home. Before leaving the barn, they petted and talked with the horses. Suddenly, Ron said, "You're too deep. We don't ever think about these things."

As Ron got in his truck, Satch walked back to the farmhouse. He thought, *I bet Ron has never stolen anything in his whole life. I know he would give you the shirt off his back.* Ron was honest to the core. As the gravel crunched under Satch's boots on the way back to the farmhouse, he thought about the many different family cultures in the world.

A good week passed before Satch got to Momma Smith's for lunch. Ron extended the invitation. Larry was going to be there. Satch wanted to talk to Momma Smith because of all of her experience: raising ten children, watching one die, working a farm, burying a husband, starting public work after raising all those young'uns, and living with Larry.

Larry was fifty-seven, lived with his mother, did not work unless he had to, had no insurance of any kind, coon hunted every night, and slept in every morning, waking to eat his momma's good country cooking. He probably was the sharpest one of the bunch and had done something lots of people are unable to do. He rejected the values and traditions of his family system, and it didn't faze him.

Momma Smith served black-eyed peas, corn, ham, potatoes—sweet, round, and mashed—roast beef, pork chops, beets, cabbage, loaf bread, cornbread, toast, biscuits, bacon, and sausage. Then she followed that with peaches, brownies, Twinkies, tea, Pepsi, root beer, Dr. Pepper, apple pie, coconut pie, ice cream, and assorted cookies—and she said she didn't know Satch was coming! She said, "Or I would have had something good to eat." Her mind was still as sharp as a briar, and Satch was dying to get into the family discussion. And, yes, all that food was there!

The problem was Ron and Larry would not let her answer any of Satch's questions. They answered for her. Satch was amazed at the role reversal occurring right before his eyes. The only thing she got to say about religion was that the "Bible was always important to my parents and to our family growing up; but when I got married, after a while, my husband led us away from it."

Larry chimed in, "Yeah, but we all still know you are supposed to do what is right."

Ron immediately added, "And we know it is important to read the Bible and to believe in God and to go to church." Satch looked over at Larry. He moved back and forth from the kitchen to the den. He was watching a football game, talking all the time, and trying to put on his hunting overalls. He buckled the straps on his overalls and then unbuckled them and threw one back over his shoulder.

Satch said, "Larry, light somewhere or leave, 'cause I want to talk to you, and it is going to take more than fifteen seconds. If you have to go, just go; but if you want in on this, be still!"

He peered at Satch and said, "We don't talk about this kinda stuff. Man, you are telling me something about yourself. You are struggling with something. What is going on? We don't know about things such as this."

"Larry, you are right about my struggling with some issues," Satch admitted. "I am and have a lot of questions. So, help me. Tell me how you have been able to reject some of the values and traditions that your family held out as so important."

"What are you talking about?" asked Larry.

Satch began. "Well, you won't work. You live with your mother, and you coon hunt every night. And you are fifty-seven years old. All your brothers and sisters are married with children. They work hard every day and go to church, and it doesn't even turn your head. How did you do it?"

"I don't know," Larry stated. "That stuff just never bothered me, and it don't bother me now. I don't care what the rest of them do. I am going to do what I enjoy, and that's it. They can do what they want. I work when I have to. I wish I had some insurance in case I get sick, you know, but I'll make it."

Satch turned investigator. Larry had no idea how despite rejecting what his family valued, he in some ways was the healthiest of the lot. So, Satch decided to use a back door approach. "Larry, what are you afraid of most?" he asked.

Larry was standing by the kitchen sink and turned straight toward them at the table and looked Satch right in the eyes. Without hesitating he said, "Hell."

"Why are you afraid of hell?"

"Well, I can't stand getting burned here, you know, on part of my arm or leg or something," Larry admitted. "But burning for eternity—I can't handle that. It scares me."

"So, you believe in life after death." Satch continued. "But why an eternal fire? Why do you think you will burn forever if you go to hell?"

"Merle died last week, and I was a pallbearer at his funeral," Larry explained. "In fact, I have been to too many funerals lately, and every one of them preachers is up there reading from the Bible and talking about dying and going to hell, burning for eternity. I don't like it. I know I need to get right. I know I need to get back to going to church."

"Why?" asked Satch.

Larry just glared at Satch, not knowing what to say. Satch tried to help. "Larry, I have learned something. The church is not a building. You can't 'go to church.' The church is the people of God. They may assemble together, but attending a church meeting cannot keep you from going to hell. Do you really think your attendance and good deeds carry you to heaven—that getting to heaven is based on your good efforts?"

Larry just kept looking at Satch, not saying a word.

Satch broke the silence. "How many people were at Merle's funeral?" he asked.

"More than I have ever seen," Larry exclaimed. "Their cars were parked all the way down to Save-A-Lot. I couldn't believe it. People everywhere. He was just a trader, but he sure had a lot of friends. I heard there were more people there than at Mr. Baxter's funeral a month ago. You know, the man who owned the bank."

Satch dug deeper. "Why do you think so many people came if he wasn't anybody?" Larry looked at Satch with a serious countenance, then pondered a few moments.

"Well, for one of two reasons," Larry clarified. "Either because of Merle, or so other people could see them there. Don't know which one it was."

Satch could tell he didn't want to talk anymore. Those overalls were buckled tight now, and both knee length rubber boots were on. He was on his way out the door saying, "Ron, put another log in the wood stove so it won't be so cold when I get home. Momma likes it hot in here."

Momma Smith, Ron, and Satch all grinned at each other.

CHAPTER 8

Family and Church

I am telling you that Satch could not get the conversation at Momma Smith's house out of his mind—mainly how Larry was able to reject most of his family's values and traditions despite believing in hell. The more he thought about it, the more Satch wondered if his thoughts were guiding him to try the church thing again. He considered it a long time and decided to visit the church where he had been a teacher and deacon several decades before. They had ordained him into the ministry. It was a good drive to that town, so he made up his mind to try and decided to go to a Wednesday evening service. It would be more relaxed.

The day came, and Satch left early enough to eat at one of his old-favorite restaurants. As usual it was busy. He saw old acquaintances and a few former clients from when he had practiced law there. They greeted him kindly. None of the church folks were there. One old friend and her husband surprised him by asking him to close a loan for them. Amy Lynn and her family were moving back to town. He told her he had not practiced law in a long time, but she was insistent. "We trust you. Please do this for us."

He didn't want to comply but could not say no. He asked the details about the bank they were using and the time frame.

They exchanged phone numbers, gave each other a hug, and he finished his meal. As he left, he wondered why they would move back to that town, but he was now close to the church. He had to find a place to park. As he walked toward the church building, he decided to go into the dining room. Maybe he would get a dessert and see how the group he used to sit with would respond. He saw ten to twelve old friends sitting together. One of them had been a prayer partner. When they saw him, they all dropped their forks, stopped eating and talking, and just stared with incredulous looks on their faces.

Then he tried another tactic. He walked into the sanctuary from the entrance at the front by the piano. People were standing in the aisles and visiting in the pews. He knew them. As he walked down one aisle toward the rear of the sanctuary, those in the pews dropped their heads. The people in the aisle turned away. He walked to the back, across and down the other aisle to the front. He retraced his steps back up the first aisle and to the back door. Not one person acknowledged him. The surprised visitor believed he had embarrassed them. They felt uncomfortable being around him. They had ordained him, and he had failed, which means they had made a mistake. They didn't know how to accept him, so they didn't.

As Satch walked back to the front and out the opposite door by the organ, he thought about speaking to the pastor. He was new, having been there only a few months. Satch found the office, and the preacher was there. He knocked and introduced himself. Satch told the preacher that though he was the new pastor there that he already knew his story of failure. He also told the new preacher that he supported him and would help in any way he could, and he meant it. It's a tough job. Then he asked him if he would meet him for a short visit after the service for some hot apple pie and vanilla ice cream. Satch could tell the preacher did not want to do it, but he reluctantly agreed.

They met at the restaurant, were served their desserts, and chatted. Satch felt the tension and decided to get straight to the point. He said, "You know my story, but I want you to know my heart. I would like to know from you—what do you think I can do? My heart is to be in the ministry. What do you think?"

The young preacher didn't blink an eye. Immediately he stood and tersely said, "I don't know anything you can do!" Then, he turned, left his pie, and walked out. That young pastor, less than half Satch's age, seemed to be developing into the type of person Jesus described as thinking too highly of himself. More likely, he was becoming a stumbling block mill-stoner. Satch paid for the desserts and returned to his truck.

On the drive back to the farmhouse, Satch felt alone—maybe the saddest he'd felt in a long time. He was glad to leave that church in Stabhurt. How hard it was for church people to forgive or be kind to one of their own who had sinned, particularly the scarlet-letter version. Shame and rejection covered him up again. Going to church no longer seemed a source of help or hope for him. As he climbed into bed that night, Satch wondered what options were left. He wondered if it were possible that God in some way was protecting him instead of rejecting him. Could that be so for him? He didn't know how, if He is an arbitrary predestinating God.

The next morning, Satch spent the day taking care of his dogs and horses. He curried, fed, and hugged his horses. Music and Son were special to him. He talked to them as the dogs lay at his feet. They were his only sounding boards as he talked through his struggles. At one point it seemed the older one, Music, was trying to tell him something. He tried but couldn't understand. When done with the chores, Satch sat on the swing and relaxed. He was about to doze off when he heard the gravel crunching on the driveway and saw a car slowly navigating along the drive past the farmhouse to the barn on the back of the property. It was Joe Carley.

Satch first met Joe Carley (or JC as they called him) when their sons were playing high school baseball. What a thrill it was when the boys ended up winning the state championship and in Legion baseball the following summer went to the American Legion World Series in Oklahoma. It was a fun time. They knew each other well, but that's not the point.

JC had talked to Satch for several years about his struggles at work and issues at home with his children, but never about his father. That day he stopped by the barn for a visit. At work, he felt squeezed. As the CEO, JC saw the situation clearly that caused major deficits, impeding the financial success of his company, but he was not allowed to speak to the issue let alone address the problems. Instead, he received the blame for them. Eventually, the board of directors scapegoated and fired him instead of dealing with the issue. The problem is people tend to blame someone else, not themselves, rather than deal with the root issue.

There was more. JC's family was in turmoil. With four children from two marriages, a lot can happen—especially when the father is consumed with his career. JC worked as hard as any man could to get it right. He was darn good at his job too, but things were headed down at work and at home. He felt low about everything.

That night, Satch saw a depth of pain that had developed into a despondency approaching resignation. JC talked about his job, his wife, and his children, but he had a hard time looking at himself. He did not have a clue as to how to deal with the horrible sourness of soul that was about to disable him.

Satch had been working on the original manuscript that became this story and asked him if he would read a portion and give his opinion. He hesitantly agreed and the two friends walked up to the farmhouse. Satch turned on the computer, found the spot and asked him to have a seat.

As JC peered into the glowing monitor, Satch sat in the chair across the room to his right under a small lamp—the only light in the room except for the computer screen—and pretended to read a horse magazine. As Satch continued to observe, the corners of JC's mouth started to twitch a little. Then, Satch saw tears begin to well in JC's eyes. When Satch saw his friend's chin begin to quiver and his head drop, he knew JC had read something that hit him right in the gut. To that point JC had never mentioned his birth family or how his father treated him.

"JC, you need to talk about this," Satch said. JC just sat there and looked down. After an almost intolerable silence, he whispered, "I don't think I can do this."

"JC, you are too valuable to not look at what may be eating your life from the inside out. Talk to me. I don't care what it is, but it is killing you. These things do not go away, I know. I am in the middle of living it. Talk to me, JC."

JC did not respond. Rather, he sat, head down, hands in his lap.

"I don't know what you saw or what you felt but talk to me," Satch insisted. "You matter. You are worth too much to me. Now talk to me."

The silence was so quiet it throbbed.

Satch sat, hoping his words would sink in. He continued, "I know the feeling. Like looking back out the window as you are backing up your truck through a tight group of trees with low branches and getting slapped in the face by a hanging tree limb. You never saw it coming."

JC finally mumbled, "What if I can't? What if I can't talk about it?" They sat in silence for the longest time. JC's jaw was quivering, and tears were running down his face. He rubbed his hands together in his lap. Then he spoke, stumbling over his words. "I was the oldest. My dad beat me down, favored my siblings, and never has had anything to do with me, except making sure we were all in church every Sunday. He criticized me all the time. I got married the first time not long after I started college. That would be the end of it, I thought. Got married to get away. It didn't work. All I ever got from him was rejection. I got a master's degree and have done well in administration. I was determined to prove myself. My dad's rejection of me is devastating. Now, he is about to die.

"In his will, he has left me nothing but has put me in charge of everything. My little brother took over the business from which I will not realize anything. They won't speak to me. They reject my wife and children. It is an awful tangle, and I got gored at work because of board members favoring their personal friends in spite of its negative impact on the business finances. They refuse to acknowledge the truth about what is going on in the company, and I get nothing from church. My soul aches with sourness—sour at home, sour at work, sour at play, sour in my core. Satch, where is God in all this? I cannot find Him. What is the God we believe in truly like?"

JC could not talk further about it that night. He just cried. Here was another earthly father who smashed the mirror of God's face to his child.

Satch walked with him back to the barn to get his truck and gave him a hug. In parting, Satch said, "JC, when you are ready, let me know. I have experienced what you are going through. You need to get all of it out. We will come up with a plan for you to face it. Tonight, you took the first step."

Satch walked back to the farmhouse thinking about how often this issue came up with people all around him. It was like a plague. As he went to bed, he felt worn out thinking about it.

The sun rose the next morning. Satch hoped today would be a good one. He ate breakfast and took care of the animals. After his chores, he sat in his recliner to read. He was going to call Scott when his old friend Pick showed up looking disheveled and unshaven. Satch knew something was wrong.

Satch had known Pick Greenwood for about fifteen years. He got his nickname while making a catch playing wide receiver in a high school football game. Pick has an advanced degree, is married with three daughters, and is successful in his profession. Pick grew up in a very religious church-attending family. Pick always wished for more accomplishments on the athletic field than he was able to achieve. He was deeply involved in his local church—Sunday school teacher, deacon, committee member. He participated in Bible studies and prayer meetings. He had toyed with going to the mission field.

That day when Pick walked up, his tone and demeanor told Satch something was very wrong. Pick admitted he was having an affair and was struggling terribly with it. It had gone on for months, and it was killing him.

Pick had always suspected something was off with his father. He had personally guarded his own daughters and other girls when he knew they would be around his father. It turned out his suspicions were confirmed when he received word that his father had sexually molested one of his brother's daughters. The problem was compounded because his father worked from before daylight until after dark every day for his brother's pharmacy store, all for no pay. His brother couldn't make his business go without the help of his father, compounding the problem.

On top of all this, as a medical professional, Pick had the ethical and a legal obligation to file a written report about a child being molested. His brother and wife had taken their little girl for a physical. The medical report confirmed the sexual abuse. Was he or his brother to be the one to turn in their own father? If he did, how would his brother pay his bills? For reasons of her own, Pick's mother essentially pretended it didn't happen—and so did his brother. For the sake of appearance, they continued their lives within the shadows.

One evening after a meal out, Pick, his wife, and Satch were sitting at the farmhouse by the fire and the subject of church came up. Something in the conversation triggered Pick. His face turned red. He sat on the edge of the chair and said, "I've got to tell y'all something that happened." He asked Satch if he knew a man named Frank. Satch knew Frank pretty well. He had been in court with him and his son on a criminal charge. Frank's wife had filed for divorce against him and had moved another man in the house with her and Frank's two children. Frank did not want the divorce and certainly did not want another man living with his wife in the same house as his children. One day Frank went to pick up his children, including his son from a previous marriage. He pulled in the driveway where his wife and children were living only to find the other man's car parked there. What ensued was not pretty.

Frank and his son ended up facing simple assault charges. They paid the fine, and that part was over. One day in that lengthy process, Frank came to Satch's law office. He confessed his life was in disorder. He voluntarily told him that he had seen the error of his ways and had recommitted his life to God. He said he had been and would be in church on a regular basis from that point forward. Satch had seen Frank's truck parked in the church parking lot on several Sundays and Wednesday nights. Frank was trying.

Pick brought up several other names Satch did not know, good friends of Frank's. Being single guys in a very sports-minded community, on Friday nights in the fall they loved to attend high school football games. The team was a championship contender. One week, they invited Pick and Frank's pastor to join them in what was the highlight of the small town's week. Pick said that everyone had a blast. They cheered for the home team, laughed, and had a grand time—the preacher included.

The next week, Frank and the boys invited the preacher to go with them again. He declined. They asked him again the next week and the week after. He continually begged off. Frank couldn't understand the preacher's response. Pick didn't either, so he confronted the pastor. The pastor confessed that in a meeting with church leaders, he was instructed that he should not associate with certain kinds of people in the community. Pick was drop-jawed.

During Pick's journey of restoration, he came to the farm several times to talk. He and Satch talked into the wee hours. Occasionally he would drop by on Sunday afternoons. One afternoon Satch was working on the story and wanted his input. He asked Pick if he would mind looking at a section and telling him what he thought.

Pick had not long sat down to the computer and started reading when he literally sprang from the chair. I mean he jumped straight up, knocking the chair backward to the floor. He started walking round and round the room, stomping and ranting over and again, "This is radical. This is radical. Satch, this is radical!"

"What do you mean?" Satch asked.

Pick just kept walking around in circles almost uncontrollably repeating the same phrase. Satch had not seen this side of him. Pick repeated his line like a trained parrot. "Radical, Satch, that's what this is. It's radical. That's what I mean. This is radical."

Satch countered. "Pick, Pick, stop! Tell me what you are talking about."

"This is radical. Radical stuff," Pick repeated. He was breathing hard now. "It is just radical."

"Pick, I don't care if it's radical," Satch said. "Is it true?'

Pick finally stopped his walking in circles and stomping and dropped his head. He just stood there with his hands on his hips looking at the floor. He took a deep breath, looked up at Satch and said, "Satch, you are writing about my life."

Pick had never understood or accepted the damage that came from his family system and religion. But it was happening to him. It was all bottled up inside of him, and he had no place to put it and no place to hide it. He had chosen to live with the secrets and pain but didn't know how. In Pick's view "radical" meant the topic could not be talked about; it could only be shoved under the table with the pretense that it does not exist. But he was living with the quandary, and it was eating his life up.

Yeesa said, "Satch, you should tell about the loan closing with Amy Lynn and Cork at the grocery store."

"Okay," agreed Satch.

I picked up the phone and it was Amy Lynn about the loan. The bank had given final approval for closing, so I had to prepare for that. I was tired of this already, but I had to move forward. The next day, I called the bank, and they gave me the details. I decided to go ahead and check the title and look at the property. I found the property, but the house was still under construction. I was astounded at the size and the price. On the way to the land records office, I called a lawyer friend and asked if I could borrow a room in his office to conduct the closing. The attorney agreed and offered the help of a secretary.

In a couple of weeks, the bank sent the paperwork for the loan. I set a date and time. I was in the lawyer's conference room when his legal secretary asked, "Do you think they are coming?'

I want you to know we had worked hard on this one, and it was about five minutes before the time for their appointment. The lawyer's secretary asked me if they were coming. I just smiled, "They'll be here, don't worry."

"And how do you know that?" she questioned.

"I know the family. I have known this family for a long time. One thing they do is keep their appointments. They will be here." I told her, "Let me tell you what will happen if they are late. If they are just two minutes late and come in that door two minutes after two o'clock, the first thing out of her mouth will be an apology. She will apologize profusely and give a good reason for making us wait, and she will convince you she means it, because she does."

At exactly two minutes after two p.m., they walked in through the glass door and into the conference room. Amy Lynn apologized. The secretary looked over at me with a quizzical look. I just smiled. Family systems are usually predictable, but then the unexpected happened. Neither Amy Lynn nor her husband, Danny, would sit down. She said, "I need to explain to you why our loan is so big, and why we are in the situation we are in."

"Amy Lynn, you owe me no explanation," I replied. "Danny, can you and Amy Lynn afford this?'

"Yes, and in some ways maybe it will be easier for us," he replied.

I did not understand that because the loan was huge, especially for someone who was essentially an associate pastor in a small town. I had confirmed the house existed and was worth the appraised amount, but that was not my issue. My question was about an issue other than money. If they were okay, then it was okay. So, I told them, "If you guys have dealt with this matter within your own hearts and you are okay, then any problem is someone else's, not yours."

"But I want to talk about this," she insisted.

"Are you certain that you want to go forward with closing on this money?" I asked.

"Yes," she replied emphatically.

"Well, sit down, and let's get this done," I said. "Then we will talk, if you still want to."

They sat down, we went through the loan package, and they signed all the papers. When the secretary notarized their signatures and left the room to make copies, I asked, "Amy Lynn, do you still want to talk?'

Without hesitation, she said, "I need to explain this to you."

"You don't owe me an explanation," I emphasized again.

"But I will feel better if I talk to you about it," she exclaimed.

I got up and closed the door. She wasn't going to be easy until she had talked about it. And this is her story:

Danny and Amy Lynn were pastor and wife in a town on the other side of the state. They had started a church there, which had grown from zero to almost a hundred in average weekly attendance. They had lived and worked for ten years with the same group of people. It had become a satisfying partnership. They were happy. They loved the people. Most members of the congregation had college degrees, which was "unusual for one of our congregations," she explained. They were close to several of the families, and their children were able to attend a private school.

I said, "Tell me about your decision to move."

Amy Lynn's whole tone changed, and her eyes started to fill with tears. She paused and lowered her head. Her sentences became more broken. She gathered herself and said, "We got the invitation and felt that we should move. It is a good church, and we felt like we could be used of the Lord here. I grew up here and know so many of the people. They love Danny and me and the children. They are very good to us. I feel so bad even thinking, much less talking about these things, but we had friends and a great house in our former town. It fit us. It was good for us.

"When we looked into moving, we tried to find a place but could not find anything that would work for what we needed for the children and for us. Then we found this lot that adjoined the country club. It was the only one we could find. It's not within the club property. Well, we decided we wouldn't find anything else. We had our house plans that were about the same square footage of the house that we had just sold. We felt good about everything and believed we were doing the right thing.

"Then, one day the builder called us to come to the site. Keep in mind, at this point the plumbing was laid, the slab was poured, and the framing for the first floor was up. The builder told us that our second floor would not fit on this house as it was drawn. He told us we would have to change the layout of whole upstairs and the entire roof structure to make it work. That was going to increase the cost substantially. It was going to take a whole lot more money. I went to see Carol, who draws plans. Do you know Carol?"

I nodded.

"Well, she confirmed exactly what the builder had said. We also talked to two other builders and got the same advice. So, we did, and it is costing us so much more than we ever expected. This is so hard for both of us. We did not intend to have a house that costs this kind of money. Do you think we are doing the right thing?"

I had known Amy Lynn since she was a teenager and Danny since before they were married. I had known Amy

Lynn's mom and dad for at least twenty years and had spoken to their congregation several times. They were some good people. I asked her husband, "Danny, where are you living until you can move into the new house?'

"With her parents," he replied.

"And was it her daddy that called?" I probed.

There was silence.

Her daddy, the pastor of the church, was the one who had invited them to move. He had been the pastor there for over thirty years. When he was younger and managing one of his businesses in another town, the church was down to one Sunday school class of three older women. One day his phone rang, and they asked him if he would be their teacher. From that beginning, her father had worked for years to build the congregation, and it had steadily grown to a weekly attendance of over two hundred. The church occupied a set of buildings on twenty acres of land.

Amy's father was one of the most respected men in the northern part of the state. I had learned the story first-hand from her dad and one of the three ladies that first called him. I respected him. He was a dominant personality in their denomination. I related the history of the church where Danny was going to be the pastor. "Do you know why your daddy called you?" I asked. Silence, so I continued, "Your daddy is one of the finest people I know. He has worked so hard at building this congregation. He loves them, and they love him. But he is getting older. He is tired. He loves those people, and he wants to be sure that they will be in good hands when he is gone. If he could get the two of you to come, he could rest a lot easier. He knows with you there these people will continue to have a positive experience. They would not have the disruption that so often occurs when transitioning pastors. He also knows you will consider him and consult with him, which gives him continuing input. In addition, with you there, he has time that he has not had. He can now take the time to—"

"—Fly his plane to Destin and stay at his summer home on the beach," Danny said, finishing the sentence for me.

"Yes," I affirmed. "And there is absolutely nothing wrong with that. He and the missus deserve to have some time. But there is another factor you must understand. He has been the pastor of that church, and he will continue to be."

"That's only right and the way it should be," Danny immediately defended.

"Okay, but is what is right for him right for you?" I asked. "Are you the kind of person who can come into a religious institution and not be the leader of the people? If you can, this may be exactly the place you need to be. On the other hand, if you guys are doing this because it is what is expected of you, you really are going to have to look hard at this situation. This could be a long, painful interim."

There was dead silence. Their eyes had become red. Tears were running down their cheeks. I reached for the Kleenex. Here were two of the finest souls a person could want to meet. They love each other and their children, Amy Lynn's parents, the church, and the Lord. And they had to make a life-changing decision for themselves and their children.

So, I said to them, "You started a home fellowship in another town and grew it to about a hundred in attendance in only a decade. You have great friends, your children can attend private school, and your congregation is made up mostly of professional people, which is unusual in your denomination. Amy Lynn, isn't this what you told me on the phone?"

"It is, and we were so happy there," she confirmed.

"Now, your answer to my question is important. Why did you agree to move back, accept all the changes and this position, and take on this expense?" I knew the answer, but she needed to acknowledge it herself.

Amy Lynn hung her head, wiped her eyes, and blew her nose into the Kleenex. She couldn't look up. She said, "Daddy called, and Satch, we felt that meant the Lord wanted us to do this."

Their pain was great. They were justifying, rationalizing, and struggling to the core of their beings. They both expressed profound gratitude and said, "We just don't have anybody to talk to about these things."

I looked at both and nodded. "That I do understand."

Later that week, I had to go to the grocery store. It was always a time-consuming trip—the drive plus shopping. I tried to stock up for at least a couple of weeks. As I left the grocery store, Cork Butler pulled up beside my truck. Cork was about fifty years old at the time this happened. He and I had known each other for years. In the five or six years since I had seen him, Cork had been through hell. He was diagnosed with prostate cancer and agreed to surgery. He ended up impotent and incontinent as a talented, virile, strong young man. His wife left him, he gave up his home and farm, and he struggled in his business. He is the fifth friend I have known with that same cancer and surgery. The same thing happened with three of the five. Was it bad luck or poor surgeons? Regardless, it is so sad.

Years ago, I had done some work for Cork, and he for me. I really like him. He is straight to the point and honest, if you can get him to talk. He asked me if I would ride with him so we could visit. He had to look at a building for an installation he had to perform. Something in the conversation triggered his asking me about family and church. I began sharing the essence of the story on which I was working. He just drove, not saying a word. After looking at the building, we rode back to the grocery store. He still had not said a word. I finally asked him if any of this was making any sense. He glanced at me, but only nodded.

When we got back to the store, he parked behind my truck. We both got out. It was late afternoon. I asked if he wanted to grab a sandwich. He indicated he had another job to look at and then had to drive across the state line for another project the next day. He turned and walked to his vehicle. With his left hand on the door handle he stopped and just stood there. His back was toward me, and he was staring down at the pavement. After a long, uncomfortable interlude, he turned around and looked at me.

"I was not supposed to be here. I was an accident. I wasn't intended to happen," Cork explained.

"What do you mean?" I asked.

Cork continued. "I am the youngest of three children. My mother didn't want to have more than two, but I came along anyway. She didn't want me. Every day after she fixed breakfast and Daddy left, she would put me outside in the backyard and lock the door. I had to stay out until time for supper. Dad would go to work, and my brother and sister would go to school. I spent my early childhood days in the fenced-in yard. I couldn't get out of the yard or back in the house.

"Early in my parents' marriage, my dad had an affair. My mother never let him live it down. Dad changed due to her shaming. He caved in to her. Mother ran everything and made all the decisions. Dad would go along with whatever she said. She is dead now, but my older sister is just like her. Now my dad yields to whatever my sister says. He will not do anything of which she does not approve. I have lived across the state line for several years now since you helped me get that property. He has yet to come see me and says he can't get here; it's just too far.

"Another thing: If it was bad weather and my mother had to leave the house, she would tie me with a rope in a chair in the kitchen. She told me not to tell my daddy. She would untie me when she got back from wherever she went."

Cork then called a man's name and asked me if I remembered him.

"Yes, he was a pastor for years but is dead now," I recalled. "Why?"

"I used to go to that church, and he baptized me," Cork revealed. "I grew up Catholic, up north, but then we moved down here. I went to that church and became a member there. I used to have an occasional date with a girl who was also a member. We had seen each other off and on for about a year or so. I was eighteen. Her family was active there, too. One week they had a youth revival. I thought I would go and maybe see her after the service. It was one of those hellfire and brimstone sermons about morality, drinking, dancing, and premarital sex. The sermon was loaded with shame, guilt, and condemnation. The invitation went on and on. The preacher kept pleading and extending it.

"After singing three hymns each at least three times, no one had responded. Then this girl stood up and walked the aisle. Apparently, she was confessing things to the preacher. She talked to him for a long time and cried. When the service ended, I noticed her father go up and talk to the pastor. Then, they went into a back room. People were standing all around visiting. I just sat in my seat. I was waiting to talk to her, but she stayed down front crying.

"All this time, I just sat there. I had never been in a situation like that before and did not know what to do. When her father and the pastor came out, I noticed the pastor looking for someone. Then his eyes fixed on me. When he saw me, he walked up the aisle straight toward me. He motioned for me to come with him. I stood from the pew and met him in the aisle. He said, 'I want to talk to you.'

"He took me to a room at the back of the church and closed the door. He accused and condemned me right there for things he said I had done to and with that girl. Then, he said to me, 'You are no longer welcome in this church. Never again set a foot in here. Leave now and don't come back.' Satch, he was the one who counseled and baptized me.

"Satch, most of the things he said to me, I knew nothing about. And the rest of them were not true. I had never even kissed that girl! He kicked me out of the church that night. I have not been back in a church since."

"May I ask you a question?'

"Yes," Cork agreed.

"Can you tell me, did the girl's father hold any leadership position in that church?" I queried.

"Yes, he was a deacon," Cork stated.

"That's what I thought," I said.

I asked Cork if he had anybody that he could talk to about these things. He said, "Yes, my brother who lives in a town north of here. He understands. Sometimes we talk, and sometimes we just cry."

"So is that why you asked me to help you buy that property and you moved to another state?" I asked.

"I had to," Cork admitted. "My gross income has gone down from $700,000 a year to $150,000 a year, and it was the best thing I have ever done. I had to get away from all this. Satch, you are sitting on a gold mine. What you were talking about earlier isn't just my story. It's everybody's story."

CHAPTER 9

Hell and a Horse Ride

That night I could not stop thinking about my friends' experiences. Their pain was severe. Family and religious abuse abounds. I cannot tell you how many stories like these I have been told. Cork was right. In some way it's everybody's story. Then there were the conversations with Ron and Larry. My four friends were living in a different hell in their own lives that came out of domestic and spiritual abuse. Larry was living in a fear of the burning of an eternal hell. On earth we describe intense emotional pain and catastrophes as being a living hell. Was hell something we experience on earth or was there also an eternal hellfire after we die? Or both? Were they the same or similar? Is it even possible that God is so good and liberating that you can be in the fire of eternity's hell while actually being in a part of heaven experiencing the reconciliation of God's redemptive justice? I went to sleep as confounded as ever.

As I slept, I was walloped again by a dream I had had only once, years before. It was the second time I dreamed of being seized while walking out of the gym on seminary campus. I was strapped into a strait jacket, wrapped in a hooded robe, and tied up. My captors chained my feet and dragged me through the woods. When I woke, I sat straight up in the bed. I remembered the whole dream. It shook me. The dream was a picture of the judgment, of a physically burning hell. I had been bound and was being thrown into an eternity of scorching fire.

The first time I experienced the dream was when I was working on my master's degree in seminary. It all began with my Baptist history professor and friend who was from the same state as me. He kept hounding me about God's sovereign election of chosen ones with the rest being sent to damnation. In a diagram of views on the subject, my prof assumed an extreme position more severe than Calvin's darkest view of predetermined election.

My professor and I attended the same church and had gotten to know each other, along with our families. My professor had three sons. One day, I asked him, "If you believe your view of election is so solid, what do you tell your sons?"

"They are either among the chosen, or they are among the damned. There is nothing else to tell them," he replied.

Having a hard time with this theology, I sought the views of several professors. Some drew extensive diagrams on a chalkboard. Others gave some brief explanation of their views. None was close to satisfactory. This issue ripped me to the core. How could a good God create children in His image and likeness—only to send them to hell? I got up the courage to ask the oldest and most experienced professor on campus—a published author of New Testament commentaries—for an appointment.

The seventy-seven-year-old prof looked at me and said, "Satch, I cannot answer your question. I do not know what election means. Most students come through here and never ask a question. Most think they already have the answers. You ask questions. Satch, keep on asking questions."

Later in the semester, my history professor invited me to sit in on a class where he had invited an international spokesman, an advocate of the professor's view of election. I did not want to go but agreed out of courtesy. I sat through the lecture wondering if I was ever going to hear the apostle Paul's pronouncement of God's election of people in and through Christ—and that before the foundation of the world. I did not. At the end of the class, my professor motioned to me to come to the front to meet the speaker. I thought, *Oh, no*, but I obliged. The two professors cornered me and insisted I allow them to buy my lunch. I did not want to go. I hesitated but did not want to offend, so I agreed.

For an hour and a half, the professors grilled me with a well-thought-out logic of those chosen and condemned in their doctrine of election based on their definition of God's sovereignty. It was obvious they had picked me out as a special object to convert to their view. They were insistent and forceful in their urgency.

I was nonplussed as I listened to their joint lecture. I ate with difficulty and a slowly rising resentment. I felt ambushed and highly ticked off by the whole process. I had been summoned into a class lecture that overloaded my already full schedule. Then I was coerced into participating in a lunch with my professor and an internationally known and respected lecturer. I listened, as my food got harder to chew and swallow. Finally, the two profs announced the lecturer had a flight to catch for his next speaking engagement. Then the lecturer asked if I had any questions. The tone was filled with a confidence of having dissuaded any possible objection or uncertainty about the issue.

I looked at them and said, "Only one: Do I have any say or part to play in my salvation? Do I even get a dice roll?"

The two profs looked at each other, and then their eyes went down to the table. They said nothing while rising from their chairs. They thanked me for listening and excused themselves. I was glad I had driven my own vehicle to the restaurant. I respected both men and realized I had just listened to a well-reasoned interpretation of a serious issue. But why would neither respond to my simple question?

The two professors did not seem to consider that if God is Father, He is not like a Sultan king who controls everyone's obedience. I had read Athanasius and some of the early church fathers and mystics who wrote that God has a Father's heart before He creates. And being Father of a family and all of creation given free will means that not everyone obeys. Such is the burden that God must carry, *if* in fact He is first a Father who truly loves. I wanted assurance of that. I was torn up about this. God gave humanity free will. How can this work with their definition of predestination? So confusing and hurtful. I was glad to have another class to attend and an opportunity to go to the workout center to relieve some stress.

I was hardly able to study, visit with my wife, or play with my three children that evening. My mind was filled with the hellfire for those who had no say so or part to play in their own salvation or damnation. How could this even be possible?

Why would God give free will to mankind and simultaneously predetermine his end? The thought haunted me in my sleep and dreams. That night, I experienced the most frightening dream of my life.

I struggled to find sleep. I was thinking about the two professors' presentations when I finally slept. As I recalled my day, I thought about how I had finished my classes for the day and had gone for a short workout. That was my last thought before I dropped off into sleep. Somehow the dream began with my leaving the workout. It was dusk when I walked out of the fitness center. The outdoor lights were blinking, trying to come on as I walked toward my truck. Suddenly I was grabbed and yanked from behind by grotesque, foul-smelling demons. I fought them but could not escape. They laughed and hooted with contorted grins.

My captors bound me in a strait jacket. They jerked off my shoes. These creatures covered me in a black-hooded robe. They tied it close with a belt around my waist. They chained my feet and dragged me into a dark, wooded area. There was no way for me to resist. The demons picked me up, threw my body into a shaft in the earth through which I descended tumbling down and landed hard on a wooden floor. The area was surrounded by wooden walls that smelled of a burning. It was something like a dumping room.

I gathered myself as much as I could. Still straitjacketed, I was not able to stand. My feet were chained. Many others suffered the same fate. There were bodies all around me, dumped in a pile on the floor, all strapped in brown or black hooded robes. The bodies were stacking up. I could not tell if they were male or female. It was like they were loading people in, one on top of the other. Then, I noticed a doorway in one of the walls through which smoke ascended from below.

My eyes began to focus. The demons grabbed the robed people and pulled them to their feet. They chanted and danced around their captives and stomped on us. The demons dragged people screaming through the doorway and down a hallway that led to something like a holding room. Suddenly, they grabbed me from the back of my hooded robe and dragged me through a hallway into a holding room. As I lay there stunned, the room continued to fill with more smoke. The stifling heat rose from below. People were crying, yelling, and screaming. The demonic captors dragged the robed people across the room and flung them down a descending stairway that led out of the holding room.

The demons were viciously angry and would randomly take robed persons who were screaming in pain and fear and throw their bodies through a wall of the holding room or a wall of the staircase. There were gaping holes in the walls. Every time a new hole was made, the heat and smoke intensified. As they dragged me down the stairs, I could see the people through holes made by their robed bodies being thrown through the wall. They were falling and screaming into a chasm, descending to the depths where flames were rising and getting hotter. A huge demon grabbed me and threw me through the wall. As I descended into the abyss, I woke up.

I sat straight up in bed. I was drenched in sweat. My pillow, sheets, and underwear were soaked. With sweat running in my eyes and dripping off my elbows, I turned to put my feet on the floor. I was dizzy. Sweat ran down my legs, off my ankles, and onto the carpet. I sat for a long time on the edge of the bed, dripping. Then I turned to look at my wife. Somehow, she was sound asleep. I was glad I didn't wake her or the children up. I was grateful it was only a dream—but what did it mean?

I knew dreams can have real value. I went to the bathroom sink and washed my face—opting not to shower, because it might wake them up. So, I took a bath towel and washed and dried myself as best I could and changed my underwear. I sat down on the toilet and pondered for a long time. Would I be chosen or dammed? Was I destined to be thrown into hell's bottomless pit raging with eternal fire? How could God allow such a thing? What is the meaning of this dream?

In time I found two dry towels—one to cover my wet pillow and another one to cover my side of the sweat-soaked sheets. I lay down, staring at the ceiling—but I did not sleep. The next morning, I wrote a three legal page letter to my friend Scott encouraging him to believe Jesus. At the same time, I wondered what difference that would make.

Forty years later, at the farmhouse the dream came again. I was falling into hell again. I awoke partway through it. I sat straight up in the bed—just like before. As I sat on the side of my bed, my mind began to clear. As I tried to recover from the dream about hell, I found myself sweating again, dripping on the floor, though not as much as the first time. I never wanted to experience that again. This question of God and hell had marked me. It had become a part of me. I could not continue my life besieged by this horrendous uncertainty. I had to find the answer to the character of God and his own being. There was no way I could go back to sleep, so I got up and took a shower.

The sun was close to being up. I decided to go to the computer and write down my thoughts. They were so scrambled I had to stop. My mind was being haunted by the fear and uncertainty of the doctrines of predestination and election as well as the wreck and hell dream. If the professors were right, then no one has a choice. If that were so, then why even try? As for earning heaven, I knew I was not worthy. If it were as I was taught, then all you had to do was believe in Jesus, pray, and be baptized. Then you were saved—once saved, always saved. How did there come to be so many different doctrines and interpretations? These conflicting systems of belief were eating me up as much as the abuse and my family issues.

I decided to get on the internet and take care of as much business as I could. Mid-morning came. I was hungry. I ate a bite and decided to ride my horses. I took Son for a short ride. He was still young, and I didn't want to overdo it. We rode and I got back to the barn and brushed out his mane and tail and gave him a good currying all over. I saddled Music, and we took off. Music is a lot of horse. Not everyone can ride her, but her gait was so sweet. I named her Sweet Music. I decided to take her down the country roads and around every field to which I came down to the old bridge remains on the river.

As I rode around one neighbor's field, I looked up and saw an eagle flying. We rounded the field, and the eagle descended and circled the field above us. There were a number of eagles on the river. I had seen their nests but seeing them in flight was a bit unusual. I slowed Music to a walk and then stopped her so I could watch the eagle clearly. It took me back to years before when I was in Colorado at Operation Restored Warriors led by Paul, a friend who had been in the military. He had a special gift from the Lord to help military men with PTSD. I had been invited to attend the weeklong session.

Paul had a gift for seeing inside a man's heart. He counseled that in the ancient sacred traditions the heart has a very specific meaning. It is not simply the seat of our personal emotions, our affective life, or our personal identity, but for perceiving divine purpose and beauty, for spiritual seeing and hearing.

I was skeptical of Paul's gift of seeing into a heart until I experienced a session with him in Colorado. Several weeks later I was with a friend who had also attended the same session. We were in Tennessee and met a pastor who was very interested in what we were sharing. He was in pain and open to discuss and to pray with us. When we did, I had the same experience. I saw inside the man's heart and the cause of his pain. That let me know that Paul's gift was true.

The eagle circled the field again and flew over us a couple of times. Then the eagle turned west toward the river. The gravel road named Possum Trail led the way. I decided to follow the eagle. On the way, as I watched the eagle, my thoughts went back to my experience in Colorado with the crows and the eagle I had experienced there. When it came my turn to meet there with Paul, he prayed for me. Paul told me my heart was so damaged—surrounded by briars, bushes, and vines—that he could not even see it, much less look inside it. My heart was hidden. He told me my heart was more damaged than all the others there combined. He asked me if I would allow Jesus to give me a new heart. I agreed, but it didn't seem to work.

Later in the week, the leadership assigned me the task of taking a walk and hearing what God had to say to me through nature. I walked a long way and sat at the base of a mountain, looking over a large open field. I encountered a bunch of crows and three eagles. I came away feeling like I was a crow and could never be an eagle. Later in the week, I asked Paul if we could pray again with two others I knew who were also attending the session. That time, the burden was partially lifted, but not nearly enough. I couldn't shake those feelings. I felt I was a crow.

I urged Music forward. We hit the road and followed the eagle to the highway and across toward the river. Music was a pretty fast single footer. I had clocked her at over twenty miles an hour in that smooth gait. That day it seemed she was faster. Even at that speed we could not keep up with the eagle. When we reached the river, the eagle headed over the ridge at least a couple of miles away.

As we slowed to a walk, I saw a boat coming up the river. I loved to fish but had sold my boat. I thought about taking up fishing again. I knew I needed to walk Music to let her cool down. As I turned her to go back to the farm, I saw a man sitting across the river on the remaining part of the old wooden bridge. He was fishing. He was wearing leather pants, a shirt with tassels on the sleeves, and a headband. "Hello, young man," the fisherman shouted. "Nice horse. Do you live close to here?"

I responded, "Yes, I do; kind of you to call me a young man. You from around here?"

"No, just visiting," replied the stranger. "Love to fish. Called you young because I'm a lot older than you. Glad to see you today. I have a feeling we will be seeing more of each other. We need to talk about fishing and horses and a lot of other things."

I was surprised. "I don't know you. Do you have horses?" I asked.

The man stood up, grabbed his fishing pole and bait and began walking away down the river's edge. He waved at me but said not another word. I watched him for a minute and thought, *He seems harmless and a nice guy. What does he mean we need to talk about a lot of other things?* I turned Music back toward the highway and walked her to cool her down. When we got to the barn, I washed her down and brushed her. She liked that. I gave her extra grain and hay and a big hug. She looked at me as though she was smiling and trying to say something.

Satch and Music

CHAPTER 10

The Sinkhole

Back at the farmhouse, I grabbed a bite to eat and sat down to write. Frustration with hell and trying to tell my story rankled its way back into my mind. I was still too upset. It had taken me years to recover from the rejection of my work. My counselor friend had thrown my first eight years of work in the trash can like it did not matter. I had invested my heart and immeasurable hours into the project. I had started over so many times since then, developed so many versions, and revised them so often that I felt unable to complete it.

Truth is, I was a mess. I didn't even know where I was headed or how to get wherever that was. Whatever way I was on, I couldn't read the road signs. It was obvious I had no life compass. I felt like a worn-out and ragged paper bag hanging on a tree limb being torn by the wind.

I thought about riding Music and seeing the eagle down to the river, trying to deal with the onslaughts of hell and my difficulty in getting anything done on this writing project. The cursor on the screen just sat there blinking. I worked on the manuscript as long as I could and then gave up. I was worn out trying to write what I did not know how to communicate. I turned off the computer and sat motionless. It was way past dark now. I knew I was totally fragmented and dispirited. I had come to the end of myself. I did not know what to do and told God I had tried all I knew to try. I was desperate for help. I asked for mercy. Then, with eyes closed, things became quiet for a few moments as I sat in a dim light from the single lamp shining across the room.

All these thoughts started rambling back into my mind and kept running into each other in my brain. I jumped from one to another. It seemed my life was repeating the same questions and struggles, intensified by my inability to corral them in any sensible way. From my experience, people all over the world are being pervaded with the same colliding confusions—having no idea why, like a universal sadness. If I couldn't do this, how was I ever going to get peace or help anyone else find hope?

Then, something different and unforeseeable began. Suddenly, I was interrupted by the sound of a violent wind followed by a loud bang. It felt like the house shook. Something slammed with great force against the window next to my chair. The wind stopped, and all went silent. I raised the shade. There wasn't any damage to the windowpane. I looked out the window but saw nothing. I had to check outside. I opened the door, stepped out onto the front porch, eased down the two steps, and sat down. After sitting for a while and seeing nothing, something felt strange. I decided to assess things. I walked around the house and back to the front. Nothing.

I took a series of long, deep breaths from the cool air and felt a little better. I noticed for the first time the borrowed trailer beside the monkey tree in the front yard. A friend had loaned it to me to haul my tractor and dropped it in the front yard. *Why did I not see that when I came back from riding?* I wondered. I looked down the hill and then up. What I saw was spectacular. The sky had the clearest, deepest blue-black hue, and the stars formed a brilliant display in the heavens that I had never noticed. These celestial luminaries appeared to stand still and blink before shooting across the sky. The moon was full and bright, and the North Star was in its regular spot but larger and clearer than ever.

I stared at this heavenly light show for such a long time. Then I began to feel something different around my feet and ankles—dampness. As my eyes dropped from the sky, I marveled at the fog rolling in from the river as if peace were rolling in over the land. Fog gradually crept from the road on the north end and moved up the hill a quarter mile toward the farmhouse, like a cloud covering the earth. I could see the top of the fence in front of me and the trees, but the ground was covered in a gentle white haze. It was a remarkable sight. I just stood there, taking it in. Eventually I felt tired, yet I did not want to go back inside the house. I wanted to experience what was happening. I forgot about time.

To my right were four large cedar trees with enough space between them that each was growing to their fullness from top to bottom. I decided to sit down in front of the one closest to the road so my view would not be blocked. I became absorbed in the beauty of the sights and sounds of this amazing, marvelous evening. The anxious sadness that haunted me began to ease.

I propped against the cedar between two large branches. It felt good. The fog covered my ankles. I felt like I was floating. Weird things started happening—not frightening, just different. At times it felt like the tree was swaying, but there was no wind. Cedars in the fall and winter shed spiny, needle-like leaves. They are small, but I guess you still call them leaves. They fell in my hair and on my shoulders and arms as I pulled my knees to my chest. There was no raccoon or bird moving in the tree. The ground seemed to soften under me. I heard a creaking noise and felt the ground shift. It didn't scare me, though. It all seemed to be a part of this experience I was having.

I was now totally convinced the farmhouse sat on an Indian burial mound. I had poked around on it but was scared to dig. When I told my adjoining neighbor Terry about my suspicions, he broke out grinning and told me there were three different mound locations. He said they had recovered not just arrowheads but spearheads, tools, bowls and many other artifacts, all on his property. I just smiled and thought, *Sure, all on your property.*

On a family weekend at the farm years before, one of my sons-in-law, who loves archeology, had found arrowheads around the farmhouse. Years earlier my father told that my great-great grandmother was a full-blooded Indian, which enhanced my intrigue. My understanding was that I had Native American blood flowing in my veins.

When I was about thirteen, my dad and uncle took Fletch, our cousin, and me on a six-week trip out west. Part of the trip included visits to historical Native American locations.

I don't remember all the places, but in Arizona and New Mexico I was absolutely fascinated by the Navajo Indians and their craftsmanship and with the Sioux's in the Black Hills of South Dakota. I marveled at the way they lived, looked, and related to each other. I have always felt a kindred spirit with Native Americans. I cannot explain it. It is real to me.

So, on that foggy night, with the sky full of stars, I was worn out. I fought the feeling that I should go inside to bed. My mind was filled with nothing but questions for which I did not have answers. I just couldn't think anymore but decided to take a walk through the fog. I stood up, climbed through the pasture fence, and walked down the hill toward the road. The moon was full, the sky clear, the stars shining, so there was no need for additional light.

When I reached the road, I turned around and faced the farmhouse. The fog reached my waist. Looking over it to the top of the hill was a glorious sight. The farmhouse stood out like a singular peak. This had to be an Indian Mound. I returned slowly up the hill, climbed back through the fence, and sat again beneath the cedar.

I can't explain what happened then. I don't know. I was exhausted. My mind was frayed. Maybe I dozed off or perhaps I was sleepwalking or dreaming, but as I leaned against that cedar tree, the ground underneath me just opened up and swallowed me. I reached out to grasp something, anything. I could not have conjured up where all of this was headed.

As I fell into what must have been a sinkhole, my face and arms were scratched by all the dirt and roots and rocks.

There seemed to be no bottom. I just kept falling, falling, and tumbling. My stomach jumped time and again up to my throat. I didn't know what was happening. I could not conceive it. I was careening downward and downward, when all of a sudden, I felt pressure coming up from the bottom of my feet like an elevator pushing against your feet and then your whole body as it comes to a stop. Your knees almost buckle. It was like that. Yet this was not a slow, comfortable stop. I slammed into the ground and landed hard on my butt. Dust and dirt particles fell all around me like a dust storm on the Kansas prairie. At first, I could not see a thing because of the haze. Slowly, the air started to clear. I was covered with dirt. I looked up to see how far I had fallen, but the view above was pitch black. I could see nothing overhead. I was skinned, banged up and hurting from head to toe—especially my back, like I had just gotten another herniated disk.

I looked all around but could see nothing in front or behind. As the dust settled more, I thought I saw the shape of what looked like a man, an Indian. When I had gathered myself enough and began to get my bearings, I felt my face. I had lost my glasses.

You may be surprised but I, Yeesa, watched Satch as he fell, and the dust cloud disseminate. I knew he would not remember who I was until I told him, but that needed to wait for now.

"Hi! I found your glasses and your walking stick." I said. "You must have lost them when you fell down the hole. You may need both of them while you are here."

Completely taken aback at the casual nature of this being, Satch replied. "So, that's what you have to say to me. How did you show up here? How long have you been standing there?"

"All your life. Hello, and welcome," I exclaimed.

"Look, I think I hurt my back in the fall, and I'm all skinned and beaten up," Satch complained. "I am gonna be stove-up and swollen as Jabba the Hutt, and you say 'Welcome.' Where am I? Who are you? How did this happen? What is going on? Give me my glasses, please."

Handing Satch his glasses, I said, "You are okay. Need me to pop your back and help alleviate the pain? You erupt with questions, always have, but you do not take in the answers. You need to be right here and shut up. See and hear. Take this in. Else—"

"Else what?" Satch inquired. "Is this the end?"

"Does not have to be," I explained. "Up to you."

"So, this is real?" Satch questioned.

"Real and true, depends on if you can accept it," I noted. "Let's start again. I was going to introduce myself this afternoon, but I did not think you were quite ready. Are you ready now?"

"I have never seen you," Satch said matter-of-factly. Then he put his glasses on and was able to see better. "You were fishing in the river today," Satch said. "What is this? Really, who are you and what in the world is going on? Where am I? What is happening to me? I was leaning against a cedar tree, and now I've fallen into a hole in the ground. You are an Indian, aren't you? Is this really a mound? Is my farmhouse really sitting on an Indian mound? I knew it!"

"Hold on," I cautioned. "Can you feel your hands? Reach with your hands and touch your arms, legs, and feet. Can you walk around and hear what I am saying and understand it? If you think this is just another dream, why are we actually having a conversation?"

Satch grabbed his stick and struggled to get up. When he did, he staggered a bit and stiffly and awkwardly sat down again.

"I cannot explain where you are other than you are experiencing another realm of God's goodness but not in heaven as men speculate. You are certainly a long way from any place called hell, except the turmoil you feel inside. You described some specifics when talking about your hell dream. Does this seem like that to you?"

"Look, dude, whoever you are, tell me what is going on," pleaded Satch.

"In your dream of hell, was it like what you are experiencing now?" I asked. "The demons made weird noises, grabbed you, and threw you down toward a burning pit. Did you touch them? Were you able to speak or just feel? Was there any conversation, or were you just there experiencing it, feeling it but really only observing, not allowed to choose to participate? Did you have any options, any freedom?"

"No," Satch replied. "There is a difference. I am skinned up and bleeding here. And there were no conversations there. I was about to be burned to a crisp."

"So, does this feel like the same thing?" I queried.

"I am unsure, but no, it is not the same," Satch confirmed.

"You are going to be here a while if you choose, unless you adamantly decline to face your issues."

"I need a lot of help," Satch admitted. "But how are you, an Indian down in this hole in the ground, wherever we are, going to help me?"

"First, why are you classifying me by race? We all hurt, bleed red, wrinkle, and turn gray. We all make mistakes, harm others and ourselves. We all come from God. We all have questions. There is only one race—the human race—one human nature, and all are in a marathon to find life, as are you."

That silenced Satch momentarily. I knew he heard me, but he would not quit asking questions. I just grinned, because many of us do that when we are afraid and have been taken totally out of our comfort zones. Satch had been. Now what would he do about it?

"Yes, I am what you call an Indian, and more," I said. "Hello, Satch, how are you?"

In absolute disbelief, Satch spewed, "What in the hell is going on? Can you tell me? Who are you and what am I doing here? What is happening to me? How do you know my name? What is all this?"

"Good," I replied. "Good is happening to you, if you want it. Do you want it?" Satch stood there dumbfounded. He couldn't speak. So, I continued, "You have been asking Father, Son, and Spirit a lot of questions, have you not? You have been asking such questions since you were a small boy. So many things do not make sense to you, right?"

"You are correct, sir!" he chirped. "And this makes no sense at all."

To get straight to the point, I asked, "Do you want to know why you ask so many questions and why your heart hurts so badly? Do you especially want to know why you feel rejected and unloved? Even more, do you know what is inside you that makes you so vulnerable to deceit and seduction? You do know you got snookered, don't you? Well, your being here is no bunco. You are here because of your broken and foolish heart—and your incessant asking."

I watched as Satch fell back to the floor. He folded like a wet sack into a fetal position. It hurt my heart to see him in more pain, but that is part of the process. I knew that conviction well. He would be okay. It was a profound reminder of deep wounds in his life. He lay on the floor and wept.

"My heart feels shredded," confessed Satch. "I can't believe it. I don't know what to do. I have cried a fifth of my life, and I just don't understand. I have poured my heart out over and over again. I've tried to talk and write about my pain, but I can't. My friends do not grasp it and cannot pursue the issue. All the things I have experienced compounded—" Satch paused for a moment and then burst out, "Wait just a minute! Who are you anyway? What is this? Am I not in the least deserving of being told what is happening to me?"

"But you know when it began, don't you?" I asked. "I know your story. Something happened to you when you were really little in a women's dressing room at a swimming pool and then after that with your neighbor's teenage daughter and her girlfriends. Then there were times after that with women other than your wife. I saw those things happen to you and have read the stories you wrote about them."

"WHAT!?" Satch exclaimed. He could not believe his ears. "What do you mean you know about those events, and you have read my stories? Is that what you meant by 'been standing there my whole life'? You weren't there and NOBODY has read those stories—not even my friend who threw my work in the trash can."

"Satch, you don't understand all that was happening to you in those experiences, do you?" I said. "But you can't forget it, can you?"

"No," he admitted.

"Do you want to know?" I inquired.

"Yes," Satch affirmed.

"Father has allowed you to come here so that you can have understanding if you are open to it," I stated. "I am your brother. I am here for you."

Still skeptical, Satch retorted, "That's just great! What do you mean 'my brother,' and what are you doing here? Why am I here?"

"Snarly one aren't you, Satch?" I quipped. "Let me share something before we go any further. Do you believe in life after death?"

"Well, yeah," came the knee-jerk reply.

"By excluding death from our lives, we cannot live a full life. By acknowledging death is part of life, we enlarge and enrich life. Death must come to a lot of things in your life for you to live. Death is but a river that runs into the sea. In the great cloud of witnesses, I have always had this connection with you," I explained. "I have watched you and your struggle to understand. I was glad when Jesus asked me if I wanted to participate. He arranged this meeting. You have been asking Father for years for help in understanding your pain and struggles. You have admitted many times your sins and the pain you have caused others and yourself. You just kept asking and asking. Father knew it was time, and you are now able to begin to get answers. You have begun to develop a pocket big enough to hold a portion of what Father has wanted to give you all your life. You are gradually coming to that good place where the truth holds more value than what you have known. The truth brings freedom, but without love, it is insufferable. So, I was sent, and I am glad of it. You have ended up in another world, which you have not begun to understand. But now you are in it."

"Okay. Maybe you got that part right," noted my doubting subject. "Now look, first, you are an Indian fishing on the river calling me young and asking about horses. Then, this! So, who are you really? What do I call you? What is your given name?"

"OhiYeesa," I stated.

"Oh high what?" Satch asked.

I slowly enunciated, "O-hi-Yee-sah."

"So, you are the Indian who became a white man but stayed an Indian?" he asked. "Oh, are you that Indian who went to med school and became a doctor? Dr. Charles Alexander Eastman, that's you, isn't it! I read several of your books about your life and Native Americans. I have seen pictures of you."

"Satch, we have a lot in common," I replied.

Satch continued, "You took a white man's name and worked for the US government for the benefit of your people. What—how—what is going on? How did you show up fishing on the river? You have been dead for decades. Are you something like a re-spirited Indian monsignor?"

"No, just a member of your all-time, always family now among the great cloud of witnesses, but I'm here to help you," I said, trying to assure him. "My dad called me OhiYeesa. I was born a Sioux Indian. At least Indian is the label given to us. If I am dead and I am here, would you please explain to me the difference between being alive and being dead? And while you are at it, what is the difference between what is real and what is true?"

Satch had begun to realize he was now in another world. It was not what folks call heaven but an outskirt of one of its outer realms where redemption is in full process. He was aware that he was experiencing more than a regular dream. He was skinned, sore, and filled with questions. His shirt was torn, and his jeans were dusty and dirty. His back was injured, and he was limping. He was weak from his autoimmune disease. Physically, he was a wreck. I pushed him. "If I am dead, how come you see me and are talking to me?"

Suddenly, Satch reeled off biblical examples of supernatural encounters. "I've heard of things similar to this and read in the Good Book about angels. Moses talked with the presence of God. Elijah and Moses met with Jesus. The angels Gabriel and Michael appeared and talked to people. Balaam's donkey talked. Jacob wrestled with God's angel. Daniel and Ezekiel experienced wonders and wrote about them. I've also had visions and dreams. I have a vivid imagination, but this is not my imagination. Am I asleep? Am I dreaming? That's what this is, isn't it? It's some kind of participative vision. I'm confused. You're not real, are you? I'm just hallucinating. I am becoming paranoid. So, go away, GO AWAY! I mean it, right now. How can I get back to the farmhouse?"

"Gosh, you are a prickly one," I noted. "Satch, you are doing right now what I just asked you about. You just said, 'You're not real, are you?' Why don't you come closer and see for yourself? Come here, close enough to touch me."

I could tell he was scared. He tried to stand. His back hurt. He struggled and sat down again. I could see he was banged up pretty good, and a couple of the cuts were bleeding. I pitched him a cloth.

Changing the subject, I asked, "So, tell me where the name Satch comes from? What is your full name?"

"My little brother called me Satch," he said. "When he first started to talk, he could not say Satcher, so he called me Satch. His name was Fletcher, so I called him Fletch. He is dead now. He died several years ago. I miss him."

"I know your brother," I conceded. "Sometimes, we play golf or shoot hoops together. He is quite an athlete. From what I know, he's a better athlete than you. He doesn't complain nearly as much either. So, what's the rest of your name, your full name?

"Wait, wait, wait just a minute!" Satch exclaimed. "You know Fletch? What are you talking about?"

"You still don't realize where you are, and you have not been listening to me," I chided. "You need to clean your ears out. Fletch and I, your parents and grandparents, and all those you say are dead are here in some form or another. Those who trusted Jesus are in the great cloud of witnesses. It is time for you to wake up and pay attention. Stop your brain and your tongue. Now, what is your full name?"

"Satcher Bond Condwell," he disclosed. "That's what they tagged me. Been called a lot of things, but Satch stuck."

"Fascinating," I replied, "Hmm, that says a lot! Now, are you ready to listen?"

"I think so," he conceded. "Can I stay sitting here? I don't feel too spry."

"Sure, you can," I said. "Satch, it is time for you to know a part of my story. That may help you understand why I am the one here for you. We have more in common than you know. My immediate family was killed or taken into captivity. For my safety, at age four I was turned over to be raised by my uncle. Years later, one day in the woods, I saw a man walking. He was searching for me. It was my father. He had escaped captivity. I was the last child born to my parents. My mother named me Hadakah. It means the Pitiful Last. She died soon after I was born. My father changed my name to OhiYesa, which means the Winner.

"My dad told me I was going to have to live in two worlds, that I would have to be strong and wise in both—it would be like a war. I was to be a warrior. I did that. I went to college, studied hard, and became a medical doctor. I worked with my people and the government. I fought for progress in spiritual matters and the treatment of Indians by the white man. I loved my people and their way of seeing and understanding. The differences between our customs were irreconcilable, but I always hoped understanding could prevail.

"My battle involved bringing two worlds together. The Christian religion in my day, like today, was driven by money. The church's income and the local parish priests' or pastors' compensation was based on the number of converts and tithers made. Too many of the workers were after quantity rather than quality of spiritual conversions. I learned not to blame the gospel for the damage caused by those who misused and preached it. You need to do the same.

"You also have been in a battle all your life, trying to reconcile the teachings of your religion with your life experiences: lack of acceptance, applause, and love with the deceit and seduction. You know something is bad wrong. You have fought and fought. You have gotten your butt kicked big time. You kept getting back up. I know that feeling. I was married for a long time, but I had an inner longing that my wife could not understand, nor could we resolve. We divorced. The battle between the trade civilization of the white man and the spiritual revelation given to all humanity, which was understood by the Indians, resulted in an incompatible difference. I moved to the northeastern United States and did all I could. I wrote about it as best I could and left there for good. I too was beaten down and disheartened. I understand you, Satch.

"Take your time and relax. It's okay. Calm down. Stay seated. You may want to lie down for a minute." He lay down.

"Satch, you said you wanted to know who I am. Are you ready yet?" Satch lifted his head and looked at me. "Do you want to see me as an Indian or a white man?" I switched from one dress to another instantly, which is easy in the "cloud."

"How did you do that?" he mumbled.

"Relax! Wasi'chus or Indian?" I persisted.

"Indian," Satch said. "I have never gotten to know a real Indian."

"Okay, first I want you to describe me, what you see," I instructed. "Then come touch me."

"I see a tall man with dark and piercing eyes and long black hair over his shoulders," Satch said. "You are strong, with a firm and defined jaw and distinctive nose. You are wearing a headband and beaded necklaces over a leather shirt gathered at your waist by a leather belt. A knife in a leather sheath is clasped to your belt. Your belt has eagle feathers woven into it. Bear claws dangle from your belt, down over your tasseled leather trousers. You're wearing moccasins. Your shoulders are covered with a large buffalo hide. You are holding a woven wool blanket across your arm that falls to the ground. You also seem at peace. You appear confident, assured, and brave. You look like you would be a capable fighter and wise leader of your people."

"You gave two descriptions, one physical. Satch, what is the other? How is it you know qualities of a being beyond what you see with your eyes? Where are those other eyes?"

"Now, wait a minute." Satch paused. "I never thought of that. Do you mean a second set of eyes? Come on, I just know it. I don't know where it comes from, and I sure can't locate it somewhere in my body, or can I? Am I about to understand that I don't understand?"

"You are. It is a gift, a gift of the Spirit," I explained. "Everyone has a degree of discernment; few have eyes to see what you have seen and are able to describe it because you feel it. Where do you feel from, Satch?"

Befuddled, Satch replied, "Man, I'm sorry but I don't know what you are talking about or what—I mean who to call you. You've got two or four names and are—help me. What should I call you?"

I reminded Satch of his previous preference. "You said you prefer the Native American."

"Yes, sir. I do," he confirmed. "But the four syllables are a mouthful all the time, so I could go with 'Oh' or 'Oh High' or 'Yeesa' or some other combination. How about 'Hi Yes'? A 'High Yes' for me would be most welcomed. But there is one other option I also like: 'Oh Yes.' I long for some yeses. I have had so many nos. Would you help me?"

I laughed and almost dropped my knife. When I gathered myself, I told him, "We all need each other, even in small things. Coming to wholeness takes a fellowship, a community. Your opportunity is now higher than ever, but you need to realize that I am not higher than you. I have only walked longer. And you and I both know the One who can say 'Oh Yes.' I can't do that on my own, but I have seen him face to face. He sent me. Let's settle on Yeesa, pronounced 'with a long 'ē', Yeesa,That's easy."

Satch approved. "I'm good with that, Mr. Yeesa."

Correcting him, I said, "No sir or mister, just Yeesa. Okay?

"Sounds like a good nickname," he said. "I like it. I don't know what's going on here, but you have my attention. Can I touch you?"

I motioned him closer. "Of course! Come here."

Satch was tentative. He took half a step and stumbled, so I reached for him. When I did, he grabbed my hands and held them, turning them over and back again, rubbing them the whole time. He clutched my forearms, grabbed my elbows, felt my biceps, and squeezed both my shoulders at the same time. He looked me straight in the eyes, put one hand on each side of my neck, then both sides of my head. Then, he touched my face. He ran his hands down through my hair to the back of my shoulders. Suddenly, he jumped back. (He later told me before he touched my head, he felt a breeze flowing through my hair, but it was not blowing on him. He was yet to learn about the breeze.) He regained his composure and looked at me. He stepped toward me again, and we both grabbed each other in a hug. He went limp and collapsed in my arms. I picked him up, laid him on a rug on the ground, and put a leather pillow under his head. I covered him with a blanket. He needed to sleep.

CHAPTER 11

Grumpy

Satch slept, but something happened during the night. I don't know if it was a dream or a reversion to total flesh, but Satch was not the same the next morning. I know what a bad mood is. I understand being angry. I have known being pushed out, dragged down, orphaned, criticized, judged, and ostracized. But you talk about a sour attitude. Whew! He was so hurt; he could not let it go. He was swinging at and fighting everything!

Satch would not say a word to me. I had fixed breakfast, but he didn't like it. He paced around the cave, turned around and came back. He was red-faced, and I'm not talking about Indian red. Something was wrong.

"What is going on with you?" I asked.

"Look, you might mean well, but your being dead and all of this happening, it can't be real. I cannot wake up," Satch lamented. "This has got to be some vision or fantasy or something. Yesterday, you claimed to have watched me all my life, know my little brother, Fletch, and all my history. That makes no sense to any logical mind, none at all—and I'm not crazy. Then, I started thinking about what my grandmother, my dad, my mom did to me. I guess you know them, too. I resent it, and I am bitter about it."

Then, he talked about his hometown and classmates that turned against him, the deceptions, lying coaches, betrayals, and the church. He could not forget all the things that were forced on him when he was so young. These memories angered him. He kept waking up during the night thinking about them. He knows he's supposed to forgive, but he cannot. He was really incensed and could not do anything about it. He was mad and depressed at the same time. He said, "Whatever is happening, what good is it!?"

"You sound like a combination of Jonah, King David, and Saint Peter—fussing, complaining, doubting, asking God to hate all their enemies and Gentiles, as well as denying Jesus. Yesterday, you appreciated, but today you are hacked off. If you are looking for title and reputation, you are in the wrong place. Until you have genuine faith and forgive, you cannot get well. Forgiveness is letting go of your chokehold around someone else's neck, whether dad, mom, girls, or church. They are unaware and are trapped just like you have been.

"You are the one that hurts. Letting it go is for your benefit. Why do you hold onto a past life you cannot change? You don't live in the past, so why do you stay in it? Holding bitterness, blame, hatred, and resentment will break you. You want to retaliate, return the favor, but do not know how. Those resulting emotions move you away from appreciation, admiration, and praise. Something happened, and you lost sight of what you once believed was the truth about some others. You can live shattered as a dead man or choose to be alive before you die. Forgiveness takes the dirt out of your soul. Satch, how much and how many times have you been forgiven?"

"Yeesa, why is letting go, forgiving, and so much of this life so hard?" Satch asked.

"It is hard, sometimes close to perilous," I replied. "Your heart is badly damaged; you have many wounds, but they are sacred wounds. It's not all your fault. Children are not faulted for the sins of their parents and family, despite the consequences to them. You did not ask for the life into which you were born. You have tried, partially. But you have not given your best. You are the only one who can do something about it now. It's your choice. Satch, you must accept the past, your mistakes, the harms from others—whether primary, secondary, or tertiary abusers—marital defects, as well as the incongruences in almost everything. You must accept what is. There is a reason behind all of it. Your capacity for self-delusion is amazing. You're the king of your own shrunken world. It's exquisite selfishness; self-focus only says 'me, me, me.'

"You do not know that you do not know. You stick your head in a hole in the sand you dug yourself as you search for relief from misery. You continue to doubt God and second guess yourself. Then you deceive yourself into returning to harmful passions fueled by deception. Temptation always comes to the door like a seductress hidden in the corner of your mind. You are the one who lets it in and clings to it, but you act like the victim. You disrespect God.

"God will test you, not tempt or deceive you. Struggle will come with challenges intended to develop and make you stronger. That too can hurt and be hard. Temptation lures you. It is a lie wrapped in candy. When you agree and yield to it, inside you are going to suffer and feel pain because you have acted against your true self. God even uses that to teach you. You cling repeatedly to the experiences and feelings from participating with the deceptions and are injured more.

"You hold onto the old, being afraid of the new. You grasp for relief through fame, money, pleasure, and power. Having those does not give you wholeness. You want control while still being a poser, like a boat adrift in the ocean without a sail, motor, or anchor. You cannot reach the shore, much less a safe harbor. Will you ever be free of yourself? You must give up your life to find it. Adam and Eve took their identity as separate from their Source, listening to the deceptive spirit. They pointed and aimed at the wrong target and missed the mark of their identity to live under their own terms. Their nature became sin-willed, self-willed—they became bent and that attitude of bentness has been passed down.

"You can recognize inside you that it is true and just not believe it so. It is easier to blame. You must change your perspective to the reality that God is using this for your good. You participated in putting yourself in this situation, but He is allowing you to move beyond it. It is called surrender. Without seeing that, you are the 'Pitiful.'"

"So, this is all my fault?" Satch asked. "All this stuff is on me, huh?"

"Stop just a minute," I cautioned. "You're thinking about the past again and your family and dad. Why don't you tell me about your father's dream that night when you talked to your family years ago at the farmhouse and you gave them the Blue Bell Homemade Vanilla ice cream."

"Well, Yeesa, I was taken aback. My dad had never opened up. Suddenly he did and spoke about this dream he had. He said he died, and Jesus came to him, picked him up in His arms, and took him to heaven. When they arrived, he looked up and saw God high and lifted up, sitting upon His throne. Jesus carried him up the steps to the throne and placed him in His Father's lap. God held him and smiled. I asked him why he had never told us about that. He said he had never told anyone."

"Satch, What does that tell you about God's true character? You must stop blaming. God has called you so many times, but your phone doesn't ring. It's like you have blocked Him. When God calls you, He calls you to Himself rather than to some position or to prove yourself or your worthiness. His is a call of reconciliation, drawing you toward a life of bringing together. Yes, you resist. Like Adam and Eve in the garden, you stand against God's growing you from a child into a son. You'd rather be deceived and choose the twisted. Adam and Eve ate the apple (or a fig) from the tree of the knowledge of good and evil and were separated in their minds from the source of life in order to live as their own self-gods. Then afraid, they covered themselves with leaves, perhaps from that same tree.

"The fruit represented their desire to be like God. They took that into themselves, and it possessed and controlled them as it has all human beings since…the fruit of self-destruction. This desire commands and dominates us, and we become less than we were meant to be. That's childish, not childlike. The childlike are vulnerable and have no illusion of self-sufficiency. You are afraid and angry, and hostile toward God. You put the ultimate blame on Him. Satch, is this blaming others and God what caused the music to die in you, the day the sun went down? Do you not know God has asked for your forgiveness, so you can let go of your blame?"

Startled and confused, Satch replied, "What! God has asked me for forgiveness? You gotta be nuts."

"Do you not feel He owes you something for the way your life unfolded?" I asked. "After all, it was His idea. He started it all, set it all up. Is He not responsible?"

"Indeed, He is!" Satch agreed. "Where else could it lie beyond the all-knowing Originator of all things? I just do not understand His reason behind it or what He intended by predestinating it."

"Then, you do not truly know His deeds, believe Him, or believe His promises," I insisted. "They are pure and true. You doubt Jesus. Has He not affirmed your destiny?"

Then, Satch spoke forcefully. "I know the teachings, which have many interpretations that conflict drastically. God predetermines up or down, and you have no choice. He decides who's in or out. Love or wrath, He flips a coin. I cannot accept that. Or humans have to pray the prayer, get baptized, join the church, show up, and tithe. Once they do that, they are set. That cannot be the truth. Another is that the Trinity has predestined that all are included in Christ regardless of the part they play and somehow redeems them. Another depends on your works—how well one performs in doing and not doing according to the rules of a particular sect. Then maybe He leaves it to individual humans as to whether or not we choose to participate in His offer of salvation. Of one thing I am sure: God started it and knows how it all ends. One can take that to the bank. Yeesa, how can predestination and free will coexist?"

This time I spoke strongly. "Neither God's wrath nor His discipline is rage against a sinner but vehement opposition to and destruction of the evil besetting His child's tormented soul bound in hell's strangling grip," I declared. "Prayer begins not by 'repeating the prayer." Prayer is the awareness and acknowledgment of the presence of God with and in you. You have not grasped the fullness of what Christ has accomplished. The predestined in Christ includes you. You may call it destiny or redefine foreordained and fate, as long as you do not include luck or chance in it.

"Without a sense of destiny, you have no authority. His providence and promises are inviolable. He grieves over the situation of the world as it is and has said so several times in the Scriptures. At the same time, there is no forcing—you freely choose. Look backward, and you can see predestination. You look forward with free will with your own decisions. In time, you will see how divine providence and free will merge. You work out your own salvation. At times you think you are running away, but you are running toward. All the while, God thinks you are amazing."

"Yeesa, why is this so divisive and controversial?" Satch queried. "If what you say is so, why such resistance from static religion to being open to identifying oneself with a Father who loves and believes in you and always is by your side working for your benefit? Your description is compelling, but I have not been able to accept it as so. Why does this struggle have such a hold on me? I do not feel like I am loved. Why do I feel such contortion and unworthiness? Is this what life is? Look, Yeesa, I know that I'm not enough. I'm not anybody, I fall short. I do not have what it takes. I do not measure up. I don't fit anywhere. I do not belong. I have messed up my life. I do not know who or what I am. So, you tell me—what can be made out of a zilch zero?"

"Satch, you are mankind, entrapped in a deluded toxic mess," I explained. "Everyone likes to be in control and determine how they will get back to God, believing they are not in Him but disconnected and estranged. They feel they must make their own way and hate to consider even the possibility that they may be in error and way wide of the mark. To see you are wrong is an upending experience, a felt disaster.

"Jesus never considers man as disposable, as rubbish to be thrown away. He gave His blood for His very own prized and precious treasure. You are worth it. You are His beloved. Satch, you need to rethink your life for the sake of your spiritual, emotional, mental—and, yes—your physical health. God did not make us Swiss clocks in a world without love, freedom, creativity, or meaning. God put us on a razor's edge, so full of godly fire that we are capable of both martyrdom and murder. We are not puppets, robots, or machines. He gave us freedom to do as we please. Such is the burden God carries. Our Father wants His children to share love and know good. He does not control the free will He bestowed on us.

There is no determinism manipulating our actions. So comes your burden: choices.

"God cannot make things easier, for He gave us as much liberty, creativity, and free rein as possible—likely even the desire to survive. He didn't play it safe. He unflinchingly gave us a flexibility with which even He won't tamper. God does not limit ingenuity but tolerates the misuse of free will. God allows evil, a deception of what is good. He is perceived as silent because He allows people to make their own choices. God respects the power and right to act, speak, and change as one wants. He does so without hindering or restraining, while He is willing and able ultimately to redeem whatever goes wrong.

"Once you see the truth, you will realize that God's providence and your free will are not contradictions or opposite halves but cooperating partners in a paradox. God can do anything, but His nature and choice is to love. *Love seeks the safety, good, and wholeness of the other while allowing you to make wrong choices and learn.*

"He lives through the pain with you and empowers you to overcome even the consequences of your choices for your benefit. No question, it is terribly hard at times and fraught with danger. Until you perceive that invincible love and stop blaming Him, you cannot know or be grateful for His gift, and your life will be filled with sadness and at least a low level of anger. Keep up the rancor, it must be very important to you. This stifling malice may let you live until tomorrow.

"What you need is a total overhaul. Your body has had several operations, but your mind and heart need to be rebuilt.

You feel you are a victim, unvalued, not knowing intimacy. Seldom are lectures beneficial, but you need a deep clean. Your eye is bad, your ear is clogged up, and your mirror is tarnished. What you want to hear is not what you need to hear. You cannot control your anxiety. Your brokenness needs healing, but there are times when the fracture needs a more severe breaking before proper healing can take place. If you cannot receive what God is showing you now, well, possibly you have suffered a shipwreck in regard to your faith. Perhaps trending as a servant of evil you should be delivered over to Satan for the destruction of your flesh so that your spirit may be saved in the day of the Lord Jesus."

"I did not fall with the rain yesterday," Satch retorted. "What are you talking about?"

"Look it up. It is a loving detachment for your benefit," I said as I pitched to him a shoulder bag I was carrying with a copy of the Scriptures in it. "You feel essentially alone, like an outcast, wandering and surviving in virtual solitude without any real companionship. You think that brain of yours knows stuff. Yes, STUFF! You keep chasing. You also have not accepted a second dimension of forgiveness. You have to forgive yourself. You have experienced shaming from the outside since you were a child, and you have added to it as an adult. No one is worthy. That is the point. All are in the same boat. But you do not have to tote that sack of rocks. Redemption is not temporary. But you can stay forlorn as you are.

"*Forgiveness is to let go of the hope for a different past.* The past can hold you like a slave. True freedom is liberty from anything that prevents your wholeness. Faith has to come before any freedom that finds the fullness of unity. The more of God you receive, the more authentic you are, and the freer you will be. In one sense, one cannot know freedom until he has been a slave, possessed by something else. You have been and still are in bondage to experiences of deceptive feelings. Truth is what it is, and acceptance of it leads to great freedom. Forgiveness heals, but it includes accountability. Are you a believer and follower or are you something else, like mutinous? Have you really got sand? How about perseverance, dignity? Yes, the pathway is inconvenient, uneven, stony, and briar-filled with a continuous unfolding. It is a struggle."

"No kidding!" Satch exclaimed.

"Satch," I continued, "you want to eliminate the struggle. You would take the wolves out of Yellowstone Park. You would remove the temptation. It is a struggle to grow, to trust, to find peace, to learn how to fly. It takes wings to fly, and you need God's help. I hope you fight to unlearn deception and learn how to fly. I so want God to teach you how to relax, be vulnerable, and experience how to play. Father, Son, and Spirit know how. You must choose to participate in the process of salvation and redemption or not. Decide what you want. When you choose to take part in something way bigger than yourself, with help, your will can control your desires. Alone, Little Chief, you are sunk. Know the feeling? God has gifted you in many ways, and He desires a return. Hiding your talents will not bring joy to you or help anyone else. Rather, you dam up the river.

"If your life is not about something bigger, a wholeness, much larger than your autonomous, feckless, scant life, you have little and give less. You are truth rationing. Life is meant to be more than a test. You play small and unanchored while seething with a quiet rage inside. Extreme heat either forges or melts you. You are like gelignite or nitroglycerin, ready to explode if you are not handled gently. It seems easier for God to assure bread and wine of their essence and identity than to convince you."

"Well, you are correct," Satch agreed. "I am not assured. I feel like an unplugged grenade sits inside me, and I keep waiting for it to explode. But what is this about wolves in Yellowstone and temptation being necessary? Did not God create Satan, the chief of tricksters, deceivers, and hornswogglers?"

"Satch, you still do not hear," I said. "Clean your ears! You cope with life and blame others out of shame and fear when your faith and trust are dormant, filled with pessimism and faintheartedness. In faith, when one knows the Lord's will, he goes and does it. When one does not know it, he stands and waits or walks away. A double-minded person with a clouded and divided heart knows only a denigrating force. Death is not the same as perishing, but the lusts of the dark spirits that bring inner death are upon you. If you want the love, you must undergo the pain. If pain weren't a blessing, why would God allow it?

"It takes time to know love. Walking that path is not for the naive or self-reliant but for a wrestler. You think you are unnoticed and have slipped off God's radar, that no one has your back. You can sit there smoldering in your pity, without virtue, or you can keep forging on, walking the path of who you truly are. A follower cannot get what he wants without effort.

"Do not be gullible or guile filled. The journey is tough, teeming with fire. The destination is far. The way is constricted, narrow, troubled, but also bursting with many blessings. You need preparations because many things are missing. God supplies everything necessary, but the journey requires faith and a strong heart. Are you winning on this road? If you listen to your passions or hold to your failures and blame, you will dither, finding no peace. Neither your desires nor regrets will ever be defeated. One cannot find oneself with values not discovered internally. You learn more from experience than advice. The remedy is hidden within and only found by one who seeks it. Look for the helper, the quencher of thirst, not the harmer. Decide what you want.

"A false humility does not fool anybody, not even yourself. Your thinking belies who you are. You are not a self-sufficient being. You live in an intrinsic wilderness while beating yourself up. Do not dwell in the darkness when you have seen the light's flame of forever. You are participating in your own degradation via self-indulgent self-pity. When will you learn who you are and realize you belong, and be grateful? You can deny who you are and dress up like a clown or flower or play the poor orphan. But you are not. You can run away, but not from your destiny, the calling of your genuine self. You should think about your own people, not just yourself.

"Should you get thirsty, water is outside in the river. Bread will be outside with the sunrise, should you wake here. If you're in your own bed tomorrow, either way, you should take a long, penitent walk. You need a radical heart examination. I'm going away for a time so that you can be alone.

"You need to determine who you are. Better, whose you are. Dignity and virtue are in you, not earned but discovered. You wear yourself out, frothing and swinging wrongly. When we meet again, it will be time to face yourself, if you have not by then. Even death would be too ashamed to take you now. Feasibly the bird of your life is ready to leave the cage for the room being prepared for you. Know thyself. Get honest. Resolve. Wounds only heal with the truth. Follow that where it takes you. For now, I leave you to you."

At the conclusion of Yeesa's exhortation, Satch retorted, "But you still have not answered my questions!"

I left. Satch later said I vamoosed like a mist riding away on the north wind.

CHAPTER 12

Tunk

You talk about hardheaded, confused, and proud. Gracious sakes! It is going to be rough with this one. Gees, did Satch ever do an about face all of a sudden and after what he had already experienced here. Some people are that damaged and afraid. He felt so lost and unloved from all the pain he had experienced. Feelings of resentment and despondency from betrayal are so hard to overcome. They depredate the soul in lieu of the beauty gratitude. He was entrenched in it. Satch was still asleep. As he lay there, I wondered if he was pondering how he knew what he knew that he knew, and didn't know how he knew it and wasn't yet sure he knew it. When he woke up, he yawned and started to look around. He had to be sore from his fall. He stretched and rubbed his muscles and his back. I was sitting behind him and noticed that his scrapes had stopped bleeding and were beginning to scab over.

He turned to me and said, "I'm not as mad as I was. I thought about your lecture last night, and waking up here in this place tells me I need to pay attention in a different way. I sorta want to apologize for yesterday. Maybe I needed that lecture. You made me think. I guess this is more than a dream, so what is next?"

"Sorta, Satch!?" I asked. "I guess one small step is good. I sorta accept your sorta apology, and I forgive you. Do you know what your two core questions are after you came to believe there is a God? I mean, the ones that are way down underneath any of the others?"

Satch pondered, then spoke again, "Well, we haven't talked about these, not specifically anyway. There is the sexual abuse, the family and religious doctrines, living contradictions, betrayals, and a lingering depression. Oh, and my failures. But at some point, I always end up asking God about these things, and what He is truly like. There are so many contradictions with all the religious and interpretive traditions, and I do not know who I am or what my purpose is."

"Satch, you talk about the causes of your suffering and the consequences to you," I observed. "The reason they impact you so is that you have not gotten to the core questions that lie beneath all that has happened to you and that you have done. The words translated 'religion' in Scripture originally referred to 'the fear of gods,' superstitions, and came in practice to mean 'external ceremonial observance of laws.' Eventually it came to refer to what we now call religion itself, mentioned only a handful of times in Scripture. *So religion ends up being a system of beliefs that determines a person's view of God and the world.* That's why James says true religion is seeking out and caring for widows and orphans and keeping oneself unstained by the world. In religion, when you have all these individual and committee-negotiated translations of Scripture, dogmatic traditions, prejudices, factions, theories, scores of Catholic variants, forty-five thousand plus Protestant denominations, and all the other religions—which only provide a shallow gaze—no question there is confusion.

"With all that ambiguity, you live in a muddled chaos and cannot prosper. Boiled down, most every institutional religion tells you its view of how you can get right and get back to God, but it's all on you. Religion is flawed because man is flawed! Men play with words and hand out crowns in a way designed for their self-benefit. You need to know what God is like in His innermost character. God is ineffable, that is, it is impossible to conceptualize God. All of our language about God is more inadequate than complete. Until you see He is Father, you cannot see. Any transformations He allows you to see here are to help you, and just for you. As you accept that, you will progress in knowing your own identity. Until then, you question and wander. To be frustrated is human. You know a lot about that."

"That is for sure," Satch agreed.

"Yes, you do," I affirmed. "At the core of all the issues on earth, if one believes in God, these two questions are the foundational ones. The others won't be put to rest until these two are decided. You are here in this world to get answers to those two questions. Before we address them, we need to talk about what that means you must do. Let me ask you a question. Do you clean your house?"

"Yes, I have always helped clean and have done it by myself for a long time now," Satch replied.

At that point, our chat moved quickly.

"Do you spill and break things in your house?" Yeesa asked.

"Of course. I try not to, but it happens."

"Do you soil and nasty up your house intentionally?"

"Absolutely not! Why would anyone do that?"

"When you realize the dirt is there, what do you do then?"

"I get a rag, broom, or vacuum and clean it up."

"What do you do with the dirt and debris?"

"I put them in the trash and throw it out."

"You do not keep dirt, breakings, and trash in your house and keep on blaming it for causing a mess?"

"What!?"

"Do you or not?"

"No. I put the dirt out and it is gone."

"Why not keep it as a reminder?"

"What are you driving at?" Satch asked.

"When you find dirt in your house, you get rid of it and have your house clean again. How long will you hold on to the dark dirt and debris and deny the goodness in your heart? Repenting is first changing your mind, seeing things in a different way, maybe the opposite way. Forgiveness is like cleaning your house; it takes the nastiness from your soul. You become clean. Is there something you have not discovered before that you are now beginning to see?"

"There is something, like another part of me that lives inside me that I did not realize. And he is dirty. I don't like him."

"Everybody carries a dark one inside themselves—a wilderness of arid, suggesting voices and thoughts. Keep listening to them and you become an expression of the dark one, and live it out, cormorant with it. To cope, some people deny the dark one. Some welcome it, some try to ignore it, but some admit it is there and face it. Are you ready for that? If you are, I am going to show you something."

"Okay. I am ready," Satch said. "But that means I need a different kind of broom."

"You are dragging something behind you. It is weighing you down. You do not recognize it. It looks like a weighted trunk or suitcase you are pulling all the time. Maybe that's why you suffer physically with a bad back."

"Yeesa, did you say I am dragging a tunk? What is a tunk?"

"Satch, I said, "Trunk—T-r-u-n-k."

"Oh, maybe it's my ears or your accent. I thought you said 'tunk.'"

"Satch, when you think you are ready to face something, you first have to see it. There is something following you. What is it? It looks like a trunk or to your ears 'tunk.'"

Satch looked around and saw nothing. "Nothing is there, what do you mean?"

"Satch, since you cannot see it, you do not know it is there. Looks like a heavy suitcase or trunk that is following you everywhere you go."

"You just called it a sweet case and a tunk."

"Perhaps to you I misspoke. Maybe it is my Sioux twang. So, since you thought I called it a tunk, you give it a name. You must recognize and name it, so let us come up with a hypothetical name so you can call it when you see it. How about tunk?"

"Tunk. You said tunk. I have no idea what you are talking about. There is no tunk or trunk or suitcase or anything else following me. Just you and me here. Explain yourself."

"Tell me what is dragging you down. Why all the questions? Heavy, are they not? Plus, they make you sad. Your shoulders slump, you crouch forward a little when you walk, your back aches like you are pulling or dragging something. Do you feel the weight inside? Is it despondency, depression, or pain in your stomach? Got a brain ache? What is it?"

"It is inside me, not behind me."

"But there is a weight you carry with you, right?"

"Yes."

"Can you see it or give it a name?"

"No. Never thought about that. But I recognize it is generally like what is called a despondency or low-grade depression. It gets heavy."

"And how long have you had this with you?"

"Since childhood, and it keeps getting heavier."

"And you have no idea what it is?"

"No, I have tried to understand but have not been able to decipher it in any clear way."

"Is it just one thing or is there more?"

"A bunch of things have happened. It has to be more than one thing eating me up like this. Is that where some of the questions come from?"

"Maybe you are beginning to get it," Yeesa said. "What you have seen so far is an effort to encourage you to move forward. But what you are carrying is holding you back. You have to get rid of that load, but you must do it issue by issue. Traumas cause emotional and psychological hurts and changes. Each one you acknowledge and face will make you more aware of how to deal with what is against you on the inside. Now tell me, do you feel the weight?"

"You already know I do. So, what is it?"

"Not that easy. You have to figure it out and put it together. You have been asking, seeking, and now you are here. When you want help enough you choose to knock on the door. If you are determined and keep on knocking, the door will open. Then, you have to have courage to walk through the door. Walk away and you will have to return again to that same door even if it comes by another path."

"Yeesa, look, I am here talking to a dead Indian because of all these questions that started when I was two and a half years old. I have been asking and seeking answers since then. The questions have kept building up. Now, here I am. Where is that door?"

"Just over here. Are you coming?"

"Darn right."

We walked through the cave a bit and entered a pathway into a part of the larger cavern. On one side of the cavern was a large stone. "Look, Satch," I said. "Tell me what you see."

Satch came beside me. We stood shoulder to shoulder. The stone was polished and looked like reflecting glass. It was so large several people could stand in front of it and see their entire bodies. We could see everything in front and to the sides of us. If one turned to the side, he could see anything behind him. I moved to one side and asked Satch to turn sideways and continue to look in the stone mirror. When he did, he stood there silent. He could see the trunk or suitcase behind him.

When he stepped forward, the trunk followed. He stepped back and the trunk moved back behind him like a shadow.

"What is that?" Satch asked.

"Is something there?"

"You know it is. What is going on?

"Do you feel the weight?"

"Yes."

"Then, you tell me."

"I have never seen this. How can I say?"

"Give it a name."

"Okay, I'll call it tunk, but what is it? Why can I not see it? What is in it? Do I need to open and see what is in it? Please help me here. I am in way over my head."

"Do you see you have been pulling a load most of your life and did not know it?"

"That's for sure."

"So, now it has a name, a tunk. Let's make it official. You have been pulling this tunk around your whole life and did not know it. Psychologists have different names for parts of it, such as conscience, subconscious, and shadow, as Carl Jung the Swiss psychiatrist has called it. The first is your consciousness, a capacity that includes awareness of something greater than you and the things you have been taught and believed. It is your compass that guides you and gives you direction for appraising and judging, defining good and evil. When you accept the rights and wrongs from your conscience, you become, behave and act according to it.

"Hidden behind your consciousness are influences of which you are not aware but which encourage or entice and try to regulate your life. You have them but cannot see them. You are unaware of your subconscious's presence. It is behind your consciousness and pops into your mind like a thought, suggestion, or dream. And your subconscious suggestions seem pretty dark, enticing, and heavy. Your mind, heart, will, and spirit comprise your soul. Your thoughts and feelings from your conscious and subconscious shadow impact and flow through your nervous system, muscles, and entire body. They hold the good as well as the dark man.

"The pound force of emotional gravity makes it heavy to pull. So, whatever you have allowed in there goes with you everywhere. At times its weight is so heavy it forces you to lean forward and push with your foot just to drag it. This unseen tunk and all its weight follows you like a shadow everywhere. Metaphorically, it is behind you, invisible to you. In fact, it is inside you. You called it your heaviness."

"Yeesa, I know the pains from what has happened but do not know what to call them. And they are heavy."

"That is what is inside your very own unique shadow. Recognizing you carry it is not the hardest part—just the first step. When you have the courage to open it up, you will already have been asking and seeking the answers. The mirror has shown you your shadow, your very own tunk. Next, you must see and identify its contents and give each temptation inside it, each suggestion, deluding passion, and affirmation a name. Each one seems like an unknown person is giving you unsolicited a thought, suggestion, or encouragement. You will have to open your own tunk of hurts and experiences that haunt you, which you have unknowingly allowed inside yourself. Your subconscious holds both good and evil. The good is supportive. Many are not able to accept the good they have done as affirmation. They avoid looking at the evil and will not address it because of guilt or shame—like a drunk or addict who swears he is not dependent on sex, alcohol, or drugs.

"In truth, he is addicted, controlled by it. Shadows can make you dependent on them and sap your life, drag you down. Emotional, mental, and spiritual shadows are heavy and eventually affect your physical body, your heart, mind, spirit, and will. *They impact your body and your soul. Your body, the custodian of your soul, discovers a time when it can no longer carry your soul.*

"These shadows sway all your relationships, even with yourself. These shadows will make you feel soul-sick. Satch, these are analogies or metaphors, symbolic language giving meaning to what one otherwise cannot grasp. We have to get beyond logic. Stories, symbols, and figures of speech guide us in the world of imagination and transcendence. They stretch your mind. That is why you're here. Are you beginning to get that?"

"I am, at least a little," Satch admitted.

"Well, right there behind you, the tunk holds the source of pain and questions. Your life has had little happiness, joy, or peace. This ol' tunk has dragged you down. What you have allowed in there is the burden. You choose when to open it and look inside. That takes facing the fear and pain with character and courage, and you will realize that you are the new broom. As you use it, your journey continues. You will be putting together your very own Cadillac, one piece at a time, just like Johnny Cash's song. You have to put it together in your own garage once you sweep it clean. It is first taking the log out of your own eye. Then, you can assist others, and your tunk will be empty and gone."

Satch sat down on the tunk and looked in the stone mirror. Now, he knew it was not only real, but it became true for him. He needed time to feel, think, and process all this.

"Yeesa, help me here," Satch said. "I think I understand what you are saying, but how do I unpack this burden I am carrying? It has snatched my life away. The same thing has been and is continuing to happen to my friends. I have also seen it in both churchgoing folk as well as non-church folks. What is the solution?"

"Your very own 'tunk,' as you have agreed to name it, or your shadow, has both positive and negative aspects. The good is positive but hard to accept as true about yourself. On the other hand, the bad is negative—evil—and that includes both what has happened to you and what you have done. One does not want to admit it or face it, and it takes you down. It is heaviness, as you say. So, both are hidden in your subconscious. You become aware of it when you see, smell, or hear something that triggers a memory or impulse to come forward into your mind or consciousness. When that happens, it is thrust into your awareness again.

"When that happens, you need to STOP what you are doing right then. Don't avoid the emotion, the memory, suggestion, thought, or temptation. Face it, confront it, give it a name, and find the truth in what happened and how you accept and overcome it. Discover the source of the impulses, thoughts, suggestions, and voices. Until you do that, it will follow you and hang in the darkness as you carry it with you. When you have a feeling, memory, or suggestion—whether of evil or good—you should name it. To give a unique name to an issue that you need to face and remember is a way to have power over it.

"Language is important; its precision is necessary for clarity. It is important to name your emotions. For example, shame is a feeling we experience when our ideas are met with derision or we are disparaged by others, or when we disdain ourselves. Guilt is remorse, contrition, or acknowledgment of fault or wrongdoing. A prerequisite for shame is feeling you are alone and keeping it to yourself. Shame has two sources: other people or ourselves. It is important to distinguish between shame projected onto you and shame that is justly felt for some wrongdoing. Shame and guilt can be dispelled when you acknowledge them to others, for then you no longer bear them alone. There are scores of feelings and experiences we encounter. Become aware of what you are undergoing. Address and identify each by naming it. Then go to the source and unravel it.

"But, Satch, there is something deeper. The core source of your pain is not the women, your grandmother, father, mother, bad religion, betrayals, or mistreatment by the church and communities. How is it that *you* sinned and missed the mark?"

"Which time?" Satch asked. "It seems I do wrong over and over again."

"You missed being who you truly are. Do you remember the last scene in the TV series *Return to Lonesome Dove*?"

"You mean the one between Captain Call and Newt, when Newt chose to leave and live his own life? He quoted his dad, something like 'A man can't live a dream and life he does not choose for himself'."

"Yes," Yeesa said, "several things are happening there. His dad never would acknowledge him openly, even though finally he told Newt his name Call had no dishonor—a pathetic way to affirm your own son. His hurt from feeling unloved, the seduction from the married woman, and the deceptions by her lying, murderous husband caused him to leave and go his own way. His father tried in his limited way to acknowledge him, but that was not enough for Newt. So he left to live life in his own way. He would not even say goodbye to his friends. He felt less than, alone, like you feel.

"That is similar to what Adam and Eve did. They chose to go their own way. They took Satan's deception into themselves. They absorbed it. It became their very consciousness. They felt both their vulnerability and lostness from their free will choice. There is much more going on with this fruit. Jesus also ate that same fruit on the cross and died, providing the way of redemption for Adam and Eve and you to return to your original design.

All mankind decided to emancipate themselves from God. God knew they would and allowed it, implementing the process of rescuing us from ourselves through restoration called 'adoption' by opening the voluntary, inclusive door of 'being in God's family not as a prodigal child but as a true son who comes home.' God loves us that way. You were never left out and separated. You just left. Distance is an illusion of separation. God is closer to you than your breath.

God's Spirit comes and stirs and strokes our very spirits. We feel that and long to be loved and totally accepted in that way. When that happens the spirit of your soul responds and reaches out for that love and God Himself is touched. Then in this profound encounter the Holy Spirit and our wandering spirits engage in this soothing and trying tempest of love and our redemption. Ask the Spirit about this. If you allow, her voice will become strong in you. She will teach you.

"Now, how do you think the saying 'the devil made me do it' came about? Satan is the tempter, but how does he get in your head and influence you to doubt God and to do something? When God told Cain that 'sin is lurking at the door,' what is the door? The tempting delusion comes from our consciousness or subconscious, the shadow. The hurts reside in our subconscious. It is the devil—evil. Do you see it? His suggestions to miss the mark of our authentic selves enter our heads. *Thoughts come unbidden. You do not think your thoughts, you can only think about and respond to them.* The devil does not *make us*. Rather, we choose, but in a confusion, lacking the discernment to know what is good and what is not. We are guided by our senses, our feelings, what we have been taught and experienced and hold them as actuality. We do what feels good and avoid what hurts. If a man does not fight evil's suggestions but buckles to its desires, he cannot be single-minded or reach the faith of truth.

"Cain's issue seems to have been jealousy. His subconscious pushed him in anger to remove and murder his brother Able who he thought was causing his pain. The consequences caused even greater agony and disaster. We think we control our lives, but we become controlled by our emotions, desires or fears in the moment. We often cannot resist the pull. When we judge people, we cause a myriad of incessant conundrums, and participate in a corporate network of continually unfolding sins and the results—a world filled with moral and relational ambiguity.

"Sin is like poison. Satan poisons our consciousnesses. When we believe the deceptions, it causes us to follow through with his suggestions. The malaise enters your awareness and imprisons you. The subconscious, in a manner of speaking, is pushed away out of one's consciousness, pressed out of mind and into a trash can. It becomes filled with the hidden suggestions and temptations rattling around inside like tin cans discarded as expendable waste. But they are there. When your tunk trash can gets bumped by dreams, feelings, odors, sounds, and thoughts, the contents are jolted out.

"The fallen angel Satan is a worm-tongued snake. In deliciousness of pride, he abandoned truth and lusted for power. His heart became enraged because of his frightful demotion to the earth world. Out of bitter hatred, he obsessively and viciously spread his wretchedness by twisting and contorting goodness into evil. By your God-given free will, you accomplish the same when you doubt God and go your own way. It becomes a part of you, as hidden suggestions spring into your memory. When you feel that and follow those urgings, you should recognize you have kissed the devil's ring. A fire that ruins is the devil's only friend. His lies burn as hellfire inside you."

Satch was considering what I said. "Yeesa," he asked, "are you saying my mind says one thing, and my heart another?"

"Exactly! That's part of what happens. The compasses of the mind and heart start pointing in different directions. They are not designed to go in separate directions yet have been forced by your choices in a particular moment to share your soul's space with evil's desires. It is soul darkness, a wilderness, and it feels like the murky blackness of a devil's hell. That's part of what's in your tunk.

"Satch, listen! What if the sin's poison can be turned into good? We have seen that the proteins in snake venom can be used beneficially to treat many conditions like cancer, pain, high blood pressure, heart attack, strokes, Alzheimer's, and Parkinson's diseases. This poison has entered because of your own choices, and it resides inside your consciousness and subconscious. You already know this happens to you daily, without realizing where the thoughts come from. What if the poison of temptation is the necessary process of growing to know and practice the good? What if Satan's purpose is needed, as Jesus said about temptation? Have you gotten that far with your questions yet?"

"Yeesa, that's dangerous territory!"

"Why? Satch. Why would God not allow temptation into the world and even create a tempter to deceive His children—whom He loves and trusts—so they can learn to choose, in faith and in failure, the good over the evil? He wants you to grow into what He intended you to be, that is, noble rather than childish. These temptations come at you as unbidden thoughts, striking you as serpents, biting then slithering back and hiding in a corner of your shadow. The Spirit will come and remind you of good and encourage you. You push Her back and send Her away because you are too ashamed to accept the good and your value.

"Nothing can disqualify you or make you unworthy of being God's child. You can deny it and refuse participation, but you cannot change the truth of His love for you. Did you not allow your children to be tested? Did you not discipline them—all because you loved them? Does He not test us and permit the temptations to help us choose the good—to choose love above all things—and discover the mark of who we are? Does he not bring good out of bad? Are we not to be overcomers?"

"Yeesa, are you saying that applies even to willful choices I knew were wrong?"

"Satch, accept the memories that hurt, the knots of failure, and your successes. All are a part of you. The bad gives you misery gut. The good helps heal your heart. Receive both. You are going to have wounds that scar and celebrations that heal. The wounds will not go away. You cannot avoid them, kill them, or cut them off. They are a part of you, but you can allow the truth about them to heal you and take away the pain. It is only the pain, not sin, that has substance, the benefit of which is the suffering, which teaches us. To heal you must accept your wounds. Then, you recognize them as your teachers, and they become sacred scars. You must confront them, name them, and clean the dirt. Only you alone can choose to do this. It is your decision to make. The truth revealed will set you free. The truth is love, and without love we cannot walk in the truth. Without knowing you are loved, there is no power to make that choice."

I took two chicken eggs I had gathered earlier from a nest and kept them wrapped warmly in my pouch. I set them out, side by side on straw in a basket and put them on the floor in front of Satch. I said, "These are about ready to hatch. Don't say anything, just watch."

At least half an hour passed, and we said nothing. The eggs just sat there. Satch kept looking up at me but didn't say anything. I took one of the eggs, placed it on the floor, and gently rolled it under my palm back and forth many times, careful not to crack it. I picked it up and repeatedly shook it hard like I was trying to dissolve powdered baby formula in a bottle. I put it back in the basket and continually tapped on it with my finger. Then I placed my forefinger on it and felt a stirring inside the egg. After I let it sit for a few minutes, I tapped the eggshell with my knife. A tiny crack appeared in the shell, and fluid began to drool out on the straw. The tiny chick inside was moving but was likely going to die.

Satch looked up at me and said, "Why would you do that? Now, there will be no chick, and the egg is a waste."

"Just watch," I said.

It took a while but then we heard a tapping sound from inside the other egg. It kept tapping. Before long, a crack appeared in the egg. The tapping continued until a little beak emerged. The chick kept tapping from the inside. The crack widened, and the chick's head popped out. The struggle continued until a wet chick broke out of its shell. The hatchling tried to walk around. After stumbling and falling numerous times, it stood, shook itself, looked around, started pecking, and even tried to walk out of the basket.

"Satch," I said, "the dying chick was rolled and shaken and tapped. Its shell was affected by external influences while it was still developing. Chances are that chick will never make it. It has not fully developed and was not ready to break out on its own from its shell. The rolling, shaking, tapping caused too much turmoil. Likewise, your life has been rolled, shaken and slapped. You must deal with the havoc in your life before you hatch and become your true self. And that comes in your own timing and effort. You want someone, something from outside yourself, external propositional knowledge and values to come and open you up and pour in a solution to your sadness. It will never work like that. It is something you must do for yourself from inside.

"What's shaken up inside the egg is analogous to the turmoil in your tunk. You must accept the development process in order to grow to maturity and deal with issues essential to growth. Until you do that, the time will not be right to break out and be whole. You must reorient yourself on your own to find the person God created you to be and experience a full life. Your life has been tapped from the outside and shaken hard, but it has not broken open. You still have the chance to break out of your own shell, to deal with your issues, but unpacking your shadow and pulling the hurts out of the tunk will not be enough. Finding yourself is not the end all be all. Living in the mystery of the Spirit is hitting the mark. That's what we do here. Are you seeing that?"

CHAPTER 13
Rooms

The cave into which Satch had fallen was only one of many caves within the mound. Like Carlsbad Caverns in New Mexico, stalactites and stalagmites were scattered throughout the cavern. It was a unique and beautiful place, illuminated by open spaces in the top and torches placed on the walls. The main entrance to the cavern faced a grand meadow on a plateau above a river. A range of mountains overlooked the scene from across the river. On top of the nearby cliff was a mesa. But it was not all safe.

Satch had given me a puzzled look after our conversation. He kept watching the cracked egg and the live chick. He had a lot to consider. He needed to rest. I covered him with a blanket. He slept for a while. When he woke, I offered him a couple of oatmeal raisin cookies and a root beer.

"Where did you get that?" he asked.

"Oh, lots of things are here, if you know where to look," I replied. "I thought you needed a little something to keep you going."

"Thanks, man, I am hungry," he said.

"Satch, you wanted to know about God's character—heaven and hell, life after death. God is not intrinsically in heaven, which refers to above creation. Heaven, hell, and this realm are in God. You will experience some things that are included in what you call the afterlife. These things are only glimpses into what can happen. If you want to understand, this is your opportunity.

"But listen to me. God doesn't demand to be the center of our conscious attention all the time. He made you free, a little wild and promiscuous. You need clothing, shelter, and sustenance. You have to give attention and effort to provide that. Your emotions vary. Your core awareness and commitment is to be to God first. Faithful compassion is a key. For example, widows and orphans, a spouse and children, and those who are left out. Remember what Jesus said: the least of these, when you care and help them, you have done it to Me.

"Finish your snack and relax. I'm going to sit over here behind you. When you are done eating, look around you, walk around and pay attention to the things around you. Inspect them as best you can. Light enters your body when your eyes become healthy. Whatever you discern, it's for you and not for discussion. Remember this from now on. Unless you are asked or know you have permission, do not keep on asking questions. Pay attention, observe, listen."

Satch finished his snack and sat down. It was quiet. He looked at me and then started to look around. His gaze fell on the cave walls, then settled on the cave floor. He ran his fingers across the floor. He looked into and beneath the floor. Yes, he could see into the floor and the walls. He looked up and up and up. He turned around and glanced in all directions and sat down with his hands over his eyes. He rubbed his eyes, stood, and sat down again. He got up again and continued to look around and then sat back down. He was totally absorbed in the scene he was taking in. I told him, "Take your time, okay, all the time you need. Do not rush through this."

Satch did not respond. He said not a word. He couldn't talk. I watched as he sat and then lay on the rug on the ground. Then, he got up again and limped around, looking through every inch of the cave's floor, its walls, and up to the top of the tall cave. He would stop and gaze a long time at each scene he was viewing in the floor and walls. When he was done taking in all he could, Satch sat back down on the rug and did not speak for a long time.

I was still sitting behind him. When I thought he was ready, I asked, "Do you want to talk?"

He remained silent for several more minutes. When he could talk, he said, "Yeesa, everything, I mean, what I saw in all those rooms beneath the floor, within the walls, and up in the ceiling, everything, everyone there had died," he observed. "Is what I saw really what happened after they died?"

"Yes, Satch, you saw a part of what happens after death. The journey does not end when your time on earth is done. Death is just another path we all must take another adventure beyond. The things you see when you first look, and the things you look at when you see in the light are different things. Tell me what you observed."

Satch describes what he saw like this, "It felt like I was sitting on the softest cloud, but it was not floating. I felt comfort and ease. My mind quit running and ruminating. I could see everything, through everything. I was at peace being able to see through that floor I sat on. When my eyes were opened, what I saw was so mysterious, so compelling that I do not have the words to describe it, but I'll try—that is, if you will let me."

"Go ahead, tell me," Yeesa said.

Satch exclaimed, "There was this enormous room with entry and exit doors. People who had died were surrounded by a great light and transported by angels through the entrance doors. They had no other way of being brought out of death. Their bodies were recognizable but looked different. The flow in and out was constant. Jesus brought some Himself but each was presented to Jesus. Some fell to their knees in worship to Him. Others stood staring with various looks on their faces—anger, bewilderment, uncertainty. Later, depending on the condition and state of their souls, angels took each one to a different room. I had never imagined anything like it.

Just behind you was a room with a short round table. There were ten little boys sitting in small chairs around the table. It was like they were my siblings, and I was one of them. We were all about the same age, like two to three years old. I can't be sure, but we were older than toddlers, able to talk and play. All of them were about the same size, and there was laughter and storytelling. They kidded and joked with each other. They liked each other.

"I knew seven of them. An eighth and ninth had similar characteristics. The tenth had some of the same physical traits as the others, especially my son and grandsons, but I had never seen him and had no idea who he was. The dark-haired boy sitting next to me was my little brother, Fletch, but he was not smaller in this scene. I was wearing the same brown-striped shirt I wore in a picture that hung in our house. It was me. There sat my dad—the same age as me. I recognized him from pictures of him at that age. From other pictures I'd seen, it seemed two of them were my grandfathers.

"My son sat beside me. This other little boy sat between my son and grandsons. My three grandsons sat next to him. He was drawing with crayons on a sheet of paper. He seemed to be writing a note. Occasionally, he looked up, glanced at me, and smiled. He bore a family resemblance, but I have no idea who he could have been. There is no question that all of us sitting at that table knew each other and felt very comfortable.

"Right next to this room—I guess it was a room—there were no walls, and I don't know what else to call it. Groups of men sat at large, round card tables in a western saloon. People would come in and go out through the swinging doors. A man played piano while Patsy Cline danced on the stage and sang to the music. Yeesa, the Beatles and the Eagles were playing their hit songs, and Patsy sang along. That great music filled the room, and everybody was enjoying all of it.

"Throngs of people crowded around other tables in the large saloon. Another bunch was standing along the bar talking. A huge mirror hung on the wall behind the bar. I saw Elvis, Buddy Holly, Nelson Mandela, John F. Kennedy, Martin Luther King, Hank Williams, Neil Diamond, and Polycarp sitting around one large card table. They were cracking each other up with their jokes and stories. Their eyes glowed bright with laughter. Every time Polycarp lifted his hand off his lap or a finger off the table, they all stopped to listen. I could tell something about him was compelling.

"I noticed other people standing around the table. Some had their hands on the shoulders of others while they chatted comfortably. This group of luminaries included Dwight Eisenhower, Babe Ruth, Jim Thorpe, Rosa Parks, Ben Franklin, both Lewis and Clark, Marilyn Monroe, Sammy Davis, Jr., Mae West, Jesse Owens, and Elton John. I know what you're thinking, but they were there. Yeesa, how can Elton John be here? He's not dead."

"Satch," Yeesa probed further, "again I ask you what does dead mean? You are not dead, and you are here. No, Elton, like some others, is not dead. He's just dreaming. I sure hope he finishes that song suggested to him about the Spirit. What else?"

"Yeesa, I was sitting on the cloud and turned around so I could see better. "Out of the corner of my eye, I had just seen something, all I know to call them is rooms, filled with people and at times animals, plants, and other things from earth. They all just looked like they were becoming clearer and more whole. But every room I saw was different, very different. Each being had a different degree of clarity. It was astonishing.

"Then, there was this one room. It was quiet, filled with beds on which people were lying. Each person was covered by what appeared to be a sheet or blanket. It was something like an infirmary. Some lay motionless on their backs or on their stomachs, and others were on their sides. Some appeared to be dead or asleep. Some would roll over and change positions on their beds. Some sat up, while others stood beside their beds. Some were eating.

"Each seemed to be under the care of someone like a nurse or doctor who treated their wounds, but they were not just physical wounds. The hurts also seemed to be mental or emotional. Some appeared to still be dealing with the grief of a loss. Some were recovering from betrayals and failures. They were being healed. Some of them smiled a time or two. Some seemed healthier than others. All of them seemed to be helped to find a way through their own pains. I do not know what more to say.

"Another room led outside to a meadow with a lake where children were playing. The children ran, laughed, and chased each other. They were somersaulting, dancing, and swimming. They hugged the animals that swam with them. These playmates did not grow tired. None of them were sickly or crippled. They had no limitations. The birds lit on their shoulders, while the horses and alligators gave them rides. They jumped off the cliff and angels swooped under them and carried them on their backs down onto the soft grass. There was no fear, except for those staring, still hiding in the wooded scope of trees at the edge of the field of joy.

"I saw another room. It had a sign posted above the door reading 'Outside-Unknown, Self-Righteous.' It was darker than other areas and filled with men in robes and formal suits with ties. Ladies were adorned in stylish robes and fancy dresses. They were dolled up with special hairdos and pricy, sparkling jewelry—including rings, bracelets, and expensive necklaces. I could tell they were not happy. None smiled. Some were on their knees and seemed to be weeping. Others were grinding their teeth. Some were holding scrolls and books they had written. A massive collection was stacked on tables as if each person had brought a library with him. They seemed to be having discussions, more like arguments, about the correct way to get right with God. They were pointing fingers at one another. They did not like each other.

"I heard groans coming from beside me. I turned and saw a room that was dark. The people there, well, they didn't have full bodies. Their muscles and organs were gone, except for what looked like a heart inside. Some skin was draping only portions of their skeletons. But I could see a red heart inside their chests, still beating. Some were a brighter red than others. Some looked like they were fading away. It appeared one of them had a heartbeat that was getting stronger.

"The next room had no light. Occasionally, there was a brief glimmer of illumination from above, allowing me just a glimpse. In those brief moments, all was still in the shadows. All I could see looked like remains of ashes still smoking from a fire. Jesus was holding the ashes. Only Jesus could redeem those ashes.

"Then, I saw rooms filled with people, birds, reptiles, insects, flowers, and even amoebas and jellyfish. There were also algae, ferns, fungi, and mushrooms. I could see their roots, the strands of the mycelium. I had no sense any were inferior, only at a different place of development.

Standing in their midst was the most beautiful being I recall ever seeing, but very small. She had long flowing silver hair. She eased from one to the next, as if influenced by a velvety wind, without speaking a word. Her eyes were soft and radiant. A blue and white robe flowed from her shoulders to the ground. She moved quietly, as a fairy floating in a gentle breeze.

"Like the people, the plants and animals had their own faces, were wounded and bruised, both inside their hearts and on their stems or cellulose. I could see the pain. Their tears were boundless. I could even hear them as they ran down their cheeks and plopped gently onto the floor. Each one looked longingly up toward the beautiful one. She was so tender. She reached for their faces, touched each one, and wiped away every tear. She took those tears into her hands and held them.

"When she touched them with her tear-soaked hands, they gently glowed, and their wounds started to heal. The bruising turned into a sacred wonder. Even their scars signaled a unique kind of glory. That is what she looked like: glory, pure glory. Everyone she touched began to be shaped into a more whole body, yet retaining his or her own distinct nature. Some kind of rapid development was going on, as they were being changed into a healthier form of being. It appeared they could graduate to a different room.

"As I stood on the cave floor below, the little lady looked at me through the glass-walled room. She smiled at me. She raised her hand and gently waved to me—not like a royal or a parade queen but with compassion, welcoming me. My knees knocked together and my legs gave way. I could not keep from kneeling. I found myself looking up to her. I cannot explain why, but while kneeling I involuntarily lifted my hands, palms up toward her. I was overwhelmed. Then, she winked at me and grinned, like she was really happy. I have never experienced anything like her.

"Each person was offered what he needed to come to Jesus, who was in each room and knew what to do with each one who was willing to hear. Still, it was no cakewalk. Choices had to be made by each one. The ones who resisted most seemed to be in the darker rooms, but it seemed they still had a chance. The room of ashes—perhaps they had faced the devils and were tormented by the crisping fires of Hell. I do not know. Only Jesus could redeem those ashes.

"While still on my knees, I heard a whoosh sound and looked up. All the rooms disappeared. Another room appeared above me that showed many universes spread across the entire top of the cavern. I recognized the earth and our universe. But there were earth-like planets in these other universes. Three people stood with their backs to me speaking to each other and pointing to the earths in the other universes. I did not know what to make of it, but it looked like they were discussing, planning something.

"I was trying to understand what I was seeing when I heard a voice say, 'Do not ask or speak of this. What you have seen is true but utter not for now a further sound of this.'

"That is what I saw. I don't know how to say more about it. Yeesa, is God really that good?"

"What do you mean?" Yeesa asked.

"Well, is He?"

"Yes, He is that good and more," Yeesa confirmed. "He provides the opportunity to become all that you are designed to be."

I asked, "If I may, I do have one question about the room with all the universes. I know the three were the Father, Son, and Spirit. Had to be. Are They hoping to find one who—"

"Stop right there!" Yeesa warned. "Some of us know They have discussions, but that's it. They are always planning. They love adventure and people. You cannot ask about this."

I, Yeesa, need to tell you Satch has no idea how long all that lasted, but it did not scare him, though he could not begin to have a handle on it. He got down on the rug and lay his head on the leather pillow. He lay still, feeling the comfort. It had been a wonderful time for Satch, not thinking but just being and seeing.

After a long time Satch began to stretch and roll over. He looked up and I was squatting beside him. I handed him what he thought was a steaming cup of coffee. He looked at me and said, "I don't much like coffee."

I just grinned and said, "This isn't coffee, it's your special blend of homecoming tea you like so much. The orange rolls are on the table with buttered hot biscuits, fig preserves, and big glasses of milk and orange juice. Do you want your eggs scrambled, fried, poached, or in an omelet? I am going outside. Finish this. You need to fill that belly up. You are going to need it. After your eggs, you'll be full. Then, we'll talk."

It wasn't long until Satch showed up.

I, Satch, was really hungry. The snack was so good. After I ate what Yeesa had fixed for me, I walked down a tunnel toward what looked like an opening to the outside. It turned out to be an opening in the side of a cliff to a whole new world. I was standing in a meadow on a mountain plateau overlooking the most beautiful valley I had ever seen. The blue upon blue of the sky, the greens of the valley, a soothing melody wafted up from a river, the quiet coolness of the breeze, it all took my breath away. There was Yeesa with his back to me and facing a fire he had built.

"Okay, Mr. Satcher," my friend said, "what are you going to call me? Remember my name? Names are important. You realize that, don't you?"

"Mr. Dr. Indian, Yeesa, I've got it," I replied. "I won't ever forget it, just like I won't forget the tunk. Now I get it—how important naming things is."

"Okay, just wanted to make sure," Yeesa said.

"I know I'm not supposed to ask more about these rooms and the things I saw, but I have got to know about those ten little boys," I asserted. "That was me and my little brother and my son. Come on! I know. That was my dad and my three grandsons. Two were my grandfathers, but who was that last little boy? He was the grandest of all. And what are they doing?"

"All I can tell you is that you are correct, and you saw yourself talking with your brother, your dad, both your granddads, your son, and grandsons," Yeesa confirmed. "As for the last little boy, you'll have to wait for that—to help you take the next step.

"What? How? You mean that's all I get?" I complained.

"For now, yes. Do you hear me? Do not ask about it again," Yeesa stated.

"Okay. What about these rooms and these people—"

"Not yet. You have seen a lot. The Great Spirit wanted you to see more than you ever have. There is so much more than you saw. Ponder what you have seen and what it means. Hold it close. *Without discernment you cannot expel or vacate what is not good; you cannot continue to point and move upward in your being to the highest you can conceive.* Know that what you have seen is good, and every bit of God's judgment is redemptive but indiscernible and incomprehensible. You have critical questions that were yours before you got here, and some answers are here for you if you are willing to face the darkness that surrounds you and has gotten into you. Isn't that what you have been struggling with your entire life, as long as you can remember?"

It was like a slap in my face. It hurt. Yeesa was right. It took me back into all the pain, all the wounds. "I want to face it, Yeesa," I said. "I have to."

At this point I believed Satch. I handed him a folded sheet of paper and told him to put it in the back pocket of his jeans. "If you read this now or before you leave, you will be shown no more. Do you understand?"

"Why?"

"DO YOU UNDERSTAND?"

"NO, but I will not read it," Satch replied.

"Satch, do you know the story of Cinderella?" I asked.

"The children's story?"

"Yes. Do you understand it?"

"Yeesa, it's just a children's fairy tale."

"Cinderella means 'the young girl who sits in the cinders, the ashes.' It is an old wise tale that speaks about the value of ashes in life. Native Americans understood this. We had longhouses—long, rectangular tents with large, sloping sides that reached to the ground. The center of the roof was open and functioned as a natural chimney. Fires were kept burning along the entire center of the longhouse, both for cooking and for warmth. People gathered near the fire to cook, eat, and socialize, but they slept away from the fire.

"Some of the men would at times go to the sweat lodge to meditate, ask the Great Spirit for a dream or vision. But anyone could sit in the ashes of the long fire. Every so often, for reasons of their own, a tribe member sat silently just beside the long fire in the ashes. They would barely eat, refrain from social interaction, stay inside, and not wash or go to bed with the others. They would sit alone in the quiet of the cinders to be restored by the long fire's ashes. They would ponder, grieve, and learn in order to be renewed, asking the Great Spirit to realign and guide them. Like the silence and ashes suggested to be used on Ash Wednesday, they are a sign of a searching humility and repentance.

"Satch, you need some time sitting in the ashes by this fire. Don't run from the ashes of your life. At some point you have to face the fractures within, let them burn and turn to ashes. Then you rebuild from there, from the ashes. Sit here by the ashes and meditate on the moments of your life that have caused you pain and anguish, and then think about them in the light and context of what you have seen today. Perhaps you will discover some assurance, hope, and reasons. Then, reform and restore. When you choose to do that, you are going to find help right in the midst of your effort."

I hoped he would not look at the note. It wasn't time. I went to get him some water.

CHAPTER 14

The Girls, Sherbet, and a Spittoon

The next morning when Satch woke up, I was looking at the river. I turned from the overlook and started back toward the opening of the cave entrance. Satch followed. As we walked, I told him, "I think you are going to bust if you don't get to ask another question. But before you start spouting, let me say one more thing about the tipping point in your life. On top of all that had happened to you before, when you thought you had found what could heal your hurts, you experienced more heart rejection and loss, you sank to the lowest point in your life.

"The Evil One used your religious culture and deceived the vulnerable sisters to get you. They may not be aware at all of what they did. Pray for them. Your joy has virtually vanished because you believed evil. When you were little, it was not your fault, but since then you have had multiple opportunities to see."

"I want to see," Satch said. "I have felt it and lived with the lie. Had I not ended the last relationship, I would be dead. I had seen who she really is, but she never saw it. I wanted her to be the person she truly is. If she could have done that—"

"STOP IT, Satch. You cannot fix her or any other person," I cautioned. "You couldn't get her there. You cannot fix anyone else. Nor can she or anyone else fix you. You have been feeding the demon. She didn't want you unless you supported her agenda. She had to be in control. You have been a dead man trying to give life to yourself through a lie. STOP IT!"

I continued, "Before you came here, Satch, in that imagination of yours, you wished you could have conversations with some people of history, did you not? You thought of people who had dealt with the same issues and questions you grapple with. Am I right?"

"Yeesa, how do you know all this?" Satch responded. "Yes, certain women in the Scriptures did horrible things. They used and killed good people and bragged as they walked away. They fought God. In strange ways some were helpful. But some of them are viewed as the worst of the worst. They broke the hearts of men and nations and led them to destruction without being fazed by what they had done. I want to believe Father's judgment is accomplished in Jesus, and that He does not condemn but redeems. I don't know how He does it. Just like in all those rooms I saw. I can't talk about that, so I want to talk to those women. I want to know why and how they accomplished what they did. I need their help."

"Okay. And who might they be?" I inquired.

"Rahab, Tamar, Delilah, Queen of the South, Bathsheba, Jezebel, Naomi, Ruth, Herodias, and Mary Magdalene to start," Satch replied quickly.

"Okay, and since we are on the subject, who else have you wished to talk to?" I asked. "Give me their names and tell me your reasons."

Satch's continued, "Enoch because he walked with God and God took him. That's about all the book says about him. Elijah because he did not die but was taken up in a whirlwind, even though he doubted. He feared Jezebel, ran from her, and wanted to die. Paul because he talked about walking in the Spirit and the mystery of all the ages—Christ in you, the hope of glory. He had this thorn in the flesh that haunted him. Father would not remove it. What really happened? How did they deal with all they faced? I want to know the rest of the story. Inside they struggled but talked about a peace that passes understanding. And I want to talk to Abraham, Joseph, Moses, Saul, David, Solomon, Jehu, Samuel, Job, and John. Also, why was Jonah so angry at a vine dying when a whole town had changed because of the message he had given them? And there are a lot more because—"

"WHOA! WHOA! WHOA! Hold it, boy," I wailed. "Geemanellie and Geronimo! How many more have you got?"

"A bunch," Satch said.

"Whew! You still got too much going on in that head of yours, and all at the same time," I noted. "No wonder you feel as screwed up as a Mongolian cluster. Just hold it. Stick with the women for now. I think it's time for you to meet the girls."

"What girls? What are you talking about, Yeesa?" he asked.

"Come with me," I said.

"Do you mean we are going to see the bitches of the Bible?" Satch quipped.

I responded with an equal measure of sarcasm. "You asked for it, so you got it, big talking Little Chief. You ready?"

He didn't know what to say. His feet stuck to the ground of the plateau. He couldn't deal with one woman. How was he going to face these powerful women who had made their way by manipulating powerful men—soldiers, prophets, and kings? But he had come too far to turn back, regardless of the shape he was in.

I picked up my pace toward the cave entrance in the side of the rock cliff. Satch followed. As we approached the entrance, I stopped, looked over my shoulder, and said, "Remember those rooms you saw with all those different people? We are going to another one of them inside the cave. I don't know if you saw this one or not."

Satch followed me through the entrance and down the tunnel that led to the mound hole. We turned left onto a path he failed to notice earlier. At the end of that pathway, the tunnel opened into another area.

I, Satch, followed Yeesa into this room in the cave. I could not have anticipated the beauty I encountered. It was beyond any loveliness I had seen. All the women were seated around one side of an oval table with one chair vacant on the opposite side. Yeesa directed me to the vacant chair. As I approached, all the women stood and remained standing, apparently waiting for me to sit down.

An elegant cloth draped the table, which was set with candles, flowers, china plates, and crystal glasses. A waterfall flowed down a moss-and fern-covered wall behind the table. Sunlight from three openings above lit the room. The most beautiful ladies stood around the dining table. They all looked about the same age. They each were elegant in their own way, with flowing hair, voluptuous shapes, and piercing eyes, and they carried themselves with grace and femininity. Each was dressed in a pastel gown reminiscent of the colors of a rainbow gently presenting itself across the sky and descending into the lush grass of a green pasture. They were marvelous. It was as though a beautiful wholeness had been presented before me without their speaking a word. I did not know what to say.

Yeesa bent down and kneeled on a colorful wool blanket that had been placed on the floor for him. It seemed like they knew each other, though they did not speak, other than with their eyes. It was as if all had been arranged beforehand. Yeesa crossed his legs, leaned back against the wall, and then looked at the girls and then at me. He just grinned. The girls looked at Yeesa and then at me. They continued to stand, as did I. I had no idea what to do. I was overcome and stood there like a stiff. They all began to smile. Their eyes were bright and deep with compassion.

It seemed as though their souls extended beyond their bodies, and the expression of who they truly were reached out to me with caring and understanding. I felt I could see inside their hearts, because no walls or defense mechanisms arose to hide any alarm. There was no pretense or charade, no mask or hiding from what was. There was no shame. I felt I should bow before them.

There stood Rahab the harlot, Tamar the seducing daughter-in-law, Delilah the deceiver, Bathsheba the bather, Sheba the proud seeker, Jezebel the usurper, Herodias the heartless, Ruth and her mother-in-law Naomi, and Mary of Magdala. Somehow, I just knew who each one was. Each was unique and in the process of becoming more whole, more of who she truly was. They were distinct, with varying degrees of life, varying shades of light from them. There were various levels of brightness, fullness, weight, as C. S. Lewis put it. Some were more totally themselves than others. What it meant, I was not sure, but the emanations from Jezebel and Herodias were not as bright or concentrated as the others. Perhaps it is true, redemption is a process that continues to go forward. Maybe we are taken to a greater wholeness, as we are able to take steps within our own freedom.

I could almost see maturity being magnified within each one. Clearly, they were not the same women who were written about in the Scriptures. They were simply amazing. I was dumbfounded.

"Hello, Satch," came the greeting in unison. "You are welcome here. The pineapple sherbet and the Fireball on the table are for you. Your spittoon is on the floor beside your chair. Relax. Please have a seat. We are delighted to meet you." Each of them took their seats.

I just stood there. I could not move. I stood frozen, trying to take it all in. I could breathe but not very well. I tried to take a step toward my chair and stumbled. I reached for the back of the chair to steady myself. It squeaked and slid on the stone floor as it caught my weight. I gathered myself, pulled the chair back to the table, and as best I could eased or fell into the chair, hitting the spittoon with my foot, scooting it, half-rolling—*ruma, ruma, ruma*—toward Yeesa's crossed legs. He just laughed, picked it up and pitched it back to me. He was grinning with his eyes, while I was thinking how could I ever take a dip and spit in front of these women. I had never experienced anything like this before. My thoughts were jolted when I heard someone say, "Satch, take it easy. We know you want to have this conversation with us."

It was Rahab. "We want to help. Yeesa has told us about your struggles. You have hurt a lot. One thing we want you to realize—and we can tell you from our personal experiences—God is not as much a rescuing God as a redeeming one. God does not protect us from pain. We are the cause of that, not Him. To be authentic means being vulnerable, which means you can be hurt. It is hard to take off your armor to risk emotional or physical safety. Wholeness requires authenticity, actual unadulterated genuineness—your absolute you—even when afraid. That takes courage on our part. God enters it with us and ultimately redeems it. Each of us have seen portions of your life. Yeesa and Baba Bengal have filled us in on the rest. Take it easy. Take your time. Eat your sherbet and get a dip. Sip the Fireball. It's all okay. Just think of this as sitting in your recliner at the farmhouse and watching a fantasy interview on TV."

"Is this a fantasy?" I blurted out.

"Well, spit and see," Mary said, as she rolled a can of Red Seal Straight Long Cut across the table towards me. They all laughed.

I caught the can and tried to laugh but was overcome. I didn't want a chew or a drink. I thought about the sherbet, but I was in water deeper than I was tall, and I knew it. Embarrassed, I took the bottle of Fireball and set it on the floor. I knew their stories, and they knew mine. And somehow, they knew my questions and issues. Getting answers to my questions had turned out to be a genuine challenge. As I looked at them, somehow even my questions hid from me. The ladies recognized my quandary. The gift of hospitality had grown within each of them and that began to change me. What happened next about undid me.

Jezebel stood up with a bowl of water and a towel. She walked around the table and stopped in front of me. She said, "Mr. Condwell, would you mind taking off your boots and socks? You have been here for many hours and your feet have to be tired."

"What do you mean?" I asked.

"Let me help you," she continued. She bent down on her knees, pulled off my boots, and then my socks.

"I don't understand," I insisted.

"May I wash your feet?" she asked.

"What? I've never . . . I . . ." came my somewhat muddled reply.

"You don't wear sandals like we did while walking in the sand and dirt all the time. Washing our feet was important and helped keep things clean—and it feels good. You must have dirt and debris all down in your boots and socks from your fall, so I want to do this for you."

Despite Jezebel's insistence, I felt very awkward.

"Satch, what is it?" she queried. "Are you sensitive to familiarity and afraid to be vulnerable? Do you not trust me?"

"I'm not sure about all of this," I said. "I have never been in this situation and do not know where I am. I am struggling with all of this and do not understand."

"Do you not long for honest intimacy?" replied Ahab's queen. "Is that not what you have longed for all your life, at least in part? There is no dishonoring here. Allow us to show your value to us. Trust me."

Still hesitant, I resisted. "But my feet are nasty."

This woman who I and others saw as an archetype of wickedness assured me. "Do not be afraid," she said.

"Let me just say this as kindly as I can. You are not described as being a woman who would want to help someone," I reluctantly replied. "At Jehu's command your eunuch servants threw you off a roof. Your blood splattered on the ground, the walls, and the horses. The horses trampled your body. Plus, when Jehu's men went out to bury you, dogs had eaten most of your body. They found only your skull, your hands, and your feet—and yet you are here. Then Jehu killed all your and Ahab's family."

"Correct," she acknowledged. "I admit that to you. You have seen what God can do. I'm not the same now. Being vulnerable even after you are dead is hard just like when you are still alive, is it not? May I do this for you?"

I was completely amazed. At that point I capitulated. "I guess so."

She shook out my boots and turned my socks inside out, wiping them until the debris stuck to them came off. She brushed my dirty jeans from my knees down. She washed my feet, cleaned between my toes, and even rubbed my heels and ankles. I had to admit it felt good. Then, she dried my feet and helped me put my socks and boots back on. I thanked her.

I had never known an experience like that. I thought, *This could be the ultimate kind of allurement.* She looked at me as if she had read my thoughts, then shook her head and returned to her seat at the table.

Mary broke the awkward silence and spoke for the group. "We know you are struggling with many questions," she said. "We may be able to help you with one you have, which is Why do women treat men the way they do? Am I correct?"

"Yes, ma'am, you are," I agreed. "And I'd like to know why such treatment affected me like it has—and like it still does. This has happened to me multiple times. I would be grateful for your help."

"Before we try to answer your questions, we want you to realize something," commented Mary, the devoted follower of Jesus. "Inside the deepest part of every man and woman exists a place that cannot be touched—a deep, abiding good at the core of the soul. It does not always come out, but it is there nonetheless."

She paused and pointed to her right, beyond the group, as though she were wanting me to look in that direction. I looked past the table, and in front of the wall stood my former wife. She was looking at me and smiling with a warm and kind expression. She lifted her hand and gave me a thumbs-up. I guess she was dreaming too.

I stood up, looked at the girls, and then over to Yeesa. They did not react, so I turned again to look at my wife, but she was gone. In that very moment, I felt hands on both of my shoulders and my neck. It scared me. As I jumped, I hit the table with my leg. I turned, and my two daughters stood right there in front of me—along with my son! At the same time, they all hugged my neck and said, "Daddy, we love you. It's all okay." I squeezed all three of them with the biggest hug I could muster. Then, it was as if they evaporated in my arms.

Mary said, "There is always more going on when you have eyes that can see. They wanted to be here for you."

Befuddled, I sputtered, "How can that be? They don't know about all this."

"No, none of them have all the details and don't need them," she explained. "They just care about you. You matter to them. They want you to be able to deal with all your demons and heartaches. They won't know they were here unless they remember their dreams, and those will likely be foggy. Their hearts are for you. They want you to know it. We hope you can accept that truth. Don't try to figure out how they could be here. You can't. That was another of Baba Bengal's gifts to you."

My head was spinning. I sat down and put my head on the table. I thought, *Who is Baba Bengal?* I could not move. I just sat there thinking of the damage I had done. I had never accepted my family's deep caring for me. I pondered that for a long time.

Bathsheba broke the silence. "We know you felt the greatest heartache you have ever known when you were rejected by religious leaders and church folks, which was made worse by being seduced and betrayed by females. It was so bad because the impact is cumulative, one thing after another without being able to decipher them. Those are the added sources of your struggle, but you will understand more on that point. Everyone has felt rejection, non-acceptance, and shame. It's the tragedy of the entire fallen world. Many are being held hostage because they do not know their true identity. You have not been able to get out of this bondage. Therein is the tumult of your heart. Now, you wanted to talk to us about what women have done to you. We are ready."

"Thank you so much for seeing me," I conceded. "I believe it started when I was two and a half years old in the women's dressing room at the swimming pool. Yeesa has helped a little with this. I see it was seduction, and when I took it into myself, I see it may have been a mimetic coveting but how can lust even exist at that age. But I have looked for that kind of attention from a woman all my life, thinking it love."

"None of us know the full story," she revealed. "What happened?"

"The incident still haunts me," I said. "I cannot forget it. Ladies, I am convinced you already know at least the essence of what happened to me. It devastates me every time I retell it. So, I ask you, please don't make me go through that experience again."

Bathsheba understood, saying, "Satch, I remember at times having to relate what I did. As you grow more, it will be easier to tell it without the hurt you feel now."

Yeesa interrupted, "But Satch, they need to know about the other things. I'm going to tell them. He was sexually violated orally by a deacon neighbor's teenage girls before he reached puberty and even knew what an erection was. Then his Sunday school teacher, a deacon in his own church, tried to have sex with him as a young teenager. So, the damage was multiplied. You girls need to know the extent of that kind of abuse that came to him."

"Yeesa, I need to ask something. Is this something that is so deeply embedded in me that I can't get past it, and I have to live with it from now on?" I asked.

"Yeesa," Ruth interjected. "It seems you should help deal with Satch on this issue and help him relax. Reliving experiences that brought this much pain takes one right back into the middle of it. You feel it all again. I think Satch needs a short break before we continue."

"I agree," replied Yeesa. "Do you ladies mind if we step outside for a minute?"

All the ladies insisted that would be helpful to me. Yeesa took me out to regather myself.

CHAPTER 15

Seduction

Satch and I sat down on the plateau looking over the river. I gave Satch some water and told him not to talk but to just sit and observe the quiet and peaceful sound of the flowing waters. I told Satch, "Let me know when you feel you are ready to resume your visit with the girls. This is a felt damage that you can get past. Just rest," I encouraged. When Satch was ready, he looked at me and nodded. We returned to the room with the girls.

The girls were conversing among themselves about what had happened to Satch as we resumed our places. I said, "Okay. Satch, the answer to your question is No, you can get past the damage by accepting it and moving on but how long you have to live with the pain is going to be up to you. It didn't pierce you to the core, Satch. Nothing can harm your core. The essence of you is pure. You may have felt it, but that's because you let it."

Exasperated, Satch replied. "Yeesa, how in the hell could I not take it in and let it affect me? I was only two and a half years old and had no defense mechanism. I didn't have any psychology or intellectual grasp of your Wakan Tanka, or the Son Jesus, or the Holy Spirit, or the Great Spirit as you call her. I was a little boy, a defenseless child. What could I do but believe what seemed so plain, so obvious? Can a child control what he thinks or feels, Mr. 'Oh-so-hi?' I'm sorry, Yeesa, it just hurts so bad."

"You are right," I admitted. "Do you know why that was allowed to happen to you?"

Clearly confused, Satch yelled, "WHAT! WHY? NO! I feel like I was cursed and am nothing more than a shard from a fractured piece of something that smells like the odor of the contents of that plastic pickle barrel in the loft of my barn. It still reeks of dill pickles after twenty years. Yeesa, I still smell inside myself, and, NO, I don't know why. How could I even begin to know why?"

"You had a deep foreboding relationship with the last woman that did you significant harm. At the same time, you had this inner premonition that somehow it was going to turn out for good. Do you recall?"

Satch admitted, "I do not understand it, but I remember."

I continued, "You then felt you had to warn this woman. You told her that no matter what happened your relationship was going to be for the good of others? You don't yet see this. You may not fully see the good that will come out of your suffering and botching things up until you get in the cloud. Most people don't see your brokenness but look at all your accomplishments and can't imagine you struggle at all."

"Yeesa, a guy said the very same thing to me a week ago, asking how could I have any problems," Satch remarked. "I just looked at him. He doesn't have a clue."

"But I do," I countered. "You have done well, but you have much more to learn and do. Do you want to participate in your own development or sit there and sulk? You have not yet resisted to the point of shedding blood, have you? Did you mean what you told that last woman who hurt you—that eventually it was meant for good—or were you just blowing smoke?"

"I meant it, Yeesa," Satch asserted. "I did not know how it was going to turn out for good, but I did believe it would. Don't play with me!"

"This ain't play, Little Chief Hustling Spider!" I quipped. "And you are still a little chief. Ready to move to the next level of understanding yet, baby injun?" Satch knew I was right. "Do you remember twenty years ago, your counselor friend looked at you and said, "Satch, I am going to say this as kindly as I know how. You are really bright, but you are not emotionally mature or wise. That is another thing and not a simple matter."

"Yeesa, what is emotional wisdom?" Satch asked. "Is that what we are talking about?"

"Yes, but no!" I noted. "The girls are about to help you with part of that. There is a connection, but we are talking about spiritual wisdom, which has emotional maturity as part of it. Your counselor friend was right, but that wasn't the core of your struggle, was it?"

"No, I knew it then and always have," Satch lamented. "Psychology can help some, but it hasn't cured my stuff, which always felt deeper. At times, doctors prescribed antidepressants for me, but I knew that was not the issue. None of that medication ever helped me. I got off them every time because I knew mine was a deep spiritual issue. Everyone I told that to, especially medical people, just stared questionably at me. They acted like I was a scarecrow pretending to be a sage."

"Ah, still a sense of humor down there in the midst of the pain," I said. "Now, Satch, where do you think the source of that is? Did that humor come from the naked woman in the dressing room?"

"You and I both know who it came from," Satch stated.

"You got it," I conceded. "See, there is music somewhere in you. Why did you name your horse Music?"

Satch looked at me with this dazed look. "Yeesa, because I lost the music and song in my life, and I wanted it back. Music was a constant reminder of my longing and determined searching. That's why! And that's intensely personal!"

Satch's horse Music

"Okay, but we are friends, here to help, and you have to get personal. Sin and solutions are profoundly personal. That desire says you realize in part what you have lost. That is a monumental step. Now, you knew when you told your friend, this woman, that it was going to end up with pain, didn't you? You didn't foresee the damage all around that was coming, but you knew. You knew it was going to hurt like hell—a pain like you had never felt before. Listen to me. Where did that awareness, that knowing inside, come from?"

"Yeesa, it was from the Spirit," Satch confirmed. "I felt what I was dealing with was so very dangerous. Even as a little boy hesitating outside that women's dressing room I had this feeling deep inside that I should not go in there. Yeesa, was that also the Great Spirit warning me then?"

"You are beginning to see," I said. "The Spirit has always been with you. She has always been there, both with you and in you. You see it. But Satch, don't let your mind take you away from this lesson. Were you not told deep inside that your relationship with your friend was going to hurt you and others, but beyond that it would help others?"

"Well, not so much in those exact words, but I knew it on the inside. I felt Her voice over and over again. I heard but still could not stop my foolishness. I felt I had to warn the woman and actually talk about the potential damage. Yeesa, what should I do?"

"Stay with me," I replied. "Do you think it was the Spirit in that dressing room suggesting you were undeserving, unworthy, and did not matter? Did She lure you?"

"No," Satch admitted. "The Spirit does not entice or neglect. Even with all the wrong stuff I've been taught, I know She never does that."

"Who was it then?" I probed. "Who was the liar, the deceiver? Who came after you with a vengeance and continued to harass you all your life? Was it the woman? Are you trying to blame the woman or women?"

"No! I don't know who to blame but myself," he conceded. "Yeesa, I did it."

"Satch, the first arrows that hit you hurt. The second arrow, the blame you hit yourself with is the worst, the god of guilt. It was not your fault," I emphasized. "Do you hear me? It was not your fault—not your fault—not when you were a little boy. It was not your fault. Satch, do you hear me?"

"Yes, it could not have been when I could not have known or been able to choose," Satch reflected. "But Yeesa, oh, the mistakes I have made since then! I have missed the mark so badly. I created some other something outside of myself, or inside myself. I still do not fully grasp how that happens. I have genuinely jumbled things up. There is no way to cure all this or make amends. No way to restore things. What am I going to do? What can I do? Is that the dark man?"

"Yes, and you can't fix it by yourself, but Jesus can—and He will," I asserted. "You have to accept His acceptance of you, His faith in you. It is yours. The only sound faith is not what you believe about God or yourself but what God believes about you. When you receive that, then you can deal with your pain. That is what is happening here. Hang with me, Satch. Don't believe another lie here. This is for you. Agree with that!"

"I do," Satch said. " I believe you."

"Satch, you were not just told one set of lies that day," I explained. "At least two happened at the very same time. The first came through your mother when she made you undress. You felt like you did not matter. Who was the other primary person in that dressing room?"

"The naked woman!" Satch shot back.

"And what did you feel her doing?" I inquired. "What did you feel coming from her? You described how she looked at you and moved her body. You told me about the look in her eyes, her words. You indicated her tone of voice. She had no hesitancy about parading her nakedness for you. She gave you compliments. She exceeded the limits of propriety without creating suspicion with your mother or any of her peers in the room. She was proud of the way she looked. Was any enticement coming from her? Did she know what she was doing?"

"She was alluring and wooing me. I realize that now, but how do I feel that at two and a half years of age?"

"You are made to feel," I explained. "That started before you were conceived. From the beginning, Jesus made you that way. You are designed like the Father, Son, and Spirit. We are of Their kind. When you recognize that you can feel, you can begin to know. The Trinity feels and wants you to feel too. At that point, you just did not know—could not have known—what pretends to be love. You can have deep feelings that come from darkness. Evil presents a tempting beauty, otherwise it would have no allure at all. If you had no desire in you, you could never be tempted. Evil takes something good and uses it in a harmful way."

"Yeesa, did she intend to do that to me?" Satch asked.

"That is a real issue, but not for us to consider now," I cautioned, "because men can seduce too. Instead, you may want to ask yourself what your own intentions were. Men view women as the seductive sex because of all the tools they have and the weaknesses of males. Beware of it always. It is a favorite tool of the Evil One. But to get to the heart of your issues let's look at how you felt. Did you feel unprotected and seduced simultaneously?"

"Yeesa, it did happen at the same time," he commented. "With both barrels. And then I substituted seduction for love."

"There is more to it than that, but you got shot twice at the same time at age two and a half," I said. "That's one thing, but there is a depth here vital for you to understand. Your mother was supposed to love, nurture, and protect you. She was supposed to take you under her wings. When she abandoned you at a time when you desperately needed her, then an alternative was immediately provided. At the same time you were being hurt by your mother's neglect of you, you were given an alternative to nurturing love and you swallowed it. What did that woman in the dressing room offer you? Do you see it?"

"She gave me attention, affirmation, and approval of sorts—some kind of acceptance and even applause," he recalled.

"So you know how to alliterate—seriously, did you ever see her again?" I queried.

"No, not her specifically, but yes, absolutely I saw women like her—especially the last woman I was with. It is astounding how much they are alike," Satch confirmed.

Yeesa interrupted me. "So, the question is: Is this all about her or about you?"

Satch replied, "Wow! Both. I blamed her and my mother, but at the same time I thought it was about me. And I kept looking for that kind of woman, the one who would do that for me. You know the *A-A-A's*. Oh, Yeesa, she was a fake, wasn't she? A fraud, a deceiver, a pretender. Yeesa, I know all women are not like her, but that one was—"

"She was that and more," I interjected. "She was an agent of evil. Her seduction was aimed at drawing your attention for the benefit of her pleasure or purpose. You were an object to entice not to love. Conceivably she was not intending to harm you but such a person doesn't know love, so she used seduction to get even a little boy to notice her. A deceived female, or male, always tries to do it where and in a way they feel safe and when no one will know what they are doing.

"Her greatest fear is exposure. The wise will call her out for what she is. In response, she will always politely deny her actions. True manners are not being polite or nice. Manners involve knowing where you stand before the Creator's glory. Nice is one of their operative words, and other women see it almost immediately. She parades. She wears a mask. She is provocative. Her image is what she cares about, not you. Most of all, she deceives herself. You are here to see the duplicity of evil and its desire to kill you, and the way it is passed on. But I think you will be better served in getting your answers on this issue from these ladies."

Satch was quiet for a moment. Then he said, "Please, ladies, if I may, I need to say something. I apologize. I know Yeesa better than you, and I have spent your time talking to him instead of you. I've carried these wounds all my life. So, I have always looked for the kind of attention that woman in the dressing room gave me. I seldom received it, but when I met this last girl, there it was. I could not help but be drawn in. I was married and not looking, but I was attracted. I didn't know how to stop my feelings.

"After my female friend and I both divorced, we saw a lot of each other. I thought we might be together and that she could be the solution for me—though I was suspicious. I had watched her for years. I mean the way she operates. In time, I discerned the person she was and realized inside that it would not work. I ended it.

"Less than two weeks later, my suspicions were confirmed. I reached out to her to give her a gift I had previously bought. I had no use for it. She met me, sat in my lap, took my gift, loved on me, and then got in her car and drove away. That day, I discovered she already had another guy. She went out with him again that very night. She never missed a beat. This heartache took me down to the lowest place of my life. Though I understand it psychologically, it is a hurt that I cannot seem to accept in order to move forward. I feel used and stupid. It was the tipping point that fully sapped my strength."

Bathsheba was the first to speak, and she spoke kindly. "So, it was more than a physical affair," she said. "It became an obsession and by obsession I mean captivated, enchanted, spellbound. In a single word, you were fascinated, meaning you wanted to become one with her."

"Yes, all of it and a continuing one," Satch stated. "I admit I was emotionally overtaken and could not help it or stop it, though I tried."

"Satch, Yeesa gave you good advice," Bathsheba continued. "Your behavior amounted to idolatry, obsessive idolatry. And at that point, one does not control it but is controlled by it. You picked us out because of our stories and what is recorded of what we did. And you are right. We did those things to men, and some of us didn't limit our damage to men or to ourselves. We hurt and used a lot of other people. In my case, yes, I took my clothes off and took a bath where others might see me. I may have been like that woman in the dressing room. I was young and proud of my body.

"There were buildings higher than my walled garden area where we washed and bathed, and higher than my roof. I knew David was in town and that his balcony was above my garden and roof. I thought he might see me. I hoped he would. I was lonely and angry. David had sent my husband and our friends to war while he stayed in his palace. I had few ways to express my anger and even fewer ways to change my situation. I was alone and felt unappreciated and disrespected. My husband was a lead soldier and loved it. He was totally loyal to David and away from home all the time. He was more devoted to David than to me. He wouldn't even come into the house when the king brought him home from fighting. He was to see me but slept outside at the palace gate. That wasn't the first time I felt unwanted. I felt I meant nothing.

"Yes, I bathed where David could see me and intended to do it. And I went to his house when he sent for me and slept with him. It worked, but, oh, the shame and sorrow that followed. I didn't think of that beforehand. Heartache and misery soon followed. Consequences always follow our actions, and we have to endure them, good or bad. David had my husband killed. I lost the child born from that union with David. Despite the pain, I realized heartache can be an opportunity to learn. And I did learn, and God blessed me out of His graciousness. Later, our son Solomon was born. God does give blessings after failures. He continues to allow me to learn now, and my being here with you is part of that process for me. It is not easy, but it is good, and it works. I am grateful."

"It does work that way," said Delilah, "painful though it be. Yes, I deceived Samson, and I meant to do it. I used my personal charm, which all people who learn seduction possess. I cared for him a little but more for what he could give me, or what I could get from him. I lied to him repeatedly and betrayed him and did it for money and recognition. I played him. Do you want to know why? That was the one option I felt I had to advance myself in my culture, and I took it. I was looking out for myself. If you do not know this, please hear us. People do things to get their felt needs met, to get what we think we must have. All of us do it. I was the only thing that mattered to me, and I did what I needed to do. I did what I wanted to do.

"Samson was a means to better my situation and get ahead, so I used him, even if it ruined his faith and him. I wasn't overly concerned about what happened to him. I was concerned about myself. But you do realize who was with those people who died when blind Samson pulled down the pillars and roof—me!"

Rahab interrupted, "And most of the time it seems there is nothing you can do to stop the destruction, like the walls of your city crumbling to the ground, which mine did. I felt I was partly to blame because I embraced my culture and became a prostitute. Then, to save my entire family, I turned on my own people. I hid the spies Joshua sent and snuck off with the Hebrews as the city walls of Jericho crumbled and crashed. A woman alone, what can she do? My justification is that I had to earn a living and save myself. I felt responsible for my entire extended family. That was the only way I knew. I felt I had to do something. We women were relegated to specific roles and did not have the opportunities afforded to men. So, I used men in order to survive and protect my family. But Satch, they were more than happy to use me too.

"The male-dominated culture has used women and prevented them from advancing. This is one reason why women have used their own free will to exercise their power of seduction. Luring men is a way to get some power back, though we must compromise ourselves to achieve it. You are now feeling the reversal."

"That's right," said Tamar. "My father-in-law, Judah, chose me as wife for his first son and then his second son, both of whom died. He blamed me without cause and would not give me to his third son to be my husband. He forced me to return to my parents. I pretended to be a harlot and became pregnant by him. I had twins. He was going to kill me until I showed him his signet ring, cord, and staff that I had made him give me as security for payment. He would not do what was right. I had to turn the tables on him. Then he said, 'She is more righteous than I.'"

"I tried to use Solomon," Sheba said, "but he wouldn't let me. I had all the material things I wanted and gave him great gifts. He had even more material things than I, but he also had what I did not have—profound wisdom. I wanted his wisdom and did everything I could to get it, but he saw through my deceit. Yes, he saw through it, at least with me. I don't know about all the others he had. A lot of women got to him, but not me, though I tried. There are rumors of a more intimate relationship, but they are just that—tittle-tattles. Satch, what man have you created in response to your felt loss? A nightmare, is it not? Satch, it's important you don't give up your true self, your legitimate man card."

Jezebel chimed in. "Or we will certainly take it," she said waving her hand toward Herodias.

"You know what we did," Herodias said. "We both seduced and usurped our husbands."

"We used our powers to take what we wanted," added Jezebel.

"They were too weak to do what we thought needed to be done," continued Herodias.

"Our hearts were cold partly because our men would not be the men they were designed to be. We took advantage of that," said Jezebel.

"Neither King Naboth nor King Herod nor Elijah nor John the Baptist nor God would be allowed to stand in our way. We commanded prophets to our liking, and manipulated the deaths of anyone who stood against us," confessed Herodias.

"So, one thing you might consider is whether or not you have been the man you were designed to be. That question applies to the heartaches you feel from women and others and to your actions in response to the pain. If you are not strong as well as wise, some woman may take what you do have away from you. You need to realize that some women will lie, steal, cheat, and kill to get what they want without caring who they hurt. Not all women are sweet precious little mothers who just want to love our children and be taken care of. Probably that's the lessor glory you see in the two of us. We still have a long way to go, but now we know it and feel very grateful for the progress Jesus is providing us. You are part of that. So, we thank you."

Satch couldn't look at them anymore. His head dropped, and his chin fell against his chest. He didn't want a chew or a drink. He just wanted to cry. He tried to understand what they had just told him.

"Satch," Mary added, "not all evil done by women or men is done intentionally. I didn't ask for those seven demons, at least not knowingly. I lived with them and was influenced by them, but I did not want them. Perhaps at times I did recognize the power they gave me and was glad I had it. But most of my life was absolutely miserable because of their influence. In that light, I guess I did use men, but they also used me. Jesus is the greatest man I have ever known. No one is like Him. He removed those demons and their influence from me.

"Did I love him? Yes, I both loved Him and fell in love with Him. I wanted to marry Him and would have in a minute. You know, I tried to grab Him that resurrection morning, but He wouldn't let me. He was true to his pure self. He would not give up his genuine man card or His sonship to our Father. Because He was true, my life is different and so is the entire world—and so you can be too."

Ruth said, "When someone has a question like yours about the actions of other people, we have learned to ask ourselves, 'What is my part in this?' These men we used could have prevented what was done to them. Each man opened the door to being ensnared and received the hurt that ensued. Did you not open the door, Satch? Do you know the answer to that question for yourself? Is it really the whole fault of the woman? Were you looking at what you could get from her?"

Satch was downcast. He couldn't talk and could hardly sit. The girls stood up and moved toward him. Each one bent down, hugged him, and kissed him on the forehead. After the last lady encouraged him, Satch generated enough strength to lift his head as they walked toward the waterfall.

Satch saw Ruth stop and turn toward him. She said, "When you get back to your space-and-time world, you may want to pick up Scott Peck's book *People of the Lie.* He has a lot of insight into human evil."

"Satch," Mary said. "One last thing: It is one thing to read the tea leaves of others; it is another to read yourself. Nothing is more fragile than a man. When deceived, you become one with the thing. Self-knowing is most vital. You may need to process with Yeesa. We can meet again tomorrow if you wish but come ready."

With that they were gone, along with the table, chairs and decorations. The waterfall was the only sound remaining. Satch sat in the chair, still holding the can of tobacco in one hand while the bottle of Fireball rested on the floor. He looked over to me as I continued to sit on the rug. I smiled. The dialog resumed.

"Well?" I asked.

"Well, what?"

"Bitches of history, wasn't that your description? Satch, four of those women are listed by Matthew in Jesus' ancestorial lineage."

Satch just looked at the floor.

I pressed, "Well?"

"I didn't know, Yeesa. They were horrible then. But now—"

"Satch, one last thing: Seduction is multifaceted and not always bad. God seduces. He draws you to Himself. Do you not feel that here? Sometimes, it is compelling and wonderful; other times it is very painful. You need to know the motive, which means discerning the character of the one seducing." I stood up, stepped forward, and said, "It's time to go. The girls and the boys will help you more." I reached for his hand to help him up. When he stood and got his footing, he looked across from where the table had been and saw the girls. Smiling, they said in unison, "You can do this!"

I took Satch by the arm and led him toward the exit. As we left the room, I sensed that Satch wanted to express his appreciation but could not bring himself to speak—except to mutter, "I feel anesthetized. I'm such a profoundly foolish and weak man."

I helped him lie down. He closed his eyes and just lay there.

I waited for Satch to rest on the floor of the cave. I could tell he was going to sleep, so I told him I was going outside. I knew he would be safe. I left him resting. Once outside, I built a fire and cooked some grub. About suppertime, Satch stumbled out of the cave and maneuvered to where I sat. He was silent. He ate and thanked me for supper. I laid out the blankets to sleep. He lay down and just looked up at the stars filling the sky and listened to the rumblings of the river. Then he said, "I had no idea. This is going to take more time."

"You will have more time with them tomorrow," I replied. "It may not be like today, but who knows? You are here to be supported, even if it's hard to take it in. Time to sleep. Tomorrow will be another challenging day."

CHAPTER 16

The Revenant

The brisk morning air stirred Satch who got up, stretched, yawned, and rubbed his eyes. "Not sore from yesterday's direct conversation are you?" I asked. "You must have a pretty hardy constitution," I quipped.

"Come on, Yeesa, don't start on me this morning," Satch pleaded. "I'm still in recovery. Oh, didn't the girls say we could meet again today? I forgot to tell all of you something. I'll tell all of you when we meet, if that's okay."

"Yes, I wondered when you were going to realize that," I noted. "Come wash up and eat and we'll go see them."

"Hey, Yeesa, who is this Baba Bengal I keep hearing about?" Satch queried.

"You'll find out. Now eat something."

We finished our breakfast, cleaned up, and headed to meet the girls. The table and furniture had returned. They were already seated and visiting with each other when we walked in. I had a feeling he would catch a load today. All of us knew his stubbornness.

Yeesa took me back inside. He sat again on a blanket against the wall, and I took my seat across the table from the ladies. The table was refreshed with a bowl, plates, water glasses, and a container of fruit. I sat down, and the ladies spoke.

"We are very glad you are here Satch," Mary said.

"We were delighted to receive the invitation to meet with you again," said Herodias. "We know why you are here and that our conversation yesterday was incomplete. We will be frank with you."

"We care for you and therefore will pull no punches," said Delilah. "It is probable it needs to be said in many ways. Are you okay with straight talk?"

"I am. I prefer it," I replied.

Ruth asked, "What is in the bowl?"

I looked. The bowl was clear glass. The contents held a golden liquid, but I could not determine its makeup, so I guessed. "It looks too thick for beer, more like honey," I said.

"How do you know?" she asked.

I acknowledged, "Only from appearance. Beyond that I cannot say."

"You are correct," Ruth confirmed. "Until you put your finger in it, you cannot know its consistency, only its color. Only when you taste and swallow it can you know its benefit and nature. But if you have been smelling acifidity bags and eating licorice and sauerkraut all your life and swallow the honey, you likely will not get the true benefit. When you have taken in the sour bitterness of deceit for as many years as you have, it is hard to taste the sweetness of the honey of forgiveness and grace. That is why you are here, to counter the acrimony you have taken in for so long. For you it will take a lot of honey. Because we care about you and want you to grasp this luring thing, we are going to be kind, not nice. God's benevolence is the seed that leads you to change your mind."

"It's okay to be direct with me," I replied. "I realized I should have confessed something to you before, but I didn't know how to adequately express myself. Please go ahead and say what we didn't finish yesterday. I agree I still need more correction."

Rahab said. "What man wished for, woman wanted to provide, to be what he needed. You men plant a seed. We receive because since the exile from the Garden of Eden our desire for you became as your being over us. When women receive the seed, we nourish and give birth. We care for and teach. We are mothers of all the living. It is very simple. Men treated us as less than them, like objects without honor."

Tamar said, "We grew tired of it. So, we women have learned to use men's objectification to our advantage. It's not pretty to experience or even watch. For both men and women, the corollaries are the same. Objectification and seduction can be killers, like a malignancy—and it inhabits all of us!"

"How does that happen?" I asked. "Help me. How does the weaker sex go about enticing?"

Sheba interjected, "Satch, women are not alone in being what you call the weaker sex. Do you not remember? Eve was the first to be deceived and used. Wasn't Adam there? He did nothing to stop it, or to help her. At least Eve was honest about it. Adam blamed her and God. We remember. You do it too. You have been blaming women and God. One learns from being the object. What men admire and do not admire is important to women. We have seen your weaknesses, we have learned about giving gifts and how to use our endowments to our benefit.

"We learned how men are sucked in. Men are enamored by shapes and form. You are captured by movements and a glance from the eyes rather than substance or character. We can mimic, mask and pretend pleasure when it comes to our emotions—even with intimacy. We can weaponize them. You cannot do that like us. What difference does it make if you change your clothes but do not change yourself? So, there are times when you become like us, objects to use for our advantage and welfare."

"Queen Sheba, please hold on a moment," I requested. "Apostle Paul wrote about Adam being deceived and Eve being beguiled. He made a distinction in the meanings of the two words, and the positions that men and women should hold. Eve was taken from Adam and given to him as an equal yet adversarial helpmate. Eve participated in ushering in death by taking the fruit and then became mother of all the living. I do not understand all he meant, but his descriptions in part intensify the tension between male and female. He seems to hold Eve more responsible. She did invite Adam to join in the choice that led to expulsion from the garden and to death. Though he described women as the weaker vessel, many if not most men still tend to defer to and favor women, as did Adam. Some men even revere them in certain ways. My own life is an illustration of this. Women have a profound impact on men. Some men even fear certain women. I know about that. Sounds like you do also."

Jezebel jumped in and said, "Your woman can become a she-wolf. An upward marriage is the only way for some women to secure their future. Do you now see how misuse can bite, claw, and injure a man? She can take you down. What you call seduction in your world is just tit for tat from another perspective. For men it becomes a blood stream fire, a nervous stream intoxicant blazing through your body. Few men ever allow any woman to sit on any throne unless it is a toilet. Women must fight back, whether through commission or omission. You should realize there are many ways to control the occupier of a ceremonial chair."

"Ladies, there certainly is toxic masculinity in some men against women," I admitted. "I've got a lot wrong with me, but that sickness I do not own. What I am asking is seduction, a woman's teasing and climbing, a response to that noxious objectification by men? Do women feel like they live in a world hostile to women, 'a no-woman's land,' and execute role flips against historical patriarchies?"

Bathsheba replied, "Some do, and a lot of us did. But there's more. Seduction is not limited to women and is but one item in temptation's inventory and revenge's pantry. Look how some men court and then contrarily treat women—as though we have no inherent value. One must learn how and when to flip the burger patty so it sizzles over the fire. It is not enough to have a spatula. You must know how, when, and where to use it. Timing is important. Those who approach wickedness can be the most dangerous of all humanity. They are hell-bitches. As you know, hell hath no fury like a woman scorned. The man you should be afraid of is that woman."

Naomi appeared in front of me and said, "Listen, Satch, you have read the story of what I told Ruth to do with Boaz. The euphemism 'uncovered his feet' doesn't fully uncover it. When it comes to sex, men tend to be engaged physically and often emotionally, but women can be aggressive and engage without feeling or attachment and often do so with another objective. God, for His reasons, used my euphemism and Ruth's actions for a higher purpose. A woman's words and actions are often just smooth and flattering. You must learn to be wise in these matters. Women do not have to be emotionally engaged with the man in the act. They may have another agenda. A man's blood has to get hot, not so with a woman. Women can play that game easier and better than men. Hardly anything is stronger in humans than the joining of emotional and sexual desires except hatred and vengeance—unless it's the profound longing to find your true home. We found that here."

"Look at Jezebel here," Herodias interjected. "She was eaten by dogs when Jehu threw her off that roof, but she has been through her own redemption process—some of which you partially viewed in the rooms you saw. She has not mentioned how she learned that revenge is a dead end. No one benefits—not the victims, not the people who cared about them, and not you. Revenge diminishes us. There is no honor in hatred or revenge.

"Did you not grasp death's teachings, the ways of restoring things after death? Death comes, and life goes on, but very, very differently. Death does not pay your debts, nor does it make you immediately whole. You yourself must participate.

For some, physical death is the only means towards salvation. Jezebel has been changed. I have too. We see in Christ there is no slave, no male and female, none less than another—but all are equal and without distinction. In earth's realm how does it feel to be used, betrayed? Was she attractive?"

"Attractive?" I responded. "That's not quite the right word. Maybe provocative, ritzy, or an admiration seeker. She was an expert in triggering the instinct to chase against a coarsened heart, an inaccessible wall—so hardened from fastening her fist around her own heart. She cultivated for herself some kind of mirage identity and reputation. For me, she was the strange woman identified in Proverbs as having her feet in death. But I could not resist."

Jezebel replied, "A lot of people hated me for things I did. Do you hate these women who hurt you? The meanest thing you can do to yourself is to hate someone else."

"I do not," I stated. "In fact, I am beginning to learn I cannot blame her. This last woman reminded me almost as a video image of the woman in the dressing room at the public swimming pool. It was another visit from the strange woman."

Delilah could not restrain herself, "Woman or man," she said, "when a person tightens his or her fist around one's heart for so long—often from the pain of a lost love or an abusive relationship—it will become like stone. Such pain cuts like a knife. For love people will betray a friend, cut their hair, stab and slice, or when heated love's knife can cauterize and heal. The Greeks had seven words for love. In English, you have only one—it is terribly vague. They had a distinct word for the self-giving love you are seeking. If one knew real love and trust, there would be no need to search for one's identity or to use hyphenated descriptors and divided last names. Finding this love is the test of life. You need discernment."

"I know," I agreed. "I have not kept it a secret. I thought I knew what love was. I was wrong in more ways than one. But even when you think you know what love is, or could be, you think that it is real. When you lose even an untrue love, or it gets taken from you, that pain can flatten you. You want to know the truth and that knowledge would change things. It is awful not to know the truth. Can you help me?"

Ruth joined in, "I will try. Any love that does not include compassion, empathy, and good will is not true, though it may seem real. Such a love is a lie. To love someone long term involves attending a thousand funerals of the people they used to be. It is our job to travel with them between each version and to honor what emerges along the way.

"You must distinguish between what is true love and what is seduction's lie," Ruth continued. "Many manipulate and plan their attacks. Everyone has seductive ways, some of which are approved in many cultures. Some seductions are for the good, to move people in the right direction. Everybody also has secrets. *Three things are hard to hold: a secret, a wound, and your true self. If you hold to secrets, wounds, or your false self, they become your masters.*

"The difference is the amount of damage secrets can inflict when the truth comes out. Yours came out, you admitted, and you experienced great loss. Inner harm comes when your life's lexicon does not yet grasp unconditional love and acceptance—even in failures. We have to empty ourselves to nothing before we can begin to see and experience who we are. If you truly understood love, you would not fall for a devious, emotional triggering. Each time that happened, when you began to come to yourself, what then?"

"I felt manipulated again—betrayed and shattered and back to beneath where I started," I explained. "A broken heart with a besieged mind has no words and can hardly breathe. I feel only sorrow and deep regret for my foolishness."

Mary could be silent no longer. "Good!" she exclaimed. "You are certainly not a flower that bloomed too quickly. You get stuck in catastrophe loops. You wither. I am not measuring you. In fact, I did the same thing. In a way, seduction is a woman's way of retaliation, which only takes one down farther. That is hurtful, wrong. You often have been the subject of ensnaring lies. When will it stop being your fault?

"You are a slow learner because you look at women as possessions. Do that and sometimes you get but sometimes you get got. You cannot know the truth when you are simply a tribulation truck portering head knowledge. You haul around and live out of what you have been taught and felt from external and subconscious sources. If your hand is only a funnel from your mind to paper, you do not know what you write. Your head is still unwary. It does not matter if it stays on your shoulders or not. You have words you see with your eyes, hear with your ears, interpret with your mind but you do not have the language of a true heart. Maybe that's why you cannot finish your story. You wander around thirsty while beside the spring.

"You refuse to make a foundational choice about whose you are and who we are. You have been too obtuse to understand the truth, though you have been shown over and again. In these moments, you are being given another window of favor to recognize within you the evil woven as truth's distortion. You carry this burden like a saddle and pack weight within your heart. Some pass the test; others go back to the vomit or the mud.

"A man who is certain does not sway between varying opinions. A rose is trying to bud in your heart. Will you allow it room to be nourished and tend to it? Guard well your heart for from it flow the springs of life. Trust cannot be given to an untrusted one. Satch, where is the music in you? *You need your wanter fixed.*"

At once another lady appeared from a corridor in the cave I had not seen. She moved quietly and slowly from behind the others around the table and stood in front of me. I could tell she was courageous and wise. She held out her palm beckoning me to stand and come toward her. As I stood, she said, "I am Esther. I have come to you for such a time as this. We have something to show you."

The others stood and eased quietly around the table, surrounding me in a circle. Each one smiled at me as they put their hands on my shoulders.

Mary said, "Satch, you are loved. Niceness is a subtle social virtue, but it is not kindness. Kindness in the purity and honesty of truth can seem harsh and unpleasant. You have spent enough time in 'nice,' polite society, filled with hypocrisy, a social pretense to be liked and accepted by others."

Esther slowly offered her hand. "Satch, do you know the fruit of the Spirit that the Apostle Paul described?"

I took her hand and acknowledged, "I do."

"And what is the last in the list he gave?" she asked.

"Self-control," I replied.

"Are you able to exercise that?" she inquired.

"I have not been," I confessed.

"That is because you cannot do it in your own strength," controlling your self, she advised. "Being in control has in its essence protecting oneself. It takes the Spirit's help. Self-control is far above just self-discipline and self-restraint. We know this has been hard on you. But it has been tough love and chastisement with the intent being restoration. You are looking for affection and mercy. All desire mercy. We now live in it. Sometimes mercy can actually feel like vicious cruelty. There are those who need a fierce mercy, the fire of God's love. This could be the dawn of the sun rising on your darkness—should you so allow it." Esther stepped back into the circle with the other girls.

I had to tell them, "Before you go, please let me share something. Last night, I realized I haven't described what I have come to recognize is desirable in a relationship with a woman. I believe women want the same thing, but we don't know how to talk about it with each other. I don't believe we differ significantly in what we genuinely want. I know some people say there are different ways people can show love—different love languages. They say there are many ways to express love: words, time, gifts, service, touch, kindness, gratitude, paying attention, and listening. So many of us are in bondage to the traditions in which we were raised and to the values which were implanted in us. We don't know how to free ourselves and cannot express love."

"That's true," Esther affirmed. "What else?"

I continued, "I wish I had come earlier to know I want her to have a vibrant spirit and know more than fleeting happiness. She deserves to experience complete acceptance and assurance. Hopefully, she would then be able to help me find that. At the same time, I want her to know that I cry and value her being able to share her own tears with me. I wanted her to like and want me for myself, not for just what I can provide for her. I want her to like and care for herself, as well as believe in and express herself—and believe I can communicate too. I long for one who would be a compass of truth for me and us, for each other. I want us to allow each other to have different opinions and listen to each other, both being honest and vulnerable. No yelling, mutual respect. I want her to be playful, spontaneous, with positive vibes—not bound in captivity, including in the bedroom. I want us to be in sync and to be companions with compassion and understanding."

Esther reflected, "Every one of us wish we had known a man who understood that. We are still learning the things you are talking about. We agree both men and women truly desire the relationship you describe. Let's see if we can together carry this further.

"We want a man to bring his full self to the table," she continued, "without judging or being afraid to talk about his fears or what upsets him. We want him to be respectful, not contemptuous. We long for honesty, vulnerability, and be open to new things. We want our relationship to be filled with intrigue, enjoyment, and expressions of intimacy—not just physical or sexual affection. We long to receive from him positive emotional reinforcement. Tell us your felt needs. Talk to us. Listen. Talk about real things that matter. Don't try to force or manipulate. If we hold on to the same rope, we will not become divided. How does that strike a man? What do these things mean to you?"

"Does that woman or man even exist?" I asked. "If so, I want to meet that lady."

"Well, that person just happens to want to share with you," Esther noted. "You have seen her and heard her voice but do not truly know her yet."

Suddenly, an elegant, ethereal feminine form appeared out of a cave wall, but I do not know from where or how she came. It was the tear lady, but becoming a full-sized human being in front of me, not a miniature as I saw before in the rooms. The vaporous, fairy-like being rose from behind and over the girls. She moved wherever she wished, unhindered by anything physical. I thought about how Jesus could just show up in a room or on a shore. He could be anywhere at any time. He just showed up. She seemed to be like that.

Her form continued to take shape as she lowered toward me and stopped inside the circle of women just in front of me. As she presented herself, she appeared as had the glory lady! She reminded me of the Blue Fairy who came to Jiminy Cricket in the story of Pinocchio. All I could think to call her for a name is Glo.

"Satch, you do not have to say a word," she said. "I am here for you. I saw you in the cave when you were looking at the different rooms of restoration and wanted to be closer to you and share something with you. Remember the tears you saw from all the little people? You saw that, but you did not know truly who I was, though I have spoken to you many times. It is okay. After today, I sense you will be more aware of my being with you. Please have a seat. I want to do this for you—just you. You matter, Satch."

I was so overcome; I could not speak.

Satch was totally overwhelmed. The sounds of music poured into the cave from all directions. He remembered a tune that seemed to fit the words. Glo began in a soft tone, almost a whisper, a hum and sang to Satch as a poet:

> You jumped from crashing bridges watching life's hope turn to dust.
>
> Living a nomad thirst in a desert makes a heart turn to crust.
>
> Got the vibes in you, Satcher, tell me how.
> Got the tune in you, Satcher, tell me why.
> You've been tied inside forever, why won't you bid it goodbye?

Tears fall from your eyes on the pillows wrapped in your arms.

You keep hoarding them in the darkest places in your heart.

Got the chords in you, Satcher, tell me how.
Got the tones in you, Satcher, you gotta try.
You've been tied inside forever, why won't you bid it goodbye?

You recant; I plant. The Revenânt.
You can't; I grant. The Revenânt.

Come, I'll swim us through the river waters rising on your knees,
Oh, please,
You know you've fought me;
You know you need me.
You know you've sought me.

Hiding all your secrets kept inside since you were a kid.

Sleeping poorly with the gloom clenched so tight n' close like a fist.

Got the song in you, Satcher, where's your voice?
Got the music in you, Satcher, make your choice.

You've been tied inside forever, why won't you just bid it goodbye?
You've been tied inside forever, and it's time to say goodbye.

Ooh, oh when you're all alone, I will dwell with you.
When you're feeling sad, I'll be holding you.

The music faded. Glo smiled, and then she was gone. Satch was bowled over. Esther said, "Satch, do not respond. Just breathe and take it in. We will give you a moment. Would you then follow us to the meadow?"

He was completely overwhelmed and could not take in all that just happened to him. He stammered but could not speak. He nodded affirmatively.

The girls moved slowly in front of him. Satch sat for a minute to collect himself. He stood, then shakily followed them through a passage that wound into and through several arched roofs in the cavern. The walls were colored and had a mix of various sheens ranging from glossy to matte finishes—and he saw within the finish what looked like people. He thought he recognized some faces, but in his state he could not be sure. As they exited a large opening from the cave, they entered a meadow. Satch could see a plateau of green pasture with flowers and mountains in the distance—beyond what seemed to be a part of the same valley he had observed before. He heard a river flowing below him and birds singing above. All of a sudden, the girls stopped walking and parted, opening a path between them. Esther walked back through them directly to Satch.

"You just heard the sound of the river of living waters down in the gorge," she explained. "You most often find it in the lowest point—down in the deepest, darkest valley of your life. In our walk here, have you also seen faces in the walls? Do you also see them in trees and clouds and floors, maybe faces in still waters?"

"How did you know that?" he asked.

She just looked at him with a kind smile and said, "Pay attention to them. Now as we leave, know you may undergo emotional highs and lows, like a window shade repeatedly being pulled up and let down again. Potentially you will experience ambivalent sensations and unforeseen physical experiences during our time here, and even after our departure. You are not crazy; it's just the human reaction to being in the process of becoming. It may be grueling. Do not panic. Face it and decide who you are and the life you want to live." Then, she turned around and proceeded across the meadow toward the valley's edge.

The rest of the girls followed and were now walking several yards in front of him. Satch looked up and saw an eagle flying above the meadow and circling around them. Shortly after it completed three circles, the eagle began to fly upward toward the mountains across the valley. When it did, the girls at once followed the eagle in the air, as though lifted on the wings of angels. Satch stood watching them rise. There were blazes of light reflecting many colors surrounding each of them as they proceeded higher through the air with melodious musical harmonies.

Satch gazed for a long time until he felt the air slowly becoming hot, and a strong and forceful wind rush down as if blown by flames like a powerful Foehn wind. The powerful wind blew grass, limbs, and dust everywhere. To protect himself, he ran back into the cave to the meeting room. The wind gushed through the cave's passageways and upper openings. The mysterious wind blew over the table where the ladies had sat. The blistering wind hurled glasses, honey, and bowls into the air and smashed them onto the floor all around. One slammed against Satch's face and left him on his back in a stupor. Satch was bleeding from the blow. It ached like a migraine, and the gusts of increasingly hot air continued. The heat rose both outside and inside him. The sound of this wind was no lullaby.

I observed as he began to come to himself. He held his head and blood ran from his nose. "Is this what she was talking about?" he muttered.

I was still sitting against the cave wall on the blanket and asked, "Do you have these Foehn winds down south?"

"Come on, Yeesa, you know better than that," Satch scowled. "We do not have mountains, but we have hot summer breezes that are only a little cooler than the heat index. Leave me alone for a minute. Do you have something to stop this bleeding?"

I got him a towel. When I handed it over, I said, "Satch, you were warned this could be tough. Remember what Esther told you. Be prepared. I'm going outside to stoke the fire and start cooking some of the fish. Come on out when you are up to it."

After Yeesa went outside, I lay on the floor for a time, trying to stop my nose bleed and deal with my headache and get relief from the awful heat. When I felt better, I got up and started outside. I was not familiar with all the corridors and tunnels in the cave. Still being a little groggy, I took a turn into a longer tunnel I thought led to the outside where Yeesa was cooking supper. I had to touch the walls occasionally to keep my balance. As I approached an area I had not seen, I began to focus a little better. I came to a large opening with two corridors that led in different directions. The one to the left seemed bigger. The opposite one looked longer. I concluded I was lost and chose the wider path.

I did not walk far before it felt increasingly damp; I seemed to be going deeper into the cave. Then I saw a light that came from around a bend in the tunnel. As I rounded the curve, I ran smack into a stalactite, which knocked me to the ground. I thought, *What in this world is going on?* When I recovered, I got up and saw light coming down the pathway. The path led into a smaller, lighted area. It was decorated extravagantly, complete with ornamental rugs. There were stuffed chairs, a candelabra, and ornate lamps. Expensive paintings hung on the walls.

Then, I noticed the quilted couch. Suddenly, she appeared. It stunned me. I stopped dead in my tracks. It was the woman in the dressing room. No, it was the last woman who I felt had betrayed me. No, it was both of them as in one person! It was like they had merged into one. The woman was lying on the couch, focused on her smart phone. She wore nothing but a silk robe, revealing her cleavage and her entire thigh. She smiled as she stood and started toward me with arms opened wide.

Then in the wall behind the woman I saw the images of my dad and mom shaking their heads. "No," my dad pleaded, "Don't be like me!" My mother held out her arms and said, "I am so sorry; I did not know." I saw Glo's image pointing to the cave's entrance. I heard her say, "Turn away. Leave!" The woman had almost touched me when the prior seductions all flashed through my mind together. I began to cringe. I saw them as never before. Before the woman reached me, I turned and ran back the way I came down the opposite tunnel and out of the cave, making sure to avoid the stalactite.

Outside, I bent over, breathing heavily. My head hurt even more. I looked for Yeesa and saw him sitting on a blanket beside the fire a little ways away. I ran toward him. I bent over again, gasping for breath and still holding the bloodstained towel.

Yeesa said, "Looks like you finally found your way out of the cave. What a knot on your head!! Did someone hit you with a baseball bat? Are you okay? You don't look too good. Did you just go troppo with all that heat or did something else happen?"

"You know it did," I retorted. "I ran into a stalactite. You knew it was coming, didn't you? You knew that woman would be there! You didn't warn me!"

"It seems to happen like that, does it not?" Yeesa replied. "Blessings come—followed by tests. Want to sit down? How do you feel?"

"Blasted, exhausted, relieved, honored," I exclaimed. "With the help of my parents and Glo—I saw them in the stone walls—I resisted and ran from it. But what were the images of my parents and then Glo in the walls of the cave? Were they actually there? And why were you not?"

"Oh, I was there," Yeesa confirmed. "You didn't see me. You can't see it all, but you can see enough. How many times do you have to be told? The images you see, well, you are not paranoid—it is your spiritual receptivity, another blessing you have been given. Remember? It is called *pareidolia.* You will not always see me standing next to you to bail you out. I sure hope you are getting your wanter fixed.

"Now, I have made something for you. You need a place to stand, a standard. Here is a representation that you can wear. We Sioux had many symbols we wore. This bracelet is like those of my tribe, and it is for you. Let it be a physical reminder of who you are and your standard of authenticity. You wear it on your person as a symbolic reminder of who you have chosen to be. Once you do that, ask Jesus to give you a brief description, a phrase that is a motto of who you are. That, little brother, will help you, like this bracelet—more than you imagine."

I put the bracelet on. It was a handmade, multi-colored, beaded bracelet stitched onto a piece of leather with closure snaps. It fit perfectly and reminded me of the Native American jewelry that fascinated me as a child. I looked at Yeesa and didn't know what to say, except, "You really are my friend! If those fish are ready, let's eat."

Yeesa told me, "You keep sweet-talking like that and I'm gonna get a cavity. Okay, sit down, if you can be quiet. I'd like to enjoy my meal."

CHAPTER 17

Crows and Eagles

Yeesa cooked those fish perfectly. We spoke little. That's the last thing I remember after the meeting with the girls and then the temptation. Then I slept. When I woke, I still felt a little bewildered, but I was hungry again. I don't know how long it had been—a night, a night and a day or two. My stomach knew it had been too long. My head knew it had not been long enough.

How Yeesa always seemed to know beats me, but he was cooking something over a fire that was producing a tantalizing aroma. I could hear the sizzling. "Want some grilled frog legs and pheasant with eggs?" Yeesa chirped. "Been gigging and checking nests, my little semi-Indian buddy. River catch is the best and more than even you can eat. Crawl over here, fill your belly, and relax. You need some recoup time, so eat up. A skin of fresh river water is hanging on that limb above you. Grab it and come have a seat."

"How long have I been out?" I asked.

"The rest of yesterday, last night, and today," Yeesa said. "It's about an hour before dark thirty. I wasn't worried about that hard head of yours, but your body needed additional encouragement and rest. You got shot with a wad, like nine mothers plus on your case, telling you the truth all at once and

Glo and a Foehn windstorm and then that strange woman. Spiritual and emotional discoveries can hit you harder than physical injuries. Being convicted and then blessed and then tested physically, emotionally, and spiritually is painful and exhausting. Don't try to talk about it yet. Just let it simmer. Hang your lip over a couple or more of these frog legs."

We ate and watched the sun set over the mountains. Saying little, we listened to the river run over the rapids and down its course. I pondered my own choices that ultimately brought me to this place. They made me sad, yet I was also glad, for they had brought me here. That was a brand-new perspective for me. By the warm fire, I felt safer and had experienced things I had never known. My blaming had been so wrong. I felt the bracelet on my arm. It reminded me of my wanter. As the fire flickered and the moon rose in the sky, I rested and eased off into slumber.

The next morning the sun beat warmly over my body as I began to wake. I felt a little more collected than I had in a long time. I lay with my eyes closed, enjoying feeling protected and watched over. I did not want to let it go. Then came the aroma of biscuits and bacon making another hole in my stomach. My hunger pushed me to turn over and sit up. I stretched and yawned as I tracked smoke rising from the fire.

Yeesa had been looking out over the river valley. He came over, and we sat down by the fire and quietly consumed the victuals. Neither of us was feeling talkative. I thought I was past my convolutions; I was wrong. Then something happened, again. I saw three eagles flying! Yeesa was watching, too. He said, "Satch, have you seen that before—three eagles at once?"

"I did in Colorado over ten years ago, and what happened was not good," I noted. "Yeesa, I have this uncomfortable feeling it's about to happen again—if the crows come."

Yeesa looked at me and said, "I hope they do. You need to see through this. What happened in Colorado?"

"I was at a PTSD spiritual recovery retreat. I was told to go out alone and listen for what God might tell me through nature. I was told to look for affirmation. I had an experience with three eagles and a cacophony of screaming, cawing crows. The crows circled over me and squawked like mad—caw, caw, caw—it was loud and offensive. They kept on circling, a concerto of disharmony, loud, offensive. It was an entire clan, right over my head. I listened to the three eagles communicate with each other though they were miles apart. One sat on a fence post close to me and spoke encouragingly to me. I wanted to be like them and fly. The crows made me feel shame, dishonor, unworthiness. It was awful. I concluded I was like a crow not an eagle. If the crows follow them—Yeesa, here they come AGAIN! This is déjà vu!"

The eagles and crows did the same thing again. The crows were cawing and screaming as they circled above us, over and over again. I exclaimed, "Yeesa, do you see what is happening?" He just looked at me unconcerned.

"Satch," he said, "look at me. Stop looking at the crows. Listen to me. Some people are so insensitive, they do not appreciate nature and creation. It is like they have little or no spiritual insight. That is not you. You decided wrongly before. Do not do that today."

"It is like something is wrong," I admitted, "like a condemnation. It is a sense inside. I feel again like I did that day in Colorado—like I'm nasty, sorry, just like a crow and could never be an eagle! That's what I decided about myself."

Yeesa dug a bit deeper. "Do you mean you feel like you felt outside the women's dressing room or in that meeting with that judge and the lawyer, or when they threw beer bottles at you when you played ball in New York?" he asked.

"What!? I can't get over your knowing about these things," I said. "Yes, this feeling is similar but not the same. The swimming pool was like a warning that I should be uncomfortable about what was coming, but there was nothing I could do about that. The crows cause a feeling of condemnation, like I am rotten and should be ashamed of myself. That message constricts me on the inside, reduces me and takes away all freedom. I want to be free, to be able to soar in my spirit like an eagle. But I am not good enough."

"That's your subconscious giving you two messages at the same time—one positive and one negative. You reject the good and accept the worst," Yeesa explained. "Don't be a dipstick. I mean just yesterday, the Spirit sang to you that special poem-song just for you, encouraging you. She never puts you down. Pay attention. If the Holy Spirit doesn't condemn you, then who does? If you can, describe the feeling."

"It's like a hollowness, a sinking feeling, like the emptiness of disrepute that grows, constantly getting bigger inside me," I explained.

"Is it fear?" Yeesa probed.

"No. Fear and warning was the swimming pool," I said. "The judge and lawyers were anger. The New York fans are rejection and avid to the point of regrettable dismay. Today the feeling is not fear. With them screaming all around us, I just feel unfit, like I am not good. Honestly, the crows make me feel I am unworthy."

"You are not, Satch," Yeesa noted. "Do you know what a group of crows is called?"

"No, sir," I acknowledged. " I have no idea."

"Not sir, Satch," Yeesa said. "We are equals, but your saying that speaks of your humility. Your heart is good but confused. Praise loses its validity if it is not accompanied by honesty. The Spirit is telling you to beware but not afraid. She wants you to fly. You have been shown how much you matter and are loved. You don't discern; you vacillate. Now you are reverting to an experience of shame and disgrace. This is tunk stuff. You must sort out each one of these past experiences and conclude who you truly are—resist the denunciation. A living parable is going on right now, and you are in the middle of it. This is a temptation not to believe in yourself. It will take your life away.

"The message being sent through the crows is that you are no good, undeserving. You have carried that feeling from the shaming you received repeatedly as a child. Today, over a decade since Colorado, they come again with the same message—right after you have been so highly affirmed. Do you see how evil is working you? A related test happened to you yesterday. Decode and decide who you want to be. You must deal with these things if you want to find your genuine life. It's part of the reason you are here. A group of crows gathered is called a murder. Evil is trying to kill your life."

"You gotta be kidding me," I exclaimed. "A murder of crows!?"

"Man, you are one hard-boiled dude!" Yeesa chided me. "Listen in your spirit to what is going on around you. What you think is your origin is not where you're from. The negative thoughts popping in your head are not where your deepest and truest thoughts originate. You did not come from your parents. You came through them. You belong to the Lord. You have been His from before the beginning of time. You have been designed to live from your heart, not from the evil stored in your subconscious.

"Your heart should teach your mind. When your heart is truly converted, your mind can take the teaching of your heart and then understand enough to be able to communicate to others. Your mind matters too. Use your mind to recall the Scriptures. They are specific on what is good and what is of evil. Many examples are given, and the consequences of choices made. Let your heart absorb and long for what is good. Believe in your true self. If what triggers your negative thoughts controls your mind and heart, it will confirm the disapproval you feel about yourself, not what the Spirit is affirming in you. Satch, we have talked about this. Now, when you think about a crow, what do you feel?" Yeesa asked.

"Not good," I moaned. "I don't even want to be around a bunch of crows. They must have some purpose, but it feels shadowy. They are repulsive, invasive, and seem nasty. I understand they will eat anything and steal whatever they can. They rob other birds' nests of eggs and baby birds. I don't like them at all. I also know they are very smart but scheming and deceitful."

"And what was the message you got about yourself in the women's dressing room?" Yeesa asked. "What about the message from the women who you feel rejected you when done playing with you? What did you receive from being banished by the church? And did you learn anything from the meeting you just had with the girls?"

"Yeesa, how do I learn how to distinguish between these feelings?"

"You will never feel good about yourself until you strangle these negative triggers," Yeesa instructed. "Focus on the affirmation you have received. It is hard with the damage you have experienced, but you must try to choose to rediscover the music within you and let it play."

I looked at Yeesa and said, "Why do I do that to myself? There is no way I could be a crow, is there? Why do I still feel this way?"

"Because you believed it was true about you," Yeesa explained. "You live and behave out of your beliefs. Your beliefs proceed from your perceived identity. Your feelings and conduct grow from what you rely on. When you believe a lie, as a child and as an adult, it stays with you, growing and feeding off you like a parasite. You have to want it burned out. Allow me to give you an example. Tell me what happened when you attended that retreat when you were about to graduate from college but had another year of eligibility in athletics. How old were you then?"

"I had just turned twenty-one," I said.

"And in the women's dressing room, you were just over two years. Okay, tell me the retreat story," Yeesa enjoined.

"Well, spring practice had ended, and the semester was to end soon. I would have completed all my requirements for graduation in just a few weeks. I was through with college but had another year of eligibility to play ball. I intended to play, but I didn't know what I was going to do about school. I knew I had to be enrolled to play.

"Every year, there was a spring retreat at a state park. I had always attended. I wasn't excited about it but didn't have anything else to do. I packed up for the weekend and headed for the park. It was not a picturesque place where the beauty helps heal your soul. It was a primitive group of cabins and a meeting hall. We used it because it was convenient and cheap.

"I have no recollection about the retreat except what happened the last afternoon. It had been decided that moral issues would be presented and then debated. Imagine that at a religious retreat! They chose teams and each side debated the issues in turn. I avoided making a presentation. I just sat and listened. A couple of the presenters were law students.

"The subject of homosexuality was debated. I remember hearing some of the dumbest arguments I had ever heard. One of the law students was an egotistical jerk. A couple of times, I chimed in with my two bits. He snapped back. I didn't think much about it but was surprised when someone—actually several people—I don't remember who, came up to me afterward and said, 'You really make good arguments; you ought to be a lawyer!'

"Now, I can't explain it, but something happened to me right then. I knew of but one lawyer and only knew his name because he was an acquaintance of my father. I had never been to a lawyer's office or in a courtroom. I had no idea what a lawyer did. Law school had never crossed my mind, but all of a sudden, a pathway was unfolding before me. The comment pointed me in a direction that I had not considered. As I look back, the fascinating thing is that those words provided the motivation for my going to law school.

"When I heard that off-the-cuff comment, I simultaneously heard an inner voice say, 'As a lawyer, you could be somebody!' That is exactly what I felt, and those are the exact words that came into my mind. It was as if I had been given a word of advice for my future. It was like, 'Yes, that's it! You are not anybody, but you could be somebody *if* you became a lawyer.'

"I could apply for law school without applying for graduation and could begin law school while playing my last year of ball. I had the grades, would be on the same campus, and could start in the summer. It just seemed right—a great fit. I had no interest in the law or any specific idea of what it entailed, but law school would allow me to play ball one more year. But there was more.

"It felt exactly like God had planned it. Since everything seemed to fit so perfectly, I thought, 'That's why I came to this retreat.' Later, law school meshed well with pro football: football in the fall and law school in the spring. This strategy seemed to be just right, but all this time the reason behind the decision was that I wanted to be somebody. I mean, what do you do with an English degree with additional major hours I had completed in poly sci and sociology?"

"Did it work?" asked Yeesa.

"Work?" I asked.

"Yes, did it work out that you then became 'somebody?' Did becoming a good lawyer, pro ball player, and then preacher fulfill you, cause you to become 'somebody'?" Yeesa queried. "When you fell in that sinkhole just a few nights ago, you were still looking for yourself outside yourself. Best I can tell, you still feel pretty much like a crow. And how old did you say you are now, over seventy? You are one sensitive, softhearted, hardheaded semi-Indian dude. But I like you. Do you feel like somebody yet? Or does it feel like you are still being killed, like you are dying or dead inside, like a murder?"

"Oh, no!" I exclaimed. "That's the crows' message, isn't it?"

"Or you are refuse, valueless. Am I close?" Yeesa asked. "You continue to draw the same conclusion about yourself. Once again you are feeling like a crow. So a crow, is that what you are? The evil in your subconscious has just triggered you, and you took it in as true. As you look back now, and in the days ahead, you have the opportunity to see how God takes evil suggestions and turns them ultimately into good. That is how predestination and free will cooperate. It is one of His specialties."

"Yeesa, how long will it take me to grasp that?"

"You cannot rush it," Yeesa cautioned. "Give it time. Let it simmer. It will become clear."

"Okay. There's no way I'm a crow—never have been!" I declared. "I've gotta be more than crow crap."

"Well, now that you've brought up the subject of elimination, have you had experiences where you could not control your bowels?" Yeesa asked.

"What!?" I yelled.

"Tell me about the episode several years ago at Lowe's," Yeesa urged. "You remember. Otis and Jootsie were with you, actually a good distance behind you in the store. You rushed as fast as you could to the men's room but didn't make it. You messed all out your shorts, down your legs, and onto the floor. You dribbled out all the way into the john. Jootsie screamed out in the store, 'What is that smell?' Otis followed you, recognized your predicament, and hustled to your truck to get your change of clothes. Remember?"

Befuddled, I asked, "How do you know about that? Yeesa, that was one of the most embarrassing things that has happened to me. It was in the middle of the store—absolutely humiliating. I wanted to stay in the closeted toilet for a long time and wished my friends could leave and shoppers would scatter. Then maybe I could go out unrecognized, without sneers."

"The point is, that day you couldn't hold it," Yeesa stated. "What about the time at the bank?"

"Yeesa, this is not funny," I said with chagrin.

Yeesa seized the opportunity to poke fun. "Sure, it is. The way you told that story at the annual men's gathering at your farm was funny! You had them rolling on the ground. Do you remember that?"

"Yeah, but that was a group of grown men out in the country at my farm," I argued.

Yeesa continued, "But you had a point to make, didn't you?"

"I did," I admitted. "And I made it too!"

Yeesa pressed, "And your point was…?"

"That Jesus knows about you, loves you, and stays with you even in the middle of your mucky crap," I explained. "Yeesa, it was a bunch of adult men, out in the country!"

"The truth, Satch, is not about propriety but about true freedom," Yeesa explained. "Just thinking and speaking about God's compassion does not mean you have heart freedom. You talk about it but still don't have it. Head talk, not heart, not authentic. First you have to confront yourself. You were trying to get these men to believe because you had not believed yourself. You continue to hide your face from Him. You don't believe it. So, what happened to you in the bank and then in the shower a few weeks ago?"

"Yeesa, this is about to get to be too much," I resisted.

Yeesa capitulated—slightly. "Okay, I won't embarrass you about the bank, but what about the shower?"

"I was taking a shower and couldn't hold it," I confessed. "I thought I could but didn't make it. I had to clean the shower, the bathroom floor, and the toilet. Then I had to get back in the shower and clean myself again. Why are you doing this to me?"

"I'm not doing it to you," Yeesa stated. "You are doing this to yourself, just like with the crows. You are having a hard time accepting the truth. Many people want to hide it when the truth makes them look inappropriate or embarrasses them. This is what you do."

Out of mounting frustration, I replied, "Do it to myself? Look, I couldn't help it!"

"Not in the shape you're in, with your guts always in turmoil," Yeesa noted. "Do you realize your emotions, your body, and your health are affected by your beliefs? Look at your autoimmune disease. You took something into yourself at two and a half years of age and a bunch of times since. The wounds were still there and growing at twenty-one and continuing through all your decades. It is eating away at your life, and NO, you can't control it. It has a firm grip on you. It owns and possesses you and will stay there and hound you until it is destroyed by someone much greater."

"Is this about getting my wanter fixed?" I asked.

"Yes, and the cause was not just the abuse and the women," Yeesa stated. "Your mother was there, and you received the message that you didn't matter. Not even God could see you. And if He did, you still didn't matter. Same thing when your parents didn't affirm you and with the legalism and spiritual abuse and the rejection from your classmates. You were stopped from playing receiver because of your knee and were restricted to kicking a ball. You felt left out, standing alone on the side, watching everyone else be engaged. Then you were drafted last, traded twice. Then you had two busted law partnerships—because you stood up to them. You were used by women, had affairs, were fired from two churches, then went through divorce. And that's not even the half of it. Repeatedly you have felt rejected and unworthy.

"So, you think negatively about both yourself and God. The two are inseparable—and your doubting of both remains. You feel like a crow, even though He sees you as an eagle. You cannot be at ease around people because you fear they see you as being unworthy. You can't even dance. You hardly ever smile. Do you even know how to laugh? You can't enjoy a party. How are you ever going to soar? You are going to have to change your mind, the way you see and understand. That is true regret, remorse, repentance. Only then can renewal come."

"I thought I *had* changed my mind, repented," I said.

"Satch, you do not apologize to be forgiven. You confess and apologize to repent. Repentance is a lifelong process," Yeesa explained. "You feel the way you feel until you feel differently. You see as you see until your eyes see deeper, more clearly. You think the way you think until your mind changes and your heart is renewed. Genuine repentance is like a tree with its roots in a wrecked and routed man's heart. With drooping branches he slumps, his limp leaves fall, and his eyes weep from regret. Unable to lift his face, the repentant man's heart has only a solitary grief, finds no peace. He feels estranged from the world with no place to hide—with no one left but God alone.

"Without deep regret, words are only withering, peeling branches. Repentance contains no self-pity, no excuses. It is a daily, recurring need. Regret unto repentance is an utter admission of the destruction one has caused, resolving never to commit again the abhorrent ugliness of such acts. It is utter brokenness. Forgiveness is a gift from the one to whom you apologize. These are two different issues. Repentance is for you. Forgiveness is for the one who forgives, and there are no limits for either. When done, both the unworthy self-blamer and the one who resents can be renewed and restored. If not, both the offender and the offended end at the same door, with different issues.

"Discoveries come every day. Just because you once walked an aisle, prayed a prayer, got dunked in a pool, and joined a church does not fix everything—in fact it does nothing. Neither does playing ball or being a lawyer, preacher, or businessman. The true temple, the place that is sacred, the privileged place where the ladder that runs between heaven and earth, upon which angels ascend and descend, resides inside you. The real church is not a building or a holy site but a place of conscience and Spirit inside you. It can be found everywhere. Nature itself is a cathedral. Inside each of us, there is a worship center, the temple of God.

"Listen to me Satch. If you could relax, be still enough and get quiet so that you can sense and hear God in you, you don't need any priest, preacher or church. Perhaps any of these could help, but none of them are a must have. Be silent and realize God is in you. And if you realize God is in you, when you go to worship or for a walk in the woods, you'll find God to be there. The burden of proof is in your own awareness.

"The Greek word for church, *ekklesia*, is another dimension of Christ's expression in the togetherness of all who believe Him. It was used to refer to the called-out people of God, who assembled as one body, a gathering of kingdom citizens called to participate in this new kingdom community with one another. God intends for them to show the world a glimpse of His kingdom and with compassion point people in that direction. Jesus also said where two or more are present He is there with them. So, what your people call church and worship is everywhere.

"You step into the knowing and live out of it. You believe it is so, agree it is so, and act as if it is so. You stop believing the lies and being drawn in by that which steals life. Divine therapy heals from the roots. Being loved removes the fear of admitting our wrongs. Grace isn't a gift for getting it right but for getting it wrong! *Humiliation is the way to humility. Exposure the way to healing and vulnerability, then authenticity.* What you have believed about yourself and carried is a fraud. It is false. You have to start listening to your healing heart instead of the malevolence in your head. That will take being loved at a level you have yet to fully accept. Come with me."

"Now, wait," I protested. "I've been listening, and underneath what you said, it sounds like you are talking about evil. Do you mean I am participating in evil? That I am evil?"

Yeesa continued, "Yes and no. You got attacked, which is not your fault. It hurt, and the pain stayed. You tried to deal with it by following religious rules. You knew about right but chose wrong. That doesn't work. It can't work. It's an inside job. So, you couldn't win. When things got worse you believed again and again you were not loved, not safe. And you had reasons—and chose alternatives to find relief from your pain and to get your felt needs met. The alternatives became your medication. Then you were participating in evil. Yes, evil has been in you and using you, primarily against yourself. Do you want it gone or would you rather hold onto it, keeping it stuck back in the closet where it can trigger you again?"

"Gone. I want it gone," I exclaimed.

With a consoling tone, Yeesa replied, "Satch, all of us want it gone for you. Think back to our talk about your tunk. It's vital for you to open it up, look at the contents, and name them. The pain and hurts, the abuses, the passions, the temptations, anger, rejections, exclusions, betrayals, bitterness, resentments, your failures, guilt, and shame. You get the idea. Identify and name each one of your hurts and pains. Identify and get to the bottom of the sources of your agony. The crows are just one metaphorical illustration that appears, and you interpret it as unworthiness; and they are tied together with many other put downs. Take these damnable hauntings out of your life! Face and eliminate each one, one at a time. You live and behave out of what you believe. Decide who you are and the life you want to live."

CHAPTER 18

Stay Stuck or Fly

Oh how Yeesa had slapped me again. I knew he was right. I knew I still needed help to get the self-degradation out of my soul. Then he said, "Come with me." He motioned me to follow him. He turned and began to walk down the plateau in the direction one of the eagles had flown. I followed slowly. Yeesa looked over his shoulder and said, "That food will take hold, and you'll feel stronger shortly."

We walked a long way—at least a mile. He did not speak but kept a strong pace, always walking ahead of me. I worked hard to keep up, glad for the food he had prepared. Despite the rigorous pace, my mind remained active. First, I thought about Yeesa. *He's an amazing man.* I thought of the way the Native Americans lived totally in nature, and it was their home. They carried their houses and animals with them and made home wherever they went. They loved the land and the earth and called it their mother. They saw how their Wakan Tanka provided for them through all that was around them. They were a hardy people.

Is he about to kill me with the pace of this hike? I wondered. Finally, my guide slowed his pace. As I caught up and trekked just behind him, I could see the edge of the plateau beginning to define itself in front of us. Just before reaching the edge, he stopped.

I thought the scene I had viewed earlier was a wonder, but as I looked below, I saw this intersecting river flowing into the main river flowing in the long valley along the path one of the eagles had flown. The river running below us through this adjoining valley was a fierce tributary. It merged into the larger river and together they became an even mightier, single force. This feeding river was a torrent flowing down out of the mountain over rocks that it was molding into smooth stones. It crashed against them with thundering force. Whitewater sprayed above the riverbed and moistened the riverbanks. As the sun shone down through the vapor a rainbow continually graced the surrounding area.

I was wrapped in wonder when Yeesa said, "Do you realize deeper means higher?"

Clearly caught off guard, I muttered, "Huh?" What are you talking about? Those are opposites, are they not?"

Yeesa continued, "The deeper your understanding, the lighter and higher your spirit will be lifted. Do you recall that dying means living, and doing so is totally up to you?"

"You are scaring me, Yeesa," I confessed. "What are you talking about?"

My trusted mentor replied, "Satch, do you want to experience flying?"

"I sure do!" I exclaimed.

"First, you hardly smile, don't know how to laugh or play, and don't feel others accept you." Yeesa explained. "Are you free enough to dance?"

Without hesitation, I stated, "I am not. Never have been secure in it."

Probing, Yeesa asked, "Not even in a relationship with one you knew well?"

"There has always been something holding me back," I lamented. "I have always been too self-conscious and afraid to let myself be unmasked. I feel all my failures would be exposed. I have always feared that I would be seen as the unworthy and incapable fraud I considered myself to be. I could not allow myself to be uncovered and totally unprotected like that. When I tried to play or dance, I awkwardly pretended but not very well."

"Is that because you felt you would not be accepted but instead would feel humiliated?" Yeesa inquired.

"Were you watching then too?" I complained. "Yes, I have been degraded and rejected so many times I do not want others to see me as I feel I am."

"Satch, *the only person you should ever compare yourself to is the man you were yesterday*," Yeesa explained. "Every single body looks the same once the maggots get to them, and the grave has walls you can't climb over. Few opinions from others have value. Do not let society judge you. Listen only to those who love you and whom you respect. That will never be more than a handful of people. You can count the number on your fingers. If you have more than that, you have too many. Opinions of the rest don't matter.

"Remember what your friend told you when sitting on the swing: 'Man you are so intense'? Then, you asked him what you should do about it. His answer was, 'Nothing. Be yourself and let the others deal with it.' To do that, you must reach the point where you are okay with you.

"Now, would you like to be free to play, dance, and fly—to be completely at home with yourself regardless of what other people's opinions might be?"

"How could that happen?" I asked.

Yeesa resumed, "Would you like to experience that?"

"I sure would!" I agreed. "But where is that?

"Do you trust me, Satch?" Yeesa asked.

"Yes, I think I do," I confirmed.

"Well, this is not the time to think," Yeesa cautioned. "You either do or don't. What does your heart tell you? You need to decide. If yes, climb on my back."

My mystical friend turned around and stood on the edge of the plateau looking down into this deep gorge. The cliff went straight down to the river and the rocks, just like places I have seen in Arizona, Colorado, and Wyoming. We are talking about Grand Canyon deep. This one was like half a mile down to the river bottom. On the edge, you could feel the wind. His leather pants and the tassels on the end of his shirt sleeves flapped in the breeze. He looked around at me as if to say you coming?

Yeesa crouched and stretched out his arms like he was going to take off. He had been right about everything so far. I trusted him. I jumped on his back, wrapped my arms around his neck, and locked my legs around his waist. Just as I locked in, he jumped straight off the ledge like an Olympic diver. Together we fell directly toward the rocks in the river below.

I felt like I was holding onto a bomb dropped from a B-52 bomber at five thousand feet headed straight for a target. Faster and faster we descended. My whole life flashed through my mind all at once. Then, I don't know why or how, but I recalled his last words before taking flight: "Deeper means higher." All I could do was hold on. And I did, while squeezing both eyes shut tight. I was scared!

Then it happened. About halfway down, Yeesa grabbed my right wrist, yanked me off his back, flipped me over and said, "Just hold both arms out."

What does a body do!? I did what he said, and suddenly I was fall-flying—but upside down and backward, and we were going fast—down, down, down. This strange ride was morbidly thrilling and utterly indescribable. I could not see. I began to feel moisture blowing up from the river. Soon after I felt the wetness, Yeesa jerked me again into position on his back.

He stretched out both arms at the same time just above the river. As he did, his arms became like wings, and I was riding on his back—flying! We swooped over the river at a tremendous speed. Then, he arched his back, and we began to ascend as we approached the mountain. We lifted to half the height of the peak. Then, he turned to the right, and we flew back over the joining of the rivers. We flew up the main river and approached the plateau where we previously walked. As we approached, I noticed an object heading our way. It drew closer. It was the eagle flying toward us. It looked at us and pulled slightly ahead, flying just in front of us. Another eagle who had been sitting on the rock above the plateau and the cave entrance joined us in flight. We turned and soared toward the tall mountain.

We glided past the where the rivers joined and continued down until we passed the large mountain. Then, we turned and circled the top of the large mountain again and again. We were flying. I was really flying! We flew through clouds. I saw the wonders. They were all in view at the same time. Oh, how they complemented each other and merged into a wondrous, beautiful sight! Despite the euphoria of these new experiences, the wonder of feeling free transcended all.

Gradually, we turned again toward the large mountain and began our descent. The mountain peak rose above a layer of clouds. As we descended, a unique spot arrested my attention. The clearing before us was unlike anything I had ever seen. Giant trees, shrubs, and flowering plants dotted the landscape. In a nearby field, I spotted various animals together—some predators and others prey. There were birds singing, fawns playing, and big cats sleeping in the shadows. The sun shown on the grass and prolific fruit trees gave life to this massive garden. Another eagle called from the distance. The two eagles in front of us responded, and we turned slightly, lifted a little, and headed for the sound.

The largest eagle that was calling was on the mountain and stretched his wings and flapped as he landed on a large flat rock above the clearing, overlooking the small paradise on the side of his mountain. There was plenty of room to light in a level area just below his perch. As we eased down, I noticed a fire encircled by stones. I watched the other two eagles land

and walk a few steps toward the bigger mountain eagle. They seemed to be talking.

As Yeesa landed, I slid slowly down his back 'til my feet hit terra firma. Trying to stand on my own feet took some adjusting. I stumbled a couple of times as I tried to take some steps. Slowly I gained my strength.

I looked at Yeesa. He stretched, looked at me, and said, "You trusted me from your heart. Now, trust me again. You are about to witness total freedom and acceptance."

As I peered at the eagles, they looked at me and seemed to smile, however an eagle does that. Then, they began to change. The rock eagle turned solid white with red spots for a moment before turning black again. The smaller eagle from the plateau that first met us and flew in front of us was, well, pink then blue, then a rainbow, then chartreuse, then small, then large, then up, then down, like everywhere, then invisible, here then there, unpredictable, then black again. I don't know what else to say, except this one had to be feminine.

The third and largest one, the mountain eagle became a cloud, then a whirlwind, a mist, a fog, a flame, a shape I cannot define, and then black again. They talked, laughed, jumped, touched wings and circled around and around with each other like they were dancing. They flew up and around. They played with each other. I knew this was God playing and dancing. That's all I know to call it. Suddenly, they stopped and turned into persons standing beside each other and pointed to me. I knew who each was.

"Watch this," they said as they began to dance. Well, it was like clogging on that big rock. They seemed to be together in total oneness but were obviously distinct. They moved in a circle, no circles, in and around one another, at times looking like they were a part of one another. I don't know how to describe it. The merry three twirled, circled, clogged, danced, smiled, and took turns leading, yet simultaneously following the others. This spectacle was beyond me.

Then they stopped and waved to me to join them. Yeesa put his hand on my shoulder, urging me to go. Somehow, I joined them. They said, You are just fine. Loosen up. Clog with us. If you don't know how to dance, don't worry. Your soul knows the steps." They took my hand and started clogging. After loosening up I found myself smiling. I was not embarrassed. My feet just started dancing. I stumbled. They grabbed me and said, "It's all okay; just stay loose." They were laughing with me. I was having a good time.

Out of the corner of my eye I saw Yeesa motion to the eagles. We stopped dancing and walked toward Yeesa. But I wasn't expecting what happened next. Jesus, who was the rock eagle, said, "Satch, let's sit around the fire. We know you like to do that. Just have a seat where you feel most comfortable, and we will join you. Yeesa, would you get the boy a drink and some sweet cherries, strawberries, blackberries, and blueberries? And bring some butter and pie dough, a pan, and his Dutch oven. Oh, and some cinnamon sugar. I hope he will make us one of his berry pies. All that flying and dancing made us hungry!"

I stood there speechless. Yeesa went over behind a rock and brought out all those things and set them down in front of me beside the fire. Looking at me, Yeesa asked, "Is this okay—I mean to put them here? Is this spot okay for you?"

"Certainly," I said, somewhat involuntarily, as I sat down in front of the fruit, fixings, and my pot. I mean what else was I going to say? Yes, it was my pot—I mean, Dutch oven with my pie pan in it, just like I had left it in my horse trailer in the cooking trunk. How did this happen? I didn't know what to say to the Godhead, who were a lot more than just eagles. There I was sitting on the side of a mountain in a paradise, having just flown in on the back of a dead Indian.

Glo, the eagle from the plateau, broke the silence. "I've heard about your pie and can't wait to get a bite of that. It was Jesus' idea to add the sweet cherries. We think you'll like that little additur—mixing both sweet and tart flavors. We don't have charcoal. Home delivery screwed up the order again, so you can't count out the right number of charcoal bricks. But we're pretty sure the heat will be just right. So, get after it; we are hungry."

"Can I ask a question?" I inquired.

"Go for it," Glo replied.

"Why in all the world would you want a berry pie that I make?" I asked. "You can have anything and have it put right in front of you with just a thought. You could just speak it into being and God-rowave it hot. It would be ready to eat instantly."

"Because of you," Glo explained. "You are valuable. We know how hard you worked to learn how to do this and do it just right. And we know how lip-smacking good it is. What you help to fashion and create is a joy for us. You join with us when you craft things. We enjoy you. We are here to assure you—even with all your failures and foibles. Though your sins be as scarlet, they shall be white as snow. Let the queasy discomfort go. We know the good that is going to come of your failures.

"They are helping make you who you truly are. We see the progress and your efforts. You can't get it all right. The only thing perfect is love. You are here with us and still act like you are alone. We will not give up on you! Do not miss being present with us. Lose this self-conscious fear of rejection and unworthiness. It is a lie. You are beginning to trust us. We long for those who do. Come to yourself. Do not be ashamed or afraid.

"Satch, you have a profound goodness in you. But you are absolutely annihilating your true self and denying who you are because of guilt and felt shame. Overcome guilt and shame by taking them out of their hiding place. Confront them as the perpetrators and become their executioner. Get brave. Be courageous. Your soul has the potential to embrace others effectively and bring light to their lives and healing to their hearts and minds. Now, would you like an appetizer, a little something sweet, like a prune?"

"My mother used to say that to me," I recalled. "How do you know that? What is this? You're an eagle and God and you're talking to me and telling me what my mother said to me when I was a little boy! What is going on here? Please help me."

Glo continued. "You know we are not only eagles. We can be whoever, whatever, any concrete substance or person, or hypostasis. Well, Jesus being the Son of God who became the Son of Man remains the Son of God—but He is still human. He does have flexibility. He always will be man. He's met with a lot of people who thought He was something or someone else. He's perfect at it, don't you think? We do this whenever we choose and for a reason. It is perfectly okay within each of us and with each other. That's what being loved and loving goodness does. We are here to show you how you can laugh, dance, play, and fly—how you can be yourself. Relax! We will never stop helping you. Just never stop trying. Please start the pie. Now, do you like prunes?"

"I do, but not really for something sweet," I said. "They do, or some of them, have sorta a sweetness, but that's not really why I would choose them."

"I hear they can be a natural laxative," injected Father God. "What do you think?"

"I've heard that too, but I can't say they have worked for me that way," I noted. "I do eat them but have never noticed they have really helped me when I needed to—you know—clean out."

"Do you need to be cleaned out?" asked Jesus, looking me straight in the eyes. All three were sitting and looking directly at me—not harshly or judging, just totally focused on me. Yeesa just smiled and sat down on the ground beside me, crossed his legs, and said, "I like this."

Incredulous, I asked, "You like it? What? My needing to be cleaned out? I don't get this, but it's pretty obvious the three—no four—of you are in this together!"

"No question about that," said Glo. While one word used in the Bible for God, "Elohim," is plural and used with a singular verb. It is an affirmation how the Trinity always acts as One. "We are delighted with each other and you. And you are in it with us. So, let's get on with it. What about the cleaning out? A long time ago, we used the term 'consuming fire.' What do you say, Yeesa?"

"Yes, it's close," he confirmed.

"Yeesa, we think he's getting ready," Glo stated. "Take him to see the boys."

Yeesa stood up, looked at me, and said, "Let's go Satch, hop on!"

I was flabbergasted, flummoxed, totally thrown off guard. I looked at the three and put the fixings in the pot over the fire. Then, I climbed on Yeesa's back. In an instant, we were gone, or at least I thought so until I noticed Jesus the rock eagle flying alongside us.

He said, "Don't worry, your pie should be just right at the right time. We can't wait! Oh, and Yeesa, help him. It has yet to sink in who he truly is. He is ready to be put in the wind himself and then learn how good is often backward. So, squeeze him."

I did not hear clearly what he said and did not know what he meant.

On the flight back toward the plateau outside the mound, I held on tight and asked Yeesa, "What was Jesus wanting you to help me with? Was it to explain what just happened? I heard something about 'squeeze.'"

Yeesa responded, "Satch, you were just shown you are okay. You are loved and accepted just as you are. Come on, let this tight-ass stuff go. Now turn loose of me. Either do it, or I'll throw you off."

"What!?" I shouted.

"Take your arms and legs from around me. Spread your arms and fly with me. Do it on your own, or I'll pitch you right now. On three: one, two . . ."

What could I do but obey? I released Yeesa, spread my arms, and suddenly I was flying beside him. A slow, tentative grin sneaked across my face. I really was flying. What a wonder! I glided down the mountain, across and back over the river, then down the plateau toward the cave. Abruptly, I realized I had to land.

"Yeesa, how do I stop?" I yelped.

"Ease behind me and watch," my mentor explained. "Relax at the waist and drop your legs some. Lower your feet but keep your arms out, not together. Lean back easily and you will begin to slow down and descend. Stay behind and pay attention to me. As you get closer to the ground, your speed should continue to reduce until you put your feet on the ground, and then start walking until you stop. You're an athlete. You can do this."

"But I'm an old broken up one," I protested.

Yeesa persisted. "Do what I am telling you or crash!"

You talk about scared. But I followed Yeesa's instructions, slowed behind him and mimicked his every movement. As we got closer to the ground, I didn't freeze, but still I didn't know what was going to happen. Regardless, I had to do this. I got progressively closer to the turf and hadn't slowed enough. When my feet hit the ground, I walked and then tried to run, but my bad knees would not hold up. They buckled. I fell but remembered to roll.

I finally stopped, face down in the grass. When I was able to look up, I noticed Yeesa bent over laughing, but it didn't matter. I was so excited. I had flown in the sky like an eagle. Then, I started to laugh. Oh, how I laughed! We had the best time with no hindrances. I don't remember ever feeling that good and light. I realized the deeper my trust, the higher my spirits. It was all so simple, yet so very hard—but so wonderful. At no time during my whole life had I known that—until this day! I wondered if I could hold on and keep that assurance.

CHAPTER 19

Backward Good

After we settled down, Yeesa hit me with a question I wasn't expecting. I had been trying to fathom what I had just experienced, when he asked, "What if good comes backward? Jesus threw the backward spear when he spoke of faith the size of a mustard seed. It has medicinal properties but grows so large it could take over an entire garden. So, Jesus is planting a weed in the world—faith that overcomes the world. That's backward good; it's opposite the world's view.

"Satch, there are so many people who recognize the good in you and have affirmed it. Think of the good that has happened to you. Remember that boy's camp up in North Carolina? Your second year there you received a position that had never been given to another camper. You couldn't believe it or accept it as true."

"I felt like I didn't deserve that kind of recognition," I replied.

Yeesa continued, "And when you were in your forties, the only time your mother actually talked with you, she told you she knew you were special before you were born. Did you believe her?"

"She had never said anything affirming to me. I wanted to but had no way to know what that meant," I explained. "A friend once told me I often used that word *special*. Guess there is a longing deep within me to feel that way."

Yeesa provided more evidence. "Remember your first interim pastorate where the people repeatedly said to you that you were the best preacher they had ever heard? The same thing happened to you in every other church, didn't it?"

I protested, "But—"

"Remember when you entered the doctoral program," he interrupted, "and took those tests? The head admission counselor, who reviewed your admission tests, wouldn't tell you how smart you were. Then, he said that you were going to make straight *A's* in that program. His advice was for you to learn to rest and relax."

"I did relax, at least for that degree," I rebutted. "Somehow, it became easier. But it didn't last long. It didn't sink in deep enough. Hardly ever have I relaxed."

Yeesa kept firing. "How about the graduate professor that followed you to your car. He said your presentation was the best that had ever been made in any doctoral class he had ever attended or taught. You outlined seventy-seven sermons from Amos 6, and he told you he would come to hear you speak every week!"

"I cried, but after the seven-hour drive home, I couldn't imagine it was so," I recalled. "The bitter comes back with the sweet. It continues that way. Yeesa, I never learned how to hold any affirmation. It always got pushed away."

"What about the coworker you respected who worked for you in that last church?" Yeesa asked. "She came to you regularly for five years seeking advice about personal and work situations. She told you that you were right about each one."

"I felt like she had never had anybody really listen," I explained. "It wasn't my first walk around the block. That wasn't a big deal. I had already been through a lot of the things she brought up and had an idea of what needed to happen."

Yeesa probed, "And how did you learn those things you told her?"

"Mostly through mistakes I had made or observed and experiences of pain and heartache," I stated.

Yeesa persisted, "And what about getting traded and finding out from news on TV, the splitting of your partnerships, and getting fired for standing up for what you thought was right? What did you tell your friend? It was grit, wasn't it? Yep, grit! Where did that come from, Easy Street or Baskin Robbins?"

Yeesa turned my mind into a clouded maze. He was right. I had received a lot more goodness—including provisions and health—and approval than that, at least until now with this autoimmune disease and two bad knees. I had friends, opportunities, and a lot more, but I had not known how to see them as blessings and be thankful. I felt so ashamed of my self-centeredness, as if I had been chained in a prison inside myself.

I was reclining when I felt Yeesa's hand on my shoulder. At this point, the pace of the dialog accelerated.

"Sit up, Satch, and look at me!" Yeesa demanded. "You have caved in long enough. You don't see how good works backward yet. The darkness, the formless, the void has to come before the light. Always has, from the beginning. However much it takes for one to come to see."

"Backward good!?" I asked.

"Yes, and positive bad, up by down, strong by weak. Listen. Do you know about right or wrong, good or bad?"

"Of course. That's what I've been taught all my life—pessimist or optimist, half full or half empty, negative or positive, one side or the other side, black or white, yes or no, one way or the other."

"What if there is another way to look at all that happens?" Yeesa asked. "What if there is such a thing as free will that lies between the either or—and has to be educated? Are you free?"

"Well, I guess so. I am freer now than ever. Before today I would say land of the free, you know, but I have not felt free before, not free on the inside. I am still partially bound up on the inside."

"Maybe, just maybe, that kind of freedom can go whichever way," Yeesa said. "We are free to choose, but our choices are influenced by suggestions both internally and externally. Then, we make our decisions based on what we think is best for us in the moment. Is that a waste? Do you sense that all your years with all your mistakes are wasted?"

"Not all of them. There has been some good but more pain. And pain is bad!"

"And what then about suffering?" Yeesa asked.

"That may be worse. It extends the pain. It's like there's nothing you can do about it."

"The truth of a person cannot be known until he has been tested," Yeesa said. "That's what happened today. You certainly passed. You want to talk to the boys, don't you?"

"Yes, if I'm able."

"Why don't you remember to ask them about that? But you don't think good at all applies to you?"

"How could it?" I asked. "I was born a sinner, depraved, separated from God; I was not nurtured by my mother, not empowered by my father; I felt like a failure, rejected. All I have known is to perform. I hope I am learning how to be. I'm still not sure what I am or who I am. Whatever, it still doesn't feel like good."

"That's what you told the graduating class when you were chosen as the top student out of the five thousand at that seminary, isn't it? When you were asked to speak at the closing ceremony. 'Teach us how to be!' Is that not what you said to all the professors? And you are still trying to learn that. What just happened with the eagles, the pie, and flying? They all occurred for that very reason: to teach you how to be. Your request has been answered today. You have seen it. Satch, you are a blessing. You have blessed so many people. See and accept that.

"Have you not made choices and felt they were the best, acted on them, only to look back later to see that those choices brought ill? And what happened to you when you learned that? Did it change you? Do you understand now more about that issue and its significance in your life? Have you not counseled others to avoid following a particular intrigue? Have you not warned people of dangerous actions the results of which you had personally experienced based on your poor choices? You were able to warn them because you knew it hurt you and so choosing a like direction would hurt them. And you call the consequences of your actions what? Pain, suffering, the wrath of God, God's justice, anger, judgment, punishment of sin, retribution, payback, retaliation, revenge? WHAT!? Don't just sit there, talk to me!"

"I'm getting confused."

"Okay, let's go a little further," Yeesa probed. "What happened to your freedom and life when it went through such pain? And what if all those things that seemed like condemnation and destruction were on the same team with love? Did freedom learn from its teachers?"

I froze like a corpse. I held my head in my hands, elbows on my knees. The idea of a connection, a link between what I had always thought of as opposite concepts of life had never entered my mind—not once. Things were supposed to go one way, either up or down. But Yeesa just said that going backward could be what assists you to go forward, good could come from bad, up could come from going down, falling behind could move you ahead.

"Yeesa, are you saying that these stories you know about me and my experiences that damaged me and other people transpired for my good, my improvement, my learning?"

"Well, did anybody compel you to choose or react the way you did? Did they force you?"

"Sometimes I felt pressure, yes."

"Okay, but does outside pressure force freedom to submit to the force? You have known times when, in your words, you stood up for what you thought was right."

"Now, wait just a minute, Yeesa. You carry this 'everything connected' deal so far and that approach could eventually mean that—if you carry if far enough—this is even hard to say—what we call hell in life and after death could end up being used to teach us."

"Sometimes your memory is very short. How about the rooms? All are intented to remove the trash and bring out the golden good in you. Satch, how else do we learn and grow and understand what really counts and lasts—that which is meaningful and whole? This really is not that hard. *Freedom does not exist outside of love. Who made everything that exists? If all has the same ultimate source, is it all not in some way connected? And is there not some purpose for everything?* Do you think the Creator wastes what He has made, or even your mistakes? And since the Creator is Father, does that not mean love for you is at the root of it all?

"Look, a few of the stories impacted you negatively, hurt your heart, damaged your thinking, your feelings, and concept of yourself. Is there another way to look at what happened and how it may have benefited you? Is there another message there? I have already shared this with you, hardhead. *Instead of asking Why is God doing this to me? why not ask What is God trying to teach me? What is He doing for me?*"

"Because it sounds like you are saying that seduction, rejection, failure, a false gospel, withholding affirmation and validation is helping me," I stammered.

"You are here, aren't you? Did those things give you what you performed to get?"

"The opposite, and if I got anything it was temporary or a deeper heartache."

"Satch, You do not yet accept that you have an origin and design that precedes, by a long way, your parents and your family. You go all the way back to before time and the beginning of all things. God planned, designed, and put you here, knowing you before you were an embryo formed by the sperm-egg union of your parents. You then ate the fruit of your family and your ancestors. You took it in. One day, you must choose for yourself. Don't the failures and damages cause you to look deeper, to another source? Ponder on this and think back through your life experiences. I've got to set up an appointment. I'll be back in a little while."

Yeesa stood up, walked across the plateau, sauntered up the hill beside the cliff, and ventured out of sight. I sat there quietly meditating on his words, recollecting memories forever etched in my mind. *Why do I remember these things? They seem to haunt me.*

I thought back to my parents and how they never gave me the affirmation I craved. Neither my mother nor my father ever seemed to change. Rather, they continued in their patterns and seemed to become even more fixed in them. I thought back about when we egged that neighbor lady's house my senior year in high school, to college experiences, to the affairs. Seduction drew me in but never gave back. I was looking for love in all the wrong places and thought I was experiencing freedom but was just being stupid. I thought about the rejection by the church, the labor of law practice, the years of futility with that last church. I thought about how all the praise of my good performances was fleeting. *What have I learned? I have got to change the way I think*, I thought. *What a convoluted mess. I have been a frigging idiot!*

As I chewed on all that, an eagle flew over and quickly disappeared in the distance. That drew my attention back to my surroundings. I wanted to join him and fly again. Then it was quiet. I sensed a gentle breeze and the purity of the air. I wanted to hold those sensations inside. Yeesa's comment about preceding design and origin was affecting me. I came from before. The only one there in the before was God, so I came from Him. I am His idea.

Then, I was startled by a whizzing sound. I jumped to my feet.

Yeesa was announcing his return. "I like to do that every once in a while. It's like being a little boy again. *I just love being a little boy. Do you know what I mean, Satch?*"

"Yes, but not the same as I was before. I wish I was a child again but loved and free to be me. You scared me. What was that zing sound?"

"I threw a rock down to the river. Saw where it splashed. Bunch of fish jumped too. Fun. Are you making progress with yourself?"

"I'm trying to get past being nothing, wishing I knew how to change my way of looking at things."

"Ah. That is progress!"

"Progress?" I asked.

"Sure. *If you are nothing, and those you have looked to can't make you something but end up hurting you, and your performance isn't cutting it, then you have three options.* The first you have tried. You could keep trying it. That is *ego*, which makes life all about achievement and attainment. Maybe it'll work, but it hasn't so far, so keeping down that path is just insanity. The second is to just sit where you are, empty, doing nothing; you know *Que será, será*. The third is to *face things in a different way*, like your experiences here in these few days and in your tunk. Are you so thick you don't remember where you are and why you were allowed to come here, and what just happened to you?"

"You are talking about all my questions."

"Yes, and your neglecting true answers you are being given here. All these years, look where you have been seeking answers from this world! You will not get the truth about yourself from the world. Just saying, Mr. Freedom, you know—a lighthearted reminder between friends. And while I'm at it, since we have been over all this before, I've got a new twist for you. You were sitting here thinking about fixing your brokenness and damage. What if the pain and suffering you have endured, the darts of fire in your heart, stuck and burned so deeply that they created wounds?

"What if the lies borne by those arrows crawled up like poisonous snakes, bit you, slithered inside those wounds, and hid there, unrealized? And you believed them, and took them inside in your subconscious—they then control and own you. You could even say they possess you, like a demon. The feelings that you have may not be you. They may be lies inside you that you believed. If so, those feelings have you instead of you having them. Unaddressed, they can become like a hydra with many heads causing internal chaos, inner tyranny with relational strife.

"It doesn't seem like your people know how to deal with the deceptive misrepresentations about the character of God. The consequences to life are devastating when you believe in an all-controlling, judgmental omni-solo non-relational god who is out there somewhere in the unknown. That smothers a life. *Religion is not relationship.* It seems many of your people are afraid to challenge that concept of God for fear of being ostracized. My people did not have to overcome that lie because as children we were initiated to the spirit world and what it meant to be a man in our culture. We knew about the Great Mystery. As men, we would seek the Great Spirit in somber, quiet, heart-felt vision quests. Centuries before your time, the older tradition in your faith understood this. They were called mystics and practiced meditation and contemplation.

"They accepted mystery. At large, your people have never recognized it. If they have, they don't pay attention. They may in some repetitive mechanical, written, or memorized way, practice some form of prayer, but it lacks a quiet, meaningful, personal, relational heart connection. Genuine prayer does not begin with your need but with acknowledging God's nearness. Prayer is a heartfelt search and conversation with God with whom you feel and know a personal connection. Prayer must be more than a ritual habit of 'supposed to' duty. Unpretentious, authentic praying is deeply earnest, genuine, and personal for oneself and for others. It is gratitude and trust, not just words being repeated because it is a religious obligation, and you should say them. You must help change this, but first change it inside yourself.

"Feelings are a big deal. Don't avoid or neglect your feelings. Pay attention to them instead of identifying with or brooding over them. Look at them, even when they hurt or bring forth exhilarated passions. When your body or gut hurts or your fervor is heightened, the pain or excitement is a physical sign of something happening, and you immediately know it. When you feel emotional reactions—excitement or negativity—it is an indication something deep is going on. When it happens, it should be a sign to you. Don't ignore it or move away from it. Pay attention to it. Stop, let it be there with you no matter how ugly, unpleasant, tempting or pleasing. It may be the lie and not you. Again, that's what's in your tunk.

"Dealing with your emotions is on you. It is vital that you pay attention to your emotions. It's something you and your people in their freedom desperately need to learn how to do. You are being given insight here because of your honest questions. Learn both here and when you leave. Learn how to deal with your issues if you want to be fully cleansed of these hauntings. As that happens, you will sense your ability to respond to the connectedness of all things and people around you. Then will you be able to help not only yourself but your people.

"Many of these deep wounds to your soul produce hurtful feelings that originate from defamations, smears, and falsehoods about you, even people gaslighting you. You could accept and believe these untruths were true about yourself or other people. What if that wound was intended to take away your giftedness? What if you were accepting being diminished to keep you from being more? *What would happen if you learned from that and faced your feelings?* What if you grew, matured, if you looked to the true inner source of your being instead of looking outside to get other people or things to give it to you or tell you who or what you are? What if you were better prepared now than ever to stand against the deceptions?"

"Are you saying that the wounds, once healed, can turn to strength and reveal why I was born?" I asked.

"I didn't say that, but they can. Discovering one's true self is both compelling and painful. However, before you think too much about that, you wanted to spend some time with the guys, right? Of course, you always have the freedom to say no. You don't have to agree to do it. Don't want you to be uncomfortable."

"Aren't you so thoughtful! So, who is it now, Mr. OH HI YEESA?"

He laughed at my sarcasm and said, "Come and see."

CHAPTER 20

The Boys

I couldn't help noticing how Satch walked a little funny and kept pulling at his jeans. He was wobbly from his aerial experience and meeting the eagles, but he looked like he was beginning to put himself back together. He still moved slowly, but he was adjusting. It can be brutal getting right, but he was trying. We walked across the plateau back to the opening of the mound cave following the same pathway as for the meeting with the girls. We entered the room and walked through it, past the waterfall and down a corridor. We could see light at the end about twenty yards away.

Satch's jaw dropped when he saw the entrance into what I would call a cove. It was like an arena on the plateau. Its rock walls extended wider as they sloped back gradually receding toward the height of the mesa above it. It looked like an amphitheater carved into the rock walls.

The floor had the appearance and texture of something like zoysia grass, which was short, cushiony, and a perfect green. It grew to the outer walls, filling the entire circle of the cove's floor. We stopped in front of the entrance. I noticed Satch staring. To the left was a tall rock watching over the entrance like a palace guard. Satch caught a glimpse of Rock, now an eagle sitting atop it.

Satch looked spellbound with his thoughts. I said, "Come on, Satch." We turned and noticed three men sitting on a flat stone in the back of the cove. They were deep in conversation and seemed not to have noticed us. Satch will tell you about it.

Yeesa and I were not halfway across the cove when all three men turned, looked up, and began to grin. They stood and made their way around a flat rock and walked toward Yeesa. All three hugged him. There is nothing quite as raucous as male laughter and companionship. These guys knew and loved each other. I was taking all of this in when they asked Yeesa, "Is this the one?"

"Sure is," Yeesa replied. "And he is chomping at the bit to talk to you guys. We may be here three weeks trying to answer his questions. He asked to meet first with you three men. Hope you are up to it. Good luck."

I was trying to figure out who they were, and if, in fact, it was the three I mentioned that I wanted to talk to. One was more rugged looking than the others, with a beard, long hair, and wearing a mantle. I guessed he was Elijah.

Compared to Yeesa and me, they were at least half a foot shorter. But one was a lot shorter than the others, bow-legged, and his eyebrows almost met in the middle. He was virtually bald. He fit the descriptions I had read of the Apostle Paul. The third man had a full head of long white hair but did not look old. None of them did. I guessed he was Enoch. All wore robes and sandals.

"Satch, proud to see you, man. I'm Lige. This here's Paul and ol' snow-top is Enoch. You guessed right."

All three of them gave me a pat on the back. Paul reached up and grabbed both my shoulders, looked me in the eye, and said, "Come, let's sit on the rocks to visit." The apostle's encouragement eased me a bit.

Enoch and Elijah sat on either side of Yeesa on a rock, which was part of the amphitheater's ascending walls. Paul sat across from them and offered me a seat next to him, facing the other three. Paul pointed toward my feet. "Your favorite sausage biscuits and grape jelly are on that rock table beside you. There are two skins on the floor by you. We each have two. One skin is water, the other wine. Hope your religion is not too offended. You are free here. You don't have to pretend. So, where do you want to start? Any question is a fair one."

They all looked straight at me, smiling, and grabbing their skins for a drink. I don't know how long I sat there thinking about how I had popped off my big mouth and there I was sitting with three of the major characters in biblical history. I felt tongue-tied and embarrassed. I noticed Elijah tapping his foot when Enoch broke the silence.

"Well, little brother, just open your mouth and let it run out, whatever is tickling your mind. Take some wine, it'll take the edge off and ease your stomach. Tell us, you didn't buy that nonsense that it was grape juice Jesus made and drank, did you?"

"I did not and thank you for accepting me," I said. "It helps me feel a little more at ease. I guess, Enoch, my first question for you is because we know little, if anything, about you except that you walked with God and were no more because God took you. And Elijah was picked up by a chariot and taken up. Nobody else. Well, Moses was buried by God and no one knows where. How come? What did you do differently from everybody else? There has got to be something you knew or did that the rest of humanity has no clue about. Were, I mean, are you just better than the rest of us?" All four of them shook their heads. Enoch put his hands to his mouth at the same time. They looked at each other and simultaneously broke out in laughter. "Did I say something wrong?" I queried.

"Not at all. We just have not thought to compare in so long that we don't know how to do that anymore," Enoch explained. "No one here is better than another. There are distinctions and uniqueness but no classification system of comparison of who is up or down. We accept the seat at the table Jesus gives us. It's all good."

I continued, "So, Enoch, help me then. There's got to be some reason. Come on, you walked with God, pleased God, and did not die because he took you. What does that mean?"

"Well, I guess I'd first have to address the issue of what it means to die. But I'm not going to do that. You have to figure that out yourself. But have you ever read some of that stuff that has been attributed to me, like, say, *The Book of Enoch*?" he asked.

"I tried, but it was kinda floaty," I admitted. "I had a hard time following it."

"I like your word *floaty*," Enoch said. "I was, still sorta am, that way. It is part of my uniqueness. I did write down some things I imagined, dreamed, or saw in visions, but not everything some say I did. Don't know that anybody understood it. I did not fully grasp much of it either. Perhaps like your experience here. But I loved to stay in that state of silence, opening my imagination. You should keep trying it, being quiet. It's the best way to hear Father and to talk to Him. It is so intriguing, peaceful, and scary on occasion. But I felt comfortable there, because in that silence I became consciously aware of the presence of God. Nothing I experienced in my years was like it—nothing!

"It is not that I did not enjoy living on the earth. I loved to eat and enjoyed time with my wife—as well as her companionship, if you know what I mean—and our children. That was fun, but for me the mystical was compelling. Those times were so gripping that I carried them with me. In God's presence everything fit together and had meaning. Being consciously in His presence consumed me. It also caused conflict within my family and friends who could not figure me out, and I could not explain it. Can't now. I do know that sensing the presence of God opened whole new worlds and awareness to me. That became the dearest of all things to me; I was committed to walking with Father."

"What do you mean by mystical and sensing the presence of God and everything fitting together?" I probed.

"You mean you are here and do not see this?" Enoch asked. "Has your spirit imagination not yet been baptized enough after meeting with the girls and having Glo sing to you, and flying with Yeesa to meet the eagles?"

"Well, yes and no," I said. "You mean everything is connected, that everything is linked together in God?"

Enoch elaborated, "Let me approach this in a different way for you. Do you ever see faces in things? I'm not talking about seeing people or animals but seeing faces, forms, and objects in other things."

"Esther asked me about that, and I do," I confirmed. "But I have never understood it. I just see these things and faces in various materials."

"How do you feel about that? Have you ever talked about it to anyone?"

"I once asked two different friends both of whom looked at me weird, so I dropped it."

"So how do you feel about *pareidolia*, which is what they call it now."

"I saw and heard my parents and Glo in the walls where the strange woman tried to seduce me. But I don't comprehend it at all."

"Pareidolia is a phenomenon in which the human brain perceives familiar patterns or shapes in random or vague stimuli, such as clouds, shadows, or patterns on a wall or floor," Enoch explained. "It has been discovered that folks even find it in sounds. It is the tendency to find meaning in seemingly ambiguous stimuli, as part of the normal human experience. People who are more spiritual, or believe in the supernatural, are more prone to pareidolia. It is not a psychosis. Some studies now show artistic, musical, and spiritually minded people tend to see more than others. I guess I was just before my time. Da Vinci and Shakespeare talked about it. It is like *apophenia* or *patternicity*, the tendency to perceive meaningful connections between unrelated things or random things. I did it all the time. Folks thought I was nuts. Have you ever had animals, trees, insects, or flowers communicate with you?"

"What?" I asked.

"Go ahead, tell me."

"Well, when my horse stiffened up, he was about to buck, meaning he was not happy. Or when my dog growled or my cat hissed at me, they were upset, and I backed off whatever I was doing. At times, I have felt they were saying something to me through the look in their eyes or their body language, but I have not heard them speak in an audible voice or a language I could hear and understand."

"What about the crows or eagles?" Enoch asked. "And did you not, at least once, think your horse Music was trying to say something to you? Do not be surprised as you become more sensitive to the mystical when that happens to you. It's feasible that she is telepathic. When you think she is communicating, be quiet, listen."

"Do you mean—"

"Look, do you not yet accept where and who you are? Best not to ask more about this now. Just remember what ol' Floaty told you. But as for why God took me, maybe it had to do with my writings. I know I projected some things. Maybe He decided I was creating something too soon or saying more than others were ready for—or was speculating about what I did not know, and it was going to cause major problems. I sure caused some problems in my community. Everybody thought I was pretty much out there. I had faith in God because He had faith in me. *God's goodness does not demand faith. He supplies faith.* That changed me. You have not yet fully received that faith for yourself. I did see that the Lord was coming with thousands of His holy ones to convict ungodliness.

"You too have been shown a lot already, but you are asking me a question that I cannot answer. God took me through a transition to non-space and time before I physically died. I know He did do that. Maybe part of the reason it was written that God took me is so that question would be asked, so that people would search out answers.

"Satch, you have got more requests than Santa gets at Christmas. Two things here: Your questions reveal things about you. Even Larry told you that back at Momma Smith's house. Remember? Your questions are good; however, you keep asking more questions before dealing with the first one. Life is like an onion. You have to peel off one layer before you can get to the next. The same goes for the experiences in your life. You have to deal with the first experience before you can move on to the next. Instead, you want to get to the center and have a quick fix. That isn't going to happen. You must deal with one layer at a time!"

Elijah jumped in cautioning, "And be careful about always needing a reason. You cannot always immediately know the reason. You may have to wait. I was able to learn that, and it made all the difference. You are still stumbling."

I blurted out, "Elisha was a witness to your going and you left him your mantle, but I see you have it back."

"Yeesa, you didn't tell me he was a sassy bloke. Just kidding, sorta," Elijah quipped.

"I told you he was filled with some audacity," Yeesa added.

Elijah smiled. "Satch," he said, "I'm a pretty wound-tight guy—maybe the opposite of Enoch. Now, you tell me: How is it a guy who called down God's fire from heaven to consume altars, stones, and water and then kills seven hundred and fifty false prophets on Mt. Carmel goes on to run away and hide in a cave and ask to die out of fear of the woman Jezebel? How does he deserve to keep living? I told God I was the only one left. Ever thought about that? I told Him I wanted to die. Talk about giving up. How does that please God? Learn to listen for the gentle whisper.

"I cannot explain how or why God took me. But it certainly was not because of merit or accomplishment or because God loved Enoch or me more than, say, your grandma. I have a quick fuse at times. I don't know the answer to your question. Father has His reasons, but Paul and Yeesa are sitting here with Enoch and me, and you are here too. Everyone is invited to the party. You won't find anyone who has not messed up and fallen short. Why don't you try and explain God's invitation for you to be here with us. Do you have an answer for that?"

I immediately reached for the wineskin and kicked back about a third of it. I was glad then for the sausage biscuits. I grabbed one, smeared jelly over it and ate the whole thing before I could even look up at my companions. A few gulps of water helped wash down the food. Soon, I began to feel less lightheaded.

Enoch jumped back in and said, "You have asked why. Most also want to know how God does what He does. Is that another of your questions?"

"It wasn't the next one, but, yes, I would like to know how He does it."

"Well, now, let me see, hmm, can you explain momentum?" Enoch asked. "You played sports. Give it a shot; explain it to me."

"It's a rushing emotion that happens all of a sudden. A player makes a good play—or doesn't. It's a single event—a tackle, an interception, a rundown, a catch, a base hit, a double play, a steal, or a goal. It's an extraordinary effort of some kind. The fans either jump to their feet or hang their heads, and everything changes. Everything starts to go the other way."

"How does the energy from the single player's effort or error transfer to the team and fans?"

"I have seen it, felt it, and I experience it now—even sitting in front of the TV. The spirit of the entire stadium changes, so does the atmosphere in a room where fans are just watching the game. It is contagious, up on one side and down on the other. Everyone can sense it."

"Okay, that's good. That describes it. Now, how does it happen, how does it work, how does it energize or deflate? How does it change the spirit?"

"I have no idea."

"Let's continue this a little further," Enoch continued. "It's like a barometer shift. It's almost universal in all of nature. For example, when you get home, your dog starts wagging his tail. It's also like stepping in a fire ant bed. Watch out, they're all coming after you! Similarly, the work group gets an unexpected invitation to a party and all are excited.

Sharks smell blood and go into a frenzy. One coyote howls, and the whole pack starts screaming. One cow gets scared, and in ten seconds you have a stampede. Either good news or sad news alters an entire crowd.

"A bad play, one dropped ball, a turnover, a blocked kick, one foul, a missed free throw—any one of those events can change the emotional environment. Jesus told the disciples to stay where they were, to pray, and not to lose heart. Then He went off by himself to pray. When He came back, they all were asleep from sorrow. When He showed up after His resurrection, they could not believe for being overcome with joy. Or consider the scene at a music concert. The whole crowd is moved by the mimetic of emotions. Is that true?"

"I see it happen and feel it, but I can't explain."

"We are emotional beings," Enoch continued. "Emotions are grounded in our beliefs and desires and our search for identity. We respond to them almost immediately. Notice how they are triggered by circumstances—instantly. We sense hope or failure through our beliefs or desires, individually and collectively. Boom, up or down. They feel real. Now, do your up and down experiences here reveal what is real or what is true?"

"Maybe, it's…Enoch, I bounce in my emotions."

"Emotional momentum shifts. The truth doesn't bounce. You cannot even explain how what happens with momentum inside you and your world every day, though you experience it. And that is an earthly thing, not a heavenly thing."

"I see and feel it, but I cannot explain how it happens. It moves me and moves between people, like instantly."

"And this movement, this connectivity, what if that is a part of the designed union between everything?" Enoch asked. "What if that's only the tip of the iceberg in trying to explain how God does what He does. You are not going to get to the how. *That's mystery.* You may want to consider the basics of what you believe. Emotions feel real, they prompt you. They are not the same thing as truth. They are just feelings. Deal with your emotions. That could change your life. These things I have observed, but of the how, I cannot say."

Paul reached over and gently grabbed my knee. "It's okay, bud. No meanness here. You picked three direct shooters. You need it. You're like that too. It took me getting knocked to the ground while I was headed to imprison believers. I was struck blind before I realized I did not have it figured out. I could not figure out all the reasons. Some of the things I saw, I could not even talk about. Other things I saw I was told not to discuss."

"Do you mean like the third heaven, paradise, and your thorn in the flesh?" I asked.

"Those are three good ones," Paul said. "Plus, the light I saw; then I could not see at all for three days. That light and voice were Jesus Himself. It took a long time to regain my sight, at least in part. My natural eyes never fully recovered. My spiritual eyes grew stronger. What I saw turned things upside down. At times, I had no words. The words I found could not fully contain what I had seen and knew to be true. People misinterpret many of the things I wrote. You too know about that. It was hard for me, just as what you are seeing and hearing is strange and difficult for you.

"I started telling what I knew and then I had to take at least three years to try and sort it out. After that, I taught in my hometown of Tarsus for about fourteen years. I understood but only in part and tried my best to share it. Spiritual insight can be difficult to translate with the limited word containers we have available. At one point, I had a huge disagreement with Peter and James. We finally worked it out and agreed on our different directions. Some things were way too big for me and us to find common parlance to hold it. That's the way it is with the mystery of all the ages."

"Can you tell me anything about the third heaven?" I asked. "We have so little knowledge of heaven."

"Satch, I can tell you this," Paul said. "You have all the info you need. The heavens are above. Heaven, though, is not just a place you go. It is also a state of soul awareness that begins when you become aware of who you are in Christ. It never has to end, even during your time on earth. You have been told this once already. *Heaven* is just another word for *above*. God is not *in* heaven. All heavens are in God. It is not the number. Rather, it is Him."

"Well, you did mention the third heaven and paradise," I said.

"I saw what I called the third," Paul said. "I saw three dimensions, but I'm not sure what the third means or if it was the grandest. Satch, how many galaxies have been discovered in your time? At what rate is the universe expanding? I hear faster than the speed of light. Is it not now taught there are many universes? Given that, you tell me how many heavens exist. I do not know—sorta like your not knowing how many mansions are in heaven or what a mansion is."

"Do you mean to tell me that you don't know—even you?"

"Not only do I not know, but I also no longer have to know. I am—we are—content and open. Are you?"

"You mean you do not know it all now, and you have no questions?"

"I would not say we do not have questions. I would say we are permitted to ask, and sometimes we are shown. Sometimes, we are told no or not yet, but we are at ease either way. That is part of what heaven is about. Are you at ease, Satch? Where is the music in you?"

"Not hardly. I do not know where my song has gone."

"Well, that's obvious. And we want you to know your questions are important. Some are more important than the answers, until you apply the answers. You have gotten a lot of answers already and still don't know much about the easy or light burden, do you?"

"You may not have all the answers, but you know so darn much. Makes me uncomfortable when I feel ignorant."

"Your questions that are being answered are for your benefit," Paul said. "There are no little secrets here—only the big one, and we know how to live in the answer to that. You do too; you just have not chosen to stand in the truth you have been shown. You think you must know it all, that your knowing will ease your pain. It never will. You feel you are less than and therefore, feel ignorant and embarrassed because you do not know. That is self-pride to know everything. That is fool's gold. Why did Yeesa give you that bracelet? You continue to be angry because you do not have all the answers. Your stubborn attitude is a sieve, the good truth runs through it and down the drain. You can never know it all. But there is no judgment. You should believe that by this point. Now, tell us the stories that hold your pain. But Satch, you are long-winded. You gotta shorten them."

I jumped up and exclaimed, "Yeesa, I know y'all already know! I told you how hard it is for me to relive these experiences. So, brother Paul, with all due respect, who are you to call me long-winded? You put that poor boy to sleep with your preaching. He got so tired he fell out of an upper window. You had to bring him back from the dead."

"Sure did!" Paul exclaimed. "Touché. But this is a little different. Try to give us the gist, and I think we can track it. Just summarize them. Satch, one tends to go further down and sour internally when pondering long on these things. ."

"What do you mean I sour?" I asked.

"All one has to do is look at you and listen. We are not in your world, but when we were, we came to know beyond it. And this is not heavenly information. You have been told this before. Oftentimes, people stay in darkness or go backward because they are tied to their shadow. They know what it is and have a degree of comfort therein. They would rather know what to expect instead of taking the risk of surrender. Like you, they become accustomed to it. It isn't well recognized, but it's another type of disease. Tell us why you do that."

"I try not to, but I get stuck over and again in the same cycle. A certain attraction pulls me toward feeling sorry for myself. So, help me. Why do I do that?"

"We cannot tell you why you do it!" erupted Elijah. "That's for you to answer! Yeesa showed you your tunk. You gotta deal with that! All of us had a shadow. One reason people stay stuck is they have believed something for so long, they know what to expect in that mindset even when it is a lie. It is much easier to take in a temptation that to remove it. Such bondage will take much longer to eradicate. The truth has a hard time getting through. People love the darkness and temporary pleasure. They are afraid and don't want to come to the light of life. They are afraid their doings will be exposed and condemned. *They cannot see that exposure does not equal rejection, but love.*

"Their mind's eyes cannot see in the darkness, only the heart can. That's when the light can penetrate the darkness and bring hope in the dawn. They taste the truth but are afraid to swallow it. Even if they try, they can't taste the goodness because of the damage, like the girls told you about the honey. Some people are brave because they are not afraid, but they are not courageous when they fear loss or real danger. Your sky is so low; it is holding you down every day of your life!

"You have only toyed with the truth. You have to change your mind, accept it, step out, and walk in it. The easier path involves staying with the familiar, even when it's killing you. We walked through the fear and acted. But that's up to you. And understand that decision is initially personal not public.

Count the cost as you have time to consider all these things. You don't have to go straight out announcing it. You walk into it and live it. You must act but know this: you must begin with your thinking. If you get cemented, that is likely where you are going to end. God can be loved but not figured out. When we reach the end of what we know, that's where we find God. Believe to understand. You must be broader minded. Here is your place to expand."

A long silence ensued. It hurt. The truth? It's not nice, but it's not shaming. They knew what had happened and waited on me for a seemingly interminable amount of time. I leaned over again with head in my hands, trying to understand the statement "toying with the truth." Honestly, I had never been able fully to take in the truth because the damage hurt so bad. I felt trapped as always. Even though I felt downcast, I teed up another question for Paul—one that had been eating at me for a long time. "What about your thorn in the flesh?" I asked.

"Are you asking, seeking, or knocking? Will not leave it alone, will you? Well, I've heard about several opinions floating around—most of them coming from men. Some think it was a woman. Others attribute it to my being a Pharisee, or that my wife died or left, or that I did not, for some reason, yet have one. What is your idea?"

"Sir, you wrote about your struggles and suffering. In particular, you mentioned being lashed, stoned, shipwrecked, imprisoned, hungry, and cold. I've not suffered in your ways, and I know I need help. Since I am with you, I guess I am knocking on your door. You expressed your pain and said you prayed repeatedly about this thorn. I don't believe your distress was a woman. But you are right, every time this question comes up, many people think it has to be about the pain of losing or not having a woman in your life. I do not think so."

"Okay. Explain."

"I read that letter to the church at Corinth backward, from the last chapter to the first. I saw a consistent pattern throughout."

"And that was?"

"Your heart hurt because of the way those church people treated you. They believed false teachers rather than you. You carried this pain for years with a lot of the churches you established. You were not accepted, valued, or appreciated by so many of the folks to whom you gave yourself. You described it as being poured out. You gave up everything just as Jesus asked of you.

"Fellows, he's already expanding a little!" Paul exclaimed. "Satch, why does life have to be so hard? You've asked this question too. It is hard, extremely so. Following the Way means service and sacrifice. It is unlike what the entire world believes; it is backward. The Spirit is willing, but all flesh is weak. We are asked to walk in the Spirit. Staying the course is the most strenuous, tension-filled road you will ever walk, because the path is holy. Yet, when you are truly walking in the assurance of it, it is easy. I was not exempt from temptation. I wanted to be appreciated by people, but Jesus said His appreciation—His grace—was all I needed. I had to hear that and learn that over and over again. Do you know anything about that?"

"Yes, I've always sought people's approval," I admitted. "And I really don't know His grace in a deep way, not like you are talking about, not fully yet."

"With all I saw, and all God gave me, I still regressed. I finally learned that I was fighting the good fight, and it is a fight. I kept trying, and each time I saw more clearly that my despondency and even my perceived misjudgments and failures pointed the way forward. So, again you are okay. Do not beat yourself up. Keep striving. One day you will finish the course, then look back and see it. *You can learn to abide amid trials and when in peace, but you have to keep trying. To abide means to stay connected, stay rooted.*

"Satch, no amount of learning or knowledge can make God like you more or care for you more or bring you closer to Him. Every viewpoint is a view from a point. You cannot think your way to God. You can't go anywhere He isn't, and you can know Him. But you can also have knowledge and not know. What good is knowledge if you do not know yourself or Him? It's a matter of having your heart revealed in your spirit. You can't see God, but you can hear and feel Him. You are having a hard time, and I know you've got another question. So, let's have it."

"I know I caused some of the suffering and hurting in my life, but so much came to me unbidden. I did not ask for or cause it. That's part of what makes this so hard. Why all the suffering? What's the purpose, or is it just the way it is? You wrote in your letter to the Romans that we should give thanks for our being pressed down, our troubles and tribulations. What is that about?"

"Do you know what sin is?" Paul asked. "*Sin is jumping out of the hand that loves us.* It is unbelief in Jesus, seeing yourself as an orphan and not knowing your Father's identity. Sin is real, but it's not simply doing wrong but missing the mark of your true identity. It is thinking you are unworthy. Have you missed the mark?"

"Obviously, I have, but you guys seem to have it together."

"Do not miss the point. How do you learn?" Paul asked. "Have you not already had this conversation? When you speak, you listen to yourself. When you keep quiet, you listen well to others. The issue is as much how you receive and interpret events as the events themselves. You are just like us and Adam and Eve. You took another god into your own mind and heart and taught it to your own children. When you find your identity in another god, that is a sin. Every human being has done the same. Sin is rampant, along with the suffering it always causes. Don't make sin your story.

"What if the poison of sin's bite can be turned into good? What if temptation and its consequences are parts of the process of growing to know and practice the good? *What if this toxin entered you because of your decision to be the umpire of good and evil?* Sin resides inside you, both on the conscious and subconscious level—the latter being hidden from your present awareness but all the while infecting your thoughts, feelings, and dreams.

"This time, you need to take this in. Sin, suffering, and failure are teachers—great teachers! *And you will not get to the right place without making wrong choices. You will take the wrong roads on your way to the right destination. Defeat is not declared when you fall down—only when you refuse to get up.* Life is a school, and we are its students. We live our own exam. That is the only way forward.

"God made us like Them, with freedom. We have erred. Great love and great pain are the means of getting back to the true path. You are in the middle of the crunch. Your hurting is the way back to life, and you can be grateful for it. It was through my blindness, both physically and spiritually, that I began to see. I am grateful for all of it. The pain from and ways of darkness became one of my teachers. Seem backward? You better get used to that. It is the only way to understand. Something way bigger than you is going on here—and you are growing due to that.

"God has poured out His Spirit, the Holy Spirit, the Spirit of Jesus on every person. She is there in you, for you to begin to recognize, sense, listen, and apply. It is an option, but She is there. The Spirit of God has been added into your soul, your psyche. You can grow out of your sin-willed natural man into a more spiritually minded man. As you do, your spirit develops a distinct and unique spirit within yourself that seeks to know and follow the Holy Spirit.

"Your spirit is learning from the life-giving Holy Spirit, but it also extends beyond your body and is recognized as distinguishable from the natural man. The spiritual man discerns that which transcends the natural, which the fleshly desires of Homo sapiens cannot comprehend. This deep healing and knowing, followed by a living out, is not normal in corrupted man's passions. But it is there. When followed one begins to experience true life.

"I must say a word to you about what you call the Lord's Supper. When I speak about communion and self-examination, it is not about finding your hidden sins and shortcomings. It is to challenge you to test in yourself the acceptance that Christ is in you—to probe what it means to be in the faith. Deeply consider that.

"But you wanted to ask John some questions, right?"

"Well, yes, and thank you. That explanation is very helpful, but I have more for—"

Before I could finish my statement, the Apostle John appeared in front of me.

"Hello, Satcher Bond Condwell!" John exclaimed. "Good to meet you and glad to have this conversation. I understand you've got a lot of questions. But first I am going to tell you God is bigger and better than the room in your head can hold. When thinking about God you need to start in the right place, or you likely will get stuck—like you have been. When Jesus spoke about being born again, He was talking first about the waters of physical birth, then about the waters of spiritual birth—all the way back to when the Spirit was hovering over the face of the waters. You were formed in God's mind then. That is where and who you came from. He breathed his Spirit into you. That is being born of the Spirit. That is where you start all over again.

"It is your life that must change, not water on your skin. The water doesn't change you. It is a symbol. Any 'water' accompanying a natural birth is not a regeneration but a physical birth into a darkened world. Another birth into a world of light is necessary. Baptism's physical water declares one has already experienced a genuine, knowing-Spirit baptism from above and has become a follower. It is an identification with Jesus' Way. Water baptism is not itself a rebirth, only an acknowledgement of repentance and one's having already been born of the Spirit and begun bearing the fruit of joining with Jesus. An infant baptism or circumcision is an affirmation of a child's community acceptance and assurance, having been created, designed, and loved by God but is not a new birth or being born again from above. Perhaps confirmations and bar mitzvahs are opportunities by which the older child can find affirmation assurance.

"The core issue is fatherhood. A bona fide baptism is the acknowledgement that you now know that Jesus' Father is your Father. An earthly father is to reflect the image of our heavenly Father, but His likeness to and fondness for us is misrepresented. Earthly fathers are to reflect the heavenly Father. Your dad was to be an encourager, friend, provider, helper, leader, teacher, and protector. So often in a dad's disillusions, he is wrong. His god is too small. Yours is too. You need reorientation. Jesus wants you to have the same relationship with His Father that He has. Jesus declares over and again that God is Father. God wants to be the Father you have not had. Being born again, born from above, is to have a changed life, a change in fatherhood—from orphanhood to sonship.

"Now, let me help you with your question about knowing."

"I have never heard that explained so clearly," I said. "Thank you. But John, may I ask about the first five verses of your gospel."

"You could, but I just gave you the answer. Your question in response illustrates to me that you did not think deeply about what I have just told you. When are you going to apply the answers to the questions you keep asking?"

"What does that mean?"

"You ask, seek, and knock to know the truth about God and yourself. Am I correct?" John asked.

"Yes. That's what I want to know."

"So, is knowing the goal of the search?"

"Uh, yes, I think."

"You ask all these questions because you want to know. So, ask the question about knowing, when you will know."

"You wrote that Jesus said, 'In that day, you will know that I am in my Father, and you are in Me, and I am in you.' When is that day, and what allows me to know?" I asked.

"When you know that answer, you will be able to grasp a lot of the first five verses and the rest of the book. You will also begin to see the answers to your culture's continuing issues. On the day you no longer feel like an orphan, left out and alone, you will know that God is your Father and the Father of all, and that Jesus is Creator of all. You will recognize that the Spirit of Truth, the Holy Spirit, Jesus' very Spirit abides within you. When you know that, you know that you know that you know. You will genuinely know, and this knowing will be so deeply embedded within you that your knowing will know. Every part of you will know. *You can know what you may not be able to articulate.* Your heart will be filled, your mind satisfied and quickened, and your spirit comforted. That will be the day of assured hope, rest, serenity, and peace. That is sonship. Give yourself the privilege of reflecting on that."

CHAPTER 21

Not a Kitten

John looked up and quickly stood. So did all the boys. Enoch said, "Well look who is here: the wise one and his daddy king." I stood up but had no idea who the figures were riding horses toward them across the cove.

Paul said, "Satch, maybe the reason I did not have a wife is I learned from the wise one. How many did he have? Was it a thousand or so including concubines? Welcome Ecclesiastical Proverbial Singer of Songs and the Bloody, Loving Psalmist Poet. Sol, you got over the women, but you do still love horses. This Satch dude has some sort of brio and as many questions as you did, well almost."

Solomon and David swung off their horses. Laughing, they gave all five men a big hug and walked over to me. Solomon said, "I heard you had some questions for me. Questions indicate a quest, a search for meaning. That is a good thing. You have been brought to the right place. Do not let these guys get on you too much. This bunch was filled with questions and kept asking them all their lives. Come here and give me a hug. I wanted to meet you. So, shoot! You want to start with women? Paul seems to want to talk about it."

I did not really want to talk about women but responded, "Can I ask you about the horse? How did you get a horse up here?"

"Everything good is here. You ought to know from reading Revelation that we have horses. They are something strong and special. I could take you to see them but not now.

"There is something else you seek. You don't know your own voice. Your voice is your translation of life. Whether you believe it was God who planned and spoke it into being or a spark became a big bang explosion, the world came to expression with a sound. Was it spoken and formed into being with a purpose or was there just an eruptive outburst that resulted in a continuing evolution? Does anyone really believe their children just ended up here by a long shot?

"What are the sounds you hear? Where do you find meaning, purpose, hope? Does it set your life afire with a glow? Stop and listen to everything around you. Listen for the sound of the genuine in yourself, in the world. Translate what you hear. That is your sound, your voice, your translation of life or a moment, an encounter or experience. Listen even as the silence speaks. Absorb them as they affect you, alter you, and impact others. That's your voice, the only one like it. What else have you got?"

"Oh my!" I responded. "Would you please record that! I guess women next. Seems you have a lot of experience."

"Yes, I have to admit that. You think you are slow. Just look at the mess I made, but I've got to ask this: where did this idea of 'making love' come from? Who came up with that? And this 'being in love.' How do you get *in* love?"

"I don't know. I've heard it all my life."

"Satch, you cannot *make* love. That phrase is so vague it is meaningless. You can love and be loved, but you can't make it or manufacture it. When applied to the physical, just call it what it is: being horny, lust satisfying, intercourse, sex, but not 'making love.' Love is a mutual giving, knowing of the other that is genuine. It is the sharing of yourself wholly with another for their good. It is being vulnerable, cherished.

"Sex is too powerful to be casual, recreational. Such misuse leads to one's own detriment for it affects one's soul. Sex is related to love and home, the place you most want to be for peace and rest. *Love not lust is intended to take you home. To go home after sex means something is terribly distorted.* It affects your soul, the inner place where your life is integrated, where your life is held together.

"Do we bring love into existence by shaping or changing material, combining parts? Do you think it is only an emotional feeling, a thrilling, pleasurable release? Do we produce love, cause it to exist, make love happen? Can we cause it to be or become? Do we induce or compel love? You are already inside love and have no idea what that means. Clearly more well-reasoned reflection is needed. When one 'falls in love,' he just collapsed into a feelings crater.

"There are two routine ceremonies not readily grasped that deeply relate to love. I understand you have done a lot of weddings and funerals. You don't like the way either usually are done but would prefer to do the latter. Why?"

I replied, "I've felt for a long time that weddings and funerals should be conducted differently. We actually have trepidation in both. I tried to change it. Culture would not accept it. When the marriage is done outside a worship service, it frequently is 'do you want to do this? Sign here. Done.' In worship contexts, the issue begins with us preachers. The stock phrases used make it rote, but it doesn't stop there. Married attenders have experienced the beautiful idea 'happily ever after' originated from the romance in fairy tale. Weddings are like productions controlled by wedding directors. Love is not just two persons holding hands facing each other in a ceremony, but two persons facing in the same direction and living in the same spirit. Maybe a handful listen to the promises to each other, the true meaning of the ceremony. Couples say their words or respond 'I do' before the rewards or costs are even known.

They should be lovingly advised of what lies ahead, but years of premarital counseling was largely a waste. Young couples don't want to hear it. We can 'fall in love' with all kinds of people who are not good for us. You have to sort out what love creates a 'share the rest of your life' marriage, the one that will take you home. Only a few will truly listen. When I would decline to participate after I counseled with couples, they married anyway and divorced shortly thereafter. They don't want to hear about sacrifice, character, personality conflicts, real adjustments, such as leaving your mother and father and the admonition to cleave to your spouse, which parents also do not want to hear. Many continue to interfere.

"The couple, and most of us, usually have no idea what 'til death do us part, in sickness and in health, to honor and cherish, for better or worse' means. For a time, the couple thinks now 'It is ours' which quickly turns into 'what about me, where is mine?' Hearts that start beating together fast then become slow irregular murmurs. They grow apart, looking out for themselves and tolerating the other. When the children come, it becomes even harder to abandon and forfeit self-desires, to sacrifice and give to each other. The declared contract—not a covenant—of marriage too often devolves into decades of frosted winters or scorched deserts. God help that couple and their children. Divorce rates are higher among church members than non-attenders.

"Perhaps a few more are attentive at a funeral rite, realizing they too will one day be in that box that is being lowered into a hole in the earth or in an urn to be scattered in the wind. It is offensive to listen to preachers' constantly damning proclamations of a burning hell. Attenders sing along with the funeral songs. Many sit nobly, playing along in silence or standing behind the family at the graveside smiling and whispering, leaving as soon as the preacher says 'Amen.' Funerals are to remember the deceased but are for the living to memorialize a life, to encourage the hope of reunion.

"Does not a burial confirm a passing and great loss without words? What about giving hope amid that grief? The most effective are the testimonials that emphasize the deceased's contributions to their lives. Those tell fond memories. They talk about their loved one's smile, laughter, encouragements, smell, hugs, unique identity, vigor, love, stories, their special grins. There should always be reminders that death is an end to this life but also entrance into a new world.

While both rituals commemorate the entering into new worlds, the formalities continue without the deepest reasons for them. Too often neither are more than an ineffective compromise of a valuable opportunity to remind us of honoring love, supporting one another, purpose, mortality, and eternity. We should participate in these services with honest attention, appreciation, fondness, compassion, hope, and truth. If we know these things, why would we not openly share them with the couple and the grievers?"

"Boy, you do understand some things," Solomon exclaimed. "Do you realize that you have just described one who has an attitude of meekness?"

"Huh? Meekness?" I mumbled. "What do you mean?"

"Yes, meekness is greatly misunderstood; it's perceived to be more like a weakness," Solomon added, "its usual translation is humility or gentleness, but the essence of the word means a balance between anger or indifference and the power of character and self-control. Meekness stands in the middle of self-assurance with humility; it is strength under control, a gifted grace of the soul. Like a soldier fully trained with his sword in combat, fully equipped with immense power, who does not abuse his strength or become heated and reckless. His self-control knows how to draw and wield his sword and when to keep it in its sheath. He is able patiently to balance and contain himself. Jesus spoke of a rare beauty of inner strength. I want you to know you have some."

"Me?" I asked.

Solomon affirmed, "Yes, you! Satch, they say I was wise, the wisest. Know this: what I had was some genuine insight but also a *wise confusion.* I knew God put eternity into our hearts, but I couldn't figure it out. The fullness of revelation in Jesus the Son of Man I did not have, but His Spirit gave me insights. I tried to write it. She gave me the words I shared as part of God's incremental revelation. I saw some things of which I was convinced.

"Satch, every human is messed up," Solomon said. "Most won't face it. One key to understanding things I wrote and that are attributed to me is knowing that they are from 'under the sun'—things that could be figured out on earth without seeing the full mystery in Christ. It was wisdom but only as far as it could go in earthly fashion—but it came from God. So, for this life, I saw that there is nothing better than a man enjoying his work. Don't work too hard at being good or bad. A man should eat and drink and find enjoyment in his labor. There is nothing better for a man and his wife than to be happy and enjoy themselves as long as they live. Be happy with what you have, enjoy it. That's still good advice, but you cannot, can you? Stuck you are! Open that bag of love-lack you carry and face the pain in it.

"With the totality of what mankind knows or we think we know, we still are left with ultimate mysteries, enigmas, and riddles unsolved. You must begin to hear and share the message of symbolic language, analogy, allegory, metaphor, parable, figures of speech, personification, truth swirls, mystery, the hidden. That was the only way I could begin to express the things I saw and knew to be true. That became my voice. Satch, look where you are. You gotta get in the real game here. Scripture can be understood on at least four levels: literal meaning, deep meaning, comparative meaning, and hidden meaning.

"Let me give you an example. Let's talk about time. When is soon? Is it one day or a thousand years? Does it mean suddenly, quickly, a little while, or a long time? Is it not a promise to come at the appointed or right time? At the fullness of time, when time can contain it no more, when it has reached its completeness—that's when soon is. And what does 400 years, 40 years, 40 days, or the word million mean. Is it literal or metaphorical?

"And what does 'three days' mean? Why is it written sixty plus times in Scripture? Does it mean the right amount of time? What does that mean? The ancient Greeks had two words for time: *chronos* and *kairos. Chronos* is sequential, quantitative time, referring to time as we usually mean it—a sequence of equal parts, twenty-four hours in a day, and each hour is the same length of time. *Chronos* is a clock face with hands. *Kairos* is fluctuating, qualitative time. *Kairos* refers to the way in which certain moments are more important or influential than others. A clock can't measure that. Some times are more vital than others. *Kairos* is a clock with no hands. Literalism does not give us the full meaning of Scripture. Sometimes it is literal. Sometimes it is symbolic. Sometimes it is both. Prophecy can have more than one fulfillment."

Daddy David jumped in. "Satch, this son of mine has never been easy to understand. He is somewhat floaty, but I don't think as far out as Enoch. What he says is solid as a rock, if you can grasp his meaning. For example, take his book *Song of Solomon*. What I want to talk to you about is your vacillating up and down. Do you know what I am talking about?"

I responded, "You mean your anger at God for your circumstances, then your praise and thanksgiving in the same Psalm. Your constant complaining, then outbursting in gratitude? I never fully got that."

"Exactly!" David confirmed. "Do you know anyone who vacillates like that?"

"You're talking about me, aren't you?" I queried.

"Yes," David continued. "Learn to hold your tongue! Speech may be silver, but silence is golden. You cannot say everything to everyone everywhere. You vacillate back and forth like me, but you do not take it straight to God. You complain to yourself and at times to others. I learned that I can tell it all to God—straight up. Job learned that. God wants you to talk to Him, and He's not worried about your coarse language or how you say it. Look how much blood I had on my hands. I killed or ordered the deaths of tens of thousands. I killed Bathsheba's husband so I could have her. Just say it to God.

"The deepest desire of my heart was to know Him. I learned to write it down, so I could look at it and remember the bad and how He would respond with the good. He focuses on *kairos* time as much as *chronos*. Remember what Solomon told you: Give it to God, tell it to God, write it down for yourself. You are in the lonesome valley of the shadow of death I wrote about, and like Tom T. Hall sang, 'You gotta walk it by yourself,' that is, until you can see that He is with you—and you keep walking and trying."

Then the unexpected happened again. I sensed something. All of the guys stood up at the same time. As I turned around, a tall, strong, olive-skinned figure in a dark robe was walking toward us. He had long black hair streaked with gray. His long robe touched the grass as he strode across the cove toward us with his staff in his hand. The ground thudded when his staff struck it. Each impact thumped like the hard blow of an axe splitting wood against a stump.

"Mo," shouted Lige, "What are you doing here? Great to see you!"

I stood and watched as they greeted each other. Enoch turned to me. I could hardly believe what he said. "Satch, this is Moses. He wants to speak with you."

Moses took four long steps toward me. He held out his hand to shake mine and as I took it, he grabbed me in a big hug. "Young man, I would like to speak with you for a moment," Moses declared. "Do you mind?"

"No, sir, but why me?" I replied. "I don't understand."

"Neither did I—at first," Moses revealed.

He jabbed the end of his staff into the soft grass, sticking it deep into the soil. He said, "I see you also use a walking staff." Then he looked straight at me for a long time. "You asked about Enoch and Elijah not dying. I died and God took me and buried me where no one knows. Perhaps He did not want any of us to become another icon or idol for His people. God has good reasons for all He does. Know that."

Then he said, "You didn't have a happy childhood, did you? You saw a video recently and remembered when your mother gave you a party at your house on your third birthday.

You never smiled. You knew the party was not for you but for her to show off to her friends. You never once even had a slight grin. All the children were playing, and your mom was visiting with all her friends. You were solemn when you got the presents. Then one older kid took one away from you. Your mom did nothing. You remember some of the children. They frolicked, laughed, ran, and played. You just watched. You have seen a few photos of yourself smiling, but you don't remember those times. It is as though they have melted into a pool of sadness because you never felt affirmed and protected.

"Do you ever stop and think about Jesus' life—a man of sorrows who was acquainted with grief? He was despised and rejected by men. Well, my mother put me in the Nile river in a little ark and sent me to where? She did not know. You want to compare hard lives? I grew up in the palace of a tyrant. Later, God sent me back to the tyrant's son, who wanted to kill me because I killed an Egyptian who beat a Hebrew slave without reason.

"I had to run away into the desert. I met a good woman and struggled about forty years in that wilderness working for my father-in-law, trying to understand all that happened to me. I had a lot of time to think and struggle with things you already know about. They happened to me. Why? I don't know. It was very hard for me, even with those encounters that you may call paranormal, like what you have been experiencing here. This is real too. It took years for me to believe that God was true and good, as I now know He is. It took me a lot of pain and a long time, and it's okay. Do you hear me?

"Yes, sir," I agreed.

"You feel you are like a pitiful chicken that goes around pecking in the barnyard thinking all you do is drop poopy pellets everywhere you go," Moses continued. "You make loud, high pitches like a hen or squeal within yourself like a pig with every criticism. Stop beating up yourself and others for your mistakes and for not being further along the spiritual journey than you think you are.

"Another thing, my people did not accept God's warnings and the dangers and hurts of not following His instructions and principles given for their benefit. But they found out what he meant. God had to find a person who would speak for Him. He picked me, but I fought it. He still does that. He picks people for a reason. I resisted. Like you, I felt unworthy and unable. I knew I had to have help. You need it too. That is why you are here. He chooses those in their time who will stand up. Satch, *when you see something wrong, do something right.* Then that conviction can spread to a group of people, so they can learn how to live in community and care for one another.

"When God gave me the commandments, He prefaced it by saying He was the one who set us free from slavery. He was saying when you know what it's like to be truly loved and free, here's how you live in relationships. *The ten rules or principles for experiencing life are not about religion but relationships, even your relationship with yourself.* Most people respond to the 'thou shalt nots' in the same way the people respond to the marketing slogan 'Do not squeeze the Charmin.' People instead immediately grab for it. When a line is drawn, we want to cross it. The law is a faint image, a dense shade, a foreshadowing, a pencil sketch, a precursor outline. It's not the full image which Jesus brought to you in the flesh. Jesus had four commandments: love God, your neighbor, believe Me, and follow Me. Here, Jesus reinterprets the law. He removed the veil from the law as illustrated when the temple veil was torn in two. He opened the holy of holies to all the people.

"That's what God was trying to teach us the whole time, teaching us to love Him and one another so we could have a supportive community and meaningful lives. We were to spread His message to all people in the world that God's love included them. That applies to you and your friends today. That was the purpose of us stiff-necked and stubborn-hearted Hebrews, but we remained God's chosen people. We were to be a blessing to the entire world. In your day, Hebrews are called Jews. They have eyes but still refuse to see. God gave them, gives you and all people the freedom to choose. Jews chose to reject Jesus as Messiah. They are exceedingly capable people, but law-proud, preferring the law to liberty, desiring tradition, rules, and ceremonial rituals over relationship. Yet the Jews are still God's selected people. Their task was grueling. There remains confusion today about the country called Israel. It is not the same, but Jews and Gentiles alike have a place in God's kingdom.

"Jews continue to have a significant purpose in the whole of God's design. God promised Abraham that he and his seed would be a blessing to all. Abe would love to come tell you how he was the first among pagans to hear God. He was told to get up and to walk away from all he knew! He was asked to leave everything and go to a strange, unknown land. And

Abe was old and settled when God spoke to him—like me! Like you. Young or old, whatever your age is only touches the surface of your life. God is the sovereign potter. As clay, we do not choose our task, but we can participate in it, knowing we have value. Satch, you can join in too, if you so choose, but yours will be in a different way."

"Moses, did you respond as soon as God called you?" I asked.

Moses retorted, "Hardly! There was this bush that burned and talked, then these meetings on the mountain, and a bunch of conversations. I was married by then and had a couple of kids and was trying to manage life; but in the middle of that, I really got the message when He almost killed me. And you have been on that same path. My wife saved me by circumcising my son, getting blood all over her and on my feet from my son's foreskin, which she threw at me. My son was bleeding and screaming.

"Look, you need to hear this. You need to fear God. I don't just mean reverence and awe. I mean be afraid. To fear God the most means we do not fear something else more. That's what it first took for Abraham and for me. Ask Paul about getting knocked to the ground when he was blinded by Jesus' light. His whole life was shattered. God means business. Ask Jonah. If God picks you for some critical purpose and you refuse to do what He knows has to be done, then he will deal with you in whatever way is necessary.

"What I am also telling you is that the way you were raised with all the legalism, judgment, and duty has a good side. There is a value and a vengeance in the law-ridden gospel. When raised like that, you have a fear of God. Look at the good you learned there. You learned to read the Scriptures; you listened to teachings and sermons. You made some friends. You had a community. In those ways, your parents formed you. Come to thank them, though they did not know what they were doing to you. But God did, and He keeps using that as He develops you. That gave you some boundaries and basics that you needed and have used. You must have those things. Look at all you gained by that. Now you are seeing more of His true character so you can move from the afraid type of fear to the fear of awe and reverence. Because we have missed the mark, we must learn both.

"Don't fret about your lack of progress in your faith and trusting God and in knowing you can carry out what He asks. *On both God's and your part, faith requires continually patient endurance.* Abraham was seventy-five, and I was about that age when God got after us. You are right there with us. I did the best I could. It was a long time before I began to get handles on all of it, but I never totally grabbed it. I made a lot of mistakes. It was more than me, but I was offered an opportunity to participate. I took it reluctantly. At times, I resented it. I was a long way from perfect in it. I made so many missteps, some of which had consequences that caused me to experience rejection by others, even the death of others. My anger got the best of me at times. Hitting that rock prevented my entering the promised land to which I had led the people. That is not meekness. Don't ever take credit that belongs to God. God is serious about His business, His honor and glory and His people...and you.

"And you know what? It's okay. I know that now. You can know it too. You are not condemned by your mistakes. Failures are not fatal. They are the soil of growth. The goal is for you to wake up and become aware of who you are. It is a step-by-step progression as we acquire understanding of our being loved and loving. It is a journey, a process. It is a moving ahead and a going back, but usually not as far back. It is going up and then down, but not as far down. It is experiencing bad that works for your good. That hurts but leads to progress. That is the way we learn...and we must learn."

"So, that is why it is so hard?" I asked.

"Your people did not experience, understand, or teach you the history and life of the people of Israel. You read the Scriptures, especially the Old Testament, without comprehending the Hebrew way of knowing many things. That is not your fault. What I am going to tell you now is not understood by your people or most cultures. The sacrifices were never for God's benefit. It was to teach us the pain and good of love. This lesson of sacrifice happened inside each Hebrew family.

"Don't you have an autoimmune disease, and it saps your energy and makes you feel fatigued and weak? Is this why it is hard for you to keep up with Yeesa?"

"Yes, I have had it for over a decade," I confirmed.

"You do know that stress is a major factor in the cause of your illness. Stress is killing you, boy! Do you refuse to get medical help because their symbol seems to be pagan, a serpent on a stake?" Moses asked.

"Well, no," I conceded.

"When my people were plagued by poisonous snakes, God told me to make a bronze serpent, put it on a pole, and instruct the people to look at it to face the threat, the poison's source, so they could live," Moses explained. "Those poison snakes are a metaphor for the evil deceptions weighing you down, hiding in your subconscious shadow. And don't buy into this sacred versus secular thing, like God is not involved with everyone. That snake on a pole is Jesus on the cross, the sacrificial pattern that we are to imitate. Jesus faced evil straight in the eye and ended its victory. That's what you need to do, face the threats, name them, resist and dispel them. The religious saw Jesus as poison to their power, but He defeated death. You are made in God's image, made like Him. Likeness is to grow into His image, to be like Him. Live it and reflect it to bring order to the chaos within your culture. It takes courage and sacrifice.

"Do you really know about sacrifice? The Hebrews chose the very best of the lambs they had raised—no blemishes or defects. They would not allow a sacrificial lamb to be injured or scarred. They could not allow its coat to be damaged or stained. They kept it from disease and treated any sickness it had as their own. They picked it when very young. It's like one of your colts at four months old looking the most like it will as a full-grown horse. The Hebrews knew the exact week to pick the lamb. Then, they took the lamb into the house. The little lamb became family.

"They named it, fed it milk from a skin, cared for it, held it, talked to it, bathed it, brushed it, and played with it every day. It lived with them. When they called, it came. They gave it treats. It slept with the children. It followed them on walks. It got clean water and the best leftovers from the table. It was a part of the household and was loved dearly. How did they feel the day they took it out and cut its throat? Then they skinned, cooked, and ate it, and the sacrifice became a part of them. They took it in themselves as a heartache, a feast, and a celebration. Try that!" Moses put his hand on my shoulder and continued. "Learning the deep cost of that loss, that suffering is the purpose of sacrifice. God feels it because He knows it. Whatever form God takes, Jesus' scars show. Feel that, Satch!

"All your questions come from the deepest question in life: is God really good, or is He that critical, demanding, judging tyrant who condemns as He chooses? Believe the first and you can have peace in your life. Believe the latter, and you won't even know yourself. It is obvious you have all kinds of knowledge in your head. You have read the Scriptures since you were a child and preached them, but you still don't fully grasp because you—like the stories of friends you are writing about—have yet to hear what the Scriptures are telling you. These written words reveal Jesus as The Word, God's Word—NOT the book called the Bible. Read it through Jesus' eyes. Do you get down on your knees and pray to the book? You must gain the wisdom to accept the symbolism in mystery. Then it will penetrate beyond your mind and into your heart."

I was stunned. I looked up into his face. His eyes were moist with tears. My own fell to the ground as I looked down. It made so much sense, the cost of the sacrifice. Still looking at the grass, I mumbled, "I had no idea."

I heard another thump from his staff and looked up. Moses had cupped his hands behind his ears and said, "Do you hear that?"

I saw all the guys jump to their feet. They turned toward the entrance to the cove. Then I heard it. A sound like nothing I'd heard before. They all began to shake a little. Their faces turned pale. They reached for each other.

The roar came again, echoing through the amphitheater, reverberating off the walls surrounding the cove. It was as though something was announcing its presence, a warning. Then I saw him moving slowly, lumbering directly toward us. An enormous Bengal tiger—an exceptional one at eight hundred plus pounds—the largest, fiercest cat ever approached. He emitted a light that spread across the grass and up the walls of the cove. He extended his neck and growled. His tail switched back and forth. I was paralyzed. The guys stood still. I could hear Moses' staff nervously bumping against the rock next to him. As the tiger came closer, his figure became clearer. I could see his muscles rippling as he slowly rambled toward us. He growled again, then again, then a third time. As he got closer, I heard him moaning.

"Satch, it's okay. You are safe. He's a friend," Moses assured.

"A friend!!!" I exclaimed.

"You've been wanting to know who Baba Bengal is," Moses stated. "Well, here he is. Do you want to meet God?"

"Hello, Satch," Baba said. "Your ego is magnificently astounding. It is exceptional. You must be so proud of it. Perhaps, right now, I should eliminate your obstinance and have you for supper. I am hungry!"

I could feel I did a lot more than wet myself. I stood there trembling. The tiger just stood there staring at me. After an intolerable time, He grinned at me with a friendly chuff. He said, "I'm anxious to have another visit with you. Been waiting on you to get back so we could have a little personal chat and eat that pie of yours. Guess you've been busy with my buddies here. How's it going?"

I could not speak, not a word. Bengal tigers are one of the two largest and most vicious cats on earth. And the biggest one of all was standing there growling, warning, chuffing and talking to me. As I looked, I could see red splotches on his head, like drops of blood spaced unevenly. It seemed as though they were running down his head onto his face. I noticed a scar in his side as though he had been speared. There was something different about his feet. There seemed to be a hole in each one between the phalanx bones to which his claws were attached.

The holes went all the way through—even through the bottom of his feet—as if he had stepped on something sharp that penetrated through. The radiance from his body to the ground allowed me to see it. I had seen this once before in one of my cat's feet. It healed with scarring all around it.

"Don't you ever believe I left my Son hanging on that piece of wood," Baba insisted. I never abandoned him, never turned my back on him. Moses just told you about sacrifice. That's what love does. You need to join the team. That's what I am asking of you."

"Are you God? Are you the Creator, the Father of all?" I asked.

"Father first," replied Baba. "*My Son and I planned it all. Jesus creates; our Spirit helps implement.* Or as you and your friend have discussed that God is the Author, Jesus is the Teller, Holy Spirit is the Revealer, and you are the writers. I would add Scripture is the writers describing and you are trying to describe creation to culmination. And you are our idea. Would you like to join with us? It will take sacrifice. Your brothers have told you it's worth it, but it's up to you."

"You scare me," I confessed.

"Good! You should be," Baba decreed. "I am who I am, will be who I will be, and can do and be what I choose. As has been said, I am good, but I am not always safe. Good and love always have the best interest of others as their concern, but you humans turned things wrong. I knew it would happen when I chose to give free will, but with my help you will make things better for yourself and other people. I intend for you to be a part of that. That is why you are here, to receive encouragement along your way.

"But you have a deep question. You have thought about and mentioned talking with Job. What do you want to know?"

"There are so many things I want to ask," Satch replied. "But Job, gosh, all that suffering. You let Satan in your presence and twice permitted him to go after Job. He lost everything, animals, servants, children, everything except a nagging wife. And insurance companies call those disasters Acts of God."

"Mankind is confused, but yes, I allowed Satan to do it. But you understand the difference as shown from the foundational statements you plan to put in the front of your book," Baba explained. "I knew Job. I knew he would not fold because of pain. Satan is delusional in his pride, but he has a purpose. He needed to see he cannot fool everybody. Do not fret or worry. Satan's dark mind does not know the true errand on which he was sent down to earth or his end. I am and will continue to deal with him. I wanted Job to learn. That's how I feel about you, Satch. That's why you have suffered. It is why you are here, regardless of what anyone else thinks, believes, or says to you. Job was a fault finder, a critic of Me, just like you. Then, he learned there were things too great for him, too high for him that he did not know until he went through that experience.

"You proud, strong ones are somewhat like the Hebrews—hard-headed, stiff-necked, without eyes to see. Their ears needed digging out. You fit that condition, but you are getting there. Job would be here. He wanted to talk with you, but he is on a mission to one of those prissy, pious, pompous, proud know-it-all preachers who has more charisma than character. Who people *are* is more revealing and important than what they *say*. This guy is so self-righteous, he doesn't know he is poor, blind, wretched, miserable, and naked. I will tell Job about our conversation."

"But Job was a full-grown man with a lot of wisdom and experience," Satch retorted. "I was just a child who knew nothing. Why did you let Satan do those things to me? I feel like I was hit in the head as a child and never recovered."

Baba explained, "Satch, not just your head, but your heart, too. Because you have to be wounded. This you have not fully understood. Your *self* believes falsely about itself. It has to be smashed—whatever it takes—because it is killing you. You have become a living ruin while thinking you make choices right for yourself. The false self has a tremendous ego, that says individual advancement should come above all things. It is a pawn in Satan's game—not love. Self has to be deeply wounded to heal into truth.

"Yeesa spoke correctly when he said it was not your fault. It was done to you. It was also done to the women, to your parents, to every ancestor all the way back to Adam and Eve, who passed their way of thinking to their children. You and the world's culture have passed it to your own children. Is there any dignity in that? That will go on unless you change your mind to listen to what your heart knows. Think about it! It is a continuing disaster, but each one of you prefers to be self-focused. Your anger is ultimately concentrated on Me. I accept that and continue to love you through your bitterness. I am for you.

"I know you hurt deeply and are confused. You have been blasted. There is a purpose behind all things. What would you be without your freedom to choose? You are here because I want you to see through all your pain and blame. I gave my son, Jesus, to you to show my heart for you, to demonstrate the way to true life. It is surrendering, giving, loving others. You need to focus on Jesus and what He has done for you. He gave His entire self for you! That love overcomes all things, even unworthiness, shame, blame, and death. Does love involve suffering? Yes! But amid all that pain is hope, because love sees beyond and never ends. Now—decide what are you going to do with your hurts, your wounds?

"There is a second thing you do not know. I trust you," Baba stated. "I knew you would make a lot of mistakes in your choices for yourself, but you would fight through them. Failures are part of the process. Before I placed you in your mother's womb in your earth family, We had thought a long time about you. We planned and designed you and placed you there in the middle of your time. You have a purpose. Your mother knew enough to tell you that you were special.

"That's all she knew, and she waited until your hair had already started to gray to tell you that. That does not mean you are any better than anyone else. But your background and suffering developed you to the point you are here and getting to see who I truly am and who you are. Your gifts are not only for yourself. They are for others now that they are colored by your wounds. I am calling you out. I want you to be one who tells generations the truths that you are seeing.

"That is a tough task, but you have the grit to do it. I designed you to do it and have never left you alone. I told your counselor friend to tell you, 'Just tell the story. They will get it.' He knew it and told you several times. You have been trying, but now you are going to find some folks who will come to you and help you get this done. In fact, have you not just met separately with some people? More are coming. Just saying. You lost the music in you and your song. You are about to find it.

"That's why you are having all these physical problems right now, but they have given you the time to be quiet, sit, and process the things Glo has shown you. Now you can think in truth and write. Your health and your story are two of the reasons you must release that family business. This is much bigger than a financial asset. All your family is going to be okay. In spite of and because of those problems with which you are dealing, you are about to find your way. So, join us and get this done. It matters in *kairos* time. So make it happen in *chronos*."

In the blink of an eye Baba changed into a cloud. He wrapped his presence completely around me and spoke again. "Now do you feel me?" Baba asked. "You are wrapped inside me. I have got you. Nothing that has happened or ever will happen to you will change that truth. Jesus is in me and inside you. My Spirit is all around you and in you. You are accepted, included, and securely held—always."

Then, Baba, the huge Bengal tiger, returned and said to me, "You can join Us and make a difference, or you can keep complaining and whining, feeling sorry for yourself. Or in your prideful determination, you can become like Nebuchadnezzar and have the mind of a wild animal and eat grass. Either way, would you like me to send you back to the farmhouse where you can dribble and frizzle away until your time is up?"

I could not say a word. I was overcome and mute. And he was gone. They were all gone.

It was just Yeesa and me standing there. It was dark now. The moon was rising. Yeesa just grinned again and said to follow him. I was weaker than at any other time in my life. I couldn't help it. I had talked to a Bengal tiger who was God.

Yeesa grabbed my arm to support me and said, "Come now, you need to get cleaned up."

CHAPTER 22

The Burn Pile

After what Satch had just experienced that day, he got himself washed and cleaned up. Finally, he went to sleep. Satch did not stir the whole night. But as he woke, he rolled over too far, too close to the fire, and almost got scorched. It was inches from his nose. I could see by his reactions he began to feel the burning on his face and arms. He rolled back over away from the heat. When he finally got up, he was looking straight at the fire. He couldn't see me, but I was watching him.

Satch stood up and stretched. He looked for me. He called for me. No answer. My friend, now feeling a little desperate, started from the plateau above the river to go back to the cove. Finding no one he returned and noticed what could be called a burn pile about a hundred feet away. It reminded him of burn piles at the farm, which make a wonderful but potentially dangerous bonfire; but this was different. This pile had been built around a tree. It was dying. It was surrounded by fallen limbs, branches and leaves piled high. It was surrounded and ingrown by vines and briars. The pile of debris was at least twenty feet high and thirty-five to forty feet in diameter. High above cawing crows circled the pile. Vultures were soaring above, and hyenas were rounding the pile with their inimitable laughing.

Although the tree was still alive, there were so many vines and briars, large and small, wrapping around the trunk and extending up and out to the end of every limb. The large vines were two to three inches in diameter and had grown in, through and around the tree, enfolding not only the tree but the surrounding debris and the whole pile. They were flourishing. There did not seem to be a single branch, stick, limb, or twig that was not enveloped by vines and briars and being pulled into the tree. The tree's remaining leaves were dying. Those vines and briars were strangling the life out of that hapless, seventy-year-old tree. Satch could not fathom what this pile, the crows, vultures and the hyenas were doing there. He exclaimed, "What is this?"

To the left of the cave's entrance and about halfway to the plateau ledge overlooking the river gorge, Satch spotted Elijah. He was standing by the fire where I had been cooking breakfast. We had all finished eating. Elijah was swinging his mantle round and round his head. Satch could not stop from yelling, "Please, please, do not hit the ground!" He was scared Elijah was about to split the plateau wide open, then who knows what would happen?

Elijah looked at him and laughed. "What's the matter, Satch, you think I'm gonna bust something?"

"You scare me when you do that," Satch confessed.

Elijah retorted, "Got too close to that fire, didn't you? Woke you up. Don't jump away from this next one! And Satch, I hope you are the one about to bust something."

"Me? What are you talking about?" Satch inquired.

Elijah turned and pointed to his left. There stood Rahab, Delilah, Sheba, Bathsheba, Jezebel, Tamar, Herodias, Mary

Magdalene, Esther, Enoch, Paul, and Moses. Satch did not hesitate. He walked straight toward Elijah. When he got to the fire, all were seated, facing Satch, except for Mary and Paul. They were standing.

Mary spoke first. "Satch," she said, "we are here because we want to be here. We have known about you and watched you for a long time. We have gotten to know you. You now come to a real core issue. It's time for you to face it." She sat down.

Paul continued to stand as he spoke. "The misguidance and application of legalistic, superior-feeling religious groups have eaten up your life. Jesus dealt with it. One day the hand of God will touch them again, and it will all go upside down. You mentioned the depredations of your family, church folk, and others. Those are real, but there is a bigger ugly underneath them. Do you know what it is?"

Satch pondered. "I think I do. Misrepresentation. They were taught and learned it."

"Of course they learned it," Paul confirmed. "Where? What does your culture call it?'

"All of them were 'church' people and authority figures, but they all were influenced by the culture," Satch noted.

Paul exploded, "The world's cultures are damaged and misrepresent God. You are correct. You took in a distorted bias. There are no monsters in this world, just people who are wounded and prideful. They act out of fear and pride, priggish self-satisfaction. They invent belief systems to make them feel they are right! People become attached and cling to them. These systems provide multiple ways from different perspectives on how to get right with God. Man's gospel, trying to do God's work for Him, is not good news. The core issue is fatherhood. An earthly father is to reflect the image of our heavenly Father, but His likeness to and fondness for us is misrepresented. Jesus wants you to have the same relationship with Father God that He has, so He can be the Father you never had.

"You were a judge once, right? Well, you have judged enough. Sit down and listen. Have you not said you were encouraged to witness, teach, and speak?"

"Yes, we all were," Satch admitted. "It was one of our obligations."

"Witness to what?" Paul probed.

Satch continued, "That God loved us, but—"

"But what?" Paul demanded.

"We are sinners and separated from God," Satch stated.

"And just how did you get separated from the One who made you and is in you, in whom you live and move and have your being?" Paul challenged. "You are not a 'separated self.' Hell is the consequence of believing separation. Your felt hell is only in the darkness of your mind's disjointed delusions. Darkness is not just the dearth of light. It is more frenzied, more menacing. It is not a locale. It is a gap of emptiness. Your sin does not change God's mind about you. Listen, you were not born broken. You got broken. You were not born in total depravity. You were beautifully and wonderfully made.

"One core problem you have is refusing to consider your thought process. Stop this self-image thing. Live in God's image and become like Him. One who wants the truth does not have to hear or read words. You can be persuaded of spiritual things when your soul recognizes them as true. *The Spirit speaks to the soul.* Look and get ready. Do not be afraid."

Then Paul pointed to the burn pile. Elijah took his mantle in his right hand and cocked his arm in a throwing motion. The prophet flipped it, pointing beyond us toward the rock beside the cove entrance. Satch looked, and there sat Rock the eagle glaring at him.

This time, He spoke: "You must experience what has to happen to the things inside your shadow. It's time." And then He lifted off, zoomed over Satch, and down through the river's gorge toward the mountain and out of sight.

Satch turned toward Elijah and exclaimed, "Elijah, I don't begin to understand all this. It's more than I can take in all at once. And you scare me with that mantle. What is Rock talking about…my tunk and this pile?"

"Okay, I'll put it back on, but just know I can take it off any second," Elijah cautioned.

"What do you mean by that?" asked Satch.

"You were just told—it's time. Today is the day; now is the time," Elijah decreed.

"For what? I don't understand," probed Satch.

"See that pile?" the prophet said, pointing to the burn pile.

"Yes, I've piled and burned many of them, but what is that doing here?" Satch asked. "It is different. And what's the deal with the dying tree and all those vines?"

"Same as your piles. It's for burning. You are the fuel," explained Elijah. "To experience oneness with God, to experience the profound encounter between God and one's soul requires a burning out of deception. A consuming fire, a cleaning out. Julian of Norwich used the word *oneing* to describe the divine union of man's soul to God and a unifying connection to all others and things. This term means more than intimacy. Rather, it denotes a coinhering of the soul with the very essence of divine assurance, peace, rest—the wholeness of God."

Satch offered, "Are you saying you want me to light the pile? I'll gather some dry grass and a burning stick from the fire and start it. Is that what you mean?"

"Are you sure you want to do that and fight hyenas by yourself?" Elijah asked. "You'd better think about it, count the cost. That pile is in you, inside the 'sweet case' you carry, and the tree is you. The broken branches, dead limbs, rotten fruit, dead leaves, debris, crows, hyenas, vultures all illustrate what is in your tunk. That is what is sapping your life, and it's not just your personal shadow, but also your cultural and system's psychological shadows you have taken in. You are being squeezed to death by the vines of evil's lies as they destroy your life. We have gathered them here together for you to see. It has to be burned, but the pile is you. You sure you want to burn it?"

"Are you saying if I burn it, I will burn myself up?" Satch asked.

"Satch, the debris, the vines, the mocking crows, the laughing hyenas, circling vultures all want to consume and destroy you," Elijah clarified.

"I see them now. I know about the crows, but what is this with the hyenas and vultures?" Satch queried.

Elijah explained, "Both crows and hyenas are carnivorous and will eat most anything. Hyenas even devour bones. Vultures eat dead and dying meat. You have not identified them yet as such. All have a purpose but can be nasty. None of us know how to get rid of them without burning the pile. The tree is dying because it is dreadfully wounded. Although it's not dead, it is struggling and gasping for life because life's flow is being choked and cut off. The core source of your wounds consists of the vines and briars, the tares and chaff that weaken—the darkness that causes the blockage. It takes a scorching internal fire to dispel the nasty creatures and consume the vines and debris, but not you. The object of the burn pile is not only to reveal the vines. The goal of burning is to save the tree, you, not the gloss and ashes but the gold in you. You felt a tinge of fire on your face this morning. It woke you up. That's where you have been, benumbed. Do you want to wake up? If so, you have to face this."

"Yes. I want to wake up, but not completely burn up!" Satch pleaded. "You are right—I know what you say is true. I believe you, Elijah. But is this the only way?"

"The only other option is to stay the way you are with all your damage and baggage! Your call."

Satch yielded. "I'm done with this doubting. Go ahead. Light the fire."

Moses stepped out and struck the plateau with his staff. The whole plateau began to shake like in an earthquake. Then Moses said, "The next time I do that, something else is going to happen, and you should not be standing where you are right now. Come over here and sit down with the others."

Rock appeared and flew straight down toward us. He reached down with one claw into the fire, grasped a burning stick, and then lifted into the sky. He descended like a lightning bolt until the flame from the stick resembled a blowtorch. He slowed, landed beside the burn pile and lit it on every side. Satch saw him thrust the burning stick into the pile, and then the fire would come back out to him, blazing and flaring back and forth, up and down. The crows, vultures, and hyenas tried to flee, but flames from the fire shot up and out all around and set some of them ablaze.

Then Rock flew to the top of the pile, spread and expanded his wings, and hovered above the fire, holding the torch in His uplifted claw. The fire intensified but seemed to stay in the vines and the debris with continuing flare flashes in hissing rushes shooting in and out, up and down, through and around the entire pile. There was smoke, heat, cracking, groaning, and popping flames. Although the smoke rose furiously, Rock's gigantic wings completely spanned and accepted the blaze. He absorbed all the heat, flares, sparks, blazes, and fumes into his body and wings.

Satch simultaneously felt an intense fire burning all through his innards as he watched the vines being consumed. Sweat poured from his body. He bent over and lay down from the pain; but he kept looking, feeling the wrenching torment in his own guts while watching Rock writhe in agony, taking the burning within himself.

Amid this struggle, Satch thought he heard music, laughter, and crying coming out of the pile as the smoke rose with the flames. He turned to look at the group. Everyone was smiling. He looked back to the burning. Occasional drifts of smoke were still ascending, but the vines were being consumed in the fire. The burning slowed to a progressive red glow over the debris' ashes and the vines. Yet the tree remained. Satch thought he saw the beginning of green sprouts growing out of the tree. Then Glo popped out of the middle of the pile, whizzed around it three times, stopped, and waved. Then she was at the top of the pile hugging Rock.

They started flying around the now growing tree when Satch heard a quiet growl, then a chuffing, then a moaning and laughing. The sound was coming from the entrance to the cave. Satch looked past the burn. Outside the entrance to the cave stood Baba Bengal. Then He changed form and was wearing overalls and a baseball cap and grinning from ear to ear.

Before Satch could sit up, Glo was beside him. She put her hand on his shoulder. Jesus was standing beside him too. And Baba was walking toward them all.

Baba, Glo, and Jesus sat down by the fire and asked Satch to come sit with Them. Glo leaned over and took the lid off the Dutch oven. There it sat, the berry pie. The aroma of that pie rose and must have grabbed their nostrils and stomachs hard. Jesus and Baba jumped up hollering, "Where are the bowls? That pie smells more tantalizing than ever." From somewhere, Glo whizzed out spoons and bowls for each of us.

"Are you going to sit there or serve?" Baba asked with a grin. Satch filled their bowls to the brim. He was dumbstruck. All he could do was look at them. Jesus, Baba, and Glo would not take a bite until Satch did. I am telling you those cherries must have done something.

They cleaned and scraped their bowls. Baba extended his bowl toward Satch and said, "Fill 'er up, Satch, that's some powerful good stuff."

I filled Baba's bowl again, then ate some myself. It was really good. But as I sat, I couldn't quit watching them. None of them said a word about the burning. I don't know if I have ever watched someone enjoy something so simple as a cooked berry pie. Baba grinned all over as He ate. When done eating, He laid down His bowl and grabbed a wineskin. He must have drunk half the contents. He was one big dude, but you could tell there was not a mean bone in His body—well, except He could be more than dangerous.

Then He stood up, patted His stomach, and sat back down. "Thank you, Satch," Baba chuckled. "Been looking forward to that, but it was even better to actually eat it with you being here. That was the best. By the way, gosh, something smells awful. You didn't let that out, did you?"

I turned red. Baba embarrassed the stew out of me. Then, they all broke out laughing.

Baba said, "Satch, I love to do that. It was Jesus. He belched. Whew, that was a raunchy one. Those cherries He added have that effect on Him. He does it all the time, especially now that folks really know Him. He is human, remember. Plus, the body odor from His and your sweating is pretty severe. The rest of the stench is the burning of the bodies of the evil inside you that got caught in the fire Jesus lit and Glo stirred up."

Everybody was laughing, but Jesus didn't blush at all. He just stood up, laughed, clapped, and started dancing. Suddenly, I heard this music, all these voices singing along. I turned around and behind me, all the boys and the girls, were dancing and singing together at the top of their voices that song from a movie. I remember hearing "Ooh, see that girl, watch that scene, digging the dancing queen."

They sang the whole chorus, repeating it over and again and stopped perfectly at the end of the verse. I heard Baba say, "Glo does not get nearly enough credit. How she deserves this! I want you to know you belong to us. Satch, how I do love you so!" Then all three vanished.

Satch then felt a quivering under his feet, like a huge hammer had slammed the earth. He realized Moses had just struck the ground with his staff. The plateau shook and started to split. Satch remembered Moses's warning and ran toward his friends, to the left side away from the cave entrance. All of them were looking at the opening as the ground cracked open from the cave entrance out toward the plateau's brink. The crack started small and then broadened. It crept toward the plateau's edge, growing larger as water began to flow through it. It grew until it was wider than the entrance to the cave, which began to break up. The entire cliff wall above the entrance began to separate and give way as the cliff turned into broken and falling rock.

Water began moving faster and wider, filling the ever-widening stream that was flowing over the plateau down into the river. Satch walked to the edge and watched it falling in a steady stream. He turned and saw the waterfall, which first had been revealed in the room where we had sat with the girls. It now was visible from the plateau with its continuous stream of water. Satch was trying to take it in when he heard, "When the blockage is gone, the living waters flow. *Res ipsa loquitur*, the thing speaks for itself."

Satch felt a spring emerging from within himself.

Photo by James Lee, James Lee Photography, 1322 Wheatland Ave. Pennsburg, PA 18073. Taken with Satch's permission at Satch's Farm with copies provided to the author.

CHAPTER 23

Wholeness

Yeesa was standing beside me. We stood in silence at the edge of the plateau watching the new stream catapult over the edge. By this time, the water had begun to carve its route down the side of the precipice and made its way to the bottom of the gorge, joining the river below. We watched it pummel small stones, collide with rocks, and create its own bed as it moved relentlessly toward its goal.

About ten feet below the eroding edge was a rock ledge that extended out beyond the brink of the plateau. The stream dissolved the earth beneath the edge and crashed its way down toward the rock ledge, creating a second waterfall descending to the river. The force of the falling water splashing on the ledge caused a refreshing mist to rise up and graciously greet and dampen both of us.

We got a little wet before we turned and walked across the plateau back toward the cave's waterfall. The tunnel leading out from the cave had partially collapsed, but left a negotiable path to get to the waterfall inside the cave. It was astounding to see how the room where we had first met the girls was still intact, along with some of the openings above that gave light to the entire area. I could see from that waterfall all the way to the plateau edges where a new waterfall had just been created.

Yeesa tapped me on the shoulder and motioned for me to follow him. We walked side by side into and across the cove. He pointed to the mesa at the top of the amphitheater. We said little as we slowly climbed. Had I the breath to speak, I didn't know what to say. I had no words for all that had happened in this place—the wonders and the failures all mixed in with the people I had hurt and met and the mess I had made. There was nothing in and of myself alone that could have fixed any of my issues. I was so grateful.

Then, I thought about the burning vines, the fiery ordeal I had just been through, and the Three who had been right there with me. I wasn't sure where the guys and gals were now, but I was glad Yeesa was there and that I was not by myself. He was the most kind, wisest, and honest person I had ever met.

We finally topped the hill and paused to catch our breath. We looked out over the mesa, which was so high up that the lower clouds were about to cover the tableland. I was amazed, exhausted, and hungry. With all that had happened, I didn't think I could endure much more. Then Yeesa spoke in the quietest voice, almost a whisper. "Look at those clouds moving across. If they keep coming, we'll be covered up. That'll bring a new adventure."

I watched as the clouds kept descending. The sun dropped slowly in the sky behind them. It was late afternoon now. The panorama of colors was astounding, like being in the great plains and looking to the west toward the mountains as the sun nestles behind them. What a sight to behold! But I was so tired, I was overcome by fatigue and did not see how I could appreciate or welcome any more wonder. I asked if we could rest.

We sat. How good that felt. Yeesa handed me a water-filled skin. I had not seen him fill it at the waterfall. The drink refreshed me enough to look back toward the kaleidoscope of colors spread across the western sky. That was when I saw three figures emerge from the gently rolling clouds. As they walked towards us, I whispered, "Who are they?" All around us, there seemed to be a hush, a reverence by all of nature.

"They want to meet you," said Yeesa.

"Me?" I exclaimed.

"Yes, you are highly favored, and they want to meet you."

"C'mon, man, someone else?" I quipped. "I'm worn out. I have not put all this together yet. My cup is full and cannot take more than all that has already happened. So please!"

"Just like I have said, Satcher doesn't yet fully know who he is. And you are supposed to be part Indian!" chided Yeesa.

"What has that got to do with it?" I said. "You talk like I have a gene missing or something."

"You are missing something, but it seems more than a gene," Yeesa replied bluntly.

Changing the subject, I asked, "Who are they?"

"My guess is they'll introduce themselves, that is if they have to, but most folks recognize themselves when they come face to face with themselves," Yeesa explained.

Yeesa had not said one untrue thing in these several days and nights. And if he was saying what he might be saying, it took me back to the table of young boys, healthy and strong, to the images of my parents in the stone wall. The boys looked young and resilient. My parents were different. Would I even know my whole self as I should be? But I'm now old, weak, and worn out. A breeze made me look up.

Who were these folks and why in the world would someone else want to meet me? They didn't seem to be in a hurry. They walked leisurely just in front of the moving clouds, which seemed to have slowed down once the three appeared out of its mist. The smallest was really short and stood on the right. The tallest stood on the left as they approached. They seemed to be having a conversation with the one in the middle. The mystery trio obviously saw us and seemed to know us. All of them pointed toward us and seemed to be laughing, though I could not distinguish their faces.

As they drew closer, occasionally one would push the other away with his hand, shoving the other's shoulder. When the little guy would push the one next to him with both hands, they stopped and looked at each other. They all bent over, apparently from laughter. With the descending sun's glare behind them, I could not see their faces—just their forms. As they approached, their height difference became more apparent. The one on the left was at least six inches taller and of a larger frame than the middle one, who had long hair and a beard. The smallest one now looked like a little boy.

Their gait was not the same, but they continued to walk side by side. As the three drew closer, I could tell they were smiling. Then, the tallest of the group and the boy-like one stopped moving and stood back as the other one continued to approach. The little one reached up and took the tall one's hand. All this time Yeesa said not one word. Instead, he broke out in some kind of gurgling. I said, "Yeesa, you sound like a clogged drainpipe."

Now, I really felt upside-down. There I was sitting on the top of an unknown mesa, and these three guys were coming to meet me. I didn't have a clue! The longhaired one stopped about six feet in front of me and said, "Hey, Satch, what's up? So glad you are here. I wanted to have a personal visit with you man to man."

I was stuck to the ground. I felt like I had a box of cotton stuffed down my throat but finally managed to speak. "Why did the other two stand back?" I asked.

"That is for later," he said. "They are fine. First, let's you and I get acquainted on a deeper level—even though we have had many conversations. I've always wanted to have some face-to-face time with you."

"I didn't recognize you. I could not see your face clearly," I stated. "You are—"

"Yes, it's Me," he interrupted.

I shifted direction. "What do you mean by 'wanting to have some time with me'? I don't understand."

"Satch, I have heard you confess, several times, that you didn't know who you are, meaning your whole self, right? Well, here you are—all three of you, and we will all be together. I will not have to explain much on that point. There is another lingering question. Are you up for this?'

Rather than answer his question, I diverted the dialog back to my inquiry about his identity. "You are Jesus, aren't you?'

"Yes!" He confirmed. "The real Me and the real you have always been together, but I prefer that freedom make its own choices. Do you want to put to rest your question of why temptation is necessary?"

"Yes. I've spent the last several years trying to figure it out in the context of God's purpose from the beginning," I replied. "I've gotten some help on the answers here, but it's a hard one for me to digest. The damage from yielding to temptation hurts so badly. How good can come from that still confuses me. It seems backwards. Please guide me!'

"I will," He agreed. "And you are not wrong in the beginning of your understanding. Do you better understand why I said the gate is narrow and the way is hard?

"The path you talk about is excruciating! I have not been able to get it right," I lamented.

"It is, and you cannot get it all right, not while you are still in your earth world. Some things you are powerless to do without Me. I never said you should be good, only Father is good. You are to be set apart, help and share, love mercy, and walk humbly. You are to do justice. *Justice never includes vengeance. True justice only comes when the victim is totally restored and the perpetrator is completely redeemed, and both experience it and amends are made.*

"As you try on this path, the way can get even harder and more treacherous, but it is more beautiful," Jesus explained. "You have been made a little less than God. In creating you, We made you as close to divinity as possible. Put your index finger right here under Mine, right next to Mine, that close, touching. That's how close you are to divinity. You are the very image and likeness of God. Do you feel that? You are to be like God. Since the fall, mankind has a perpetual itch to set itself against Me. Therefore, life is a training ground, a school. That is because you are free to choose, and God trusts you. It is that simple. He wants you to find and choose your original wholeness. Wholeness has been, is, and always will be God's plan and desire for you. It's who you are to be."

Satch had to ask: "Jesus, was your temptation in the wilderness when you decided as a man who you truly are?"

Jesus smiled. "Satch, first you do realize no other person was there. I had to tell of My temptations in a way my disciples could begin to understand. Now, can you see that in the wilderness, and in the garden and on the cross is found the reason for temptation, how evil is defeated—the necessity of choosing from your will? I've always known, as the Son of God, who I was to be as the Son of Man—a human being. For every man, there must be learning and growth. In those excruciating temptations, what you call the wanter, became increasingly more solid. I always had to choose, moment by moment. I knew as a man what I wanted most was to do the will of My Father. That superseded everything. Those three are illustrations of where you choose God's will because that is what you want. You will it. Make that a perpetual choice. That's how your wanter progressively gets fixed.

"We believe you can and will learn what is good and what love is. You will not get everything right, you can't—at least not in your earthly life. Father's transmitter is always perfect, but you need to keep your receiver tuned in. Just keep aiming for the mark. When you fail the seventh time, get back up—as many times as it takes—without limit. Keep going forward. You are being asked to do what you are incapable of doing. You cannot do it without Me. But you can keep trying. A victory comes when you learn to believe Me and follow Glo's guidance. You will then choose the good and make progress. You will know Baba has you completely wrapped up inside Himself and that you are free to be. You will be able to help yourself and others, but that will be up to you."

"So, temptation is allowed because I must learn to choose good?" I asked.

"Yes, and believe who you are," Jesus attested. "We believe in you. Hard as it is, We trust you that much. And We have your back. We know how it all ends. You have seen a part of that. It is necessary, because humans believe they are already gods and are confident they can accurately discern between good and evil. But they cannot.

"They and you can learn through being tempted. Satan is the one who tempts you. We allow trials that test you, but we will not lead you into evil. Damage happens when you believe Satan's lies and give into his deceptive allurements. The effects of missing the mark enter as part of your consciousness and subconscious. Satch, they make the worst prisons. You must unlearn this path. That's what causes your heaviness. Remove it all. That's the experience of the burn pile you just witnessed and the pain you experienced. I will be with you as you address each issue. We will help. You must believe Me. Each time you refuse to acknowledge and face your shadow and fears, you add more stones and emotional damage to the sack you are dragging. It takes time, but I have faith in you. That is why you are here.

"But did you not say 'No one comes to the Father but by Me?'"

"Yes, but also consider, 'When you have done it to the least of these, you have done it unto Me.' You must consider it all together to begin to understand. Now, as an illustration of that and to fill a gaping hole within your soul, I want you to meet yourself, the whole of you."

Bewildered, I said, "I know I am still somewhat of a mess and confused, but what do you mean the whole me? Am I all split up or something?"

"That is pretty obvious to everyone here," Jesus noted as He turned and beckoned the tall and short ones to come join us.

What do you say when you are looking at yourself? I was looking dead into my spitting image, except the tall one was stronger and had hair. He was my younger Satch, just like from the old films and photos when I was in my late twenties and early thirties, wearing blue jeans and a white T-shirt. It's who I tried to be and thought I was back then.

Looking down at the diminutive member of the group, I asked, "Who is this little boy?" Jesus knelt and picked up little Satch and handed him to younger Satch. Jesus put his right hand on young Satch's back and nudged both toward me. Young Satch held out his right arm with a grin and stepped toward me, holding the little boy in his left.

At this point, Yeesa could not contain himself. He couldn't help laughing aloud. As I reached for younger Satch, I lost all my strength and started to buckle. My younger self caught me and gently with one arm lifted me up. He just grinned as he picked me, his older self, up.

Then, younger Satch eased me down to the ground and looked at me. "Satch, I am a part of you from years ago. We were confused then; guess we always have been. I got stuck in the past and could not move forward. I held back and caused the tension in us about going into the ministry. I was the part of you that did not want to leave friends and hobbies. I did not want to give them up. You felt we had to. And you made the choice and left. We were both following what our wanters thought was important. We thought our intentions were good, but were akin to vanity, like two inner egos competing—no satisfaction for either. But God has used it all for good. Now, we can move into the world of peace and see how God puts things all together.

"Jesus wants every part of us to be whole. You have felt it, but somehow you could not receive it. You became a preacher, but I resisted. That's when we became divided in our desires. That's what Yeesa has been trying to show you about the good that is hidden in the bad. The good is there, and it cannot be overcome. It takes a while, and this is our time to be all together rather than in pieces. All our questions find answers—not always with words, but with encounters. Let's get out of our head and listen to our heart. Now meet our little Satch."

I looked down at the little fellow with blond hair and blue eyes—the spitting image of the little boy in the pictures I had seen all my life. He was me as a young boy.

Jesus said, "This little fellow has been wanting to get himself back together and whole since before he reached his third birthday. You do remember what happened to the two of you back then?" Jesus asked. "Satch, hug and reclaim yourself."

As He spoke those words, I reached and took little Satch in my arms. The little one reached both his tiny hands around my neck, looked me straight in the eyes, and smiled with tears running down his little cheeks.

The little guy said, "I needed you to come and get me so we could be whole." He rested his head on my shoulder and kept hugging me. Almost simultaneously, younger Satch reached both his arms around little Satch and me, saying, "I love you guys." I lost it! I reached for my other two selves and experienced the grandest embrace I had ever known.

Jesus said, "Satch, you lost part of yourself between ages two and three and then more of yourself in your early thirties. You needed to rescue these fellows and yourself, because they have been estranged from you for a long time. Now you can be whole again."

As we held each other, Jesus stood beside the three of us and grabbed us all in His arms at the same time. In that embrace Jesus became so large that we were engulfed inside Him, and my younger selves and I became one with Him. We were emasculated and empowered at the same time. In that moment all three parts of me that had been fragmented into pieces came together as a whole. In Jesus I reached the greatest wholeness of my life!

We sang, laughed, and danced until exhaustion overcame us. We sat down in a circle, the three of us—Jesus, Yeesa, and me, a whole Satch. I don't know where the meal or the fire came from, but they warmed us on the outside and the inside. With the sun now having gone down and the temperature dropping, the warmth of the embers and their flames matched the glow in our hearts. As we enjoyed the supper, we listened as Yeesa told stories of how he had come to discover his own true self. Jesus then looked deep into my soul.

I felt emboldened, so I looked up at Jesus and said, "I don't want to be out of line, but I saw Solomon and David riding horses. I didn't know horses would be here. Do you think it would be possible for me to have a horse?"

"You mean like that smooth riding red chocolate single-footer with a silver mane and tail that you saw at that horse show in Kentucky?" Jesus asked. "I've got a brand-new colt, just born off my stallion and a special mare. He is not only going to be fast, but also can fly. Seems you like that. I will ask Solomon to train him for you. I'll bring him when I come to get you, and you can ride him as we come home. You can even bring your favorite saddle with you. Better than that, Satch, you wanted to know about the little boys you saw around that table. You were right about all of them. We are going to restore all the years the locusts have eaten. When we thought of and planned each of you before the foundation of the world, we wanted you to share the life we know. We do not intend to lose a single one of you.

"You named your mare Music," Jesus continued, "because you felt like you had lost your song. You are going to get it back. But tell me why you named your second horse Son."

"I never felt I had a father who loved me the way I needed. I never felt accepted. I always sought my parents' approval and never received it. Dad was all bound up and couldn't give it to me. I named him Son because I had always wanted to be one, a son who was affirmed and encouraged."

"You need to dig back and discover how your parents were raised and what happened to them," Jesus advised. "They did the best they knew how. You have begun to see how blaming them only makes things worse for you."

"I am beginning to understand that," I assented. "Thank you for reminding me."

Jesus continued, "Remember when you and your wife lost that child in a miscarriage? Such a tragedy can break a heart. The other little boy you saw in the room sitting at that table coloring with a crayon on that sheet of paper is your other son. You have four children. When you pass through death's portal, you will see him again and know him, and all those years will be restored—and there will be no more tears. Physical death does not interfere with eternal life. You sleep and wake getting donned with a new body and outfitting. You did get the note from Yeesa?" I nodded my head. "Keep it until you get back to the farmhouse," He said and then continued, "Are you ready to move from being a hurt child to being a son, to manifest authentic sonship? If you are, let your heart's roots grow deep in the soil of belief, which you have come to know in this place—and come out of hiding!"

I contemplated Jesus' words as I glanced down at the fire. I would see and know a son I never knew—my previously unknown little boy. I nodded my head in agreement and, under my breath, murmured, "Yes!" When I looked up, Jesus was gone.

Only Yeesa and I remained by the fire. I put my head on Yeesa's shoulder. He wrapped his arm around me and gave me a hug. As he held me he said, "Do you know the Dutch word *gezellig* or the Japanese art form *kintsugi*? *Gezellig* refers to a total and perfect wonder of acceptance, comfort, fondness, friendship, warmth, peace, and togetherness. *Kintsugi* is the art of mending broken and flawed things with lacquer and gold powder to create something stronger and more beautiful. You have now experienced both. You know gezellig-kintsugi!"

Instantly, I sensed a breeze and in its well-being and wholeness—genuine hope.

PRODICAL SON Mildred Nungester Wolfe (1912–2009) Artist - Photo by the author

Satch's horse Son

CHAPTER 24

The Return

Yeesa and I said no more that evening and both of us curled up next to the fire. I gradually eased into a serene, deep sleep. I dreamed that night of the wonders I had experienced, the people I had met, the changes I had felt happening in me. I held an awe of a newly healed little boy within me and a younger self that would bring more wholeness. I would know myself for the first time. It was the beginning discovery of the authentic me without the lies I had believed my whole life. I was determined now to empty tunk completely. I was fed up with believing and being led by all the lies. I don't think I moved all night long. Sometime in my drifting off, I thought I heard Moses say, "Satch, your face is shining."

I am not certain what woke me. I thought I heard a car's tires crunching gravel as it rolled up the driveway toward the farmhouse. It startled me—a car! My eyes popped open, and I peeked down the driveway looking for a vehicle approaching from the road. There was not one. The fog was gone. The sun was high, mid-afternoon.

Wait—where is Yeesa? I turned around, and the farmhouse entered my view. I was lying curled up beside the cedar tree. I wiped my eyes, shook my head, and tried to stand up but moved too quickly. My head felt dizzy, I lost my balance and fell with my face in the dirt. I pushed myself away from the cedar tree and barely avoided skinning my face. I lay in the dirt. I just lay there. What had happened to me?

I was able to get on my hands and knees and finally stood up. My back and knees hurt. Then I saw my walking stick leaning against the cedar. I walked slowly around the house, then back, sat down and bumped hard against the massive cedar, which was leaning forward toward the sinkhole. Cedar leaves fell again in my hair and on my face and neck. I spit cedar until I was dry mouthed. I felt the ground around me in front of the cedar. The soil had dropped, sunken in a circle in front of the cedar. The ground had become more recessed and softer than the night I fell in the sinkhole. My back ached. Had the sinkhole been filled and packed? I stood up to examine it but could not be sure. Then, I remembered I had left a spade on the front steps. I got it and started to dig. The settled area was more malleable than the ground around it. I'm not sure why I was digging with the spade. What was I going to prove anyway? I quit.

I gave up, wondering about all the things that as of now seemed like a dream. I went to the farmhouse to get a drink of water. I drank my fill and looked out the window at the creek below. I watched the horses feeding in the pasture. I walked to the front door and looked down the slope of the mound toward the road. The mound? Had I just been dreaming or lost my mind? What had happened to me? I didn't know, but I had horses to feed and a business to run. I had no idea as to the day or time. But man, did I feel better! As I put my glass back in the sink, through the back window I saw three vehicles in front of the barn. I took off through the back door and down the drive. On the way I realized it was my friends Cork, Pick, and Joe Carley. They were sitting on the big swing and talking.

I yelled, "What in the world are you three doing here?"

"Looking for you. Where have you been?" JC replied.

"I guess I fell asleep outside looking at the fog and the stars," I explained. "Just woke up when I heard a vehicle coming up the drive."

"Well, it has been overcast every night here for the last week. We could not see the moon or stars. Three vehicles have been up and down the drive looking for you today, but we didn't see you," JC continued. "We beat on the back door, went into the farmhouse and couldn't find you. You look like crap. Did you sleep outside all night?" Pick asked.

"I guess so," I conceded. "But what in the world are all three of you doing here at the same time?'

"We each had a dream last night, and the night before—the exact same dream, that you had fallen in a hole and couldn't get out. None of us could shake it. Each one of us drove out here to check on you and discovered we all had the same dream," explained Cork. "So, what is going on?"

"What? Oh, nothing that I know of except I'm exhausted and have a lot to catch up on with work, and around the place," I said. "That has never happened to me before, falling asleep all night outside on the ground."

"You okay then?" Cork asked.

"Sure," I assured. "But I can't tell you how much it means to me that you guys came to check on me. You all had the same dream?"

"Listen, three guys, same dream, two nights in a row, down to the last detail. We've been sitting here on the swing comparing. Each of us had the same dream twice, where you fell into a hole and met this Indian, talking eagles, and some strange people. There was something about you being put in a straitjacket. And there was this fire and this cave and this waterfall. What's going on here, Satch?" Pick insisted.

"And how come you smell like smoke, like you've been in a fire or putting one out? And your jeans have this odor and look a nasty mess. They are filthy. Your face is all scabbed up and you've got little cedar leaves all in your hair. Your shirt sleeve is half torn off and this cut exposed on your arm," Cork exclaimed.

What was I going to say? "I guess maybe I look a little strange, but I don't know, other than I was just sitting under the cedar and got tired. I guess I fell asleep. I'm fine. Guys, it means a lot to me for you to come all the way out here. Thank you. Can I give you a hug?"

"Ain't much on huggin' guys," Cork announced, "But glad you're okay. I gotta get back to work."

The others agreed. We shook hands, and they trod toward their trucks. On the way, JC stopped me. He looked at me with a quizzical stare and said, "We are going to have a talk—just you and me. This dream deal, with all of us at the same time, is some hint or clue from God. Has to be! And the way you look! I'll be seeing you later in the week. You are holding out on us."

I thought about my many conversations with JC. At one point, he told me he was working on a children's fantasy story about squirrels. The way he talked, his imagination had really begun to develop. I wondered if I could tell him what had happened in the mound.

They all entered their vehicles and drove down the driveway, leaving a cloud of dust blowing back in my direction. It reminded me of those clouds moving toward me on the mesa. I took a whiff of my shirt. I smelled of wet smoke. Then, I remembered the horses and work. I took off to the loft to get some hay. I feed square-baled Bermuda and stack the bales in the loft. I used covered drop shoots to feed hay to the horses. When I got in the loft, I noticed I had a bunch of hay missing. I had counted the last time I fed the horses. At least ten bales were missing. I couldn't believe it, but I had to get to the farmhouse and work.

I fed the animals and went back to the farmhouse. I was too befuddled to do any work, so I locked up and headed for the truck to take a ride to relax. When I walked out the front door, I noticed again the trailer my friend loaned me. It had been moved. It was a heavy, homemade trailer that would carry a load of elephants. He had offered it so I could haul my tractor. Someone had moved it. That trailer was like his baby, and he had left instruction no one else was to use it without his permission. I had agreed.

Apparently, someone had used that trailer to haul off some hay and returned it afterwards. For some reason, I turned and looked beside the front steps where I kept a bucket of pine kindling for starting fires. I collected the kindling on my walks in the woods. It was gone, too! This was too strange.

As I drove down the drive, curiosity got the best of me. I knew one neighbor to ask. He was a good man, my friend, and kept an open eye. He was making a chair for me. I went straight to his house. He was in his shop. I walked in. He was weaving a seat on a chair. I asked Marv, "Do you know anything about a trailer, hay, or pine kindling?"

He looked me up and down and his eyes seemed to fix on something. He replied, "Why, you lost something?"

"Not to my knowledge, but I've got some things missing," I said. "Somebody has been up to my place."

"You better be careful," Marv warned. "Looks to me you may have more trouble on your hands than a trailer and some hay."

"What in the world are you talking about?" I asked.

"You do remember the game warden is up in this area all the time," Marv stated. "Those three eagle feathers sticking out of your back pocket will not make him happy. That carries a huge fine and possible prison time. And one of them looks like it still has blood on it. You may be part Indian but not enough to get you out of that! They are dead serious about protecting those eagles on the river."

I felt around my waist and, to my astonishment, pulled three eagle feathers out of my back pocket. I was bewildered. He said, "You better get outta here and hide those things. Here, put them in this paper bag."

I gathered myself as best I could. "Thank you for reminding me," I said. "Guess it was a little reckless. You are right. I will take better care with these. Do you know when you'll be done with my swivel rocker?'

"Oughta have it ready by the middle of next week," Marv disclosed. "You realize that's a big-assed rocker. I've never made one like this one for you."

"You told me that, and I am going to love it," I chirped. "It's special. Thank you, my friend. I want you to be the first to try it out, so give me a holler when you want me to come get it; but about those missing things…"

"Haven't seen you lately, you musta been outta pocket for a while," Marv expounded. "You look pretty rough, even for a farm boy, all skinned up like that, shirt ripped, and smelling raunchy. A few days ago, early one morning, I saw that trailer come by here loaded. Had a wagon on it. That wagon is sitting just up the road in front of a house. A few minutes later, the trailer came back down the road, empty. Not long after, the pickup that had pulled the trailer both ways came back without it, but the bed was loaded with hay. I don't know anything about pine kindling, but the two in the front seat of that truck who live just up the road—you used to see every Sunday morning. I have an idea you know who they are."

I did. I walked back to my truck, put the paper bag with eagle feathers on the passenger's seat and just sat there. The longer I sat, the madder I got. I was having a hard time accepting this. These two friends had snuck the use of the trailer and stolen from me. Once before one of them had come to my barn, saddled one of my horses and let someone I did not know ride it. I caught him in the act. I had helped both of them over the years, eaten in their homes, fed them, had given one a horse, and had referred people to them.

How long had I been asleep? Or was it days I had been away? How could that happen and me not know they did that in front of my nose if I was there at the farmhouse, especially lying in the yard where the trailer was? It had to be way more than one day. Marv said he saw the trailer coming by his house "several days ago," and the guys said it had been cloudy every night for a week.

I cranked the truck and for the first time noticed the clock. It was too late to investigate anything further, plus I was dog tired and not in the mood to deal with other issues right now. I was significantly over-problemed for this one day, so I decided to go back to the farmhouse and try to get myself together. On the way, I began to feel less upset and more relaxed—more quickly than at other times.

I closed the driveway gate down at the road and pulled up the mound hill around behind the farmhouse, so it appeared that no one was there. I went in, closed the door and all the blinds. I took the bag with the feathers into the bathroom that held the only closet in the farmhouse and laid the bag on the shelf.

When I did, that note that Yeesa gave me and I had put in the back pocket of my jeans had stuck to the three eagle feathers and fell out of the paper sack. I had totally forgotten about it. For the first time, I unfolded the note. This is what my youngest son had scribbled on that sheet of paper as he sat with the other little boys around that table in the room I saw. It was a note written in crayon, part in Latin. His note read:

Audi, vide, tace. "Hear, see, be silent. Then, when you have heard, seen, and remembered—choose—and do not be silent!"

Dad, you do remember those two little boys whose bodies you pulled out of the wreck that day. Well, you are right. They are precious and are now two of my very best friends. And their mom smiles all the time. They really want to see you and talk with you, but not as much as I do.

I'll tell you my name that Jesus has given me as soon as I get to hug you. And I wonder even now what name He is going to give you.

I love you, Dad.

I lost my breath. How am I going to deal with this? I read it several times and just stood there. I put the note and feathers back in the paper sack on the closet shelf. Beside the paper sack on the closet shelf, I noticed the shoulder bag Yeesa had given me that day containing a copy of the Scriptures. How did that get here? I started to fall backwards but caught myself with my hand on the sink behind me and narrowly avoided falling and hitting my head. I sat down on the floor. I was in an irreconcilable daze.

When I was able to move, I knew I had to take a shower and wash those clothes I had worn for I don't know how long. They and I were so nasty I had to go outside to shake out my boots and socks and the filth and the cedar leaves off my clothes and out of my hair. I managed to get a shower and put on fresh clothes. That helped. I locked both the front and back doors, checked that the window shades were closed, and headed toward my recliner to crash. I needed to contemplate all that happened and hopefully take a nap. I sat in my recliner and thought to myself, *What am I going to do with these eagle feathers, this note from my little boy, and a shoulder bag with Scriptures? What translation did he give me?* I could not process it. And there's that leaning cedar and the suppressed softer soil. I lay back in my recliner and nearly fell asleep when I thought I heard another car coming up the gravel drive. Someone had opened the gate. It had to be my neighbor. I was exhausted, so I pushed back in my recliner.

My mind was filled with so much. I lay back and placed my hands across my stomach to rest. I felt the bracelet Yeesa had given me. I was just about to doze off when I heard this light repeated tapping knock on the door. I didn't move, but my eyes popped wide open. I thought I knew that little knock. I said to myself, *No, not again, especially to that.* Or whoever it was did not matter. Any anxiety I had seemed to ease without my fighting it. I laid my head back. I rested, a peaceful easy. My wanter was getting fixed. As I drifted off, I heard the music and sang quietly inside myself. Now I felt safe. I went sound asleep.

CHAPTER 25

Then

Several weeks had passed since I met Yeesa in the mound cave. I had dropped a few veiled hints with Joe Carley but still had told him little about my experiences. I knew he wasn't ready for the sinkhole. Then one day I received a message. It popped up on the main screen when I started the computer. There was no return address. The message could not be replied to, copied, forwarded, or saved. It had a one hour time lapse to read it before being deleted.

Whatever I did, it bounced back to the main screen of my laptop. I tried restarting my computer. That didn't help. The message came right back up. I called my tech person who used remote access and could not figure it out. She said, "We never heard of such a thing. There is no record of this kind of thing happening. This is not possible." So, I copied it by hand onto paper.

Here is the message Yeesa had sent me:

> Satch, you can read this message but cannot reply to it, nor can you take a screenshot or photo. You can copy it by hand if you act quickly. This is not your world's technology. There will be no record of it in your world.

Just look up and nod when you see it. I'll know. The feathers, note, and Scriptures in the leather bag are yours to keep. You will have them to remember.

Thank you for letting me work with you on your story. Hopefully you will approve what you asked me to do. Now, finish it. I see and feel the difference in you. Thank you for allowing me a genuine interactive relationship with you. That is the way intended for all of us to be with each other. Hope your skinned up places have healed, and your heart hurts are being cured. Your back will get better. Maybe that autoimmune disease too. Get physically strong enough to get those knees replaced. Maybe then you will be like Caleb at eighty.

Let that hay and trailer incident go. You have dealt with a lot of stuff in your life and shadow. Don't add any more weight to it. Keep facing any issues that may remain. Smile and tell that trailer and hay duo what happened but don't make an accusation. Allow it to simmer with them. They will know that you know, and Glo will get to them. They must work through their own stuff. One day they will want to make amends with you.

As for any others who have hurt you, keep your hands off their throats and let them go. As you now know, forgiveness is for you—and it takes guts. Proud of you for letting go and coming to understand compassion and tolerance for others, as well as release for yourself. That is a big deal. We'll talk more next time we see each other.

Remember, relationships never end. You are going to have a lot of face-to-face conversations with people when Jesus brings you home with Him. And there remain a few that you have been hesitant to engage. You could speak with those before you enter the transfer portal, which is merely a change of your clothing. Pray for a happy death. Leave there with no unfinished business—no regrets, nothing unspoken, nothing unforgiven—but with peace in yourself and with others.

This is hands-on personal. Everything is personal if you're a person. Take action to apologize. Right any wrong you've done. Seek to restore the balance with other people. Engage unless anything you do would hinder and not help. Do not increase the strain, making things worse. You do not have to tote those loads anymore.

I know you still have some questions. Being a curious seeker, you will continue to have more. Bet you already have at least a couple brewing. I know you would like to meet the Inklings and George MacDonald, from whom they and you learned. They know how to tell meaningful stories. I hope that can happen.

Pay attention now! Should you have opportunity to show this to anyone, I mean, do you really think anyone will believe you? They may say you are more disarranged than before. That's said about a lot of God's folks who have experienced similar things. Remember Enoch? Wait until people ask you about this Yeesa guy. When that happens, recall your conversations with the brothers and sisters here, the things you experienced. Just smile at your doubters. You'll know what to say. Speak what you know is truth.

Don't let others' unbelief and opinions stop you. Perhaps tell no one except through your story. Be wise. Just live it. That's what counts. Signs, miracles, and what people call paranormal experiences do not create faith or last for those who hear about them. They just want more but have no awareness of God's voluminous ways of helping His children.

Remember, few folks hear, see, or receive wisdom from the hidden. Mystery is problematic for most people, even if it is a fiction-fantasy memoir. Maybe the ones you choose will have ears.

I must tell you something you do not know. This won't be easy. You have a living older sister and a younger half-brother. You can find them. They need you. Find a way to get your story out there. I'll find a way to get it to them. Baba has some plans. After all, you and this story are His idea. Go ahead, search for them. They could find you first. Your mother never told your dad or anyone else about the birth of your sister while he was away those years at war. She knew people would talk and figured your dad would doubt her. She felt it would taint not only her marriage but her entire family—especially you, treated as her first born. Before she knew you, in her way of thinking, she thought about how it would affect you and your siblings. She quietly and securely placed your sister in a good home. Several years later, your mom found out about your half-brother by your dad. She said not a word. Now your other two siblings are asking questions and want to know. Both your parents want to talk to you; so do your gargoyle grandmother and some of your hometown folks. Little Chief, they are changing. There will be time for that.

Satch, you fell into a sinkhole deep down into an unknown cave underneath an Indian mound, but you have climbed a huge mountain. You are able to accept and respond to the unexpected, unanticipated happenings. You now know trust and safety. You are connected and protected in your faith's assurance and dependence. There is always more, even for me here.

An old saying I like goes something like this:

May peace and grace be your rest.
May the sun not burn you.
May the rain not make you cold.
May no stone turn your foot.
Flow like water,
And return like the wind.

Sleep well tonight my treasured friend. The ride is the destination…and that is now.

Oh, there's a package at your front door.

—Yeesa

SAINTS PUNTER JULIAN FAGAN
Averaged 45.5 yards on four punts . . . His longest was a 56-yarder . . . Fagan, a two-year veteran from Ole Miss, has a 64-yard punt to his credit, longest in the NFC this season. He's defending NFC punting champion.
Julian Fagan
GRIDWEEK
HOTTEST PLAYER OF THE WEEK

JETS
JULIAN FAGAN
PUNTER

10 Julian Fagan P
New Orleans Saints

JULIAN FAGAN
PUNTER
NEW ORLEANS SAINTS

This story has taken over forty years to develop and has been cathartic for me. My goal is to help others who have experienced hardship and pain on their life's journey.

I want to thank you the reader, for coming along on this ride. I hope you found the story meaning and helpful. If you enjoyed this book, please leave an honest review on your chosen platform. In this way you can participate in bringing help to others.

For more information about me, go to
https://authorjulianfagan.com

You can contact me at info@authorjulianfagan.com

The book will be available in hardback, paperback, digital, and audio, which can be found at Amazon, Goodreads, Barnes & Nobel, Apple, Google, Audible, other online vendors, as well as Bookstores.

You can follow me on social media at:

YouTube, Facebook, Instagram, TikTok, X, and Threads.

Check your provider for podcasts.

www.ingramcontent.com/pod-product-compliance
Lightning Source LLC
Chambersburg PA
CBHW020937310726
48980CB00007B/808/J

* 9 7 8 1 9 6 4 2 5 1 6 1 5 *